CW00550761

Graham Plowman

THE HOUSE ON SENTINEL HILL

Internal Illustrations by Matthew Dewhurst

Cover Illustration by Joseph Kelly

Inspired by the work of H.P. Lovecraft

"Out of corruption horrid life springs, and the dull scavengers of earth wax crafty to vex it and swell monstrous to plague it. Giant holes are digged where earth's pores ought to suffice, and things have learnt to walk that ought to crawl."

H.P. Lovecraft

Special thanks to the play-testers
(may their sanity return in time)
Edward Hickey
Greg Allensworth
Darren Seeds

Edited by:
Greg Allensworth

Graham Plowman is also the Composer of

CTHULHU MYTHOS MUSIC

Visit:
https://www.youtube.com/c/GrahamPlowmanComposer

to listen to atmospheric orchestral music
to accompany this book.

For Lisa and Rebecca
(a.k.a., Spuds)

ABOUT THIS BOOK

The book you hold in your hands is no ordinary book! It is a gateway into a terrifying mystery where YOU decide the outcome. Inspired by the Cthulhu Mythos of H.P. Lovecraft and other authors, it will test your resolve, and your sanity.

The year is 1926, and you play as Frank Winston, a writer and journalist working for the *Arkham Gazette* newspaper. Your main area of expertise lies in the unusual stories and happenings that no one else at the paper wishes to write about – unexplained events, and tales of local folklore and superstition.

Though your persona is set, you can customise Frank's abilities for the coming investigation, and you will enter these on your *Investigator Sheet*. There are many terrifying dangers ahead, and only those who can overcome their deepest fears and fight bravely (or avoid danger), will survive.

Be wary, and be smart. Your investigation could come to an untimely end when you least expect it. You're not likely to succeed in your first, your second, or possibly not even your tenth attempt!

If you manage to survive the horrors to come with your health and mind in reasonable shape… you may still be forever changed when the story ends.

RULES OF PLAY

Skills and Attributes

Your abilities are a way for you to interact with the world. For example, being able to spot hidden items, sneak past a dangerous foe, or even fight an enemy. Your attributes are Dexterity, Strength, Health and Composure. Your skills are Perception, Stealth and Combat. Throughout the investigation, you will use these skills and attributes to perform *Check Rolls*. You will determine the level of certain skills and attributes when creating your character. Health and Composure always begin at 10.

Check Rolls

Throughout the investigation, 'check rolls' are required to perform certain tasks, discover clues, sneak, and perhaps even prevent an imminent demise.

To pass a check roll you must roll **2D6** (two six-sided dice), apply the *modifier* to the dice result (see the *Difficulty Modifiers* table), and if the result is *equal to or less* than the skill or attribute for the check, you have passed. If the result is *higher*, you have failed and must face the consequences. Note that all check rolls are made against the *current* value of the attribute or skill, as your attribute/skill values can be affected through the investigation by a loss of health and composure – those modifiers are explained later.

Difficulty Modifiers for Check Rolls

Difficulty	Modifier
Very Easy	-2 to die roll
Easy	-1 to die roll
Regular	+0 (no modifier)
Hard	+1 to die roll
Very Hard	+2 to die roll
Extreme	+3 to die roll

You won't need to remember the above modifiers as each check roll in the book will state the required modifier.

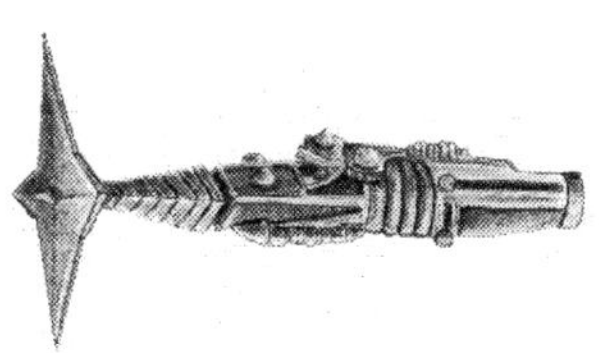

Example of a Check roll

You are talking to someone who seems suspicious. As the conversation continues, you believe you noticed something unusual about their appearance.

You make a Hard (2D6+1) Perception check. You roll 2D6 and get a combined total of 7, then modify the roll by the difficulty (in this case, +1 for a Hard check). The total is 8. Your Perception skill in this situation is also 8. You have passed, and what you discover could be a vital clue…

If the result had been 9 or more, you would have failed.

Health and Composure

You start every game with **10 Health**, and **10 Composure**. This is represented on your *Investigator Sheet* as a vertical table. The top is 10, the bottom is zero. You can circle the current level of your Health and Composure on this table.

Your Health and Composure can never go above the initial value of 10.

Health represents your physical condition, and Composure represents your mental condition. At various times you may lose Health points (due to a fall, in combat, or other reasons), or you may be asked to make a **Composure Check** against your *current* Composure level due to frightening encounters or situations. Always ensure you keep track of these two attributes using the table in the *Investigator Sheet*. Remember, if you are asked to make a Composure (or Health) check, it must be made against your *current* score, and not the initial score of 10. This represents the idea that the more your Composure suffers, the more likely it will continue to suffer and worsen, and if it reaches zero… you could lose your mind.

Further to this, the loss of these attributes carries certain penalties. On your *Investigator Sheet* you will see a **Modifier Effect**. For example, if your Health falls to 6 or less, you now must adjust your Dexterity by minus 1. If you manage to heal yourself to 7 or above, this effect is removed. Be sure to note these changes as your Health and Composure fall and rise and affect your skills and other attributes. Note, too, that as your Composure falls, you can gain bonuses to Strength, Combat and Damage. (This *can* raise that attribute or skill above the *Initial* level).

The increase represents your manic state in which you are likely to be more aggressive. If you have 7 Strength and 8 Combat, but your Composure drops sharply to 2, you now have 8 Strength and 9 Combat (and -1 Dexterity).

If either Health or Composure reach zero, your investigation ends immediately. Sometimes there will be a consequence to this that can be read for further detail – for example, during a fight it might state if you lose, turn to a certain paragraph. If not, stop reading immediately, as you have been defeated, and you must start the investigation again. You might want to adjust your character statistics based on your experience in the previous attempt to give yourself a better chance in the next game.

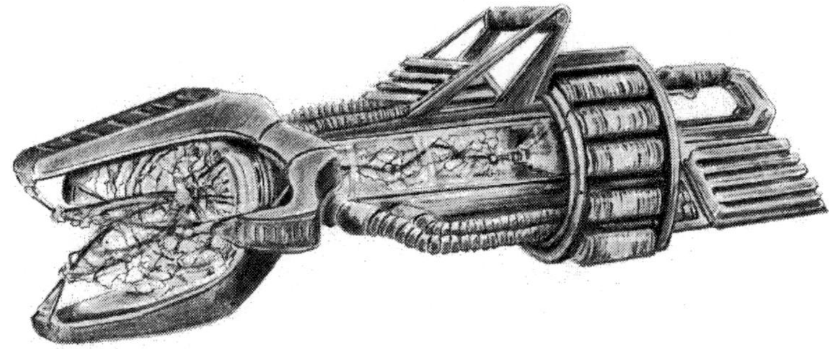

Combat – One-on-One

During your investigation you may find yourself in the unfortunate situation of having to fight for your life. For these desperate situations you have your **Combat** skill. To resolve combat situations the following rules, apply.

Combat is divided into a series of rounds. Each round consists of an attack roll for each combatant. At times (but not always), it will be important to track the number of rounds passing. Be sure to do this if the text instructs you to.

To resolve a one-on-one combat:

- Roll 2D6 and add your **Combat** skill. This is your **Attack Level.**
- Roll 2D6 for your opponent and add their **Combat** skill. This is your opponent's **Attack Level**.

- If your Attack Levels match, the result is a standoff, and the combat continues to the next round.
- If your Attack Level is higher than your opponent's, you deal 1 Damage to them. Reduce their Health by 1. (If you have any weapons that deal additional damage, add that to the damage result).
- If your opponent's Attack Level is higher than yours, they deal 1 Damage to you. Reduce your Health by 1. (If your opponent deals additional damage – this will be noted in the text – then add that additional damage).
- Combat then continues to the next round where the rolls are repeated.
- The first combatant to drop to zero health loses. If this is you, the investigation is over.
- If you win, continue with the investigation.

You may also encounter a variety of weapons or other tools to aid in Combat situations. Take note of the rules for these items if or when they are found. They can offer increased damage or even increased Combat skill.

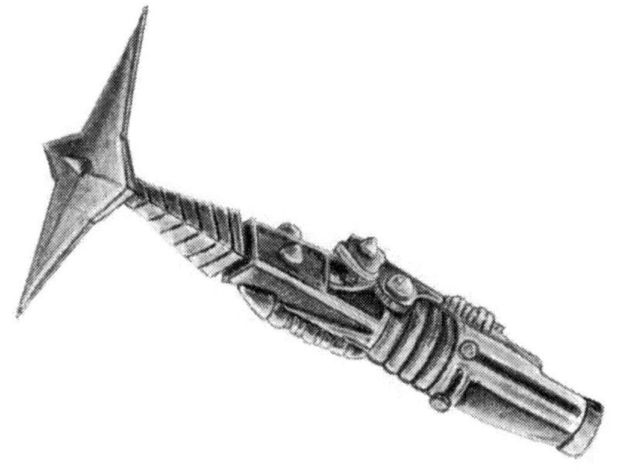

Combat – Against the Odds

Fighting two or more opponents at a time

When fighting two or more opponents at a time you will be at a distinct disadvantage. All opponents get 1 attack each in each combat round (unless otherwise stated in the text).

- Choose which one of the opponents you are fighting for the Combat roll. You can change which opponent you are attacking each round (unless otherwise stated in the text), but can only damage the chosen opponent in that round.
- Roll 2D6 and add your Combat skill. This is your **Attack Level**.
- Roll 2D6 for the opponent you are facing. Calculate the winner as noted in the one-on-one rules, and apply the Damage as before.
- Now, roll 2D6 for *each other* opponent in the fight, and add their respective combat skills to get their **Attack Levels**. For each opponent that betters your **Attack Level** (that you already rolled previously, you do not roll again) they deal 1 Damage to you. If your **Attack Level** is equal to or greater than theirs, you avoid these additional attacks, but note you *do not* damage them. You can only damage the opponent you are facing.

Example: You are facing two unknown creatures, one with Combat skill 7, and the other with Combat skill 6. You may fight them in any order, so you choose to fight #1 (the skill 7) creature first. It has less health and so killing it quicker will reduce the combat to one-on-one sooner.

You roll your attack against creature #1 and score a total

Attack Level of 13, and roll for the creature getting a final total of 12. You deal 1 Damage to that creature. Now, creature #2 attacks: You roll for it, get an 8, add the combat of the creature for a total of 14. Your original roll was 12. The second creature has hit you, dealing 1 Damage. If the creature's total attack roll had been 12 or less, it would have missed, but remember that no damage is dealt to that creature because it is not the creature you are actively engaged with.

MYTHOS POINTS

Mythos points are a *permanent* record of your investigation. They are awarded (or removed) during play for a variety of reasons – finding an important clue or item, performing certain actions, and even for the many ways you might meet your demise. They begin on zero for the very first game, and will accumulate over the course of each game you play, with the totals from your last game being your starting total for the next.

You must record two figures here, the first is the number of investigations (or games) you have played – so each investigation attempt raises this by 1, and the second number is the *Mythos* points total across all of those investigation attempts. Upon successful completion of the game, you will find out how to calculate your final *Mythos* points total.

Ensure you keep a consistent record of them. Your *Mythos* points cannot fall into a negative score – if this happens, raise them to zero.

By the end of a successful investigation, *Mythos* point totals are used to determine your final *Ranking* for the game.

Accept your fate… don't reset your *Mythos* points!

Investigator Journal and Items

You start the investigation with your satchel, containing your journal, a newspaper clipping from the Newport Examiner that has led you to the house, a flashlight, and some cash for the journey. You also have your trusty 1922 Chevrolet automobile. During your investigation, you'll be asked to record certain events, or the obtaining of various items, into your *Investigator Journal*. Be sure to note these down when received and note that some entries ask you to also keep a record of a certain paragraph number (or two numbers) for later use in the investigation. Note these very carefully. You should only use entries that you have earned in that playthrough of the book. If you fail, all entries should be deleted, only to be used if earned again in a subsequent game.

You may obtain other items and weapons along the way that don't require an entry reference. Note these down in either the weapons table, or the additional items area of the *Investigator Sheet*, as well as any modifiers they offer.

Visit www.grahamplowman.com to download a PDF copy of the Investigator Sheet that appears on the following pages.

INVESTIGATOR SHEET

Attributes and Skills	Base Value	Spend 6 Points	Initial Value (Max 8)	Current Value
Dexterity	6			
Strength	6			
Perception	6			
Stealth	6			
Combat	6			

Health (Current Value)	Modifier Effect	Composure (Current Value)	Modifier Effect
10	Healthy	**10**	Sane
9	-	**9**	-
8	-	**8**	-
7	-	**7**	- 1 Perception
6	- 1 Dexterity	**6**	-
5	- 1 Combat	**5**	- 1 Stealth
4	- 1 Strength	**4**	- 1 Dexterity
3	-	**3**	+ 1 Strength
2	- 1 Dexterity	**2**	+ 1 Combat
1	- 1 Combat	**1**	+ 1 Damage
0	Dead -10 *Mythos*	**0**	Insane -10 *Mythos*

WEAPONS

Weapon	Damage Modifier	Other Modifier
Unarmed	+0	

ADDITIONAL ITEMS

Satchel Newport Examiner Article Flashlight	

JOURNAL ENTRIES

Investigator Journal Entries / Items	Ref #1	Ref #2

MYTHOS POINTS

Number of Investigations	Current Mythos Points

ENCOUNTERS

Opponent	Combat	Health

PROLOGUE

My name is Frank Winston, I'm a journalist, and the tale I'm about to tell you is true. I can barely comprehend what happened to me in that house... and beyond. I try to forget, every day. Every day I try to hold my mind together.

I thought back to that fateful day, many weeks prior, that I happened upon the newspaper clipping in the Miskatonic library archives while researching for my column in the *Arkham Gazette*. The article was ten years old.

Newport Examiner, October 5th, 1916

> Yesterday evening, Sergeant John O'Mahony of the Newport Police Department was called out on business up north to investigate a series of killings that have shocked the sleepy town of Durham. It has been reported that three bodies were discovered by the local Reverend Thomas Downe, in a house five miles west of the town. In his report, Sergeant O'Mahony has stated that the victims were members of the Turne family, who have been residing in the house for three years before, having recently moved to the locale from Vermont. The locals say they were decent folk but certainly kept to themselves, with no known grievances with any other local or person known. Further to his investigations, Sergeant O'Mahony has revealed that only three of the four family members remain accounted for at this time, and a search (possibly a manhunt) is underway to find Edward Turne, the eldest son of twelve years.

At the gruesome scene, Jacob, the father, Melissa, the mother, and Sara, the youngest child of five years, were all found with a strange puncture wound on their abdomen, and very little blood remaining. There was no blood at the scene. The police would not elaborate further on this matter.

The police are also looking for a stranger to the town who was seen acting suspiciously the day before the bodies were discovered. He wandered out of town on foot, seemingly dazed and confused, and avoided the locals. He had an unkempt appearance, with some reporting it looked as though he had been in an accident. Thus far, he has not presented himself for questioning and the police would like to eliminate him from their inquiries.

The house, which sits atop Sentinel Hill (named for its far-reaching view in all directions), is no stranger to bad tidings. It sat empty for fourteen years prior due to events in 1899. It was previously the scene of more gruesome murders, which saw a whole generation of a family wiped out by unknown killers. Could it be the same killers returning after a seventeen-year absence? Professor Albert Peabody of the Miskatonic University doesn't believe so, but his keen interest in the developing field of forensic science has led him to the house. He is aiding the police with their investigation.

At his request, and by order of the Newport Police Department, the house will not be deemed

> habitable again. Also, after the initial investigations, Professor Peabody has asked that the house remain standing to preserve the crime scene. "Forensic Science make take years to mature, but when it does, we would be able to walk back into that building and study the evidence contained within its walls with new perspectives. One day, we may discover the truth."

I had tried to contact Professor Peabody at the university, but he'd been away on a research trip for years. An old friend of his, Professor George Stein, hadn't heard from him in all that time, but had remarked that Albert had initially been obsessed with that old case with the house for a long time, but eventually just lost interest in it and suggested to all to forget about his own pointless interest in the place. He remarked he was ashamed he wasted so much time on the worthless endeavour. Then, one day, he just left the university grounds to travel for research. The university wasn't funding his trip and so no one could say where he was. There was no paper trail to follow.

I decided to indulge my curiosity and plan a trip to Durham. As I mentioned, I write for the *Arkham Gazette*, with unsolved mysteries, folklore, and local legends, being my main interest. My column, 'What Lies Beneath?' was rather popular, and this tale seemed like a quite a find. I felt compelled to see this place for myself… how I wish I never had such inclinations or morbid predilections.

How I wish I never found… that accursed house on Sentinel Hill.

NOW, TURN OVER

CRAFT TIRES
EST. 1890
PETE'S FUEL DEPOT
CRAFT TIRES
EST 1890
ETHYL GAS
NO
MOTOR OIL
ZEPPELIN
PREMIUM
GAS & OIL

1

The year is 1926, September the 23rd, the time is 4:45 p.m. The fading sun casts a grey silhouette across the crumbling road as your Chevrolet bumps and crunches its way through the falling leaves. The multicoloured tree line sways in the early fall breeze, with most of their leaves still clinging on. The roadside thickets and overhanging trees clip the side of your automobile every few feet. You hear cracks and snaps as the twigs that strayed too far break off, or are snapped under the wheels. The town of Durham must not get many visitors, at least not using this route. The birds are singing, however, with chirps and songs aplenty, seemingly taking no notice of your intrusion. You are thankful at least that the area is not silent, for if it weren't for the birdsong, you fancy that it would be slightly foreboding to the outsider. You shrug off those fanciful thoughts and emerge from under the canopy of leaves.

The trees thin out and become meadows, extending far on both sides of the road. The tall grass sways in some, while others are clearly victim of the harvest, bare and flat. A beaten-up old sign nailed to a thick post reads 'Durham'. Squinting through the glare of the low sun, you see the town up ahead.

You enter the town and pull your vehicle in to a garage. The sign over the place reads *Pete's Fuel Depot*. You don't need fuel just yet; you've more than enough for the time being. You're looking for directions to Sentinel Hill before it gets too late. You had hoped to arrive hours earlier, but took a wrong turn in Kingsport. The garage has just one pump and looks a little rundown. The paint is peeling from the wood-panelled walls and there is no sign of any attendant.

Stepping out of the automobile, you look up and down the street, thankful for the opportunity to stretch your legs. It's quiet. You spot an elderly lady shuffling along on the other side of the road, paying you no heed. There's not another soul around. What will you do?

Approach the old lady for directions, turn to **8**.
Ignore the woman and enter the garage, turn to **59**.

2

Unsure as to why this tunnel has no lights, you decide to turn down it regardless. As the light from the tunnel behind begins to fade you curse Edward again, and the fact that your flashlight is back in the attic of the house.

If you have recorded in your Investigator Journal '*Have a glowing mushroom*', then turn to the reference you noted with that entry now.

If not, turn to **76**.

3

Edward hugs you. "Thank you... thank you so much!" He falls to his knees, tears running down his cheeks. You've managed to save everyone from the hell on Yuggoth.

You remain with the family for a time, masquerading as a helpful stranger that Edward sought on the road when the family took ill from a strange malady. Both you and Edward agree to deny all knowledge of what really happened. You both maintain that it was a fever dream. Melissa has little enough recollection to disagree, and the young child, Sara, seems unscathed.

But Jacob, the father, is a changed man. Moments of lucidity reveal details of a visit to the hills of Vermont, where he discovered the machine, and whispers of an unusual individual that showed him how to use it to help his farm prosper. You and Edward bury the machine deep in the woods. Not much else Jacob speaks of is worth delving into or makes sense. You know it contains a hideous truth – of the mi-go and their possible influence on Earth – but you cannot allow those thoughts to become threads of a new story... for you, too, might eventually go hopelessly mad. Over time, Melissa and Edward thank you for your help, but soon the need for a doctor is discussed.

The date is October 11th, 1916. The newspaper clipping that brought you here remains as before, but tells a story that is no longer what actually happened. Your car is gone... or never existed. Only that which you brought with you to Yuggoth and back, remains as it was. The machine was more than just a way to traverse across space, it also had the power to transcend time. Edward and Sara hadn't aged because no time had passed for them. The machine sent you to Yuggoth ten years in the past – possibly only moments after the family had been brought there. Now you realise just how powerful this device was for the mi-go, and why they were so tenacious in trying to recover the lost power source.

You settle in the town of Durham, get a job working as a store clerk for Mrs. Wilkins, and remain there as both support for the family you saved, and as a way to stay away from... yourself. A young reporter by the name of Frank Winston starts to write an article for the *Arkham Gazette,* which you have delivered by post especially to your door.

On September the 23rd, around 4:45 p.m., in the year 1926, you stand on the main road of Durham and wait for a Chevrolet to trundle down the road. You contemplated writing to yourself, anonymously of course, as a warning to stay away... but instead felt that you would simply be compelling this other version of yourself to question the warning and turn up anyway. When you thought about it, you know that is what you would have done. No one arrives... there are no strange flashes of green lightning, and no voice on the air. The killings have now never happened, the original article was never written, and thus the other version of yourself remains in Arkham writing for the paper. It is highly unlikely that your paths will ever cross.

If you have recorded in your Investigator Journal '*Received a gift*', then you must turn to the reference associated with that entry now.

If you do not have this entry, turn to **36**.

4

You wave your hand before the professor. He doesn't even blink. "Are you feeling okay, professor?"
A moment passes, and he suddenly speaks up. "Yes, why yes. I feel quite good. If you will," he gestures for you to take the stairs.
He did not seem to hear or acknowledge your request to leave.

If you want to repeat again your desire to leave and head towards the door, turn to **149**.
Or change your mind and do as he asks by climbing the stairs, turn to **225**.

5

You follow the left branch which, to your relief, starts to climb upwards again. A series of stepped ledges about five feet in height are easy enough to climb over, like a giant staircase, and eventually the way opens out again into a much wider cavern. However, you pause to take in the sight before you, and even consider turning back!

Ahead in the cavern is a forest of white glistening threads suspended from the cave ceiling. You look up and see that the ceiling is completely hidden from view by a thick white mist. The threads descend from the mist and almost touch the cave floor. Across the opposite side of the cavern is another opening which appears to rise upwards. It could be the way out.

What do you want to do?

Tug on the thread nearest you. Turn to **263**.
Cross the cavern, taking care to avoid the hanging threads. Turn to **68**.
Change your mind and return to the fork, and take the right-hand tunnel instead. Turn to **481**.

6

You creep out from behind the containers and approach the mi-go, ready to strike.

Make a Hard (2D6+1) **Stealth** check.

If you pass, turn to **114**.
If you fail, the mi-go turns at the last moment as you approach and rears up on to two legs to fight. Turn to **505**.

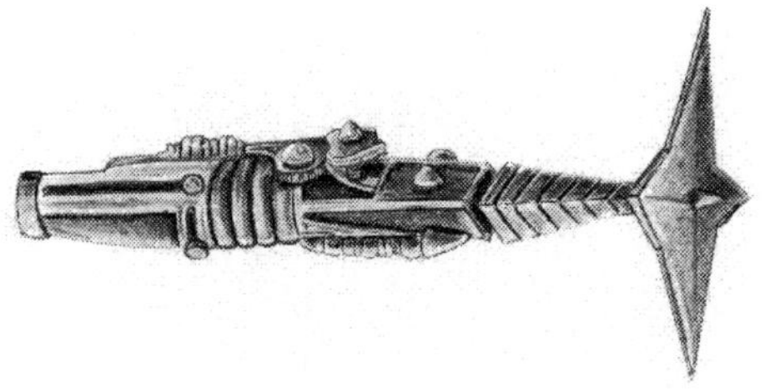

7

The door opens into a small, elongated room, with rows of curious items running down both sides. It appears to be a storage area full of odds and ends. There are large empty cannisters and various metal joints, cables, and other unidentifiable pieces of equipment.

Make a Regular (2D6) **Perception** check.

If you pass, turn to **189**.
If you fail, turn to **51**.

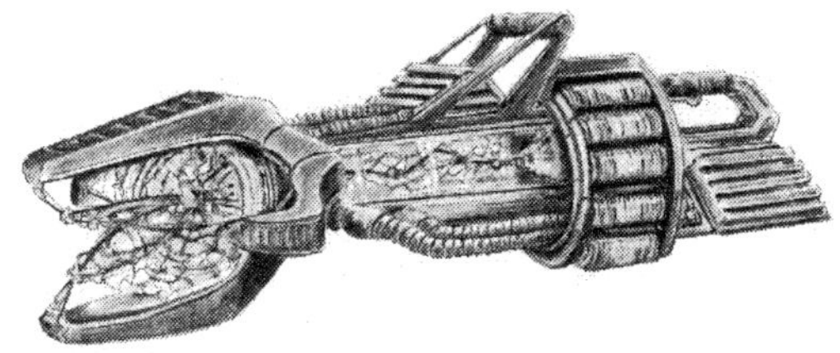

8

You take a few steps towards the old lady which prompts her to stop walking.
"Good afternoon ma'am. I was wondering if you could help me. You see I'm not from around these parts and..."
"You don't say," answers the woman, cutting you off.
Her head is bowed. Her heavily lined face remains fixed on the path in front of her feet. But you can see her eyes and heavy brow rise to look at you.

What will you ask her?

Tell her you're looking for Sentinel Hill, and ask if she can direct you (turn to **152**), or inquire about the town and the absence of people (turn to **560**).

9

You insert the two plugs into the sockets of the second cylinder and wait, unsure of what is supposed to happen. You are suddenly startled when a strange mechanical sounding voice starts to speak from the connected speaker box.

"Am I awake? Who is there?" It speaks in a strange metallic and emotionless tone. There's a whirring sound as the lens device turns slowly of its own accord and stops when pointing directly at you. It speaks again. "A man? Who are you and where are the mi-go?"

Can it be? Is this 'brain' speaking and looking at you through this miraculous device?

You explain who you are and how you came to be here.

"I am Charles Glover Barkla, a physicist. I have learned much, and seen many miraculous sights in the company of these beings, the mi-go. I offer that I, too, have taught these beings some worthwhile avenues of exploration in the field of quantum mechanics. Their technology, as you have no doubt seen, is far ahead of our own."

"But where is your body? Why did the creatures do this to you?" you ask, incredulous.

"They asked, and I was honoured. My body is in suspended animation, and my visit to this world is almost at an end. They will return me to my body. I will be honour bound not to speak of this, but will use the knowledge discovered to further mankind. Would I have known they were successful in transporting our kind without the need for such measures, I would have certainly been obliged to accept that method upon which you found yourself here on Yuggoth. Perhaps my esteemed colleague, August Möbius, has been instrumental in this endeavour."

"Tell me more of this 'Yuggoth'." you ask.

10

"I see you know little of your predicament. You are on Yuggoth, a currently undiscovered ninth planet from our sun."

The eye-lens whirrs again, turning to the empty cylinder. "Ah, I see the good Herr Möbius has already been returned. We were often allowed to speak to one another to theorise upon matters of space and time. I'm afraid he would be of more help to you than I, but I do know he was allowed to work in the laboratory quite often. You might find some answers there. It is the central tunnel in the main chamber just outside."

"Now if you'll excuse me, be a good chap and disconnect the aural and visual apparatus, for it is quite wearying upon the mind to operate them for extended periods of time. I wish you well. The mi-go aren't so bad, if you have something to offer them, that is."
You do as he asks, and shudder at the thought of those horrid mi-go creatures doing this to people. What could possess anyone to accept this fate?

You return to the central chamber. Turn to **235**.

10

You back away coughing and spluttering, rubbing your face in an attempt to clear the spores away. Some of the spores have made their way into your lungs. You gasp and wheeze for a few moments, and manage to eventually catch your breath.

You don't feel well due to the effect of the spores and must lose **2 Health**, and reduce both **Combat** and **Strength** attributes by **1** to reflect your weakened state.

Cursing your curiosity, and this place, you need to decide your next move.

Approach the well in the centre of the room. Turn to **327**.
Head for the door in the far opposite wall. Turn to **546**.
Head for the door over on the right-hand side. Turn to **7**.
Investigate the ramp going up to the next floor. Turn to **433**.

11

You make your way across to the cube and it is just within reach when Yar'ith's voice echoes across the cavern. "Huuuumaan betraayer..."
You glance back and see Yar'ith crouch low and enter the cavern, its head the tell-tale deep red of an enraged mi-go as it skitters with surprising speed across the cavern floor. The distraction is enough that you fail to notice a brush against one of the threads – it attaches to your jacket sleeve. You reach for the cube and unwittingly tug on the thread. You glance with fear into the mist above only to see your worst nightmare made flesh. Silently, like a shadow of death, a giant, vaguely spider-like thing, flows down from the mist.

Suddenly, a wrong move by the mi-go sees it ensnared by a thread. It sticks like glue to the creature, and as it thrashes about, Yar'ith becomes hopelessly entangled.

The visage of this bloated purple monstrosity bores into your very soul. If you have recorded in your journal '*Been inside the* cavern', then you do not need to make a composure check. If you do not have this entry, make an Extreme (2D6+3) **Composure** check. If you fail, you must lose 2 Composure. If you pass, lose 1 Composure.

Mercifully, the ensnared mi-go draws the spider-thing away from you. It changes direction and descends upon Yar'ith. This is your chance to get the *Tok'llian* and escape! You try to pull yourself free from the thread that holds you...

Make a Hard (2D6+1) **Strength** check.

If you pass, turn to **260**.
If you fail, turn to **280**.

12

You hear a 'pop' sound and then the spilling of liquid off to your left. You turn to search for the source, and it's almost as if one of the eggs just blinked out of existence. Watching closer, you see another egg turn black and vanish, then another! As you continue to observe, a living black slime envelops egg after egg, bursting it, then absorbing its contents into itself. Is this the creature you unwittingly released from the container in the storeroom? It moves along the wall, devouring the eggs one by one at an alarming rate. It grows larger with each one it absorbs.

Record in your Investigators Journal *'The black slime devoured the mi-go eggs'*, and note the reference 180. +2 *Mythos* points.

You don't wish to linger here while this creature feeds.

Will you make a dash for the opposite side of the chamber and leave (turn to **267**), or sneak carefully across the chamber while the creature is busy feasting on the eggs (turn to **448**)?

13

Using the flashlight, you scan the basement. Loose stones, pieces of wood and dirt litter the floor. Rotten wooden shelving rests against two of the walls, and contains nothing of interest. Empty and broken bottles, and various containers of junk. Piles of wooden crates lean against the south-facing wall. Seeing nothing of interest here, you head back up the steps. Suddenly, you're surprised by a figure at the top of the stairs just as you're coming out. A man, possibly late fifties, steps in front of you and jabs you with a syringe. You fall backwards, tumbling down the steps, breaking your neck in the process.

Record in your Investigator Journal *'You were killed by an unknown assailant on the basement stairs.'* -5 *Mythos* points.

Your investigation ends here.

14

You're not as quiet as you endeavour to be, which you become acutely aware of when one of the larger armed mi-go turns to face you. Its head changes from purple to a dark red as it raises the gun. You must think fast.

Dash for the junction on the right as it's just a few feet ahead. Turn to **178**.
Turn and flee back through the egg chamber. Turn to **113**.

15

"Yes, er, I am looking for Sentinel Hill. I found this article you see... " you call back in reply, holding up the newspaper clipping.
"You're so curious you've come all the way out here to see an old place?" He reaches into his coat pocket. "That doesn't sound right to me. You're from the university, aren't ya? I'll have no interference from the university here!"
"Are you Professor Peabody?" you ask, suddenly realising

the connection with the house and the Miskatonic University.
"Come to put a stop to my work? I won't return those *Necronomicon* pages. They hold the key to all this!" He gets very agitated, pulls a revolver from his pocket, and starts waving it around at you. "Leave, now, before you can't leave at all."

Record in your Investigators Journal '*You were warned to leave the house alone*', and note the reference 335.

You try to protest, but the gun changes your mind. You feel you've no choice but to leave. Turn to **210**.

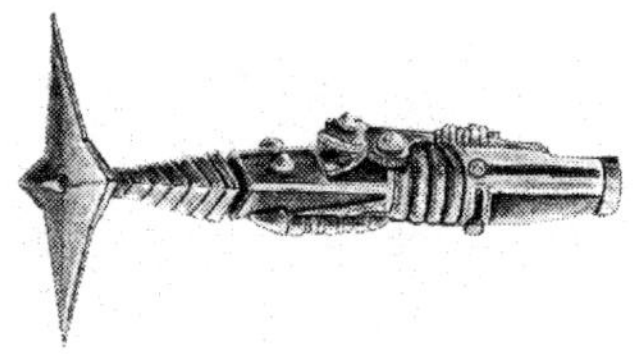

16

You pick up the journal and start flicking through the entries.
"That's private," says the professor, without any sense of emotion.
"We'll see." you reply, continuing to look through it. Skipping to the last entries you see it's dated just recently.

> 14th September 1926
> I've decoded the equation! Now to use the numbers and see what happens. I knew that blasted book contained knowledge far beyond our understanding or reason – but I'll show those fools in Miskatonic now. Cowards, locking away secrets that would change our

very existence. Bah! They'll be crawling at my feet soon... begging for the answers.

21st September 1926
I'm close! I know it. The numbers are degrees for each dial!!! How did I not see it until now? 190 is not 190 degrees, its dial 1, 90 degrees, dial 2, 37 degrees, and dial 3, 121 degrees! Three-dimensional space! Dial 4, I have no reference for. I will leave that alone on zero. By my calculations I was only two degrees off as those dials are so sensitive. At this distance though (roughly 3 billion miles) two degrees is enough to miss the barn right before you! I've made the adjustment – the next test should hit!!!!

23rd September 1926
I've managed to open it! GLORIOUS!!!! The lights! The glorious lights! Green and intense, yet somehow you can stare right at it without the need to blink. There's something on the other side. A room? Soon I can prepare for the crossing.

Record in your Investigator Journal '*Dial 1, 90 degrees, dial 2, 37 and dial 3, 121. Dial 4, leave alone.*' +5 *Mythos* points.

The professor is growing impatient behind you. He insists now that you've read his journal, you know enough to stop asking questions and come see for yourself.

You decide now is the time to follow him upstairs, turn to **229**.

17

You step over the threshold of the door, and it slides shut behind you, making the tunnel that much darker and uninviting. The humidity in the tunnel is high, and you loosen your collar a little to compensate. The ground is slick with moisture – you tread lightly and carefully. You follow the tunnel for a few minutes until it opens out into a huge cavern about one hundred feet wide, and so tall you cannot see the ceiling as it fades to darkness. Slicing the cavern in two is a twenty-foot-wide chasm running through the centre from left to right. You approach the edge and peer down into the murky depths. It's a sheer drop, and just as with the ceiling, you cannot see the bottom. Just how far underground are you? On the opposite side is another tunnel, but there's no way to cross. For all intents and purposes, it's a dead end.

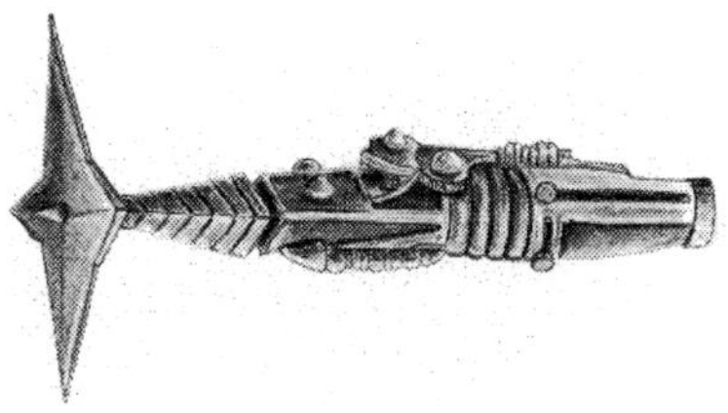

You suddenly hear a strange clacking and clicking sound from behind you... the sound of something hard hitting the stone floor of the cavern. You turn to see a lone mi-go creature standing in the tunnel entrance! It takes a few steps towards you – its hard, pointed feet, clacking on the stone. As it skitters slightly to the left, then the right, the bulbous head of feelers turns a luminous purple. Its wings beat momentarily, then rest again. It's a hideously unnerving sight in the dim glow of the cavern, and with the chasm behind you, you're trapped.

What will you do?

Try and talk to it. Turn to **155**.
Rush it and attack. Turn to **301**.
Try to edge your way around it so that the chasm isn't to your back. Turn to **243**.

18

Outside, Pete lifts the hood on your car, and pulls a wrench out from his belt. "Your radiator wouldn't last too much longer with this valve loose the way it is." He tightens it, and closes the hood. "Now, no charge for that." You thank him for the repair. He bids you good day and heads back into the garage.

Record in your Investigator Journal that '*Your car radiator was fixed*', and note the reference 94.
Later in the story, if asked have you earned this information, you will turn to 94. (Do not turn to that now).

Do you want to head on your way in the hope you can find the house (turn to **557**), or head to the post office in the hope of getting better directions (turn to **218**).

19

You pull with all of your remaining strength and manage to get up far enough to swing your leg over to catch your foot on the metal walkway. From there, the rest is relatively easy as you haul yourself over the edge onto the raised floor. You take a few moments to catch your breath.

The walkway leads out of the main room through an opening in the right-hand wall.

As soon as you enter this passage you instinctively duck. On your right there's an open doorway looking into a side room where two mi-go creatures are busy attending to tasks. One is operating a console and the other is examining a variety of items on a metal slab in a corner. Various containers with specimens of meat, organs, and even a brain, line a shelf nearest to where you are. At the far end of the corridor that you are in, there is a closed circular doorway. You suspect the creatures would hear or notice if that door was opened. What is your next move?

Prepare for battle. Enter the room and surprise the creatures. Turn to **420**.
Stay low, and sneak out of the area through the door ahead. Turn to **74**.

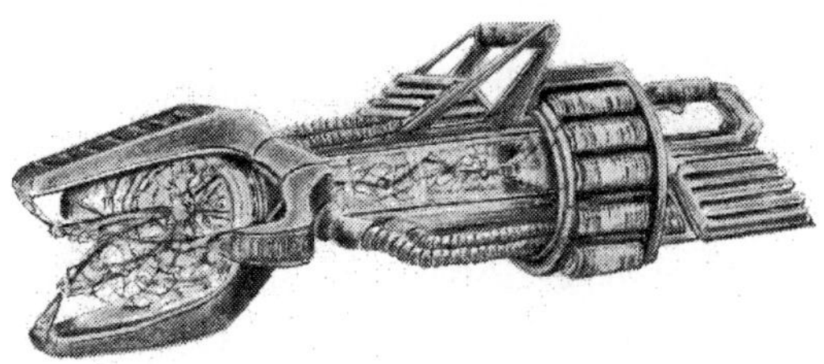

20

She eyes you up and down for a moment. Her lined face locked in a curious stare. Then she speaks up.
"Tragic, that was. Poor family. T'was the boy that did it, didn't ya hear? Young Edward, eh, Turne, yes that was it. Turne. He turned on his own." You hear a raspy sound emanate from the old woman. You realise she's laughing at her pun. "Never did catch that boy. Tragic."
"Did you know them, the family?" you ask.

"In a roundabouts way. The mother, don't recall her name, was a sweet enough thing. A painter she was. Went about painting the land hereabouts. What was her name?" She raises withered a hand to her chin, and bows her head in thought.
"Melissa, ma'am," you offer.
"No, no, or was it, mayhap... anyway my boy, I need to scoot. I don't rightly remember the way, but definitely take a left, young man, as it's out that-a-way," she says pointing to the west.

And with that, she shuffles away mumbling to herself. What will you do now?

If you want to enter the garage, turn to **59**.
To call it a day, look for a lodging and get a fresh start in the morning, turn to **372**.
Or return to your car and drive on. Perhaps there will be a sign to point you in the right direction towards the hill. Turn to **331**.

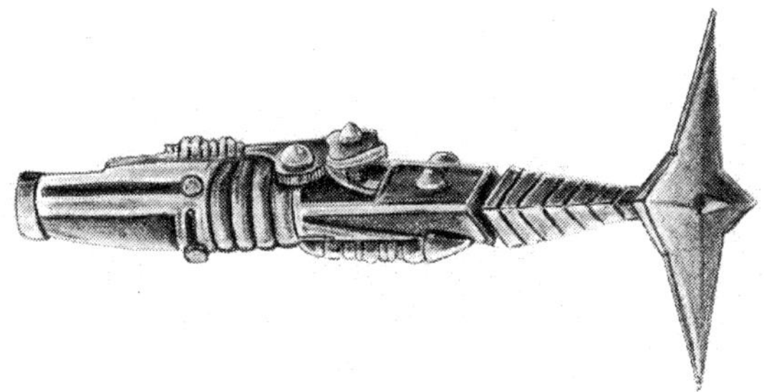

21

You approach the door to listen, but have forgotten that your presence close to the door activates them. The door slides aside revealing a terrifying sight in the corridor. Standing there is one of those hideous insect-like creatures. It turns towards you, emitting a buzzing sound, with the noise of its many feet clicking and clacking on the hard metal floor. The creature enters the room, forcing you to back away.

You will have to defend yourself! Turn to **48**.

22

You take the left fork, the road getting a little bumpier. You soon arrive at another junction.

If you continue straight on, turn to **46**.
If you turn right, turn to **563**.

23

Glancing down you see his hand is covered in grime and oil. You decide not to shake it.
"Frank Winston, pleased to meet you," you say whilst nodding.
Pete leaves his hand out for a moment longer, but then his smile fades and he lowers his hand. "I see, then that'll be two dollars for the repair on your car. Then be on your way. This is no car park."
You apologise, but he doesn't want to hear it. "Two dollars, mister. Working ain't for free."

If you wish to pay him the two dollars, turn to **270**.
Or refuse to pay on the grounds you didn't ask for him to touch your car in the first place, turn to **413**.

24

The tunnel twists and turns, but you're able to see ahead due to a glowing fungus that covers the tunnel wall in small patches every few feet. The tunnel runs on for a few minutes before it starts to narrow to the point where you need to crawl. You eventually see a small opening ahead just large enough to fit through.

You drop a few feet down from into a much larger tunnel. Turn to **455**.

25

You leave the dial alone, set on zero degrees.

How do you want to set the fourth dial?

To leave it as it is, set to 17 degrees, turn to **70**.
To set it to zero degrees, turn to **447**.
To set it to 100 degrees, turn to **364**.

26

For a few moments the creature doesn't respond, then it leans forward. The closer it gets, the more the mind-shredding dread becomes almost unbearable.

"An unwitting traveller. A worthless offering. Begone."

The void falls away like a curtain tumbling to the floor. Turn to **29**.

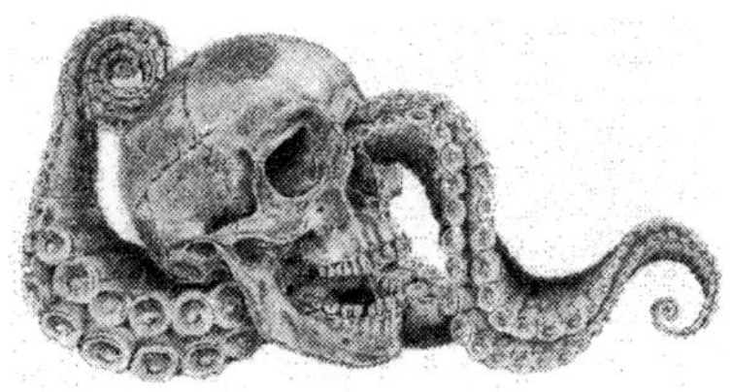

27

The chamber here is a dead end, but would seem to be a guard station, perhaps for the protection of the egg chamber behind you. Numerous large containers, each with a yellow sweet-smelling liquid, line a low shelf on the wall to your right. On your left sit a variety of odd-looking contraptions, possibly for maintaining the care of the eggs, but you cannot be sure. There's nothing else here. You glance back down the tunnel, conscious that the gelatinous creature may come this way.

What do you want to do?

Examine the strange contraptions, turn to **288**.
Taste the sweet-smelling yellow liquid, turn to **583**.
Leave and make for the side tunnel while you still can, turn to **138**.

28

You charge at the mi-go as it attempts to turn the gun in your direction.

Make a Hard (2D6+1) **Dexterity** check.

If you pass, turn to **266**.
If you fail, turn to **281**.

29

You are standing by the bowl and statue in the temple once again. Somehow protected in the void from the effects of the creature's malice, it now all comes rushing at you. You fall to your knees and scream.

Mercifully, the almost overwhelming feeling subsides quickly, and your senses return to you. However, you have not returned from the void unscathed.

Make a Very Hard (2D6+2) **Composure** check. If you pass, you lose **1 Composure**. If you fail you must lose **3 Composure**.

You need to decide what to do next. Turn to **235**.

30

The mi-go falls to the floor, dead, just as you hear those unmistakable buzzing tones coming from the opening to the walkway above. More are coming!

It's then you notice a long metal rod next to the dead creature. It must have brought it down with it. You decide to take the metal rod for yourself.

Record in your Investigators Journal '*Have a metal rod*', and note the reference 283. +1 *Mythos* point.

Now you must think fast and get out of here.

The large door is opened via a panel next to it set into the wall. If you want to try this way, turn to **504**.
Or take the faster but less desirable route, and follow the conveyor through the wall. Turn to **110**.

31

"You said your name was Edward. Edward Turne?"
"Yesssss... You alreaady knoooow thissss." You notice a hint of confusion in his voice despite the unnatural qualities it contains.
"Come out into the light, Edward, if you could, please."
He moves forward, allowing more light to fall across his misshapen body. You can see him more clearly now but can't understand how he could be Edward Turne, for he would be in his twenties if still alive. His face is that of a boy, as reported in the article to be twelve years old. He looks gaunt and sickly and of similar size for a boy that age, but hunched over, and slightly twisted. His right foot is turned in and looks to be dead weight, dragging behind

him. His right arm is elongated, nearly twice the length as his arm should be, and worse still, at the end in place of a hand is a hideous engineered prosthetic of a metal claw. The claw is articulated, wired, and jointed. It looks jagged and sharp, and quite dangerous. His left arm looks normal, at least what you can see of it.

What do you want to ask?
To inquire about his 'claw' and other physical changes, turn to **571**.
Ask where he has been all this time, turn to **90**.
Or to inquire how come he is still only twelve years old, turn to 77.

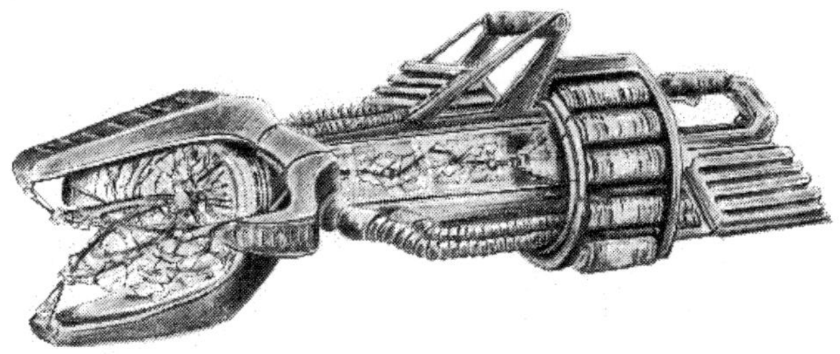

32

Nyarlathotep places a huge hand across your forehead. You try to recoil but are held fast by his indomitable will.

Suddenly, you feel stronger and more capable than ever before as a surge of energy passes through your body. Restore your **Health** to its *initial level* and regain **3 Composure**. However, you also feel a little light-headed and must reduce your **Perception** and **Stealth** by 1.

The void falls away like curtain tumbling to the floor. Turn to **344**.

33

The devices make little sense to you. One of them appears to be for extraction of the larvae, an articulated claw on the end of a tube. A single button on the tube extends it slowly before it snaps shut and retracts. It's too big and bulky to carry with you so you place it back down.

You can make for the side tunnel now. Turn to **138**.
Or try some of the yellow liquid on the other side of the room. Turn to **434**.

34

He catches you off balance on the step and pulls you down the remaining steps to the hard stone floor, knocking the wind out of you. Before you can regain your balance, he takes the syringe and injects it into your back. "I'm debating whether you're worth the effort now." he says, crouched down beside you. Your vision blurs and as the drug takes hold. Peabody continues talking, but his voice becomes an echo, then you fall under.

The drug takes effect. Turn to **120**.

35

You ask about the lack of people around and mention that the only other person you saw outside was an old woman wandering down the street.

"Aye, old Mrs. Barnes. She's a dear. Well, yeah, isn't a lot of folks about these days. Been that way for many a year now. Sure, if it weren't for this being the only route onwards to Dunwich, I don't think anyone would come this way. I'd sell no gas, and I'd be outta here myself. Speaking of which, you need some?"

"Sorry, no, I've more than enough I'm sure," you answer.

You decide it's time to ask about directions to the hill. Turn to **373**.

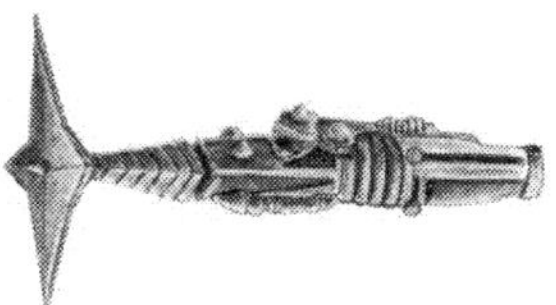

36

In February 1930, the planet Pluto is discovered... but you know it, and fear it, by another name – *Yuggoth*!

The discovery brings back a lot of painful and horrifying memories, making it difficult to sleep. You retreat for a time, gather your thoughts, and endeavour to carry on a normal life despite knowing that the mi-go are out there... *waiting*... perhaps constructing another power source for that accursed machine. Perhaps they have a score to settle with mankind... perhaps one you started!

Your story ends here. Now, turn to **586**.

37

Crouching down to look inside yields nothing as it is completely dark. You curse Edward, and the fact that your flashlight is back in the attic of the house. You move in, taking care not to hit your head. In the enclosed space your breathing sounds heavy and laboured as you move deeper.

Up ahead a light suddenly appears. The faint white glow of a teardrop shaped light flickers on and off with an unpredictable rhythm. Something doesn't seem right about this.

Make a Regular (2D6) **Composure** check.

If you pass, you can choose to turn back (turn to **368**) or continue toward the light (turn to **137**).
If you fail, you immediately turn back and exit the tunnel to explore the larger chamber. Turn to **368**.

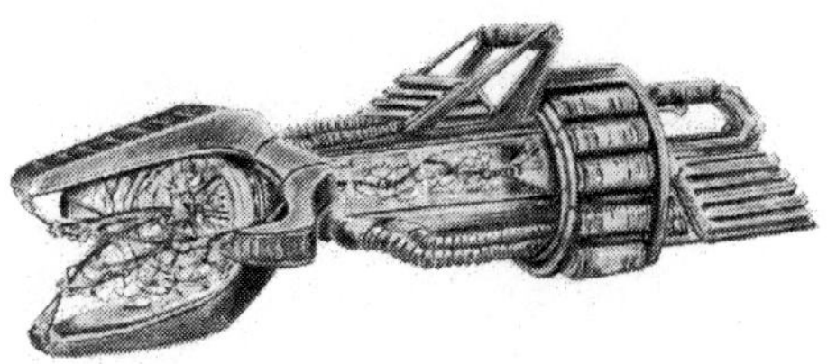

38

"Perhaps it'd be best if you explain first, professor. What's in the attic?" you ask, looking about the hallway.
He closes the door behind you, seemingly ignoring your query. The hallway darkens. Slivers of light still manage to penetrate, though, making it just bright enough to see. He stands there motionless again. You take a step back, feeling uneasy and justified in your defensive motion.

"Are you sure you're okay, professor?"
His eyes glint with a sickly green colour in the dull hallway. You've seen that shade of green light before. Suddenly he lunges at you brandishing a syringe.

Make a Regular (2D6) **Dexterity** check.

If you pass, turn to **409**.
If you fail, turn to **421**.

39

You follow behind the mi-go as they lead you through the intimidating maze that is their city. Continually moving upwards, one takes a moment to fly across a chasm and then extends a walkway so that you can follow. It seems that despite their ability to fly, there are methods to reach many areas by foot if necessary.

As you are led on, you see hundreds more of the creatures, sorting through rock and ore in vast quantities. It is a huge mining facility. You pluck up the courage to ask where you are and what are they doing, but the creatures do not answer.

Your final stop is a huge chamber filled with rows upon rows of cannisters lining the walls. Two armed mi-go bring you in, the others returning to their original duties.

"Our visssitor chammber of knowledge," one of the mi-go announces. This mi-go remains to guard you as the other turns to leave.
"I willl reeturrn with ooour... massster," it utters as it disappears through a door.

What will you do now?

Wait for the mi-go to return and speak with their 'master'. Turn to **352**.
Try to speak to the lone mi-go and get some answers before the other one returns. Turn to **185**.
Look for an escape route then launch an attack on this lone mi-go. Turn to **366**.

40

You try to recall the settings that got you here and set each one to the best of your recollection. When you get to the last dial, you move it, then recalling the machine in the attic, you set it back to zero again. The machine bursts into life. The low thrum starts up as you move away and clamber to your feet. The beam of green light shoots up from the sphere on top just like it had done in the attic of the house. It then bends downwards to rest parallel with the floor, striking the wall to form a shimmering portal. The entire room is bathed in the eerie pulsating light. It's difficult to see through the haze of the portal.

You rush back to Edward and explain how you can all leave this hellish place. Just as you are trying to convince him that you can help carry his unconscious family members into the portal chamber, the door on the opposite side opens – and in swarms a horde of mi-go. You're out of time! You grab Edward and tell him you must flee. He refuses. You tell him that you'll come back for his family, but he doesn't listen... he cradles his mother. The mi-go ignore him for the moment. You turn and run as a blast from a lightning gun ionizes the air! With one final push, you leap through the portal... and into the cold blackness of space. The machine was set incorrectly.

Record in your Investigator Journal '*You died in the cold blackness of space.*' -20 *Mythos* points.

Your investigation ends here.

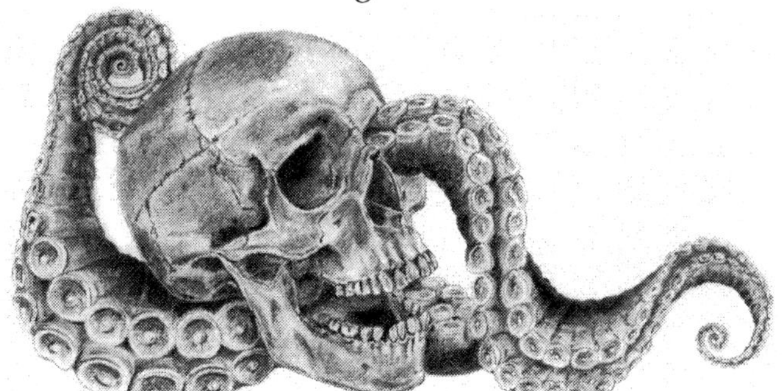

41

You search through the collected remains scatted around the Byakhee lair and find a metal rod next to a dead mi-go. If you haven't already found this item, you decide to take the metal rod for yourself.

Record in your Investigators Journal '*Have a metal rod*', and note the reference 283. +1 *Mythos* point.

From here you find your way across a rocky ledge that leads back to the main structure. You head inside. Turn to **170**.

42

You can't quite place what is troubling you. He closes the door behind you as you enter, dulling the sound of the heavy rain outside. Slightly on edge, you turn to face him, trying to smile. You almost felt he was reaching for you just then, but you pass it off as your imagination due to clearly being on edge over the whole situation ahead of you. The hallway is dark due to the boarded-up windows, but slivers of light penetrate just enough to make things visible. Peabody seems to be waiting for you to do or say something.

Ask him which room you should enter. Turn to **241**.
Ask the professor about the strange green lights you saw last night, assuming of course that it wasn't a dream. Turn to **257**.
Or tell him you've had a sudden change of heart, and wish to leave. Turn to **129**.

43

You approach the alcove and see that it contains a variety of unusual tools. Each one appears to be medical in nature. One of these is a large scalpel-like blade. You decide to take the scalpel. You may use this as a weapon and add +1 to the Damage you deal in combat while you have the scalpel (note this in your journal).

You're about to approach the metal slab by the opposite wall when you suddenly hear a strange clicking sound. It appears to be coming from just outside the door. What will you do?

To exit the room to investigate the sound, turn to **321**.
Listen at the door instead. Turn to **21**.
Or find somewhere in this room to hide. Turn to **118**.

44

Your attempts to defend yourself are in vain as the creature lashes out and spears you in your eye socket with a swift blow. You cry out in pain as your second eye is then plucked from its socket. "Huuumaaan vissson sphere!" it rasps with unnatural delight.

You await a killing blow, but it doesn't arrive. Instead, you are dragged away screaming. Still clinging to life, the creatures begin to experiment on you, slicing off body parts before you pass out.

You awake with a strange sensation and cannot feel your arms or legs. Turn to **564**.

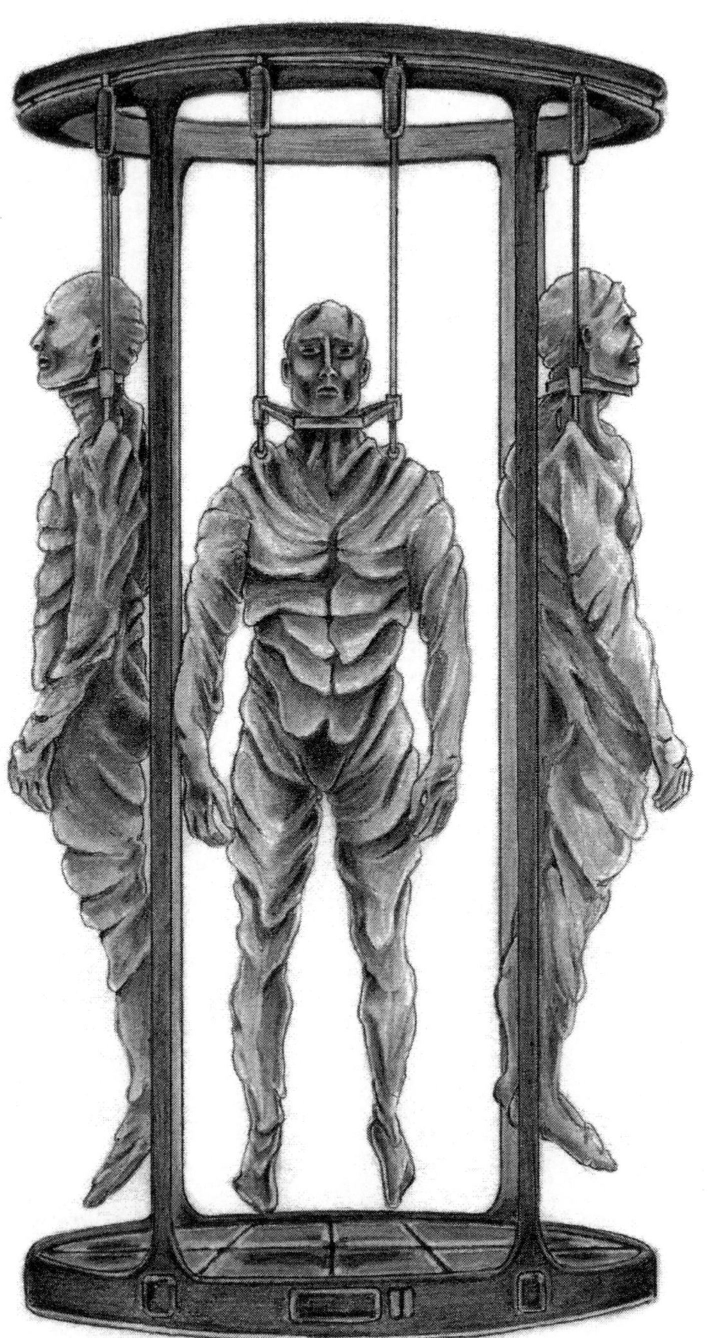

45

There's an unsettling look to the misshapen and loose hanging skin that is suspended from the metal frame. Next to them is a small table with a pile of human clothes. It consists of a variety of suits, overalls, and other workman's attire and three wigs. Are these disgusting creatures capable of disguising themselves as human by wearing skin and clothes? You shudder at the thought. Gain +5 *Mythos* points.

Make a Hard (2D6+1) **Composure** check. If you fail, you lose **1 Composure**.

There's nothing else of interest with these, and you certainly do not want to touch them.
If you haven't already, you can examine the exoskeleton (turn to **176**), or leave this room through the door in the far wall (turn to **317**).

46

As your car jostles its way down the uneven road, you come to a turn off to the left. You can take this turn or continue straight on.

To turn left, turn to **286**.
To continue straight, turn to **357**.

47

Climbing the stairs, you step out into the main hallway. The professor suggested that answers await in the attic.

If you want to go there now, turn to **172**.
Or instead, to search the remainder of the house first, turn to **326**.

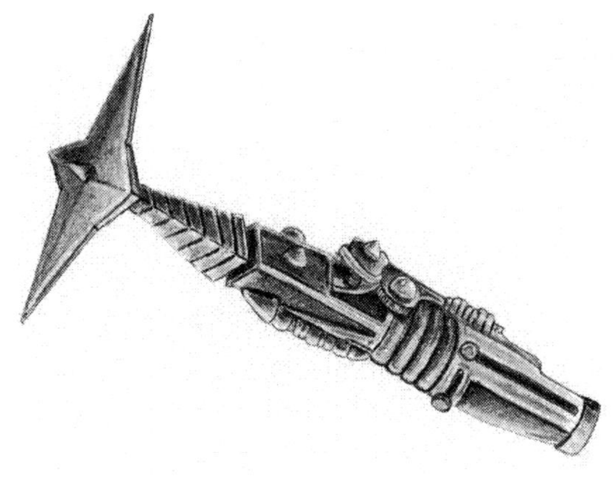

48

It points a claw in your direction and again emits that buzzing sound, but this time forming a word you understand. "Intruuuuudeeeer!" The creature's hideous head of writhing antennae changes to a deep red colour as it advances. You have no choice but to fight it.

Mi-go Worker
Combat 6
Health 5

If you win the fight, turn to **223**.
If you are reduced to just 2 remaining health, turn to **457**.

49

You turn and flee, but the creature seems to relish this chase. It takes flight again and attacks you from behind, running a clawed talon across your back.

Lose 1 **Health**.

If you continue to flee, turn to **193**.
Or to stand your ground and fight, turn to **313**.

50

You are about to give up and back out, when you notice an object covered with slime. You pull it loose, then retreat from the hole. Examining it in the light, you can see it's a black, flat metal disc with a series of unusual symbols on it.

As you grip it, it starts to glow with a bluish hue, and you feel your fatigue partially fading away. You can choose: either gain 1 **Health** *or* 1 **Composure**. You have used one of the healing disc charges. The disc has *5 charges* remaining, and each charge heals either 1 Health or 1 Composure. You can choose which each time you use it. You can use a healing disc charge at any time *except* when in Combat. When all 5 charges are used, discard it.

Record in your items, *'Healing disc. 5 charges. +1 Health OR +1 Composure per charge'* (and add +5 *Mythos* points).

Grateful for your good fortune, you exit through to the next tunnel. Turn to **147**.

51

You search through the various materials and equipment but don't see anything that could be of use, or anything to tell you more about this strange place.

Finding nothing of use here, you head back into the main chamber. Turn to **167**.

52

"Let's start at the end of the hallway," you suggest, pointing the way. "You first, professor."
He walks slowly down the hallway and opens the door.
"You hungry, lad?" he asks as the door opens to the kitchen.
"Nothing of interest in there," he adds.

Suggest instead you examine the basement. Turn to **300**.
Or suggest the door at the foot of the stairs. Turn to **332**.

53

You casually drop in a comment about the professor's funny old ways, and ask what has the old fellow bought now?

She tells you that it's mostly copper wiring, reels of the stuff, and other electrical related paraphernalia. She jokes that she hopes he isn't planning on blowing the place apart.

"Not that it'd be a loss, of course," she adds. " The place I mean, not the professor. That place has an ill air about it. It's not natural, if you ask me. Dead the area is. Dead. House should be ripped down I suppose, after what happened all those years ago."

You tell her that you're familiar with the stories from the house.

"Not stories though, sir. Fact. That Turne boy, bad 'un he was. He even gave Reverend Downe a tough time. The reverend left soon after the killings, never seen him since. But then, I suppose you lot know all this already? In any event, as much as I love to chat, I need to shut up shop."

You decide now is a good time to ask for directions. Turn to **549**.

54

Edward has managed to wake his father, Jacob, but he seems to be extremely panicked and incoherent. You rush to help calm him as Edward moves aside.

Jacob lifts his head and grips your shoulders, pulling you down close to his face. "It's my fault... I activated it... they... oh my god... THEY told me how to do it! Those... things! Oh my god! Melissa? They've taken my Melissa... and Sara? I will kill them!" He leaps up from the slab with rage in his eyes. Edward tries to reason with him, begs him to come and explains Sara is okay, but his father is both out for vengeance and suffering mentally from the ordeal.

If you have recorded in your Investigator Journal '*Have the syringe'*, then you may attempt to use that on Jacob. If you choose to, turn to the reference associated with that entry now.

If you do not have a syringe, or choose not to use it, turn to **444**.

55

The mi-go drops to the floor, dead, just as the other two reach you. On seeing their fellow scientist dispatched so easily, they both turn and flee through the door you came through – back into the large mining cavern. They're gone before you can react. Turn to **249**.

56

You deal the creature a glancing blow, but not enough to put it down.

The creature is wounded by your surprise attack, but it is still strong enough to defend itself. It turns on you with snapping claws.

Mi-go Worker (wounded)
Combat 5
Health 2

If you win, turn to **278**.
If you are reduced to just 2 remaining health, turn to **457**.

57

Using the scalpel, you slice at the worm as it bores into your flesh. You manage to carve it into shreds, but not before it has done some final damage to your face.

Lose 1 **Health**.

The creature stops wriggling and drops to the ground with a sickening splat. You kick it back into the pool in frustration, placing your hand to your bloodied cheek. The sting will remain for some time.

You must keep moving. Turn to **455**.

58

You are just a short distance from reaching the other side when you spot a small metal cube, about six-by-six inches in size, off to your left and further back into the cavern against the wall. It looks too dangerous to reach it from where you currently stand, as there is an almost impossibly thick gathering of the threads to pass through. You look up to the mist... a feeling of unnatural dread once again enters your mind. You shut your eyes and turn away, looking back to the glint of metal. Some instinct deep inside tells you it is important.

However, you feel you have little choice but to carry on and leave this cavern. Turn to **389**.

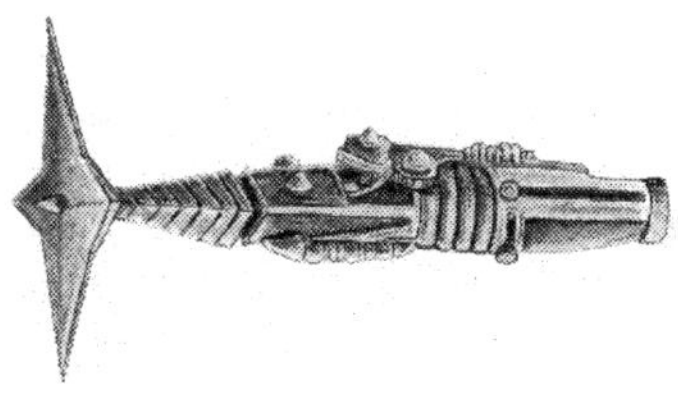

59

The door to Pete's garage is old and battered looking. The once white paint, cracked and peeling, reveals a dull grey wood beneath. A heavy rusted padlock is attached to the frame of the door. The latch is open, and bent out of shape from a countless number of nightly lockups.

"Hello?" you call out.

No answer. The windows appear to have several years' worth of grime on them, making it impossible to see inside. You step inside, the door creaking all the way, and enter a dusty dry room. Motes float through the air, illuminated by what slivers of light can make it through the filthy windows. A long counter runs through the centre of the room, dividing it in two. On your side, the room is bare. On the other side, there's more clutter than your grandmother's attic. Rotting cardboard boxes stand in one corner, stacked precariously and leaning away from the paint-peeled walls. A battered looking chair sits in the opposite corner, and various knickknacks, car parts, empty bottles, old overalls, and pieces of newspaper lie strewn about the rest of the place. The counter is bare, save for a small service bell.

Do you want to ring the bell for service? Turn to **287**.
Or decide you won't get any help here and leave the garage. Turn to **536**.

60

As you approach it, the metal slab starts to slowly rise from the floor. You pause and wait to see what happens. It stops about waist height. Reaching out, it is cold to the touch, and like everything else you've encountered thus far, devoid of marks or features. It doesn't appear to have any other function than to rest something on.

You're about to approach the alcove in the opposite wall when you suddenly hear a strange clicking sound. It appears to be coming from just outside the door. What will you do?

Exit the room to investigate the sound. Turn to **321**.
Listen at the door instead. Turn to **21**.
Find somewhere in this room to hide. Turn to **118**.

61

You come out from behind the large disc machine and keep to what little cover there is. Thankfully, the noise of the machinery will at least mask any sound you make. When you reach the first of the four conveyor belts, you hesitate. The smell assaults your nostrils as various chunks of meat, flesh, and offal trundle by. You begin to carefully climb over each one.

Make a Regular (2D6) **Stealth** check.

If you pass, turn to **518**.
If you fail, turn to **446**.

62

As you step up to the door in the left wall, it automatically opens with a swish to reveal a long featureless corridor on the other side, about forty feet in length. You step through. The door slides shut behind you, silently setting back into the wall. As you take a few steps forward the reverberation of your footsteps echoes strangely about the corridor.

Reaching the mid-point along the corridor, you see two similar circular doors on either side of you, one to your left and one to your right. Looking onward to the end of the corridor you see another door ahead.

Will you try the left door (turn to **202**), try the right door (turn to **108**), or ignore these and move onwards towards the end of the corridor (turn to **377**)?

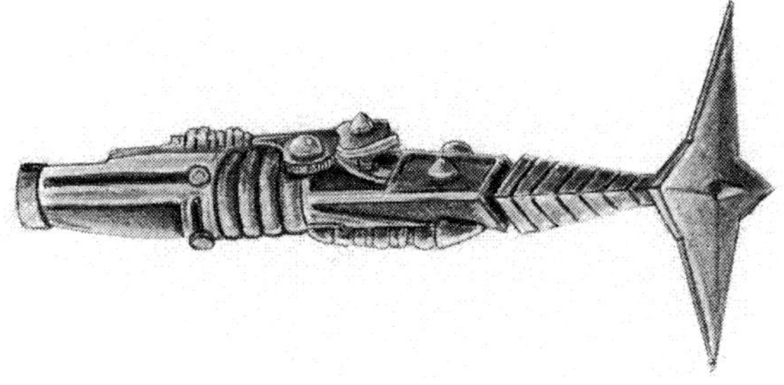

63

The machine was more than just a way to traverse across space, it also had the power to transcend time. Edward and Sara hadn't aged because it sent you to Yuggoth ten years in the past – possibly only moments after they themselves had arrived. Now you realise just how powerful this device was for the mi-go, and why they were so tenacious in trying to recover the lost power source. You mull this over in your head, trying to understand what you will do now that you are no longer in your own time.

Unable to return to Arkham for fear of running into your past self, you stay in the town of Kingsport. You have just enough money to rent a room for a week, and manage to convince a local foreman to give you a job working at a warehouse. In time, you can afford to rent a room long-term.

You pore over every copy of the Newport Examiner you can until you find news about the house.

Newport Examiner, October 7th, 1916
Missing Family in the Durham Locale

The Newport Police Department was called out on business up north to investigate the mysterious disappearance of the Turne family, who have been residing in a house near Durham for several years. The locals say they were good honest folk, but no one had seen nor heard from them since late September. On visiting the house, it stood empty, and their possessions remained at the abode. No explanation for their disappearance has been offered at this time. Searches are ongoing in the local woods.

The missing individuals are Jacob, the father, Melissa, the mother, and Sara, the youngest child of five years, and Edward, their twelve-year-old son.

There were no signs of foul play in the house, but some locals did report a stranger to the town who was seen a few days before the disappearance was reported. He avoided the locals. Thus far, he has not presented himself for questioning and the police would like to eliminate him from their inquiries.

You read it over again and again, and compare it to your article. Disappeared... the bodies are on Yuggoth. No one would ever believe you, so you have no intention of attempting to explain this.

Record in your Investigator Journal '*The entire family were reported missing.*' -50 *Mythos* points.

Eventually, you settle into a mundane existence. A young reporter by the name of Frank Winston starts to write an article for the *Arkham Gazette*, which you have especially delivered by post to your door so you can follow your alter-ego's progress.

Then, ten years later, on September the 23rd, around 4:45 p.m., in the year 1926, you return to stand on the main road of Durham and wait for a Chevrolet to trundle down the road. You contemplated writing to yourself, anonymously of course, as a warning to stay away... but instead felt that you would simply be compelling some version of yourself to question the warning and turn up anyway. When you thought about it, you know that is what you would have done. No one arrives... there are no strange flashes of green lightning, and no voice on the air. The killings never happened – the disappearances are perhaps much less intriguing, and thus the other version of yourself remained in Arkham, perhaps dismissing the story (if he found it at all) as not worth pursuing. It is highly unlikely that your paths will ever cross.

In February 1930, the planet Pluto is discovered... but you know it, and fear it, by another name – *Yuggoth*!

The effect of this does not go unnoticed on your demeanour, but you remain resolute to carry on a normal life, such as it is, despite knowing that the mi-go are out there... waiting...

perhaps constructing another power source for that accursed machine, for perhaps they have a score to settle with mankind... one you started!

Your story ends here. Now, turn to **586**.

64

As you fight Yar'ith off, neither of you notice the large dark shape descend from the mist on threads of silk. You block a blow from Yar'ith and get ready to strike back when suddenly a long black spear pierces Yar'ith's head, covering you in green mi-go blood. The spear is in fact the blade-like leg of a gigantic purple spider creature. With seven legs to spare, the bloated monstrosity wastes no time in repeating its attack on you. With a sickening squelch, your head is speared by a second leg, killing you instantly.

Record in your Investigator Journal '*You were killed by a Spider of Leng.*' -5 *Mythos* points.

Your investigation ends here.

65

You take this opportunity to flee out the door and get away from the accursed place. From a safe distance down the hill, you turn back and see Peabody standing in the doorway. His face shows no sign of emotion. He just blankly stares, then slowly closes the door.

You make your way back down the track and pass through to the road. Whatever mysteries this house holds, they will not be yours to discover. Rattled at what could have been, what could have happened, you consider finding the Durham police station and reporting him and his possible attempt on your life. You get back to your car, ever watchful of the treeline while getting the car started. Thankfully he does not emerge, and you drive away.

Record in your Investigator Journal '*You fled the house when attacked by Peabody.*' -5 *Mythos* points.

Your investigation ends here.

66

You look around the attic for something to use. The attic seems different somehow...

A pile of crates in one corner might give you time enough to escape. You pull Edward to his feet and explain your plan. The crates are full of old clothes and other odds and ends. Moving them is easy enough, but you know it won't hold the mi-go! You peer through the haze to see that the mi-go are arming themselves with the weapons from the counter.

If you have recorded in your Investigator Journal '*The black slime devoured the mi-go eggs*', then you must turn to the reference associated with that entry now.

If you do not have that entry, turn to **319**.

67

The mi-go are surprised by your tactic to ambush them. You pounce on the one holding the weapon and attempt to pull it free, but to your dismay the creatures grip is stronger than you had hoped. It pushes you back then turns the weapon on you. A loud whirring sound emanates from the weapon as sparks crackle and flow over its surface. Then, with a blinding flash and a crack that reverberates around the cavern, you are blasted backwards. Bolts of electricity shoot through your body, singeing your clothes and hair. You hit the ground convulsing, foaming at the mouth, twitch some more, then your heart stops.

Record in your Investigator Journal '*You were electrocuted by an alien weapon.*' -2 *Mythos* points.

Your investigation ends here.

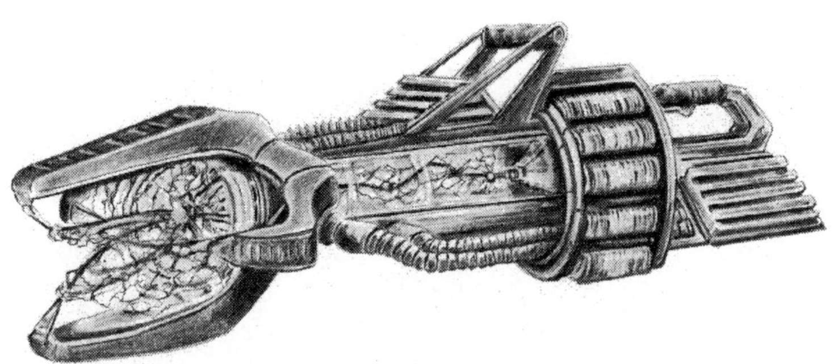

68

Making your way slowly across the cavern, you need to turn sideways at times and side-step to avoid touching the hanging threads. Up close they remind you of spiderweb silk, but many times thicker. You stop and shudder, looking straight up into the mist. As you stare, a long, thin black appendage appears out of the mist above, then disappears again. A sudden fear grips you.

Make a Regular (2D6) Composure check. If you fail, turn to **175**.

If you pass, you consider the situation carefully. You're only about one third of the way across the cavern.

If you wish to continue onwards and hopefully make it across without alerting whatever this thing is, turn to **58**.
If you wish to turn back and take the other tunnel, turn to **466**.

69

You turn and start to take the stairs when suddenly you get a sharp pain in your back. The professor has stuck a syringe in you when your back was turned. You let out a cry while trying to reach back and pull it out. "What on earth?" you shout, confused.

The professor stands back, emotionless, as your vision blurs.

You fall to your knees, then black out. Turn to **120**.

70

You leave the fourth dial at 17 degrees and step back from the device. Suddenly a bright flash of green light shoots upwards from the sphere atop the machine. A low thrum pulses in the air, and the light flickers, slowly at first, then faster and faster until it becomes a solid beam firing upwards. You back away, not knowing what to expect.

Edward stares intently at the beam of light. "Yesssssss!" he cries, excitedly. "You diiiid it!"

The beam of light tiles downwards, coming to rest parallel with the floor. It strikes the attic wall and forms what you can only describe as a doorway – and then on the other side, faint and distorted as though peering through water, a large, cavernous chamber appears.

"Goooooo, nooooow!!" Edward cries. "Goooooooo, befooore it isssss... too late!"

Equal part terrified and fascinated, you step up to the shimmering doorway. The thrum of the machine pulses through your head. "Nooooooowww!" Edward cries from behind you. You consider the possibility of dashing to the attic stairs and getting as far away from this nightmare as you can, but before you can, Edward loses patience. He advances on your and pushes you through… turn to **276**

71

A huge black leg steps from the light, followed by a writhing tentacle. It's only when the form has fully stepped through the tear do you see that the tentacle is the monstrosity's head. This is the form of the statue made flesh, only it is even larger at nearly thirty feet tall.

The aura of dread is nearly overwhelming, and yet, here you stand, your mind intact and senses alert.

"Unexpected," the creature bellows from an unseen mouth. It lowers itself to regard you more closely. "Human. A tribute? Or a seeker?"

It waits... you believe it expects an answer.

Respond with 'A tribute'. Turn to **341**.
Respond with 'A seeker'. Turn to **209**.
Ask the creature who, or what, it is. Turn to **26.**

72

You break free from his grip easily enough and retrieve the syringe. "Explain yourself! What is in this?" you demand, pointing the syringe towards Peabody. You try to sound forceful, but instead come across as frightened.
Peabody slowly gets to his feet. "It's just a mild sedative, to calm you for the wonders I plan to show you. It is in the attic if you'd like to follow me. I didn't think you would willingly take it. I'm sorry for the start it caused you."

You find his answer incredible, as though he hadn't just tried to attack you.

"I suggest you take it," he adds, "seeing as you have a fear upon you. You'll need to be calm for the discoveries to come."

You're not quite sure how to respond to this extraordinary situation.

You can threaten him to back away, and then leave the house (turn to **65**), or threaten him again with the syringe and demand an explanation of what is going on here (turn to **289**).
Alternatively, tell him you won't be taking any unknown drug, but will follow him to the attic (turn to **229**).

73

To your horror, the black slime attaches itself to your face in a vice-like grip. You instinctively attempt to scream, and it takes the opportunity to enter your mouth. Pulling your head down towards the open core of the plant, the spines pierce your skin, sending a toxin coursing through your veins. Your body is paralysed, held standing over the plant as it slowly digests you. You manage to remain alive for an hour or so as it works on your head... eventually you succumb to madness, then death.

Record in your Investigator Journal '*You were paralysed and slowly digested by an alien plant.*' -3 *Mythos* points.

Your investigation ends here.

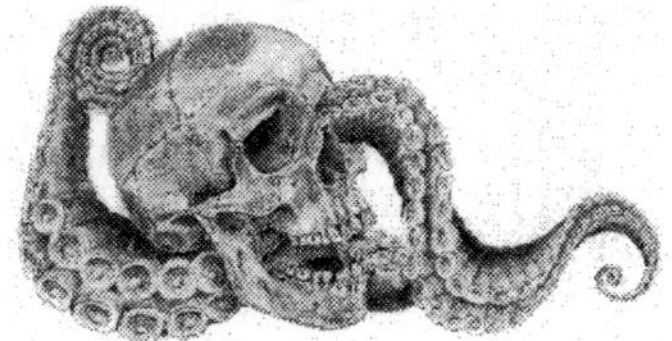

74

You approach the door past the room, staying low and hoping the creatures won't notice.

Make a Hard (2D6+1) **Stealth** check.

If you pass, turn to **405**.
If you fail, turn to **517**.

75

You listen intently for a moment and hear the beating of the creature's wings. You believe it is going to perch on the slab above where Jacob lies! You wait nervously, and sure enough the mi-go lands atop the slab – but you are ready for this eventuality. Reaching up, you grab the creature's gun, wresting it from its claws. The mi-go is caught by surprise, possibly expecting you to cower rather than offer up a fight. You turn the gun on it, and fire! The gun kicks you back a little as a white-hot bolt of lightning incinerates the mi-go where it stood on the slab. At this close range you feel the heat of the blast and are also splattered with the green blood of the creature as it explodes, leaving just a mess of slime and a shattered carapace. Turn to **222**.

76

As you continue the tunnel bends slightly; the light behind completely disappears. With no light source of any kind, it's utterly impossible to see. You move on a little further, with only the heavy sound of your own breathing for company. The air smells putrid.

Make a Regular (2D6) **Composure** check.

If you pass, you can decide to continue, feeling your way in the dark. Turn to **354**.
Or even if you passed, you may still choose to turn back by turning to **312**.
However, if you failed, you are *compelled* to turn back due to nerves, and so must return and take the lit tunnel instead. Turn to **312**.

77

"I am tweeeelve!" he replies, as puzzled and frustrated as ever. "Why doessss that matterrrr? Gooooo and ssssave my family. You promisssed me!" He reaches into a pocket and retrieves a small diamond-shaped object that glows gently, then moves toward the machine. Turn to **353**.

78

The basement door opens over a stairway leading into the darkness below. A damp mouldy smell rises from the basement, but mixed with something else. A chemical odour? You take your flashlight from your satchel and aim it down. Dust motes fill the beam as it shines on the stone ground. You can't see anything unusual from up here.

What will you do?
To head down the steps, turn to **13**.
If you haven't already done either of the following, you can try the door at the end of the hallway (turn to **484**), or call out and see if anyone is home (turn to **478**).
You can also go up the main stairs (turn to **131**), or try the door at the foot of the stairs (turn to **499**).

79

As the door opens, a pungent, earthy smell immediately hits your nostrils. Beyond the large circular opening lies a tunnel of black stone – a stark contrast to the metal room you're standing in. It leads away into darkness – with only the faintest glow of bioluminescent fungi growing along the walls to light the way.

If you wish to cross the doorway into the tunnel, turn to **17**.
Or if you'd rather try the other door behind you, turn to **62**.

80

Brandishing the scalpel, you plunge it into the back of one of the creatures and pull sharply. It tears through the beast between its wings. It falls dead, twitching. The other creature turns and immediately goes to attack you.

You are more than ready for a fight.

Mi-go Worker
Combat 5
Health 4

If you win, turn to **265**.
If you lose, turn to **44**.

81

You turn the first dial to what you would believe to be 190 degrees.

How do you want to set the second dial?

To set it to 45 degrees, turn to **521**.
To set it to 121 degrees, turn to **247**.
To set it to 37 degrees, turn to **362**.

82

Excluding Edward, which of his family members survived?

If only Sara survived, turn to **111**.
If only Sara and Jacob survived, turn to **419**.
If Sara, Jacob, and Melissa survived, turn to **3**.

83

You wait roughly two minutes for signs of movement, but don't see anything from above. The only noise and movement are from the conveyor belts. As you wait, a lump of meat slips over the side of the conveyor nearest you and splats to the floor. What will you do?

If you continue to wait, turn to **187**.
If you ignore it and examine the disc machine, turn to **220**.
Or if you wish to try and sneak across the conveyor belts and head towards the large door, turn to **61**.

84

You pull with all of your remaining strength and manage to get up far enough to swing your leg over and catch your foot on the metal walkway. From there, the rest is relatively easy as you haul yourself over the edge onto the raised floor. You take a few moments to catch your breath.

The horrid remains of the melted creatures ooze off the edge, creating a vile smell. Covering your nose, you step over them. As you do, you notice the metal rod lying on the walkway. You decide to take the metal rod for yourself. Unsure of how to operate it, or even whether it has ammunition, it still seems wise to have it.

Record in your Investigators Journal '*Have a metal rod*', and note the reference 283. +1 *Mythos* point.

The walkway leads out of the main room through an opening in right-hand wall. You peek in cautiously, looking into a side room. On one wall is a control console, and across the far end of the room is a metal slab with a variety of objects strewn across it. Various containers with specimens of meat, flesh and even a brain, line a shelf next to it. At the far end of the corridor that you are in, there is a closed circular doorway. What is your next move?

Ignore this room and move on. Turn to **405**.
Enter the room and examine the control panel. Turn to **523**.
Search through the objects on the metal slab. Turn to **316**.

85

To your left, the ledge snakes its way around the edge of the cavern, where another tunnel opening leads back into the rockface. The tunnel is short and ends in a typical circular metal door. You creep up to the door, and knowing it will open when you get close, you prepare yourself for what horrors may lay beyond.

The door slides open to reveal an end to the rock of the cavern, and a return to the metal construction similar to the area you first arrived in. As the door opens, three mi-go turn towards you. In the room are four metal slabs, and on them rest four bodies. It is a man, a woman, a young girl, and a boy – Edward. It's the Turne family! They do not appear to have aged at all. Two of the mi-go are operating on Edward – they've attached the prosthetic arm that you saw back in the attic. The third mi-go turns and skitters towards another door on the opposite end of the room.

You only have moments to act...
Despite the odds of two-to-one, you can decide to rush in and attack the two mi-go next to Edward (turn to **482**), or ignore them for the moment and rush at the lone mi-go heading for the other door (turn to **408**).

86

You wait for what feels like an age as the creature rummages through the remains on the conveyor belt. You're close to losing patience when you hear the unmistakable sound of its feet on the floor, then the beating of wings. You glance over to see it land on the walkway above and exit the room through the open doorway leading from the walkway. What next?

Come out of hiding and make for the large doorway on the opposite side of the room. Turn to **61**.
Or examine the machine. Turn to **459**.

87

Using the flashlight, you scan the basement. Loose stones, and pieces of wood and dirt litter the floor. Rotten wooden shelving rests against two of the walls but contain nothing of interest – just empty and broken bottles, and various containers of junk. Piles of wooden crates lean haphazardly against the south-facing wall.

Investigate the crates. Turn to **553**.
Leave the basement. Turn to **47**.

88

Something is moving at the far edge of the display, but you can't quite make it out. You lean in for a closer look.

Suddenly, it turns towards the screen and advances, filling the screen image with what appears to be its head. It's another of those beings – a mi-go. Its bulbous head starts changing colours in quick succession. Despite the screen being between you and it, its presence on you is felt, and it is terrifying. It has clearly seen you.

It reaches closer to the screen and then the image goes black.

You decide you should quickly leave this room. Turn to **321**.

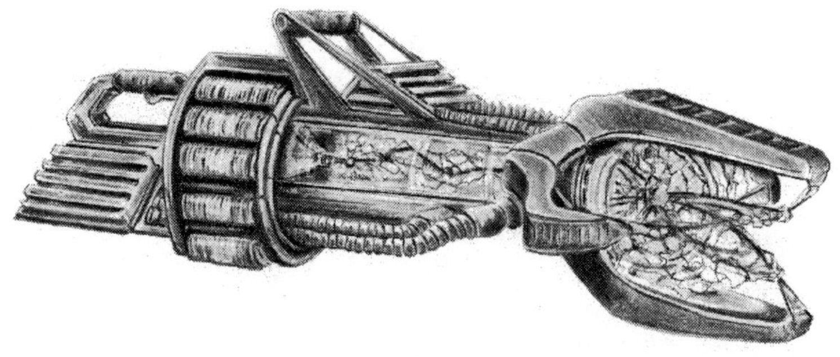

89

You take his hand and shake. His grip is firm. "Pleased to meet you!" He smiles and releases your hand. Resisting the urge to look at your hand, you tell him your name. "Well met, Frank. So, what brings you all the way out here?" he inquires, looking around at the quiet, empty town. "From Boston, I suspect?"

You take the brief opportunity to look down at your hand,

and see that it's smudged with oil. "Yes, I'm from Boston," you reply.

Record in your Investigator Journal that '*Your car radiator was fixed*', and note the reference 94. Later in the story, if asked if you have earned this information, you will turn to 94. (Do not turn to that now).

What else will you say?

Tell him you're looking for directions to Sentinel Hill. Turn to **373**.
Or ask about the town, and why it's so quiet. Turn to **35**.

90

You ask where has he been for all this time? He puts his head down and places his one good hand over it.

"Weee have beeeen there! Fightiiing theeem! You knooow thissss. You made meeee leave theeeem… had to leeeave them beeehind or dieee. But nowww you goooo back assss promised. I haaave the keeeey..."

Edward produces a small, glowing diamond-shaped object from his pocket and moves toward the machine. Turn to **353**.

91

You stop yourself, teetering on the edge, but manage to retain your balance and keep upright at the edge of the walkway. Looking to your right, the cavern fades into darkness after about one thousand feet. You see a myriad of walkways and openings both below and above you, criss-crossing the cavern like a web. Many of these extend from the structure you've just come from, and cross into the black rock face on the opposite side, about two hundred feet away. Where you stand, the walkway is missing. There is a raised control panel here.

You have only moments to decide your next action.

To advance on the creatures and fight them, turn to **145**.
Examine the raised control panel on the walkway to see if you can operate it. Turn to **345**.
Or make a leap down to a lower walkway. It looks risky but could be your only escape. Turn to **298**.

92

Wary that there could be more mi-go creatures up here, you proceed cautiously. The sponge-like material on the floor makes it slightly easier to remain silent.

Make an Easy (2D6-1) **Stealth** check.

If you pass, turn to **382**.
If you fail, turn to **328**.

93

You tie the cable around an outcrop of rock and test the strength. It should hold. It almost reaches to the bottom which is good enough to see you safely down with only a small drop at the end. It's harder going than you first thought, the heat combined with the rubber wiring are not ideal climbing conditions but with a steady slow pace you reach the bottom safely. There's no way to retrieve the cable so you leave it. Strike it from your Journal.

You turn to examine the cavern floor. Turn to **323**.

94

Your car bumps and jostles along the track but remains as dependable as ever as you trundle on.

You soon arrive at a small roadside clearing where a small truck has been pulled in. The cabin is empty. Using your flashlight, you examine the area until you spot a rotted signpost in the treeline next to the clearing. Pulling out the remains, you can see the faded paint marks of what was once unmistakably the lettering 'Sentinel Hill'.

Investigating further, you find a narrow gap in the treeline. You are just about to step through when a man appears through the gap!
"Are you lost, stranger?" calls the man from within the glare of your flashlight. His voice sounds weary and strained.

Check your Investigator Journal. If you have recorded '*You know who is in the house*' then turn to that reference now.

Otherwise, turn to **15**.

95

You manage to maintain your balance and thankfully the floor starts to level out again. You're suddenly feeling quite hungry, a feeling that brings some sense of normality to your desperate situation. You sit against the rock wall for a few moments to rest. Your thoughts drift back to the house, and Edward.

'Find my family!' he said. They are dead.

'You promised!' he cried. You promised nothing. You had never met him before. Yet, he knew your name, but surely the professor told him. His mind was clearly gone, and a sudden pang of pity for him and what he endured washes over you. But now you're in this situation, and despair follows as you feel it could be your end.

Despite these thoughts, you pick yourself up and carry on. Turn to **136**.

96

You land a heavy blow as you attempt to defend yourself, causing him to fall back against the wall and slump to the floor. The syringe falls from his grasp and smashes into pieces on the floor. You check for a pulse as best you can. Nothing. Placing a hand on his chest you check if he is breathing. Still nothing.

You've killed him.

Make a Very Hard (2D6+2) **Composure** check. If you fail, deduct 1 from your current Composure.

Record in your Investigator Journal '*You killed Professor Peabody in self-defence.*' -10 *Mythos* points.
After some moments you compose yourself, then decide to at least see what this business was all about. You find the door to the study. Turn to **326**.

97

You hail the man, and then walk towards your car. He seems to take no notice, and walks to the front of the car, all the while looking at it.
"Hello, eh, Pete, is it?" You ask as you reach your car.

“Yes-um,” replies Pete, still looking over vehicle. “She’s a beaut’.” he adds. "Not bad, sir, not bad. Iffin you don’t mind it breaking down often of course, sir.” He smiles broadly. His wit is dryer than his dusty boots. “Still,” he continues, “I’d give you a fair price all the same.”

“Oh, it’s not for sale. I need it.” You’re not impressed with his assessment of your car.

“Suit yerself, sir. Anything I can help you with?”

What will you ask?

Do you want to ask him the way to sentinel hill (turn to **184**), or ask what he meant by ‘breaking down’ (turn to **337**)?

98

"You'll never find out if you keep insisting on holding me to your will. Instead, we could work together like you wanted." He seems quite calm, far calmer than you feel. He knows everything that is going on here, and you don't know anything, yet.

"Cryptic non-answer, professor," you reply, trying to sound dry.

"What I have discovered needs to be seen, not spoken of. I again suggest you take that sedative, or you may wish you hadn't been shown anything." He seems sincere, but then, he has been rather detached and lacking emotion in your discourse thus far. That could easily be mistaken for sincerity. You turn your attention back to the room.

Will you approach the desk (turn to **214**), or examine the bookcase (turn to **417**)?

99

The archway leads into a long semi-circular tunnel carved from the now familiar black stone. The entire wall and ceiling of the tunnel are intricately decorated with a series of curved lines that twist and turn into swirls and circles before branching out again. As you examine the patterns, you suspect they may be displaying planetary bodies. It's on closer examination that you spot what look to be tiny, winged figures carved into the stone, and the figures are depicted as travelling from planet to planet.

The tunnel ends with an open archway into a much larger chamber. You carefully step through and are amazed to see that the chamber is a gigantic tower made from the same black stone as the tunnel. The patterns carved into the walls flow from the tunnel to cover the walls of the tower. You're standing at its base, and up above it disappears into darkness.

In the centre of the tower stands a roughly hewn statue, some fifteen feet tall. It is vaguely humanoid in appearance, with three legs, and is a focal point for the intricate detail of the wall carvings as they twist and turn, cross the floor, and converge on the statue. At its tip is a large, pointed head that rises a further five feet into the air. At its base is a large bowl, again carved from the stone. You sense that this is a place of worship.

There are three more archways identical to the one you emerged from, one to the left and one to the right, and the third one lies behind the statue ahead of you.

What is your next move?

Approach the bowl at the base of the statue. Turn to **164**.
Try the archway on the left. Turn to **230**.
Cross the chamber to the archway behind the statue, turn to **358**.
Or go through the archway on the right. Turn to **437**.

100

As you start walking, the metal floor sounds unnaturally loud with your footsteps. You reach out to touch the edge of the shape, and as you do it sweeps aside to reveal a passage on the other side. The passage is undefined, blurred. You step through to see what lies beyond, and as you do you suddenly lurch forward, sliding down a metal tube. The tube is slick and feels wet. Before you can get your bearings you are deposited into a dark cavernous chamber.

Your landing is soft enough, accompanied by a loud squelch as you find yourself atop a pile of offal. The smell is sickening. You try to move to sit upright, but instead slide down one side of the mound of flesh and entrails, rolling over and over. Hitting the bottom of the mound you spit repeatedly, feeling the entrails all over you. You stand up and look around.

The chamber seems infinite, with hundreds of mounds of bones and guts in all directions, and each with a single light source above the peak of the mound where an opening for a chute lies. Human skulls are evident in the masses of meat and bone.

Make a Hard (2D6+1) **Composure** check. If you fail, deduct

1 from your current Composure.

The only way out is the way you came in, through the chutes above. Impossible to reach, you spend the rest of your short life here, slowly going hungry and mad.

Record in your Investigator Journal that '*You dreamt of a terrifying pit filled with flesh and bone.*' +4 *Mythos* points.

That is, until you wake up. Turn to **500**.

101

You're not even remotely comfortable with the prospect of battling this horrid thing, but nor are you willing to become its victim. You tighten your fists, then start to advance on the creature. Its head immediately turns a deep shade of red as it clicks its claws together expectantly – it seems it wanted you to try this. It advances to meet you in combat.

Mi-go Worker
Combat 5
Health 4

If you win, turn to **278**.
If you are reduced to just 2 remaining health, turn to **457**.

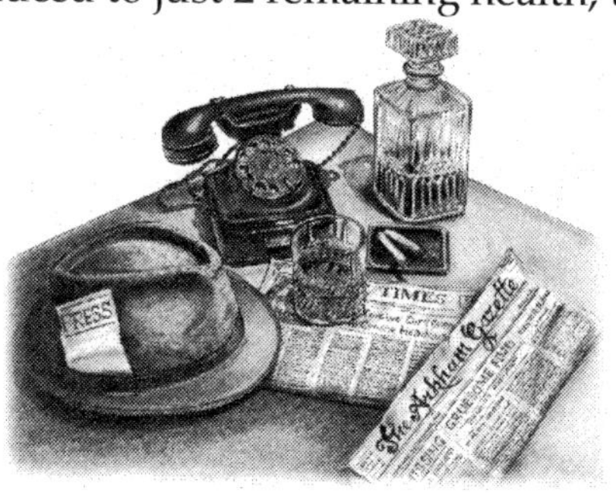

102

You curse the machine and the hopelessness of your situation when you discover it doesn't have the power source attached. You search the room but cannot find any sign of the power source. Returning to the main chamber, you inform Edward that you cannot start the machine and start searching, but it's looking more and more hopeless. You've come so far, but the one thing you really need to get out of here is the one thing you don't have – the *Tok'llian*.

The door that leads back to the enormous mining chamber opens and in rush swarms of armed mi-go. The creatures surround you as others head onwards to take Edward captive. You're taken away and placed on an operating table before being put under.

When you awake, your vision is narrowed and at first you find it hard to focus. Across from you on a metal slab lies the body of a man. One of the mi-go is leaning over it, doing something to the head, but you can't quite see what is happening. Moments later it turns towards you with a large flap of skin dangling from its blood-soaked claw. As it gets closer, the creature's head turns a deep green while it holds up the flapping piece of skin before your eyes. It is your face dangling from its claw...

You spend the rest of your life as a brain in a cylinder, occasionally given the power of sight, hearing, and speech through some devices that are connected to the cylinder, so that you may be questioned by the mi-go. You see Edward, too, but transformed even further – perhaps a more complete version of the condition you first saw him in back at the house. You beg him to let you go, but his mind appears to be too far gone – a slave to the mi-go. And after a time, the final threads of your mind begin to snap also.

Record in your Investigator Journal '*You died after many years as just a brain in a cylinder.*' -5 *Mythos* points.

Your investigation ends here.

103

You don't expect to have any benign encounters with these monsters and are prepared to fight your way out of this lair of horrors. Despite the first creature looking larger than the other, you launch into an attack.

Mi-go Soldier	**Mi-go Worker**
Combat 7	Combat 5
Health 6	Health 5

If you win, turn to **429**.

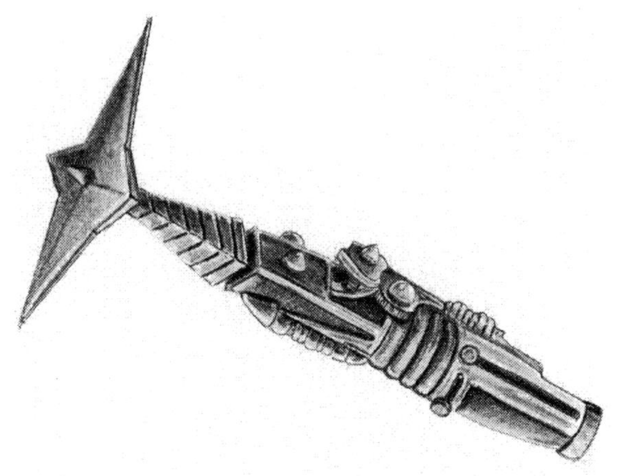

104

After a time, you look up again. The attic seems different, tidy. You examine the machine... there is no *Tok'llian* in it. Unsure what to do, you wrestle for hours with the thought of trying to go back, and never *wanting* to go back. With no power source, the decision is made for you. With a sense of guilt that you can't shake, you become reluctantly thankful that there is no other option.
But what has happened to Edward and his family?

You bury the machine in the woods and remove all other evidence that you may have been in the house. As you traverse the house, you note it looks well-kept and the windows are no longer boarded up... something is clearly not right here. You pull the original newspaper article from your satchel. It remains the same, though your eye is drawn to a paragraph you hadn't originally taken much consideration over.

The police are also looking for a stranger to the town who was seen acting suspiciously the day before the bodies were discovered. He wandered out of town on foot, seemingly dazed and confused, and avoided the locals. He had an unkempt appearance, with some reporting it looked as though he had been in an accident. Thus far, he has not presented himself for questioning and the police would like to eliminate him from their inquiries.

You tidy yourself up as best you can, borrowing some of Jacob's better garments, and head into Durham town. Your car is gone! As you explore the possibility of getting a bus from the town, you do your best to limit interactions with the locals. You retrieve a discarded local newspaper from the street. The date reads September 25th, 1916.

You quietly ask a passer-by the time... then the date. They look you up and down strangely. It is September 27th, 1916.

You contemplate your situation on the bus to Kingsport. Turn to **63**.

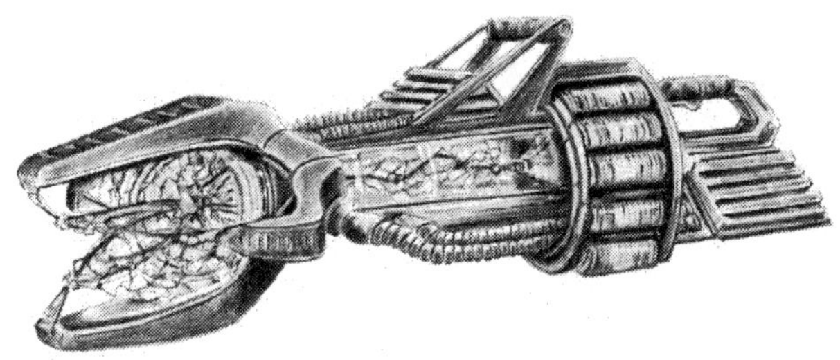

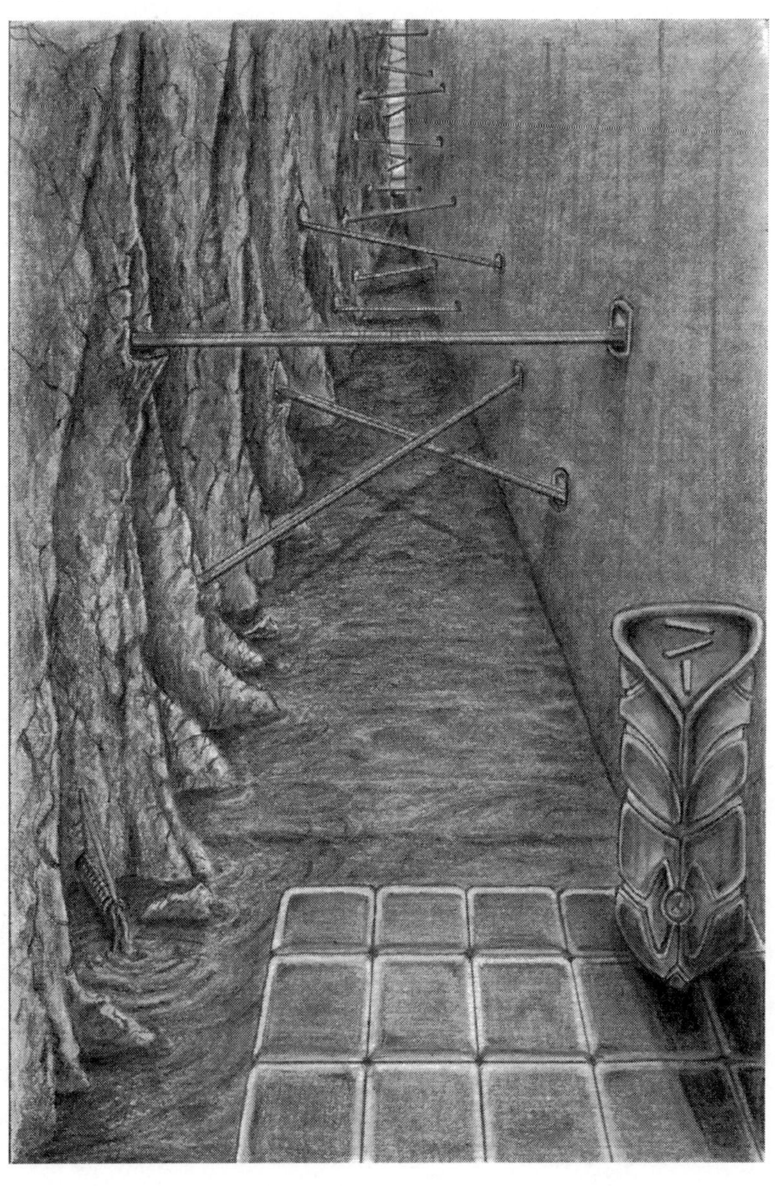

105

The door opens into a massive cavern. Looking to your right, the cavern is so gigantic that it fades into darkness after about one thousand feet. You see a myriad of walkways and openings both above and below you, criss-crossing the cavern like a web. Many of these extend from the structure you're coming from, and cross into the black rock face on the opposite side, about two hundred feet away. Where you stand, the walkway is missing, and a raised control panel is visible. Below, running through a channel is an eighty-foot-wide black river. It's slow moving, more like a black viscous slime than water. Feeding the river of slime is a series of huge pipes set along the cavern wall. A trickle of slime flows from these and joins the main artery.

You'd be in awe of the place if it weren't trying to kill you at every turn. You surmise that the many bridges are for transporting cargo or other supplies, seeing as the creatures fly and certainly would not need to rely on these for walking. You spot movement in the distance and can make out lines of mi-go, like traffic on a busy city street, crossing the width of the cavern into and out of the various caves and doorways. You note there is far less movement on the side with the natural rock and caves.

Dismayed at the size of the place and how finding a way out seems more impossible at every turn, you wonder at how this could be hidden underground.

Feeling exposed here, you look around for options. Turn to **128**.

106

Unfortunately, your fear overcomes you, forcing you to back away sloshing through the two-foot-deep fluids. The creature makes a sudden change of direction, and this only makes you turn all the more sharply and attempt to run. The cavern floor is littered with hidden obstacles beneath the surface, causing you to trip and fall headfirst into the disgusting foul-smelling mess. You cough and splutter, then try to freeze in terror as you suddenly feel the presence of the black slimy mass crawling over you.

Lose 2 **Composure**.

It lingers over you for a few moments as you shut your eyes waiting for the inevitable attack, but that doesn't arrive. Instead, the whip-like tentacles lash out some distance ahead of it, latching onto another mound. The creature propels itself away across the cavern and disappears out of sight over the nearest mound.

You climb to your feet, a filthy sullen mess. You don't feel particularly well, either. Who knows what kind of diseases you could contract here, if you haven't already?

In your weakened state you must lose 1 **Health**.

You trudge on in the hope of finding an exit from this hell. Turn to **519**.

107

You decide this way is too dangerous and turn back. However, as the door opens into the plant room, you immediately spot two of those hideous insect creatures on the far side. They turn towards you, their heads instantly transitioning from a bright yellow colour to a deep red.

One of the mi-go is larger than the other and is holding what you can only imagine is some kind of firearm, a large boxy design with multiple coils extending from its body and ending in a nozzle. Despite its unusual look and construction, it's not difficult to imagine its function.

You are immediately startled. Make a Regular (2D6) **Composure** check.

If you pass, turn to **540**.
If you fail, turn to **573**.

108

The doorway slides open as you approach. The room beyond is small, with no other exits that you can see. Straight ahead set into the far wall is a large reflective sheet of black glass. It almost entirely covers the back wall and is the only feature in this room.

You can examine the black glass. Turn to **520**.
Or if you haven't already done so, you can leave this room and try the door in the left-hand wall. Turn to **202**.
Alternatively, you can continue towards the end of the corridor. Turn to **377**.

109

You heave with all your might and the machine starts to turn, but not quickly enough.

The creature with the rod fires again. A thin shard of metal flies from the rod and pierces your shoulder, sending you stumbling backwards. You fall against the disc machine and to your horror get caught in its heat ray. Your flesh melts from your bones almost instantly, after which your bones begin to decalcify. You've barely time to cry out in pain before the end comes.

Record in your Investigator Journal '*You died horribly, melted by a large mining machine.*' -5 *Mythos* points.

Your investigation ends here.

110

You plunge headlong into a chute and find yourself sliding downwards at a steep angle among the offal, before being deposited from an opening in the ceiling of a massive cavern. Luckily, your fall is broken by a large mound of piled up refuse. You find yourself on your back staring up at the ceiling. A light above the peak of the mound sits next to the chute you fell from.

The mound is a massive pile of entrails, bones, and offal. You're covered in it. You get up and try to wipe it off, but it seems futile. You feel physically sick.

Make an Extreme (2D6+3) **Composure** check.

If you pass, turn to **216**.
If you fail, turn to **161**.

111

Edward falls to his knees, tears running down his cheeks. You've managed to save Sara at least, and with some luck she won't have any knowledge of what has transpired.

Edward's resilience falls away over time, and the ordeal's effect on the mind comes to the surface. Fiercely protective of his sister, the official story is that their parents fled under financial pressures and left the two children alone. It's not that anyone actually believes that story, only that there remains no other explanation. Both you and Edward bury the accursed machine in the woods.

The date is October 11th, 1916. The newspaper clipping that brought you here remains as before, but tells a story that is no longer what happened. Your car is gone... or never existed. Only that which you brought with you to Yuggoth and back, remains as it was. The machine was more than just a way to traverse across space, it also had the power to transcend time. Edward and Sara hadn't aged because it sent you to Yuggoth ten years in the past – possibly only moments after they themselves had arrived. Now you realise just how powerful this device was for the mi-go, and why they were so tenacious in trying to recover the lost power source.

Edward and Sara are fostered in the town of Durham, and with your watchful eye over them, they settle well. You get a job working as a store clerk, working for Mrs. Wilkins, and remain there as a way to stay away from... yourself. A young reporter by the name of Frank Winston starts to write an article for the *Arkham Gazette,* which you have delivered by post especially to your door.

On September the 23rd, around 4:45 p.m., in the year 1926, you stand on the main road of Durham and wait for a Chevrolet to trundle down the road. You contemplated writing to yourself, anonymously of course, as a warning to stay away... but instead felt that you would simply be compelling this other version of yourself to question the warning and turn up anyway. When you thought about it, you know that is what you would have done. No one arrives... there are no strange flashes of green lightning, and no voice on the air. The killings never happened, the article was never written, and thus the other version of yourself remains in Arkham writing for the paper. It is highly unlikely that your paths will ever cross.

If you have recorded in your Investigator Journal '*Received a gift*', then you must turn to the reference associated with that entry now.

If you do not have this entry, turn to **36**.

112

You notice to your surprise that Edward appears to be completely normal and unharmed. It's unmistakably him, but with none of the deformities or alterations you witnessed back in the attic. It's then you spot on a small table next to him a series of implements, one of which is the serrated claw-like prosthetic that was connected to his arm. Have the mi-go removed it? You check his arm for signs of surgery, but there's nothing. You shake him gently to wake him and he starts to stir.
"They are alive, human. I can hear their hearts... beating." Unlatha says, as she leers over you, casting you in shadow. "I would not advise waking any of them... their minds may snap." You ignore her.

Unlatha's shadow moves away as Edward opens his eyes.
"Edward, it's me, Frank!"
He stares at you blankly. "Who... who are you? Where is my mother?" he asks, groggy, but with a perfectly normal-sounding voice.
"It's me, Frank, don't you remember? We met in the attic?" you reply, gripping his shoulders.
"Attic? The light... the green light in the attic!" He starts to sound more agitated.
"Yes, that's right. But I'll get you out of here, and your family too, see?" You point over to his family. He starts to scream. Standing over his mother is Unlatha. A long proboscis extends from her head. She moves to inject it into the mother's abdomen. You cry out and run towards her. "What are you doing?"

"I must feed!" Unlatha bats you away with a swipe of her leg.

Edward gets up, unsteady on his feet, and grabs the claw from the table. "Leave my mother alone!" he screams. He looks like he is going to attack Unlatha.
What do you do?

Pull Edward away and try to flee through the door on the opposite side. Turn to **497**.
Or join with Edward and fight Unlatha. Turn to **525**.

113

Turning to flee down the long tunnel is the worst, and last, decision you will ever make. With nearly fifteen feet of ground to make up, the mi-go take time to aim before sending bolts of lightning hurtling down the tunnel. The area is ablaze with a blinding light as a bolt shoots into your back and flings you forward. Your body is scorched and electrocuted. The smell of your own burning flesh assaults your nostrils. Your body lies twitching as the mi-go surround you.

Record in your Investigator Journal '*You were shot and killed with a lightning gun.*' -2 *Mythos* points.

Your investigation ends here.

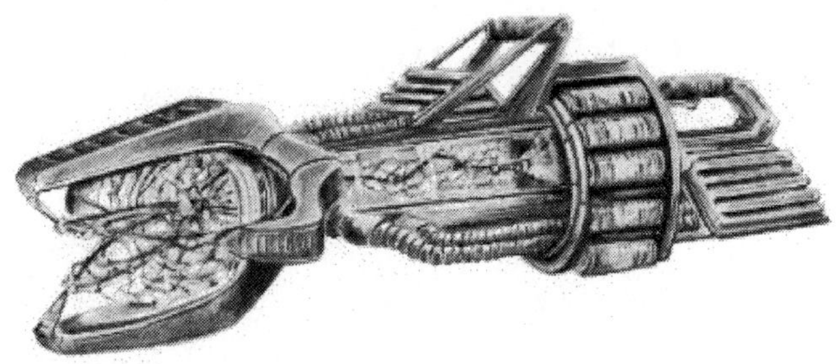

114

As you creep out from behind the container, second thoughts quickly enter your mind. This mi-go is larger than any other you've seen. It has a broad carapace and *four* fully formed arms ending in huge claws, instead of the usual two clawed arms and two smaller utility arms the other mi-go have. Still, you're committed now!

The closer you get the more your nerves build until suddenly, the mi-go guard moves to turn around. Then something quite unexpected happens. The mi-go prisoner taps on its cell wall, enticing the large guard over. It turns its back to you again, buying you precious seconds. It's now or never...

If you are in possession of a weapon, you can choose which one to use. If you haven't gained any of these weapons, you must attack unarmed.

If you are fighting unarmed, turn to **231**.
If you are using a scalpel, turn to **173**.
If you are using a forearm blade, turn to **545**.
If you are using a metal rod, turn to **487**.

115

You implore Edward to stay put and rush back to retrieve Sara, trying to ignore the grotesque creature feeding on their mother. As you pick Sara up, Unlatha's voice speaks in your mind. "Are you taking my food, human?"
"Be silent, monster. I will save who I can!" you reply defiantly as you pick up Sara.
"You... DARE?" Unlatha speaks aloud and turns to face you. A trail of blood whips through the air from her proboscis

and spatters the wall. The body of the mother convulses on the slab. You step back, clutching the child.
"Keep away, monster! You've had your blood," you declare, nodding towards the dying mother.

Unlatha rears up to strike...

A blast of lightning burns through the air from the doorway behind Unlatha. Her body convulses and crackles, smoke rising from her extremities. Edward stands in the doorway holding a lightning gun! Unlatha collapses in a heap, her legs folding in a vain attempt to protect her body. Edward fires again, the weapon kicking him backwards as he tries to control its power. Unlatha's body twitches one last time, then remains still. She is dead. Edward throws the gun to the ground and runs to his mother. She too, is dead.
"I'm sorry, Edward. You must wake your father so we can try to get out of here." You plead as you rush back with Sara into the chamber with the portal machine.

Record in your Investigator Journal '*Sara is alive.*' +20 *Mythos* points.

You place Sara down next to the machine then return to help Edward. Turn to **54**.

116

You make to move to the other side of the room, but stop dead in your tracks. Glancing back, you are horrified to see that the entire tunnel is now blocked by the gelatinous creature. It passes the side tunnel, cutting off your escape as it continues heading toward you. There's nowhere to run from the approaching blob. It reaches the chamber and starts to expand outwards, filling it completely. Having feasted on the entire mi-go brood, it is now enormous. You back up to the farthest wall hoping the creature's approach ceases, but it is a fool's hope.

It burns as it envelops you, suffocating and melting you into itself. You become one with the creature, feeling both what it feels, and what its victims feel. However, your consciousness cannot comprehend the alien nature of this being and you are quickly driven completely insane. Insatiable hunger is all you now feel.

Record in your Investigator Journal '*You were enveloped by the black slime creature and became part of its consciousness*.' -10 *Mythos* points.

Your investigation ends here.

117

You press the panel on the cell and prepare for a possible fight as the transparent cell door rises into the ceiling.
"Yesss, my human ally. You are strong to make it thisss far. But furrrrther on you will requireee my guidance."
You eye the creature suspiciously. "How do we get out?"
It points a claw towards the door on the left. "The cavesss. Ssseparated in cavesss, my former companion and I. Follow

to fiiind the *Tok'llian*." Yar'ith skitters across the floor and through the door. It's smaller than most mi-go you've seen, and as such you expect it will not be much protection should you both encounter a mi-go patrol.

The door leads back out to the sprawling cavern with the black river of slime flowing beneath it. "There, humaaan," it says, pointing down to the river. "Food for Cxaxuklutha. Also an offerrring for him... the Crawling Chaossss... " it says as it moves on, failing to elaborate on that last statement.

"Keep it down," you whisper back, "or we'll be discovered."

"Mi-go don't cooome hereee," it replies. "Dangerousssss... "

You follow behind Yar'ith as it moves along a stone ledge that follows the river flow, until it reaches a side tunnel that heads away from the river.

It turns here, following the tunnel with the familiar sight of glowing fungi on the walls lighting the way. After clambering up a series of raised ledges like a giant staircase, you eventually come to the entrance of a large cavern.

Have you recorded in your Investigator Journal '*Been inside the cavern*'? If so, turn to the reference associated with that entry now.

If you have not been here before, turn to **253**.

118

Unsure of what you are hearing, but suspecting the worst, you look about the room for somewhere to hide. The almost barren room is of no real help. Not even the metal slab would hide you. However, as you contemplate your situation, the strange noise starts to dissipate and then fades away. You decide it is best to keep moving and cautiously check back outside in the corridor for signs of life... nothing.

You move on towards the end of the corridor in the hope that what you heard has gone the other way. Turn to **377**.

119

You keep your footing on the slick stone ground of the cavern and reach the exit to the tunnel. The mi-go skitters after you. You manage to stay ahead of it and reach the doorway back into the room you arrived in.

Will you:

Attempt to get away by passing through the room and on to the door in the opposite wall? Turn to **329**.

Or head through the door and wait at the side to ambush the beast? Turn to **399**.

120

Flashes of green light pierce your vision. A pulsing thrum sends pain through your head. You try to open your eyes, but all you see is a blur, and then a flash of green forces them shut again. You hear a cry, "It's working!" It sounds distant and drawn out. You fade in and out of consciousness. In your weakened state you think you hear a terrible scream, then there's a sudden silence.

When you awake fully, you're lying on the floor. Your hands and feet had been tied, but you notice your bonds have been cut. You push yourself up to a sitting position. It appears you are in the attic. It is dark, with only one grimy window for a light source down the far end facing you. The rain beats down noisily on the roof above.

Standing in the middle of the attic floor is a strange metal device about 4 feet tall. It is a pillar of polished metal that glints in the dim light of the attic, and like tentacles, many copper wires snake their way from openings in the device, running across the floor and disappearing into the walls. A perfect sphere of the same polished metal sits atop the device, set partway into the base. In an almost perfect circle three feet around the device, lies a ring of dead animals – everything from rats, mice, flies, beetles, and centipedes. Some look fresher than others. The possibility of a bad smell is masked instead with the odour of chlorine bleach. What you see just beyond the device sends you into a mild shock. The professor is lying on the floor, his body twisted at the middle, while his lower half is facing almost entirely the wrong direction. Blood runs down into the seams of the floorboards. His eyes are wide open, frozen in terror.

Make a Very Hard (2D6+2) **Composure** check. If you fail, lose 2 Composure. If you pass, lose 1 Composure.

Something moves in the far corner. Lurking in the darkness is a small, hunched figure. You are about to ask who is there when it speaks first in a strained and raspy voice. You fumble to take out your flashlight.

"Fraaaaannnk! Where areeee myyy family? Yooou..mussst go... baaack."
"How… how do you know me?" you answer, both terrified and overwhelmingly intrigued.
"Fraaannk? It issss me... Edward... You saaaved meeee... "
"Did... did you kill the professor?" you ask, your nervousness showing through.
"Yesssssss. I had to! He plannned to stop ussss. Heee isss working for... theeeem!"
It's then that you notice blood dripping from the serrated edge of the claw at the end of his arm. Edward lurches to one side and starts to shuffle out of the darkness towards you.

What do you do?

Decide this is all too much and flee the house (turn to **198**), use your flashlight to get a better look at the figure (turn to **350**), or ask more questions and find out exactly how this could be Edward (turn to **31**).

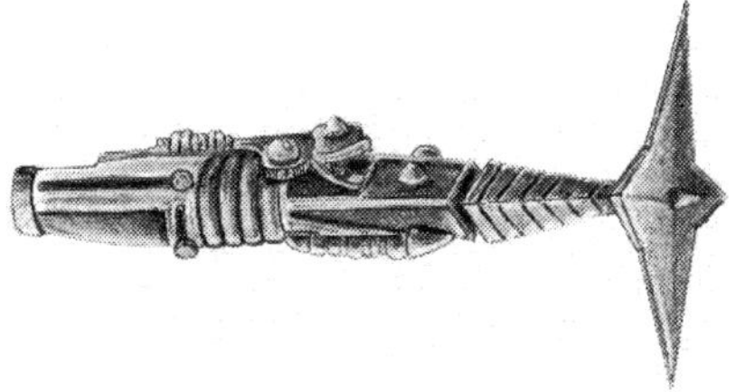

121

The floor of the cave tunnel is smooth from years of moisture erosion, and your footing becomes increasingly unsure. Stepping down from a small ledge you slip, causing an immediate slide downwards about twenty feet. You smack your side off an outcrop of rock. It abruptly, and painfully, stops your descent.

Lose 2 **Health**.

Wincing in pain, you remain against the rock wall for a few moments to get your wind back. Your thoughts drift back to the house, and Edward…

'Find my family!' he said. But they are dead.

'You promised!' he cried. You promised nothing. You had never met him before. Yet, he knew your name – surely the professor told him? His mind was clearly gone. He must have mixed up everything, and whatever the creatures did to him, clearly prevented the aging process. A sudden pang of pity for him and what he endured washes over you. But now you're in this situation, and despair follows as you feel it could be *your* end.

Brushing those thoughts away and cursing your clumsiness, you wince in pain, then continue downwards. Turn to **136**.

122

Despite some near falls, you manage to scramble your way across the line of conveyors and reach the door. You wait... it does not open! You turn to see the two creatures descending from the platform. You see only two possible choices.

You can dash for the nearest conveyor opening in the wall. Turn to **110**.
Or face the creatures in battle. You will have to engage the creature armed with the metal rod first, to prevent it firing at you. Turn to **390**.

123

The large door opens onto a platform that looks over a massive cavern stretching out directly ahead, fading into darkness after about one thousand feet. You see a myriad of walkways and openings both above and below you, criss-crossing the cavern like a web. Many of these extend from the structure you've emerged from and cross into the black rock face on the opposite side, about two hundred feet away. Where you stand, the walkway is missing, and there is a raised control panel visible. Below, running through a channel in the cavern floor is an eighty-foot-wide black river. It's slow moving, more like a black viscous slime than water. Feeding the river of slime is a series of huge pipes set along the cavern wall. A trickle of slime flows from these and joins the main artery.

You surmise that the many bridges are for transporting cargo or other supplies, seeing as the creatures fly and certainly would not need to rely on these for walking.

As you look around, you see a mi-go far below use a panel to extend a walkway, before pushing a container across it. It disappears into one of the doorways. There is a similar raised control panel here with three buttons that could be used to extend a walkway. Which button will you press?

The button with the horizontal line. Turn to **228**.
The button with the vertical line. Turn to **140**.
The button with the diagonal line. Turn to **470**.

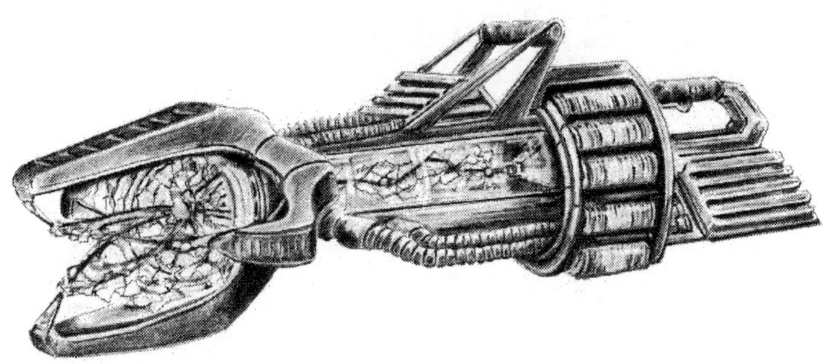

124

"Is your arm okay, professor?" you ask, pointing down.
He remains motionless. You take a step back, feeling uneasy and justified in your defensive motion.
"Are you sure you're okay, professor?"
His eyes glint with a sickly green colour in the dull hallway. You've seen that shade of green light before.

Suddenly he lunges at you brandishing a syringe.

Make a Regular (2D6) **Dexterity** check.

If you pass, turn to **409**.
If you fail, turn to **421**.

125

Your attempt to stop yourself is in vain as you flap your arms uncontrollably, and plunge off the end of the walkway. The cavern has multitudes of walkways criss-crossing its expanse. You hit one of these, breaking your leg. As you struggle to maintain consciousness, various mi-go land next to you. They seem to silently converse with each other, perhaps deciding your fate, then you lose consciousness.

You awake with a strange sensation and cannot feel your arms or legs. Turn to **564**.

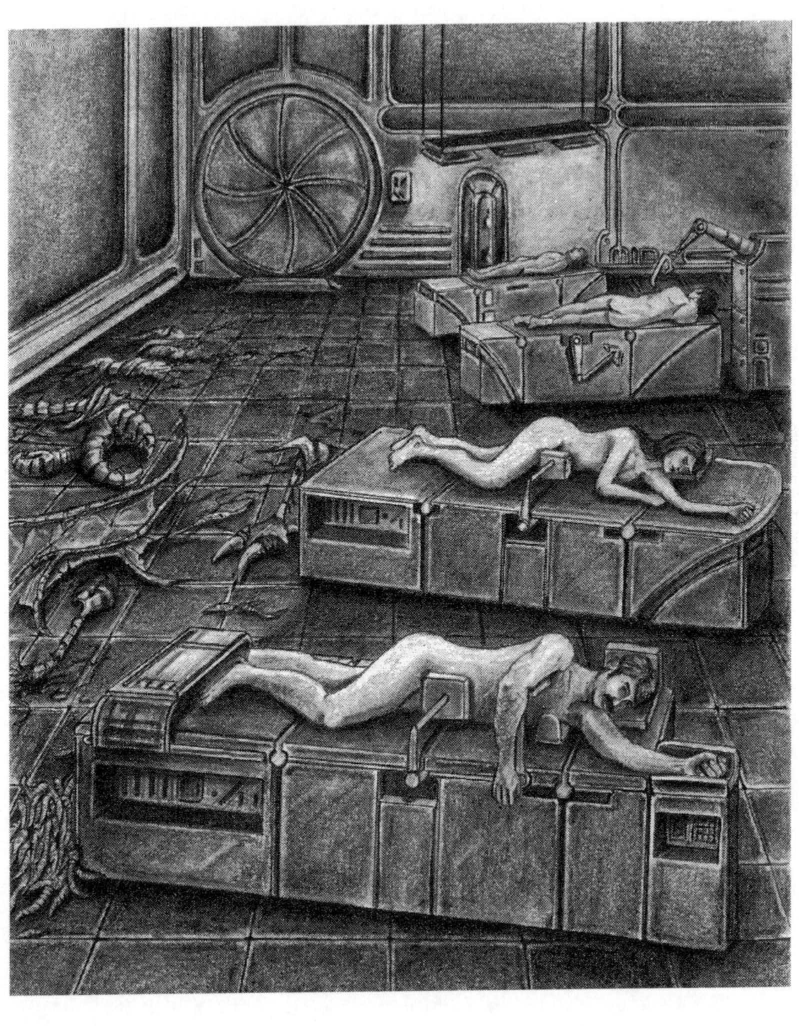

126

"Numerous, aren't they? Disgusting, vile little insects!" The voice of Unlatha echoes in your head. Alarmed, you turn about and can only just about see the vague outline of the jet-black spider-thing clinging to the sheer vertical wall of dark rock. "You have done well, human, to have travelled this far."
"I have... ", you say aloud, "and these disgusting aliens have tried at every turn to stop me. Yet here I stand," you reply with a sense of accomplishment, turning back to look across the cavern of mi-go workers.
"Though it would amuse me to push you off of this ledge right now," Unlatha says, poking your shoulder with an extended leg. "I will resist."
Such is your indifference to Unlatha's 'jest', she continues. "I am most impressed, human. I offer you more of my invaluable assistance. I found your human companions."
You turn sharply. "Where?"
"Follow me. I will move slowly for you."

The ledge branches to the left where another tunnel leads back into the rockface. You glance in to see the remains of numerous mi-go bodies, slowly starting to melt away. They appear to have been dead for some time and such is the carnage, you cannot tell how many of them she killed.

"I cleared the way, as I promised, human."

She enters the tunnel with you following close behind. Green blood and pieces of broken shell and flesh ooze slowly down the wall as you pass. The stone tunnel ends with a metal circular door. She passes through into a room constructed of metal, not too unlike the first room you arrived in. There is one other exit from this room, a door in the opposite wall. There are more dead mi-go here as well. But also, something else...

"Here, human. Your brethren," Unlatha says.

On four metal slab tables lie the bodies of a grown man, a woman, a little girl, and a young boy... Edward. The Turne family! You cannot tell if they are dead, or just unconscious. The two children appear to be unaged – how can they still be their respective ages from the article? You brush off that mystery as there are far more pressing matters.

Will you:
Approach Edward. Turn to **112**.
Check the status of the other family members first. Turn to **242**.

127

Back in Durham, you wander around looking for a vacancy sign. You half expect you won't find one given the run of poor luck the end of the trip has taken, but just as you reach the town edge, you spot an available lodging. The landlords are a friendly middle-aged woman and her husband who are happy to offer lodgings to visitors of Durham for just a few dollars. Apologizing for the late hour, you explain your brief visit and the need to get off the road for the night. "You're a sight for sore eyes, young man. We haven't had a lodger in six months!" she says, taking your coat.

You explain that you may not be staying long. After a late bite to eat and a long tiring, and trying, day, you fall into an uneasy sleep.

That is, until you're suddenly awoken in the middle of the night. Turn to **168**.

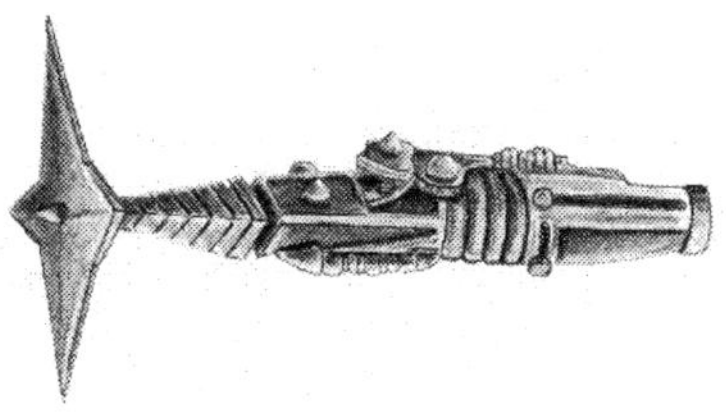

128

As you look around, you see a mi-go far below use a panel to extend a walkway, before pushing a container across it. It disappears into one of the doorways. There is a similar raised control panel here that could be used to extend a walkway. Each button on it has a marking, a series of lines, perhaps representing directions. Following the possible direction with your eyes, the horizontal line would appear to cross the cavern to a cave opening on the opposite side. The other two are harder to apply the same logic to, but you would guess the diagonal line might lead from here to either the left or right. The vertical line, you can't figure out. Which button do you want to press?

The horizontal line. Turn to **228**.
The vertical line. Turn to **140**.
The diagonal line. Turn to **470**.

129

"You know, professor, I'm really quite sorry, but I think I will call it quits, and head on back to Arkham. I feel... " He stares at you, emotionless. "I feel this isn't for me after all," you add.

Ten seconds go by, with no response.

If you want to approach the front door to open it and leave, turn to **149**.
Or if you wave at the professor and try to coax a response from him, turn to **4**.

130

You back away coughing and spluttering, rubbing your face in an attempt to clear the spores away. Luckily, you escaped the worst of the effects. Your constitution holds out, and after a few moments you feel well enough to continue.

What will you do next?
Approach the well in the centre of the room. Turn to **327**.
Head for the door in the far opposite wall. Turn to **546**.
Head for the door over on the right-hand side. Turn to **7**.
Investigate the ramp going up to the next floor. Turn to **433**.

131

The stairs creak with each step you take. When you near the top, you are suddenly shocked by the appearance of a figure stepping out in front of you. You've no time to react as a syringe is jabbed into your shoulder. You tumble backwards down the stairs and hurt yourself, badly.

Lose 3 **Health**.

You have been injected with a sedative and feel it taking effect. The figure follows slowly down the steps. "You might be of use, young man. I'm Professor Albert Peabody, pleased to... "

You black out before you can hear him finish. Turn to **120**.

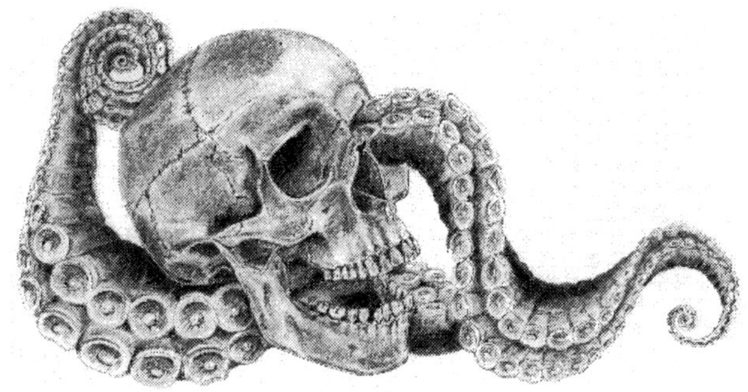

132

As the beast falls dead at your feet, its companion from the control room flees down into the conveyor area. It's swift and you gather you'd never be able to catch it. Perhaps it's going for reinforcements.

Fearing more will be coming, you decide to quickly move on, and exit the corridor. Turn to **105**.

133

You turn the first dial to what you would believe to be 75 degrees.

How do you want to set the second dial?

Set it to 45 degrees. Turn to **521**.
Set it to 121 degrees. Turn to **247**.
Set it to 37 degrees. Turn to **362**.

134

You somehow, miraculously, avoid seriously hurting yourself with each leap to the lower step, then turn down the right-hand branch. The tunnel starts to narrow, and you breathe a sigh of relief as you discover the horrifying spider cannot follow. You slump against the wall, panting heavily, ever more in shock and bewilderment at your predicament. What other horrors await you? It would seem preferable to at least be back in the mi-go structure.

You climb to your feet and carry on. Turn to **466**.

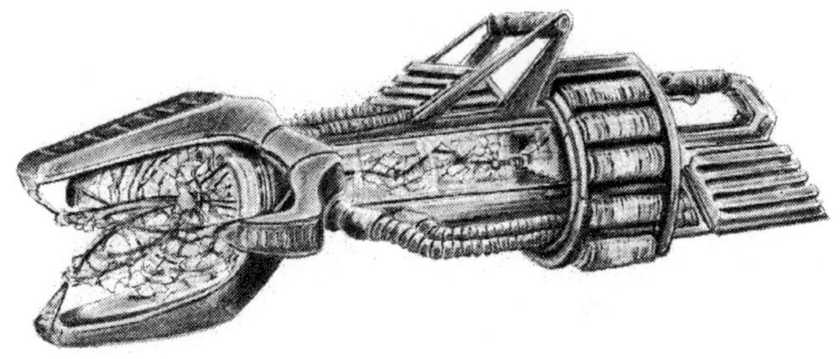

135

"Oh, okay. Didn't mean to pry or anything. Just nothing much happens around these parts, ya know? Thing is, you can't go up there. No one is allowed you see. So sorry you wasted your time. If you make a start home, perhaps you make it before it gets too late. Now if you'll excuse me."
She ushers you out, and ignores your attempts to get more information about why no one is allowed up to the house. You leave the post office, the doorbell ringing loudly on your way out.

As you walk down the street, you hear the bell once more. Looking back towards the post office, you see Mrs. Wilkins shutting the door and locking it. She's looking directly at you. She turns and hurries off in the opposite direction, disappearing around the first corner.

You return to your car – the town is quieter than ever. The garage door appears to have been locked up for the evening. You feel there's not much more you can do here. What next?

Drive on. Perhaps the house might be easy enough to find along the main road out of town. Turn to **557**.
Or call it a day. Look for a lodging and get a fresh start in the morning. Turn to **372**.

136

The deeper you move into the cave, the more the air seems to close in and stifle. It's warm, a little too warm, and all of your recent exertions haven't helped. You open your shirt collar and wipe the sweat from your brow. The cave widens into a larger cavern where a strange, bulbous fungi grow, lining the walls. In the centre of the cavern, stalactites and stalagmites create a forest of rock ahead. The fungi are varied here, with huge deep red-capped ones, small glowing blue ones (which are the only source of light), and a yellowish fungus that hangs from the rock by a long stalk.

Schreeeeeeeeeee! A distant animal call startles you, the sound echoing around the cave. You cannot tell where it came from. Instinctively crouching low against the wall, you advance slowly, watching for movement.

Make a Regular (2D6) **Stealth** check.

If you pass, turn to **398**.
If you fail, turn to **359**.

137

Despite your instincts telling you otherwise, you move up to the flickering light for a better look.

Below the light, the rock appears to undulate and peel away. You scramble backwards but it's too late. The tunnel floor below you crumbles, sending you hurtling downwards at a very steep slope. You are deposited from an opening in the ceiling of a massive cavern. Luckily, your fall is broken by a large mound of piled up refuse. You find yourself on your back staring up at the ceiling. A light above the peak of the mound sits next to the chute you fell from.

The mound is a massive pile of entrails, bones, and offal. You're covered in it. You get up and try to wipe it off, but it seems futile.

Make a Hard (2D6+1) **Composure** check. If you fail, deduct

2 from your current Composure. If your composure has dropped to zero or below, you spend the remaining days of your life having gone insane in this hell, feeding off the entrails you find until sickness follows, and eventually, death. -5 *Mythos* points. Your investigation ends here.

If you pass, you must still lose 1 Composure as the full extent of this horrifying place takes hold.

If you have not yet succumbed to madness, you steel your shredded nerves, and look for a way out. Turn to **203**.

138

You continue onwards, weary, angry, frustrated... and vengeful. If you cannot escape, you at least plan to take out as many of these mi-go as you can. If you die here, you'll die fighting.

Your anger renews your drive, and you quicken the pace.

The tunnel turns sharply to the right and then starts to rise upwards at a thirty-degree angle. You continue up for about two minutes until it opens out onto a high rocky ledge. Standing on the ledge, you look out far below at a cavern so vast, you cannot see the bottom. Hundreds, if not thousands, of mi-go crawl about like a massive ant colony, carrying ore and other materials throughout the elaborate network of caves and passageways. Large disc-shaped machines are being used to bore holes through the rock and form new passages, or to reveal new ore deposits. Glinting sliver veins of the ore snake through the rock like the central nervous system of some vast beast.

If you have recorded in your Investigator Journal '*You freed Unlatha*', then turn to the **SECOND** reference associated with that entry now.

If you do not have that entry, turn to **85**.

139

Sensing you won't make it in time if you rushed at the creature, you duck behind the nearest slab just as the mi-go unleashes the power of the weapon. A blast of lightning blasts overhead with a loud crack. The air is charged with electricity for a few moments.

"Huuuumaan... will dieeee... " utters the vile creature from behind the slab. You hear its feet skitter across the floor – it is coming.

Make a Hard (2D6+1) **Perception** check.

If you pass, turn to **75**.
If you fail, turn to **304**.

140

When you press the button, you quickly steady yourself as the entire platform begins to descend. It comes to rest on a ledge that runs along the bank of the black slime river flowing through the cavern. The air is warmer down here, making you sweaty and uncomfortable. The river is on your left, and flows ahead of you before disappearing into darkness through the cavern wall.

Will you go back up to choose a different route (turn to **269**), or explore the ledge (turn to **182**)?

141

A quick flash forces your eyes shut, then you open them again as you emerge on the other side. A searing heat incinerates you instantly. Your calculations were wrong! You have emerged on the surface of a burning star.

Record in your Investigator Journal '*You went through the portal and died instantly on the surface of a sun.*' -3 *Mythos* points.

Your investigation ends here.

142

The professor was clearly mad, but you feel you've no choice but to believe that the syringe does in fact contain a sedative. As Jacob makes to flee back out towards the mi-go mining chamber, you rush up and inject the syringe into his back. You call for Edward to help as Jacob turns to you.

"It'll calm you down so we can get you out of here," you explain as you back away. Jacob pulls the syringe from his back, then falls to his knees, and finally, his eyes roll to the back of his head as he slumps forward. You catch him as Edward arrives. "Just a sedative, Edward. I knocked him out so we can try to get out of here before those mi-go arrive!"

Record in your Investigator Journal '*Jacob is alive.*' +20 *Mythos* points.

Edward nods. The boy is remarkably resilient to everything that has happened. With his help, you drag his father to other room. The machine stands silent. You examine it and find the slot for the power source – the *Tok'llian,* but it is not here. Do you have it?

If you have recorded in your Investigator Journal '*Found the Tok'llian',* then you must turn to the **FIRST** reference associated with that entry now.

If you do not have the *Tok'llian,* turn to **509**.

143

You set the fourth dial to zero and step back from the device. Edward looks at you expectantly. "Weeeellll, issss it working?"
"I don't know. I've never seen this thing before!"
Edward is about to protest again when suddenly a bright flash of green light shoots upwards from the sphere atop the machine. A low thrum pulses in the air, and the light flickers, slowly at first, then faster and faster until it becomes a solid beam. You back away, not knowing what to expect. Edward stares intently at the beam of light. "Yesssssss!" he cries, excitedly. "You diiiid it!"

The sphere starts to tilt, sending the beam downwards, coming to rest parallel with the floor. Where it strikes the attic wall it forms what you can only describe as a doorway, and on the other side, faint and distorted as though peering through water, a small empty chamber appears.

"Goooooo, nooooow!!" Edward cries. "Goooooooo, befooore it isssss... too late!"

You step up to the strange doorway. Turn to **426**.

144

The door opens into a darker area, and the floor seems to be soft, almost sponge-like. The walls are made from a black stone and are slick with moisture. The faintest of light remains as the door closes behind you, but your eyes adjust somewhat, allowing visibility of about ten feet ahead. The floor is covered with fungi, much of it already trodden and crushed. A trail leads ahead and to the left through the fungus, as though something was dragged.

Will you follow the trail where the fungus is disturbed (turn to **558**), or walk straight ahead into the fresh, untrodden area of the chamber (turn to **368**)?

145

Given the dead end, you concede that fighting is your best chance. You advance on the mi-go to give yourself the advantage and keep away from the dangerous walkway edge. The creature armed with the metal rod points it towards you. You must try to dodge this attack.

Make a Regular (2D6) **Dexterity** check. If you pass, you successfully dodged the shard, which flies harmlessly past you into the vast cavern behind. If you fail, you are hit square in the shoulder, and must lose 2 **Health**.

If you were hit and survived the damage, you now must face them in combat. The corridor is narrow enough to ensure you can fight them one at time instead of both together. Fight the first mi-go, and if you survive the second one steps up.

Mi-go Worker 1	**Mi-go Worker 2**
Combat 6	Combat 7
Health 5	Health 4

If you manage to win, turn to **227**.
If you lose, turn to **385**.

146

He sighs. "Very well." He holds up a syringe. "Take this and inject yourself," he says, matter-of-factly.
"What? I will not!" you respond, taking a step back further into the hallway.
"I'm afraid if you do not, then what I will show you upstairs might be damaging on your psyche. I really must insist." He holds out the syringe for you to take.

Will you take the syringe, but instead turn it on him and demand answers (turn to **289**), or take the syringe and smash it underfoot (turn to **199**)? Alternatively, you can take the syringe and do as he suggests and inject it (turn to **206**).

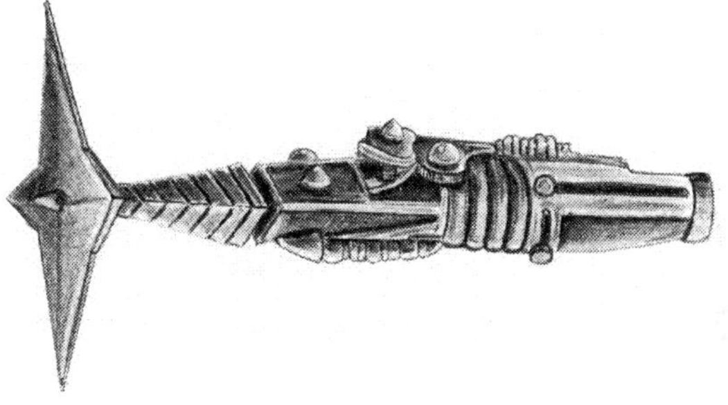

147

The cave starts to slope downwards and becomes increasingly more difficult to traverse. You're not exactly equipped for this, and it gives you pause to consider that you're either getting further away from your goal of getting back home than when you started, or you are eventually going to find a way up to the surface and will be able to orientate yourself and figure out exactly where you are once you do.

As the cave begins to level out again, you come to another

branching tunnel. Both ways appear equally illuminated, but you sense that the air smells fouler from the left branch compared to the right one. It could also just be your imagination. Which way will you choose?

To take the left branch, turn to **5**.
To take the right branch, turn to **481**.

148

You make a dash for the large door, hoping it will open as swiftly as the others you've encountered. But first, you'll have to leap over each of the conveyors that cross the floor. The two creatures above call out for you to stop in their terrible affected tones.

Make a Very Hard (2D6+2) **Dexterity** check.

If you pass, turn to **122**.
If you fail, turn to **513**.

149

You make a move towards the front door and add, "So if that's okay, I'll be going. So sorry to have... "

Before you reach the door and finish your sentence, he lunges at you!

Make a Hard (2D6+1) **Dexterity** check.

If you pass, turn to **409**.
If you fail, turn to **421**.

150

Crouching down, you leave your hiding place and approach the creature's back. With the element of surprise on your side, you attack first, wounding the beast. The mi-go's head turns red as it whips around. It lets out a shrill cry unlike what you've heard before from these monsters, and prepares to defend itself.

Now you must finish it off.

For this combat, you must record the number of rounds it takes to fight the creature. If you haven't won by the start of round *seven*, turn to **239**.

Mi-go Worker (wounded)
Combat 6
Health 3

If you win in 6 rounds or less, turn to **30**.
If you lose in 6 rounds or less, turn to **461**.

151

You quicken your pace, the imagination of what could be in the water taking over and driving your actions. In your panic, your foot gets caught in a crack in the stone, sending you crashing down into the water. You splash wildly for a moment before pushing yourself back up. As you rise, something in the water latches onto your cheek. You feel a sharp sting as you stumble onward, letting out a cry of pain.

Lose 1 **Health**.

You reach the other side and instinctively reach for the thing. It's a kind of tube-like worm, similar to a lamprey, with its sucker-like teeth it's attempting to bore its way through your cheek.

Do you have a scalpel? If so, you can try and cut it away by turning to **57**.
Otherwise, you will have to try and pull the creature off. Turn to **458**.

152

"I'm looking for Sentinel Hill. You see, I read about this old house up there, and wanted to take a look." You pause to allow the woman to respond. She lifts her head slightly, looks you in the eye, but remains silent. "Eh, you see, I couldn't find it on a map, but I read it was close to Durham," you continue, her stare making you feel on edge. You're about to continue further when she speaks up suddenly.
"Sentinel Hill, you say? What would your business be with that old place, eh?"

What is your response?

Tell her you're writing an article about the murders ten years ago. Turn to **20**.
Tell her you're curious because you are thinking of moving out of the city. Turn to **163**.
Or ask why the town is so quiet. Turn to **560**.

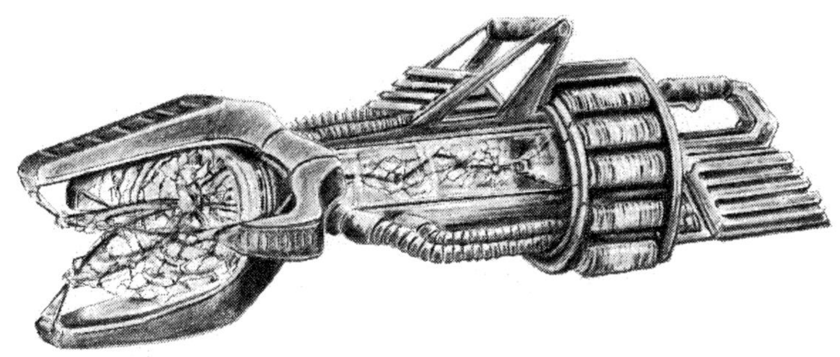

153

You sense that any possible movement from you at this stage would alert this horror to your presence. You don't see any eyes, but that is not to say it has none, or other means of sensing you are there. You keep as still as possible and watch as the *Formless Spawn* crawls, walks, then slithers around before you, morphing itself at will to the changing terrain. It moves further away before suddenly changing direction and turning back directly towards you, only to again change direction at the sound of another chute opening above. Rapidly forming long whip-like tentacles, it launches itself with surprising speed away to your right and disappears over the crest of another mound.

When you feel it's gone far enough away, you slowly continue onward. Turn to **519**.

154

The noise of machinery is unmistakable as you enter a wide chamber. You see a large device which is dominated by a metallic disc that stands upright, roughly ten feet in diameter, facing a wall of rock. The remaining walls of the chamber are the familiar metal construction. The noise you heard is coming from a series of conveyor belts that run across the floor of the room. There are four of them, and each one runs from an opening in the right-hand side of the chamber and sends its cargo into another opening on the opposite side. You wince when you notice what they are transporting... various lumps of bone, flesh, and other offal. The smell is vile.

Make a Very Easy (2D6-2) **Composure** check.

If you pass, turn to **325**.
If you fail, turn to **512**.

155

"What do you want?" you call out to creature.
It remains still, its head flashing through a multitude of colours... then it speaks.
"Huuumaaan... sssshould noot beeeee hereee... " It takes a few steps towards you, its feet clacking off the ground.
"I want to leave. How do I get out of here?" you ask.
"Hoooww, huuumaan? Hooww are yooou hereee?" it asks in return, and again takes more skittish steps towards you. It's only about ten feet away now.

Do you wish to continue talking to it? Turn to **395**.
Or take its advances as a precursor to attack, and strike first. Turn to **233**.

156

The creature, a juvenile *Byakhee,* is too engrossed in its meal to notice you. You deal a blow to its neck and are relieved to see it crumple quickly to the ground. It already had multiple wounds, likely a result from its battle with the mi-go, and perhaps other encounters before that.

With the beast dead, you search the area. Turn to **41**.

157

You sense that any possible movement from you at this stage would alert this horror to your presence. You keep as still as possible and watch as the *Formless Spawn* crawls around into full view, then slithers around before you, morphing itself at will to the changing terrain. It moves further away before suddenly changing direction and turning back directly towards you, only to again change direction at the sound of another chute opening above. Rapidly forming long whip-like tentacles, it launches itself with surprising speed away to your right and disappears over the crest of another mound.

When you feel it's gone far enough away, you slowly continue onward. Turn to **519**.

158

You take cover behind the large metal disc, but what now? You listen for the creatures and one of them lets out a shrill series of short cries. Then you hear the tell-tale sound of their feet clacking on the metal floor. Then another, and another. You stay behind the disc, but it appears you are being surrounded by reinforcements.

The situation is desperate. You raise your hands in surrender and come out from behind the machine.

However, it appears the creatures are not impressed with your gesture. Each one attacks! Claws nip and slice at you then back away, only for another to repeat the assault. You find it impossible to defend against. A claw pierces your eye socket and plucks your eye clean out. You've barely the strength to scream as another repeats this with your second eye. Slowly but surely the creatures take what they want, clipping fingers from your hands. You are dragged onto a conveyor belt and then plunged down a chute to join the other rotten remains. You die shortly after.

Record in your Investigator Journal '*You died horribly mutilated by a gang of mi-go.*' -2 *Mythos* points.

Your investigation ends here.

159

As you take a few steps forward the reverberation of your footsteps echoes strangely about the corridor. You reach out to touch the edge of the shape, and as you do the wall opens before you. It is a door. In one swift motion it sweeps aside to reveal a chamber on the other side. The chamber is undefined, blurred. You step through to see what lies beyond and the chamber reveals itself. The door closes behind you.

At the far end of the room stands a group of four pedestals that appear to be moulded up directly from the floor. Atop each pedestal rests a tall cylinder. To you right, four horizontal metal platforms line the wall like a row of low tables. In the left wall is a large round window that looks out to a black sky. A faint green light shines in through the window, bathing everything with a sickly green tint.

What will you do?
Look out the window. Turn to **416**.
Examine the horizontal slabs. Turn to **422**.
Or examine the cylinders at the far wall. Turn to **192**.

160

You push on the door and to your surprise, it opens. Easing it open further, there's a loud creak from the old, neglected hinges. You step into the darkness beyond the door and wait for your eyes to adjust.

You are standing in a dim hallway. Old picture frames line the wall on the left. The main staircase runs up on the right-hand side. At the foot of the stairs on your right is a door. Facing you at the end of the hallway is another door. Finally, there's a door under the stairs which likely leads to the basement.

Where do you want to explore?
Open the door nearest you at the foot of the stairs. Turn to **499**.
Try the basement door. Turn to **78**.
Go upstairs. Turn to **131**.
Try the door ahead of you at the end of the hallway. Turn to **484**.
Or stay put, and call out to see if anyone is here. Turn to **478**.

161

Deduct 2 from your current **Composure**.

If you have not yet succumbed to madness, you steel your shredded nerves, and look for a way out.

Now, turn to **203**.

162

You step away from the screen, and as you do it starts to dim and eventually returns to black.

There's nothing else of interest in this room.

You can try the room on the left if you haven't already done so. Turn to **246**.
Or continue down the corridor. Turn to **377**.

163

She eyes you even more suspiciously (if such a thing is possible), and then chuckles, her laugh raspy and laboured. "Oh, you city fellers. No clue about nothing out here. If it were the quiet life you be looking for, then Sentinel Hill would not be it. I hear it's a mess and a ruin. But enough of this chatter, I'll be late if I don't get moving. Good day to yer, young sir."

She shuffles away, slowly. You realise she hasn't told you how to get to the hill, so you inquire again. "I don't rightly remember the way, but definitely take a left, young man, as it's out that-a-way," she says pointing to the west.

And with that, she shuffles away, mumbling to herself.

What will you do?
If you wish to enter the garage, turn to **59**.
Call it a day, look for a lodging and get a fresh start in the morning. Turn to **372**.
Or you can return to your car and drive on. Perhaps there will be a sign to point you in the right direction towards the hill. Turn to **331**.

164

You get a strange sensation with each step towards the statue – a sense of growing fear and malice. It would seem fanciful if it weren't for this unearthly place. Nevertheless, despite the growing unease, you reach the statue and peer into the bowl. It's filled with a black liquid (which reminds you of the river) that trickles down from the feet of the statue, yet the level in the bowl remains constant.

If you want to touch the liquid (turn to **539**), or try one of the exits (only if you haven't already done so):
The exit on the left. Turn to **230**.
The one directly ahead. Turn to **358**.
The one to your right. Turn to **437**.

165

The creature grips you in its talons, pulling you from the ledge. In flight, it snaps and pecks at you, pulling strips of flesh from your face. It reaches an inaccessible ledge and drops you. You attempt to crawl away as the Byakhee starts to rip and tear at your flesh. You are eaten alive.

Record in your Investigator Journal '*Eaten alive by a Byakhee*.'
-5 *Mythos* points.

Your investigation ends here.

166

You turn the handle and push the door slightly... it opens! Easing it further, you take a step beyond the threshold. The door creaks loudly, competing with the rain to be heard. You wince. You can’t yet see very far into the dark hallway.

You can push the door further and keep going. Turn to **451**.
Or stop and call out to the professor. Turn to **548**.

167

Back in the main chamber, you may do any of the following (but only if you haven't already):

Investigate the ramp by turning to **433**.
Examine the well in the centre by turning to **327**.
Or head for the door in the opposite wall by turning to **546**.

168

Your eyes flick open. Flashes of green light fill the room through the window. Green lightning? The window is open, but you were sure it was closed when you retired for the night.
"Help ussss... you promisssed... " A distant voice, terrible and raspy.
Your heart nearly stops as you dart your eyes about the room. "Who... who's there? Show yourself," you stammer.
More flashes of green light pour through the window. "You ssssaid you would... gooo baaack."

What do you do?
Leap out of the bed and search the room for the source of the voice. Turn to **236**.
Try and talk to the strange voice. Turn to **544**.

169

You stick close to the cavern wall and come across another, smaller opening, in the cave wall. There's a rancid smell emanating from it.

To examine the smaller opening, turn to **277**.
Or ignore it and continue on to the larger exit ahead. Turn to **147**.

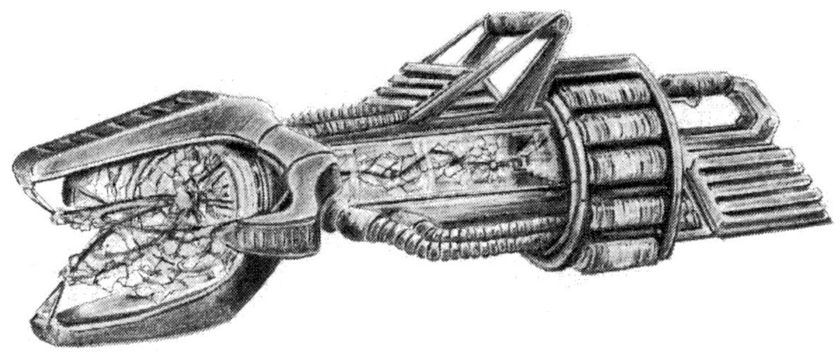

170

Back inside the structure, you find yourself stumbling down a long featureless corridor. The corridor is a mix of both the metal construction and the now-familiar hewn black rock. You reach a square-shaped door in the left-hand wall at the end of the corridor, and press yourself against the wall as it opens. Staying low, you listen for the possibility of mi-go presence. When it seems clear, you step inside.

You turn to scan the room and almost immediately jump with fright when you see three people are standing upright against the wall on the left. They are all naked, but appear to be missing reproductive organs. Their skin hangs loose, and their eyes are hollow black holes. It is then you realise it is human skin handing from some kind of rack.

On the opposite side of the room is a large mechanical exoskeleton, the arms of which are a series of serrated implements that remind you of Edward's dangerous prosthetic.

There's another square door straight ahead. What do you want to do?

Approach the skinsuits. Turn to **45.**
Examine the exoskeleton. Turn to **176**.
Or leave this unsettling room through the door ahead. Turn to **317**.

171

The mi-go is badly wounded by your blow – it collapses to the floor. You look away as you stomp on its bulbous head to finish it off. A pool of green blood oozes from its carcass. They are surprisingly fragile, you think to yourself, though still repulsed by the encounter.

If this truly is the domain of these monsters, just how many will you have to face?

You're about to step away when you notice a small metal tube with a star-shaped metal piece at the top lying next to the creature. You pick it up and examine it. A small switch on its outer casing piques your interest. When you press it, the star-shaped headpiece starts to whirr and spin. You're not quite sure what it could be for, but it's a curious enough thing that you decide to take it and place it in your satchel.

Record in your Investigator Journal '*Have a star-shaped tool*', and note these two references. The *first* is 475, and the *second* is 425. If asked about this entry later, be sure to confirm you go the correct reference mentioned, the first, or the second. +3 *Mythos* points.

After your experience going through the tunnel, you decide it would be best to try the other door instead. Turn to **62**.

172

The attic space is long and narrow, and strangely uncluttered as you would be used to seeing an attic space taken advantage of for storage. However, standing in the middle of the attic floor is a strange metal device, about 4 feet tall. The pillar of polished metal glints in the dim light of the attic, and like tentacles, many copper wires snake their way from openings in the device, running across the floor and disappear into the walls. A perfect sphere of the same polished metal sits atop the structure, set partway into the base. In an almost perfect circle three feet around the device, lies a ring of dead animals – everything from rats, mice, flies, beetles, and centipedes. Some look fresher than others. The possibility of a bad smell is masked instead with the odour of chlorine bleach.

It is dark with only one grimy window for a light source down the far end facing you. The rain beats down noisily on the roof above.

Something moves in the far corner. Lurking in the darkness is a small, hunched figure. You are about to ask who is there when it speaks first in a strained and raspy voice. You fumble to take out your flashlight.

"Fraaaaannnk! Where areeee myyy family? Yooou..mussst go... baaack."
"How… how do you know me?" you answer, both terrified, and overwhelmingly intrigued.
"Fraaannk? It issss me... Edward... You saaaved meeee... " The shape lurches to one side and starts to shuffle out of the darkness towards you.

Make a Hard (2D6+1) **Composure** check. If you fail, lose 1 Composure.

What do you do?
Decide this is all too much and flee the house. Turn to **198**.
Use your flashlight to get a better look at the figure. Turn to **350**.
Ask more questions to find out exactly who the speaker is. Turn to **31**.

173

You plunge the scalpel deep into the back of the creature's head, badly wounding it. The reaction is almost instant as the mi-go swings around with its claws ready. You jump back just in time to avoid its counterattack and prepare to fight.

This mi-go is unlike the others you have encountered. It has a broad carapace and four fully formed arms ending in huge claws, instead of the usual two clawed arms and two smaller utility arms the other mi-go have. The extra limbs and claws can deal 1 extra Damage to you for each round you lose against it. Though it is badly wounded, it is still extremely dangerous.

Mi-go Guard (badly wounded)
Combat 8
Health 4

If you win, turn to **562**.

174

As you walk cautiously through the chamber, you are just about to reach the door when a voice speaks. The effect is disconcerting as rather than hearing it, this voice spoke directly in your head. "Human, stop."

Despite the shock, you can try to ignore it and exit the room by turning to **144**.
Or do as the voice asks, and stop to see who (or what) spoke by turning to **191**.

175

You can't explain the suffocating fear that washes over you, only that you must turn back and flee this trap you willingly walked into. Something lurks in mist above, and a mere brush off one of these threads will have it descend on you. In your panic, just as you are about to clear the forest of silken threads, you do exactly that, catching the last thread. It sticks to your jacket, stretching as you move out of the cave. And your fears turn to reality as a gigantic, bulbous purple spider-thing silently flows down out of the mist!

Make an Extreme (2D6+3) **Composure** check.

If you fail, turn to **308**.
If you pass, turn to **514**.

176

The construction almost defies belief. It is a mechanical 'suit' designed to be worn around the user. Multiple attachment sockets line the arms and legs. Unfortunately, it is clearly designed for use by a mi-go, and therefore it would be of no use to you. Something catches your eye, however. There's a star-shaped indentation along the arm.

If you have recorded in your Investigator Journal '*Have a star-shaped tool'*, then turn to the **FIRST** reference associated with that entry now.

If not, you can do one of the following:
Look at the skinsuits (if you haven't already done so). Turn to **45**.
Or continue out of the room through the door. Turn to **317**.

177

The tallest of the plants droops slightly due to the weight of four small pods hanging from the stem, attached via a thin thread of silk. The black petals reflect the light of the room and the red veins running through them bulge slightly.

To take one of the pods hanging from the plant, turn to **274**.
Or if you haven't already done so, you can examine the orange plant. Turn to **386**.
Examine the spiny cactus-like plan. Turn to **190**.
Or leave this room, as you need to find a way out of here and back home. Turn to **370**.

178

Quickly deciding that to turn back down the long tunnel would invite instant death, you make a desperate run for the junction just ahead of you. A loud crack reverberates through the tunnel as it is bathed in a brilliant white light. With the wall taking most of the impact, you are just partially caught by the gun's wild discharge.

Lose 1 **Health**.

You clamber to your feet and run on with little time to consider what additional dangers you may be charging into. It doesn't take long before you run into another mi-go patrol. They are out in force, clearly looking for the human intruder who has been seen loose in their city. The patrol wastes no time in training their guns on you, forcing you to surrender.

Captured, the mi-go lead you away. Turn to **39**.

179

You struggle in panic but cannot release yourself. You're pulled into the larger cavern among the other threads which stick and entangle you to the point you can no longer move. Then, you feel yourself rising from the ground as the threads are pulled upwards into the mist. The mist envelops you, making it impossible to see the creature that bites into your torso, injecting your body with a paralysing venom that then starts to liquefy your internal organs.

Record in your Investigator Journal '*You were ensnared and devoured by a giant Spider of Leng.*' -5 *Mythos* points.

Your investigation ends here.

180

"We need to get out of here, Edward!" you call out as you pick up the young girl.
"No, we can't leave them!" Edward tries to move his mother. You glance back at the portal, expecting the inevitable. Suddenly a dark shape looms up in the background through the warped haze of the doorway.
The mi-go turn, and flashes of lightning from the guns fill the room beyond. The gigantic dark shape is the slime-creature that you unwittingly freed. Having fed on the mi-go brood (and perhaps countless more mi-go creatures since), it has grown to a terrifying size. It flows into the

room seemingly unaffected by the lightning guns' power. One by one the guns fall silent as the mi-go are swallowed whole by the viscous burning mass. A dread fear grips you, holding you in place... it could come through the portal…

Your fears are unfounded, however. As the unstoppable nightmare advances it fills the room beyond, enveloping the machine. The beam is cut off, and in a flash the portal is closed. It's over... and the mi-go will unlikely be able to follow. The creature you unleased upon them may prove beyond their abilities to stop.

Record in your Investigator Journal '*Edward is alive and unaltered.*' +20 *Mythos* points.

The nightmare is over. Turn to **82**.

181

Both creatures lie dead, and you sit for a moment, exhausted.

Content to sit and rest here, you almost feel like giving up, but some resolve from the pit of your stomach pulls you to your feet. You decide to take the metal rod for yourself. Unsure of how to operate it, or even if it is now empty, it still seems wise to have it.

Record in your Investigators Journal '*Have a metal rod*', and note the reference 283. +1 *Mythos* point.

Now, you examine the room. Turn to **197**.

182

The ledge is wide enough for two people to walk abreast and heads around a slight bend to the right. As you pass the bend it widens considerably, and the ground gets rougher. The area here is littered with debris, from rocks to what are clearly metal cannisters and other items of mi-go construction. Suddenly, you hear a wild screeching from behind one of the larger rocks. You hunker down and look.

A winged creature is feasting on a fresh kill. A dead mi-go lies at its feet, being picked apart by a vicious beak. It hasn't noticed you, too engrossed in its meal. Its leathery wings are rough and tattered as though it has been in many battles. Its body looks sickly, half-decomposed, with a head dominated by a huge beak on the end of a flexible elongated neck. Its head is more snake-like than bird-like, with little room for eyes and other sensory organs. Ignoring its wingspan, it is perhaps the size of an emu.

Make a Regular (2D6) **Composure** check. If you fail, lose 1 Composure as the creature's size and almost undead appearance induce fear.

What will you do?

The creature hasn't noticed you, so you could head back to the platform and choose another route. Turn to **269**.

Quietly search the area while the creature is occupied. Turn to **440**.

Or sneak up behind the beast and attack it. Turn to **307**.

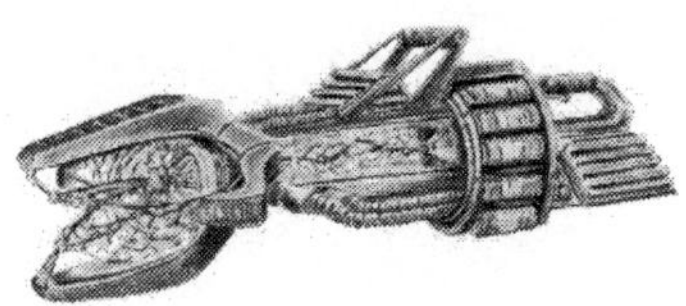

183

You wait for the perfect moment, scalpel at the ready, then strike. Going straight for the head, the creature poring over the objects doesn't see you coming and goes down easily enough as you slice it open, green ichor oozing out of the wound to the floor. The second mi-go reaches for a metal rod from the shelf (a weapon of some kind?), but you are upon it before it can utilise it. It turns to fight you…

Mi-go Worker
Combat 7
Health 4

If you win, turn to **262**.

184

You ask him for directions towards Sentinel Hill.
"Ah! Don't go out that way much. The roads are bad. I know you take a left at the fork ahead, but not too sure after that. Best check at the post office just down the street there. Mrs. Wilkins knows this area better than anyone." You thank him once again as he turns and heads inside the garage, shutting the door behind him.

You turn back to your car, then take another look up and down the street. No one is around. The place seems empty and uninviting. A cold breeze suddenly whips through the garage lot, blowing leaves up into a swirl.

Will you get into your car and head on (turn to **557**), or visit the post office and see if you can get directions there (turn to **218**).

185

The mi-go appears to be listening as you ask it a range of questions about where you are, what they are, and what are the cannisters that line the walls – but it only answers with one word no matter what you ask.
"Yuggggooth."

You give up asking when the other mi-go return. Turn to **352**.

186

Finding the only likely area to attempt a climb, you reluctantly edge yourself over the ledge and get some footing. The rock here is rough and natural, allowing for some purchase as you descend.

Make an Extreme (2D6+3) **Dexterity** check.

If you fail, turn to **318**.
If you pass the Dexterity check, you successfully reach the bottom. Turn to **323**.

187

Not convinced that it's safe to cross the floor, you continue to wait and watch. There! At the far end of the room on the walkway, one of those creatures emerges from an opening in the wall and moves to a control panel. It starts to manipulate the controls. The conveyor belts grind to a halt. The creature turns, forcing you to duck in behind the disc you are using for cover. You hear the loud beating of wings, followed by the clacking of its feet on the floor. It's close. It has come down to your level. Your heart beats so loudly in your chest you fear the creature will hear you.

What do you do?

Peek out and see where it is. Turn to **310**.
Leap out from your hiding place and attack it, you have the element of surprise. Turn to **462**.
Stay hidden and wait for it to leave. Turn to **86**.

188

The second mi-go drops dead just as the door ahead opens again. The mi-go that escaped comes through carrying a large device that certainly looks like a gun. It is almost too big for it to wield properly. What will you do?

Rush the mi-go before it has a chance to aim the gun at you. Turn to **28**.
Dive for cover behind the nearest metal slab (where Jacob lies). Turn to **139**.
Or if you found any explosive seeds, and have one remaining, you can attempt to use it against the armed mi-go without exposing yourself to the gun. Turn to **207**.

189

You search through the objects hoping to find something of use, and happen upon a long sturdy cable that could be used as a makeshift rope, should the need ever arise. You place it in your satchel.

Record in your Investigators Journal *'Found cable long enough to use as a rope.'*

There's nothing else of use here, so you head back into the main chamber. Turn to **167**.

190

You bend over to see what could be moving inside the plant. A thick slime undulates as though it were moving of its own accord. You watch it for a moment, curious, when it suddenly shoots outward towards your face.

Make a Hard (2D6+1) **Dexterity** check.

If you pass, turn to **361**.
If you fail, turn to **73**.

191

You stop and glance around.
"Over here, human." In your mind, the voice is a harsh-sounding female whisper. Inside the last display on your right, a long spindly leg unfurls from under a black mass, then another, and another...

Eight legs in total unfold as the body they are attached to rises from the floor under their support. Six eyes catch the dim light of the room, and a series of long tentacle-like feelers drop from its mouth... or are its mouth? You can't be quite sure. This terrifying thing stands nearly eight feet tall.

Make a Hard (2D6+1) **Composure** check as you look upon this horror.

If you fail, you lose 1 **Composure** and immediately move to leave through the doorway. Turn to **144**.
If you pass, you control your fear and speak to it. Turn to **565**.

192

You approach the four cylinders to find they are hollow, made of glass and capped with a metal top and bottom. Each one is filled with a pinkish fluid. You reach out to tap one to confirm your visual inspection and as you tap you blink...

When you open your eyes, you are no longer standing in front of the cylinder, but are instead looking at a distorted image of a man – who looks eerily similar to you – standing before you through a pink haze. His finger pulls away from before your eyes, and you realise the figure is you! You are staring at yourself from within the cylinder. You scream, but nothing is heard. Something appears from behind the doppelganger, a skittish glowing thing with too many appendages to count. You cry out silently as the thing rips into your body. Blood splays the cylinder, turning pink to red and eventually it is so thick you can no longer see...

Make a Hard (2D6+1) **Composure** check. If the result is equal to or less than your Composure, you have passed. If you failed, deduct 1 from your current Composure.

Record in your Investigator Journal that '*You dreamt of being trapped in a cylinder while your body was dismembered.*' +4 *Mythos* points.

You wake. Turn to **500**.

193

You attempt to outwit the beast by changing direction and making for the building doorway. The creature swoops again and again, forcing you to stop and defend yourself for brief moments. It makes another attempt to grasp you in its talons.

Make a Very Hard (2D6+2) **Dexterity** Check.

If you pass, turn to **493**.
If you fail, turn to **165**.

194

You start to make your way carefully through the forest of dangling threads. You need to turn sideways at times and side-step to avoid touching them. Suddenly, all around you, the threads begin to swirl and before you can react, you're enveloped by them as they latch on to you. You struggle in panic, and this just makes it worse as they stick and entangle you to the point you cannot move. You inadvertently announced your presence when you tugged on the thread earlier. Then, you feel yourself rising from the ground as the threads are pulled upwards into the mist. The mist envelops you, making it impossible to see the creature that bites into your torso, injecting your body with a paralysing venom that starts to liquefy your internal organs.

Record in your Investigator Journal '*You were ensnared and devoured by a giant Spider of Leng.*' -5 *Mythos* points.

Your investigation ends here.

195

"I'll try. Give me a moment," you plead, as you take a closer look at the device.
The metal of the device is smooth and polished. Four prominent dials are set into the pillar and are etched with a single point each, denoting where they can be adjusted to. Small notches encircle each dial, similar to a dial on a safe, and one notch resting directly at the east point is larger than the others. You surmise this could be denoting a zero position. There are no other distinguishing marks or numbers.

You believe they could be angular degrees based on the number of marks present around each dial. How do you want to set the first dial?

Set it to 100 degrees. Turn to **479**.
Set it to 90 degrees. Turn to **342**.
Set it to 190 degrees. Turn to **81**.
Set it to 75 degrees. Turn to **133**.

196

You simply can't trust this alien creature and decline the offer of help.
"Huuman... you will dieee here and become feed for Cxaxuklutha." The mi-go's words echo in your head as you leave through the door on the left.
You find yourself back in the huge cavern on the edge of a stone ledge, with the river of black slime below you. Looking off to your left is the way you've come from, twisting your way through this labyrinthine city only to come up with little to show for it beyond exhaustion and near-madness!

You decide to turn right and trudge on, following the river flow as it snakes its way through the cavern, before arriving at a narrow tunnel in the rockface. Turn to **389**.

197

The room appears to be a storage room with rows and rows of empty cylinders of various shapes and sizes. Each one is made from clear glass and topped with a lid. The largest of the containers are about four feet tall and have three connectors or socket-like markings on the lid. They are clearly for holding larger specimens of whatever it is these horrid creatures seem to be collecting, or searching for, and you're just relieved that they currently stand empty.

Some smaller containers sit on a separate shelf, each one containing a different coloured liquid. You examine these, noting that they each have markings on them. It looks like writing, but it is not any known alphabet that you've ever seen. They are far too big and heavy to carry with you.

You can ignore these and head for the door at the end of the corridor. Turn to **105**.
Or examine the containers of liquid. Turn to **442**.

198

You drop your flashlight before you can even turn it on and make your mind up to get out of this house of horrors. You turn and flee, which prompts a terrible cry of anguish from the unseen speaker. You suddenly hear the bounding of it moving fast through the attic behind you as you flee down the stairs. You hit the bottom of the attic stairway when that terrible cry goes out again 'Fraaaaank!!!' Only this time the cry is right behind you. It's fast, incredibly fast!

Perhaps you're a victim of its rage, or perhaps a victim of its intense desire to have you accomplish something for it that it catches you too quickly, but in the pursuit you are knocked forcibly down the main stairs. You turn and twist over and over, you neck snaps on the bottom step, and all goes dark.

Record in your Investigator Journal '*You were pushed down the stairs and killed.*' -5 *Mythos* point.

Your investigation ends here.

199

"Well, that was rather foolish," he says as you crush the syringe beneath your shoe. "Nevertheless, I will show you what I've been working on, if you will follow me, please?"

He starts to ascend the stairs. The stairs creak loudly as you follow him upstairs. He climbs slowly with laboured steps, and does so in silence. You attempt to ask for more information about what you're going to see but he doesn't answer. A sharp turn at the top of the stairs leads into a narrow, steep staircase ending with the door to the attic. He turns here and continues upward. Reaching the top, he opens the door and enters, walking out of sight almost immediately. You suddenly hear a loud thud as something heavy hits the floor. The door hangs open…

To call out to the professor, turn to **355**.
Or if you enter the attic, turn to **511**.

200

You make your move and sprint for the tunnel, but the slick rock has other ideas. The mi-go also makes its move, skittering quickly across the ground. To avoid slipping you need to slow down and regain your balance, and that is when the creature strikes. The mi-go's deadly claws nip at you – they are sharp and quite lethal, cutting deep into your thigh.

Lose 2 **Health**.

You've no choice but to turn and face it in combat.

Mi-go Worker
Combat 5
Health 4

If you win, turn to **278**.
If you are reduced to just 2 remaining health, turn to **457**.

201

You move to retrieve the syringe but suddenly the professor grabs your leg. You manage to maintain your balance but must try to break free and reach the syringe.

Make an Easy (2D6-1) **Strength** check.

If you pass, turn to **72**.
If you fail, turn to **226**.

202

The door reveals a small room. On the left-hand wall is an alcove with a variety of objects. On the right-hand side of the room sits a large rectangular and featureless metal slab about six feet long and four feet wide. It is raised only a few inches off the floor.

What do you want to do?
Examine the alcove. Turn to **43**.
Examine the large rectangular block. Turn to **60**.
Leave the room and head to the end of the corridor. Turn to **377**.
Or if you haven't already done so, you can leave this room and try the door in the right-hand wall. Turn to **108**

203

The floor of the cavern is a sickening two-foot-deep black soup of blood, guts, and other bodily fluids. Wading through it is hard going. The smell makes you retch uncontrollably until you have nothing left to give and you finally gain some control over the gag reflex. The piled-up mounds stretch as far as you can see, eventually fading into the darkness about three hundred feet in either direction. Occasionally, the sound of falling offal puts you further on edge as different chutes open above to deposit more remains into the cavern. You wade on, scanning the walls in the hope of finding an exit. It is not long before you hear short bursts of a loud high-pitched squeal somewhere off to your left.

You may not be alone down here.

Will you remain still and see if you can spot what made the sound before deciding where to move? Turn to **410**.
Or take refuge behind the nearest mound. Turn to **256**.

204

You follow the river as it snakes its way through the cavern, watching of signs of life. You enter a tunnel, which starts to narrow the further you go. Turn to **389**.

205

You take a fragment from the container in front of you and toss it against the opposite wall. It makes a loud clang which immediately alerts the mi-go. You hear the creature's feet clack against the floor as it runs with surprising speed towards the sound. You rise to attack but at that very moment the beast turns to face you! It blocks your blow with ease and rears up on two legs to fight.

You must fight it! Turn to **505**.

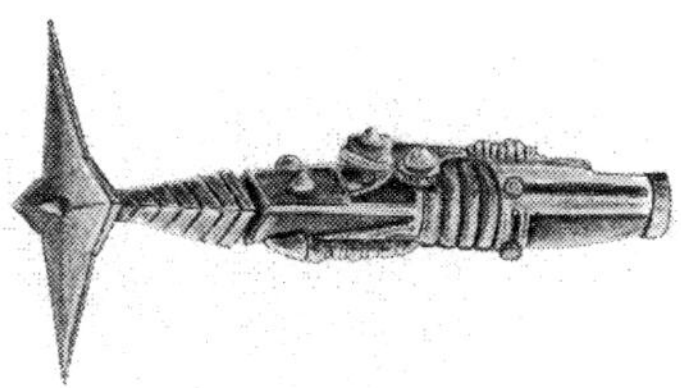

206

You agree to take the syringe. The professor suggests you sit on the stairway before doing so. You hesitate for a few moments, but then slowly inject it into your arm.

The professor stands there, emotionless, as your vision blurs.

You lie back, then black out. Turn to **120**.

207

You fling the seed at the creature. The noise is deafening in this metal chamber as the seed bursts into a ball of flame. The mi-go's volatile gun explodes, blowing the arms of the creature off, killing it instantly.

The disorientation and ringing in your ears pass after a few moments. Turn to **249**.

208

You clear your throat and walk over to the car. The man looks up and closes the hood.

“Just checking the engine, sir. Can’t be too careful out here. These things are liable to break down on ya, then you’re walking for miles.” He grins, wiping his hands on an oily rag.

"The name's Pete. This here's my place." He gestures towards the garage, and then offers his hand.

His hands are black with grime and oil.

Will you shake his hand? Turn to **529**.
Or just nod and speak your greeting. Turn to **23**.

209

"I am... a seeker," you say with a lack of sincerity that you don't intend.
Moments pass, then it leans over you. Something about this place, this void, is holding your mind together. You almost feel it wanting to break apart, but you can control it. As if knowing what you are thinking, the creature speaks again.
"No good are the maggots that wriggle uncontrollably before me, so I hold your mind in place. You, traveller, have come unprepared for your journey." It unfurls its huge hand and places it across your forehead.

"Until such a time as your kind see... I, Nyarlathotep, offer this, to thee."

Roll 1D6 and go to the corresponding entry to receive your gift.
If you rolled:
1 or 2, turn to **492**.
3 or 4, turn to **465**.
5 or 6, turn to **32**.

210

You return to your car, dejected, but can't help but wonder at the strangeness of the situation. Just what exactly is he doing up there?

You head back to Durham resolving to try again tomorrow. Turn to **127**.

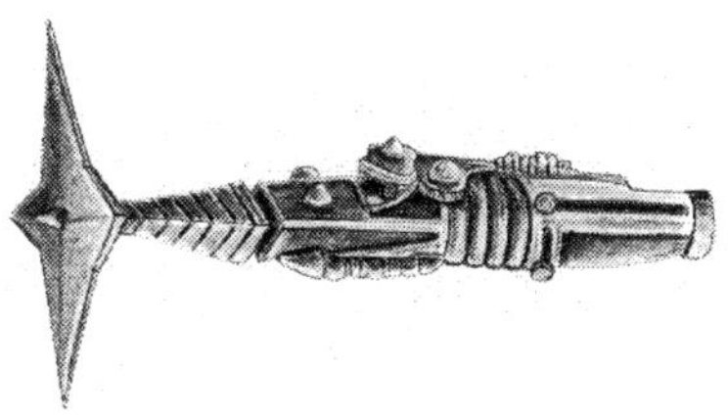

211

You shrug, then realising that Yar'ith doesn't understand the gesture, you tell it you don't have any weapons to offer. "Weee mussst dissstract the feeder!" Yar'ith says, pointing a claw upwards into the mist.

Will you offer to distract the 'feeder' (turn to **468**)?
Or suggest that Yar'ith distract the feeder while you retrieve the *Tok'llian*. Turn to **264**.

212

The door has a rusted metal knocker in its centre. You knock on the door and wait. After a few moments, you knock again. "Hello, anyone there?" you call out after you feel enough time has passed. You're about to try again when suddenly the door opens a crack, and a man's face appears.

"Yes?" he asks.
"Sorry to bother you, sir. Frank Winston. I write for the *Arkham Gazette* and... "
"Arkham, you say? ARKHAM? You're from that blasted university, aren't you?"
You're about to protest and deny it when the door is slammed shut.

University, Miskatonic… could this be Professor Peabody from the newspaper article? Did he come back to the house? You call out his name and add that you just want to talk. You're not far into trying to explain yourself when the door is fully opened. He looks around late fifties, about five-foot-five in height, and unshaven. Balding at the crown of his head, his remaining grey hair is a little long and unkempt.

"Yes, I'm Professor Peabody. Best you come in then, Frank from Arkham."
You get a sudden rush of excitement and step over the threshold. "Thank you very much, professor," you say, looking about the dark hallway ahead. The main staircase runs up on the right-hand side, and the hall ends in a door with another door to the right at the foot of the stairs.
"Up the stairs, lad, save me some effort."

You move to head upstairs. Turn to **69**.

213

As you reach the opposite side you hear that unmistakable clacking sound of multiple mi-go feet and the beating of wings. You duck behind a jut of rock near the entrance just as four mi-go rush past you into the egg-chamber. They've clearly come to defend their brood.

You can watch to see what happens (turn to **238**), or take this opportunity to leave while they are heavily distracted by the creature (turn to **537**).

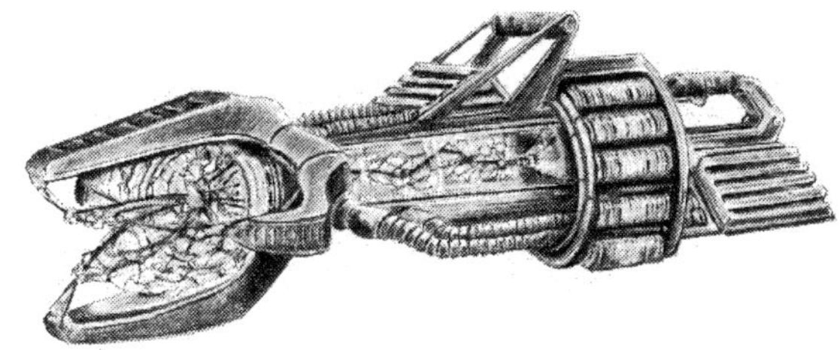

214

You approach the desk and start looking through the collection of papers and books, all while keeping a watchful eye on the professor. There's a journal filled with notes, a couple of what look like star charts held open by two large paperweights, maps of the solar system, and various books on studies of physics and the new quantum theories. Some loose pages catch your eye, old and torn as if ripped from an older book written in Latin. You push them aside as you cannot read them. Will you:

Look at the star charts. Turn to **394**.
Check the journal. Turn to **16**.
Or if you haven't already done so, look at the bookcase. Turn to **417**.

215

The door has a rusted metal knocker in its centre. You knock on the door three times and wait. "Professor? Are you there?" you call out after you feel enough time has passed.

Just as you are about to knock again, the door is opened by Professor Albert Peabody. "You have come. Good." He looks sicklier than you first thought last night.
"If you don't mind my saying so, professor, you don't look in the best of health," you say with genuine concern.
He stares blankly for a moment, then retorts, "I don't need a nurse. I need someone with a backbone... and a brain. If that is not you, then leave." He seems quick to change mood and intolerant of wasting time.
"No, no, no, I'm quite willing and able to help," you assure him.
"Then come in," he insists, stepping away to allow you entry.

Something seems different about him, but you're not sure what it could be.

Make a Very Easy (2D6-2) **Perception** check.

If you pass, turn to **552**.
If you fail, turn to **42**.

216

Despite passing, you still lose 1 **Composure** as the full extent of this horrifying place takes hold.

If you have not yet succumbed to madness, you steel your shredded nerves, and look for a way out.

Now, turn to **203**.

217

The green ichor of mi-go blood runs down the walls. Only fragments of their weapons, mixed with limbs and other pieces of the creatures remain. A yellow liquid, possibly from a row of broken and fallen containers, pools on the floor, mixing with the blood of the mi-go. The resulting smell is a horrid mix of the burning flesh, strengthened to a sickening level by the strong-smelling yellow liquid.

There's nothing of use remaining, and you don't wish to linger here. You head back and take the side tunnel. Turn to **138**.

218

The post office sign is easy to spot and also designates it as the town's general store. A second sign in the window reads 'Mrs. J. Wilkins – Proprietor'. As you enter, a small bell hanging from the ceiling chimes loudly.

"Be right with you," calls a woman's voice from the backroom behind the counter.

Moments later, the woman appears in the backroom doorway. She's short and stout, with long grey hair and a smooth plump face. She smiles at you at first, then a

quizzical look crosses her face.
"Good afternoon, sir. Have I seen you somewhere before? You look familar."
"No ma'am. This is the first time I've ever been out this way," you reply.
"Oh, strange. No matter. Was just about to close. What ya needing, sir?" she asks.

You ask about the way to Sentinel Hill. She turns around to the shelves and starts rearranging items.
"No one's allowed up there... not for many years. Why would you want to go there?" she says, her back still turned.

How do you respond?

Tell her you're writing an article about the strange murder case you read about. Turn to **485**.
Tell her that you are simply curious about the house and need to find it before it gets too late. Turn to **135**.
Lie by telling her that you've received a call from a colleague who is staying at the house. Turn to **407**.
Or tell her you're interested in buying the place. Turn to **348**.

219

You move silently across the chamber and are just about to reach the exit when a whip-like black tentacle lashes through the air and ensnares your leg. You're quickly reminded that this creature is acidic to touch. You cry out involuntarily as it burns through your clothing and into your calf.

Lose 1 **Health**.

Suddenly, four mi-go burst through from the exit. They don't appear to have noticed you lying among the fungi; instead, their focus is clearly on the rampaging creature that is devouring their young. Two of the mi-go fire large gun-like contraptions at the creature. The entire chamber lights up as sparks of lightning blast and crackle from the guns. It has little effect. You're instantly released as the creature turns its focus on the mi-go.

You don't hesitate to take this opportunity and flee through the exit. Turn to **537**.

220

Behind the huge disc, you find what appears to be a control panel. Two metal bars are set either side of the panel for leverage and turning the device. A large lever protrudes from the panel.

Do you want to try and push the lever up (turn to **282**)? Leave the machine alone and cross the conveyor belts (turn to **61**), or rest here a moment, and watch for signs of mi-go (turn to **187**).

221

He stands up again, the glint of a wrench in his hand. He twirls it around and tucks it into his belt. Closing the hood, he looks up and directly at you. You realise he knew you were there all along.

"There, sir, all done. I tightened your radiator valve. Another mile like that, and you would 'ave blown the rad! These rougher roads take their toll on those city vehicles."

"Really? Well, thank you. What do I owe you for that?" You respond, not sounding completely thankful as you wonder why you would offer to pay for work you didn't ask to be done.

"Ah t'was nothing, sir. The names Pete. This here's my place." He gestures towards the garage, and then offers his hand.

His hands are black with grime and oil.

Will you shake his hand (turn to **89**), or just nod and speak your greeting (turn to **23**)?

222

With the mi-go dead, you decide to first check the other chamber connected to this one – before you rouse the family you need to know what you're heading into. In the connecting room you make an incredible discovery – the portal machine! It stands as the centrepiece and could be your way out of here. There are no other exits from this room. Also in the room is a series of dangerous looking sharp implements and more versions of the mi-go lightning gun resting on a counter. Could it be the mi-go arm themselves here before using the machine?

Suddenly you hear a voice from behind you. Turn to **363**.

223

Your final blow fells the creature. It collapses to the floor, curling its limbs inward as it twitches and stops its bizarre resonating. You step back and take a breath. What kind of terrible place is this and how will you get out alive? At least you know there's a certain vulnerability to these things. They look terrifying, but seem less capable in a fight than their appearance might suggest.

You decide it is unwise to linger here, and head for door at the end of the corridor. Turn to **377**.

224

The recoil from the gun is more than you expected and sends your aim harmlessly upwards. You know only too well how fast Unlatha can be. With the thunder of her legs pounding across the floor, she is on you in a split second. A talon-like leg spears your shoulder, forcing you to drop the gun – the wound is quite vicious.

Lose 4 **Health**.

If you are still alive, Unlatha rears up to strike one last time...

A blast of lightning burns through the air from the doorway behind you. Unlatha's body convulses and crackles, smoke rising from her extremities. Edward stands in the doorway holding the lightning gun. Unlatha collapses in a heap, her legs folding inwards in a vain attempt to protect her body. Edward fires again, the weapon kicking him backwards as he tries to control its power. Unlatha's body twitches one last time, then remains still. She is dead.

Edward throws the gun to the ground and runs to his mother. She too, is dead.

"Thank you, Edward, you saved my life. I'm sorry about your mother. You must wake your father so we can try to get out of here," you plead as you get to your feet, and nurse your damaged shoulder. Despite your injury, you manage to pick up Sara and carry her into the chamber with the portal machine.

Record in your Investigator Journal '*Sara is alive*'. +20 *Mythos* points.

You place Sara down next to the machine then return to help Edward. Turn to **54**.

225

You turn about as requested and make to head towards the stairs. "How long have you been staying... "
You don't get to finish your question. Suddenly something is jabbed into your neck. You cry out, twisting around and instinctively reach up and pull out an empty syringe. "What on earth?" you cry.

The professor stands there, emotionless, as your vision blurs.

You fall to your knees and black out. Turn to **120**.

226

His grip is surprisingly strong. He pulls your leg out from under you and you crash to the floor, banging your head.

Lose 1 **Health**.

Slightly dazed, you move to rise, but he's already up and passes you. Quickly retrieving the syringe, he turns before you can regain your footing. He jabs you in the side with it.

The professor stands there, emotionless, as your vision blurs.

Then you black out. Turn to **120**.

227

Both creatures lie dead, and you sit for a moment, exhausted.

Content to sit and rest here, you almost feel like giving up, but some resolve from the pit of your stomach pulls you to your feet. You decide to take the metal rod for yourself. You decide to take the metal rod for yourself. Unsure of how to operate it, or even if it is now empty, it still seems wise to have it.

Record in your Investigators Journal '*Have a metal rod*', and note the reference 283. +1 *Mythos* point.

You look around for options. Turn to **128**.

228

You press the button and watch as a walkway extends outwards and connects to a cave opening in the far cavern wall. Wary of being spotted, you move quickly across the walkway as it continues to extend. As you reach the cave you glance back to see if you were spotted. You were! Two mi-go spot you and hover outside the cave entrance, but strangely, they do not approach. In fact, as you make to get away deeper into the darkness of the cave, the creatures turn and leave. You breathe a sigh of relief, but also can't help but wonder why they didn't follow you…

Further on, you arrive at a ledge that looks down to another passage below. The only way onward is to drop down into the lower passage. When you do, you can see that the tunnel starts to widen as it runs to your right, and to the left gets narrower.

Nothing but darkness lies via the left route, so you decide to head right where a soft glow lights the way. Turn to **136**.

229

The stairs creak loudly as you follow him upstairs.

As you follow him, you place the syringe in your satchel. Record in your Investigator Journal that you *'Have the syringe'*, and note the reference 142. +2 *Mythos* points.

He climbs slowly with laboured steps, and does so in silence. You attempt to ask for more about what you're about to see, but he doesn't answer. A sharp turn at the top of the stairs leads into a narrow, steep staircase ending with the door to the attic. He turns here and continues upward. Reaching the top, he opens the door and enters, walking out of sight almost immediately. You suddenly hear a loud thud as something heavy hits the floor. The door hangs open.

Will you go through the door (turn to **511**), or call out to the professor first (turn to **355**)?

230

You take the left tunnel, keeping low for fear of walking directly into a patrol of mi-go. The end of the tunnel opens into a large room.

In the centre of the room is a table with three transparent cylinders resting on it, and you gasp when you see that two of these contain a brain floating in a pinkish liquid. They are possibly human brains judging by their size. The cylinders are three-foot high and capped top and bottom with a metal seal. There are two small sockets on the base of each cylinder where it seems possible to connect something. There's also a small plaque on each base with a symbol on it.

Next to the cylinders sit two equally odd contraptions. Each one has a three-pronged plug-like component with a wire attached. The end of one wire runs to a thin metal stand with an oval-shaped lens on top of it. The other coil runs to a curious speaker that rests on the table. It reminds you of an oddly designed wireless radio back home. It seems that you could connect both devices to any one of the cylinders.

If you wish to try this, which cylinder will you connect to the devices:

The empty cylinder with the ∞ symbol on it. Turn to **290**.

The cylinder containing a brain with the **L** symbol on it. Turn to **391**.

The cylinder containing a brain with the **X** symbol on it. Turn to **9**.

Or leave this unsettling machinery alone and try another route from the central chamber. Turn to **235**.

231

Your blow to the back of the creature glances off the hard carapace body, doing very little damage. It turns around and rears up to over six feet tall. This is the most imposing and dangerous looking mi-go you've yet encountered.

Your sneak attack has failed, and now you must fight for your life against this imposing enemy. Turn to **505**.

232

You nervously place the *Tok'llian* into the machine and are relieved when it starts to thrum. As before, there are four dials on the device, and you notice that each of these is currently set at what you denote to be zero degrees. Do you have any clues on how to set the device for the journey home?

If you have recorded in your Investigator Journal *'You know how to get home'*, then you must turn to the **FIRST** reference associated with that entry now.

If you do not have this entry, turn to **40**.

233

You're not even remotely comfortable with the prospect of battling this horrid thing, but nor are you willing to become its victim. You tighten your fists... then attack first. Its head immediately turns a deep shade of red as you land a free blow, wounding the creature.

Now you must fight for your life...

Mi-go Worker (wounded)
Combat 5
Health 3

If you win, turn to **278**.
If you are reduced to just 2 remaining health, turn to **457**.

234

You maintain your composure and continue, speeding up only a little and not wanting to think what could be in the water. You don't allow those thoughts to force you into a mistake. You reach the opposite bank safely. Aside from being wet from the waist down, you feel okay. However, as you look yourself over you notice a bloated tube-like worm has wrapped itself around your ankle. Not wishing to touch it, you manage to shake it loose. It flops to the ground and wriggles its way back into the water, disappearing below. You shudder.

You must keep moving. Turn to **455**.

235

Back in the centre of the main chamber, you can explore any currently unexplored area that you haven't yet tried.

What will you do?

Explore the archway that is to your left. Turn to **230**.
Try the central archway. Turn to **358**.
Take the archway to the right. Turn to **437**.
Or examine the strange statue and bowl in the centre of the chamber. Turn to **164**.

236

You leap from the bed and look about. Quickly glancing under the bed and all round, there's just no feasible place for someone to hide in this room.

You can approach the window. Turn to **452**.
Or try and talk to the strange voice. Turn to **528**.

237

With a lucky blow, the professor manages to inject you with the syringe. The fight goes out of you very quickly. "I'm debating whether you're worth the effort, now," he says, leaning over you. Your vision blurs and as the drug takes hold. Peabody continues talking, but his voice becomes an echo as you fall under.

Now, turn to **120**.

238

You watch for a moment as two of the mi-go fire large gun-like contraptions at the creature. The entire chamber lights up as sparks of lightning blast and crackle from the guns directly into the slime. It has little effect. The creature forms a series of rope-like tentacles almost instantly and whips them through the air, sending the armed mi-go crashing against a batch of eggs. They split and spill their contents across the chamber floor. The other two mi-go fare no better as one is torn asunder in moments, and the final mi-go turns to flee, only to be lassoed by the whipping tentacle and smashed into the ground, spraying its green blood everywhere.

Make a Regular (2D6) **Composure** check. If you fail you must lose 1 Composure. If you pass, there is no effect.

You decide enough is enough, and get out of there. Turn to **537**.

239

The fight continues longer than you'd ever hope for, and soon you understand the nature of the creature's shrill cry when you first attacked. Reinforcements! Three more mi-go fly down from the walkway above and surround you. You stop fighting and raise your hands in surrender.

However, it appears the creatures are not impressed with your gesture. Each one attacks! Claws nip and slice at you, then back away, only for another to repeat the assault. You find it impossible to defend against the various attacks. A claw pierces your eye socket and plucks your eye clean out. You've barely the strength to scream as another repeats this with your second eye. Slowly, but surely, the creatures take what they want, clipping fingers from your hands.

Eventually you lie dying on the conveyor as it is turned back on... with your eyes gone, and bleeding from many lacerations, you are plunged down a chute to join the other rotten remains. You die shortly after…

Record in your Investigator Journal '*You died horribly mutilated by a gang of mi-go.*' -2 *Mythos* points.

Your investigation ends here.

240

Unlatha looms over you as you gasp for breath. You're badly wounded and bleeding profusely. Leaning down, she places her death-like skull next to you and speaks. "Less sport than I hoped for, but a fine vessel for my brood." Her long proboscis shoots into your abdomen, and moments of excruciating pain are endured before you lose consciousness.

You wake, unaware of the passage of time and still in pain lying on the floor of the same room. There is no sign of Unlatha. Something lurches inside of you, causing you to double over. You try to get to your feet, but the pain brings you down again. The family are here, and they too are crying out and writhing in pain. Suddenly, the body of Edward splits apart, and two black legs sprout from his stomach, then another leg, and another. His cries reverberate around the room before he falls silent. Then the mother, the father, and even the young girl, Sara, all suffer the same terrible fate. Mercifully, it is quick, before the same fate befalls you. The young brood of Unlatha crawl out of your splitting bodies, to join their mother and feed on your remains.

Record in your Investigator Journal '*You and the Turne family were impregnated by Unlatha and spawned her young.*' -50 *Mythos* points.

Your investigation ends here.

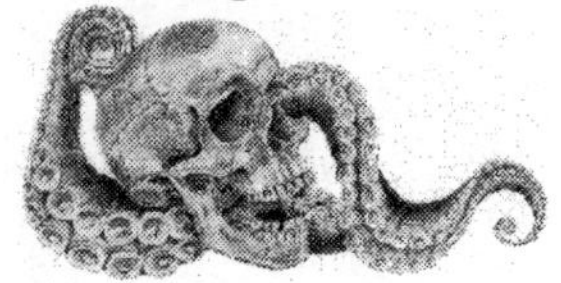

241

"Well, my boy. What I want to show you is upstairs. In the attic. If you'd be so kind... " He gestures for you to take the stairs.

If you do as he asks, turn to **225**.
Or if you decline, and insist he tell you why, turn to **38**.

242

Each of the other family members are unharmed and unconscious. You approach the father and shake him, but he does not stir. You try the mother, and she does not stir either.

"The mi-go would experiment on them, as is their way. You cannot carry all of them. Leave some with me." Unlatha suggests. You turn to look at her, suspicious of her motives.

"The small one, there. Take that one." Unlatha points a leg towards Sara, the young child.

"If I take the girl, what of the others?" you inquire.

"Leave them in my care... for I do hunger so."

You don't like what you're hearing.

"They are not food, Unlatha, you will not touch them!" you reply, forcefully.

"Do not presume you can command me, human insect."

Angry, you approach Edward, who to your surprise, appears to be completely normal and unharmed. It's unmistakably him, but with none of the deformities you witnessed back in the attic. It's then you spot a series of implements on a small table next to him, one of which is the serrated claw-like apparatus that was connected to his arm. Have the mi-go removed it? You check his arm for signs of surgery, but there's nothing. You shake him gently to wake him and thankfully he starts to stir.

Edward opens his eyes. "Edward, it's me, Frank!" He stares at you blankly.
"Who... who are you? Where is my mother?" he asks, groggy, but with a perfectly normal-sounding voice.
"It's me, Frank, don't you remember? In the attic?" you reply, gripping his shoulders.
"Attic? The light... the green light in the attic!" He starts to sound more agitated.
"Yes, that's right. But I'll get you out of here, and your family too, see?" You point over to his family. He starts to scream. Standing over his mother is Unlatha. A long proboscis extends from her head. She moves to inject it into the mother's abdomen. You cry out and run towards her. "What are you doing?"

"Feeding!" Unlatha bats you away with swipe of her leg. Edward gets up, unsteady on his feet, and grabs the claw from the table. "Mother?" he screams. He looks like he is going to attack Unlatha. What do you do?

Will you pull Edward away and try to flee through the door on the opposite side (turn to **497**), or join with Edward and fight Unlatha (turn to **525**)?

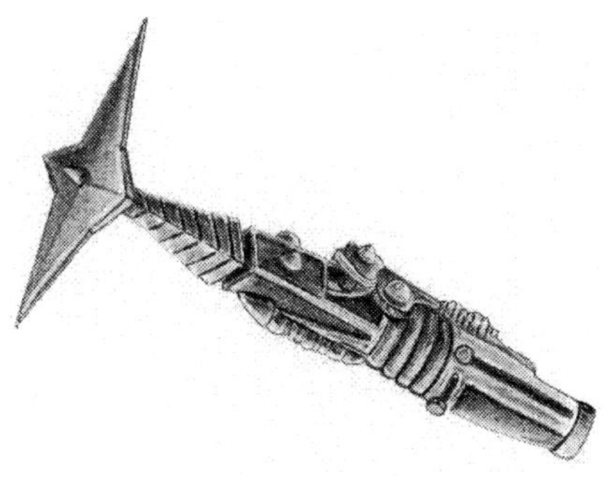

243

You start to sidestep to your right with the idea to move around the mi-go in a semi-circle. As you watch, its head changes to a yellowish hue in the dim aura of the cave. It turns to keep focus on you, its feet clacking off the stone as it rotates to keep you in sight. It moves away from the entrance into the centre of the cavern floor. Then it speaks.
"Huuuumaaan... intruuudeer. Trrry to esssscape... "
You stop in your tracks. Did it just ask you to try and escape? What will you do?

Make a dash for the tunnel. Turn to **245**.
Rush the creature instead and attack it. Turn to **301**.
Or talk to it. Turn to **155**.

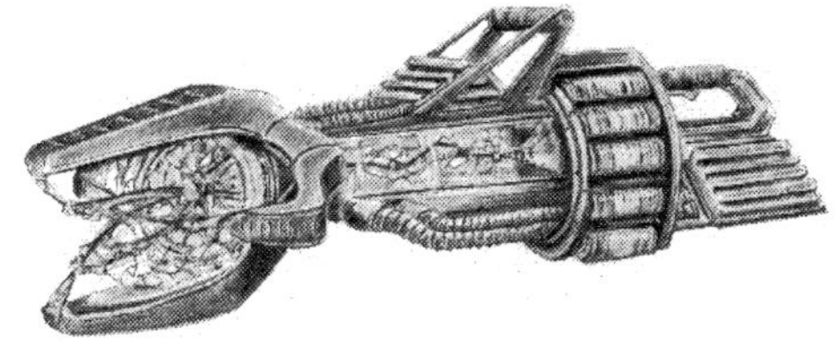

244

Feeling equal parts revulsion and pity for the thing before you, you do as he asks and turn the flashlight off.
"Yoooou... yoooou are diffff... erent. Hoooow?" His voice is lower now, sounding more scared, more like the young boy he appears to be. What do you want to ask?

Where has he been all this time (turn to **90**)?
How does he seem to be the still only twelve years old, (turn to 77)?
Or ask about his bizarre 'claw' and physical changes (turn to **571**).

245

The creature moves a little further away from the exit, as though it is goading you to try and flee. It takes another couple of steps away, and so you make your move – you run for the exit!

Make a Hard (2D6+1) **Dexterity** check.

If you pass, turn to **119**.
If you fail, turn to **200**.

246

You decide to try the other door instead. It opens into another small room. On the left side wall is an alcove containing several objects. On the right-hand side of the room sits a large rectangular and featureless metal slab about six-feet long and four-feet wide. It is raised only a few inches off the floor. You instantly recognise this room as being identical to the one you just viewed on the display, but there's no naked figure or anything else present.

What do you want to do?

Examine the alcove. Turn to **43**.
Examine the large metal slab. Turn to **60**.
Leave the room and head towards the end of the corridor. Turn to **377**.

247

You turn the second dial to what you would believe to be 121 degrees.

How do you want to set the third dial?

To leave it as is, set on zero degrees, turn to **25**.
To set it to 90 degrees, turn to **418**.
To set it to 47 degrees, turn to **467**.

248

Eager to leave this exposed area, you quickly move through the door. It opens into a long, narrow chamber. Running along both the left and right sides of this chamber are huge glass-walled enclosures, and within each there appears to be a wide array of plant-life. In amongst the thick vegetation, you can't see any animals, but their presence is certainly heard through chirps, grunts, and other animal-like calls. You don't quite recognise what they could be. In fact, the more you observe the enclosures, the stranger they seem. In all, there would appear to be ten such enclosures, five on each side of the room. At the end of the room is another door.

If you want to look at the displays more closely, turn to **460**. Of you can head straight through this chamber to the door on the opposite side. Turn to **174**.

249

You cautiously check the other chamber connected to this one – before you rouse the family you need to know what you're heading into. In the connecting room you make an incredible discovery – the portal machine! It stands as the centrepiece and could be your way out of here. There are no other exits from this room. Also in the room is a series of dangerous looking sharp implements and more versions of the mi-go lightning gun resting on a counter. It looks like the mi-go arm themselves here before using the machine!

Suddenly you hear a voice from behind you. Turn to **363**.

250

Deduct 1 from your current **Composure**.

You take a step towards the creature... then stop. You decide you can't force the attack in this situation. The environment coupled with the way this creature seems to regard you curiously puts you more on edge than you had expected. What will you do instead?

If you want to try and talk to it, turn to **155**.
Or if you you'd rather make a dash for the tunnel, turn to **245**.

251

You glance back at Yar'ith. You really have no idea if the creature is looking at you or not. Your mind is made up – you silently make your way across to the back of the cavern to retrieve the *Tok'llian*. The threads are difficult to avoid. Your very presence seems to disturb them and set them in motion, swaying ever so gently back and forth.

Make a Hard (2D6+1) **Stealth** check.

If you pass, turn to **469**.
If you fail, turn to **11**.

252

You find nothing else of interest in the rest of the house, as it's largely disused. An old makeshift bed and various unfinished meals reside in one of the upstairs rooms.

You decide to enter the attic. Turn to **172**.

253

Ahead in the cavern is a forest of white glistening threads suspended from the cave ceiling. You look up and see that the ceiling is completely hidden from view by a thick white mist. The threads descend from the mist and almost touch the cavern floor. Across the opposite side of the cavern is an exit.

"There, huuuman." Yar'ith points towards the back of the cavern. "There issss where the *Tok'llian* liesss. You willll retrieve it."

You stare into the cavern where the mi-go has signified. Near the back wall you can just about make out something small, glinting in the dim glow of the cavern. The white threads hang motionless.

"And what are those white vines hanging from the ceiling?" you ask, with an air of suspicion.
"Tooo be avoiided. Eassy for skinny huuuman."
"I will not," you reply, trying to keep your voice low. "There's something there in the mist. I can feel it!"
The mi-go's head changes to a deep red.
"Verrry weelll. Weee neeed a weaaapon!" Yar'ith's voice sounds as cold and emotionless as it ever did, but whatever passes for mi-go anger, you believe you have just heard it.

If you have recorded in your Investigator Journal '*Have a metal rod'*, and if you wish to give it to Yar'ith, then turn to the reference associated with that entry now.

If you do not have a metal rod (or wish to keep it to yourself) but have any other type of weapon, you can choose to give a different weapon to Yar'ith. Turn to **414**.
If you would rather not give up any of your other weapons (or don't have any), turn to **211**.

254

As you set the last dial, the beam of green light shoots up from the sphere on top just like it had done in the attic of the house. It then bends downwards to rest parallel with the floor, striking the wall to form a shimmering portal. The entire room is bathed in the eerie pulsating light. Through the haze of the portal, you can see the attic of the house. You did it!

You rush back to Edward and explain how you can all leave this hellish place. Just as you are trying to convince him that you can help carry his unconscious family members into the portal chamber, the door on the opposite side opens – and in swarms a horde of mi-go. You're out of time! You grab Edward and tell him you must flee. He's confused and unsure... you make it to the portal while he hesitates.

"My faaammily?" he cries.

"We'll go back Edward," you shout over the thrum of the portal. "I promise, I'll go back for your family, but we must get out of here now! They're coming!"

You both turn and run as a blast from a lightning gun ionizes the air! With one final push, you leap through the portal just as the weapon strikes the machine... you land on the attic floor. You quickly get to your feet, The portal flickers... Edward hasn't come through!

Moments pass as you watch through the haze, willing Edward to make it. You stare, feeling helpless as he approaches, leaps... then the portal blinks out of existence. You wait expectantly... nothing. He's gone.

You slump against the wall and put your head in your hands. Turn to **104**.

255

The growth on the wall is slightly soft and spongy to the touch. You press your finger into it, and it suddenly ejects a stream of spores into your face!

Make a Very Hard (2D6+2) **Health** check.

If you pass, turn to **130**.
If you fail, turn to **10**.

256

Pushing your way through the foul slop, you crouch down as much as you're willing to dare in this disgusting mess, and watch from behind a pile of entrails. After a few moments, a black slimy tentacle flops over the side of the mound to your left – followed by another, then another.

Will you duck down and keep out of sight (turn to **340**), or keep watching and see what it does (turn to **376**)?

257

"Professor, I noticed some strange green lights last night around the area of the hill. Do you know anything about that?" you ask as you look about the hallway.

"We are the lights," the professor responds, emotionless.
You turn, startled by that reply. "I beg your pardon?"
"I said where were the lights?" inquires the professor, curious.
"Oh... I could see them from Durham. All around the hill. You didn't notice?"
"I was probably fast asleep. I was very tired last night." You decide not to mention hearing the strange voice, as such confessions give credence to not being of sound mind.

You can ask him which room you should enter (turn to **241**), or tell him you've had a sudden change of heart, and wish to leave (turn to **129**).

258

Despite your misgivings, you briefly taste the smallest amount of the red liquid as you can. It tastes salty, almost like sea water. There's no ill effect that you can feel.

You feel you could risk trying one more before moving on.

Try the yellow liquid. Turn to **443**.
Try the black one. Turn to **271**.
Or decide against tasting these, and leave the room to try the door at the end of the corridor. Turn to **105**.

259

You gently pull the pod apart to reveal a black seed lined with the tiny red veins, just like the petals of the plant it came from. You decide it's of no use and toss it aside. Suddenly a low crack is heard, and you turn sharply to see the seed has created a small explosion, sending some of the other plants flying across the room, leaving a scoring black mark where it stuck. These 'seeds' are like miniature grenades. You decide to take the remaining three seeds and pocket them carefully.

Record in your Investigator Journal '*Took 3 explosive seeds from a plant.*' +3 *Mythos* points.

In the first round of combat only, you can decide to throw a seed instead of doing a normal fight action. Throwing a seed counts as your first attack action and is resolved against your opponent in the normal way. However, for throwing, you get +2 to your Combat skill. If you succeed on your combat roll, deal 4 damage to your opponent. After using a seed in the first round, you must resolve the remaining combat normally.

(Note this reference if you need to review the combat rules for these seeds)

Noting that the noise made will likely attract more of those creatures, you quickly leave by the opposite door. Turn to **370**.

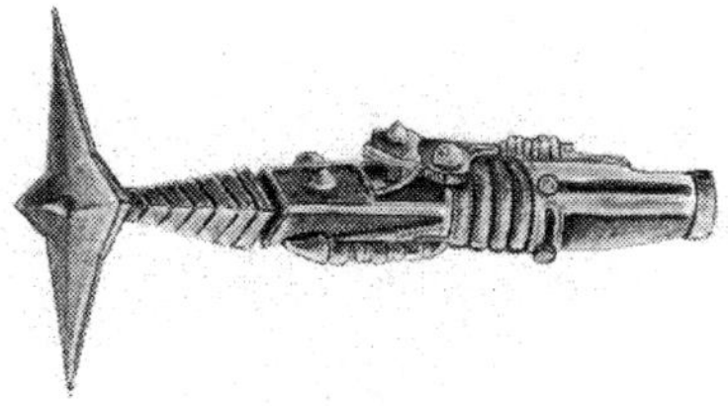

260

In a desperate attempt to free yourself, the thread snaps away from your sleeve. The recoil almost forces you into another series of threads, but you just manage to keep from getting entangled. You grab the *Tok'llian* to the sound of a mi-go being rendered limb from limb behind you. You turn away and head for the exit, praying that this thing finds enough sport in Yar'ith to allow you to go unnoticed. You manage to reach the other side and exit the cavern.

When you believe it's safe, you stop to examine the cube. Turn to **445**.

261

The final blow silences the horrid creature as it hits the cave floor with a sickening splat, black blood oozing from its many wounds.

You follow where it came from to find a smaller opening in the cavern wall. There's a rancid smell coming from the opening.

If you want to bend down and enter the smaller cave, turn to **277**.
Otherwise, you can leave and continue on deeper into the cave system by turning to **147**.

262

The second mi-go falls to the floor, dead.

You examine the curious metal rod the creature was trying to retrieve, turning it about. It is quite plain with no obvious function, but you decide to take the metal rod for yourself.

Record in your Investigators Journal '*Have a metal rod*', and note the reference 283. +1 *Mythos* point.

What do you want to do now?

Examine the control panel the mi-go was operating. Turn to **523**.
Search through the objects on the metal slab. Turn to **316**.

263

You pull gently on one of the hanging threads only to find that it sticks to your hand. The thread stretches as you try to pull your hand away, and taking advantage of being near the entrance you back out of the cavern hoping the thread will come loose.

Do you have a scalpel? If so, you can try and cut the thread. Turn to **522**.
If you don't have a scalpel, turn to **330**.

264

Yar'ith's head deepens to a darker red. "Nooo humaan. I coooommand here. Gooo... " It points into the cavern. The mi-go suggests that you must enter the cavern and distract the creature above to lure it away from the location of the *Tok'llian*.

Will you do as it asks (turn to **468**), or refuse (turn to **401**)?

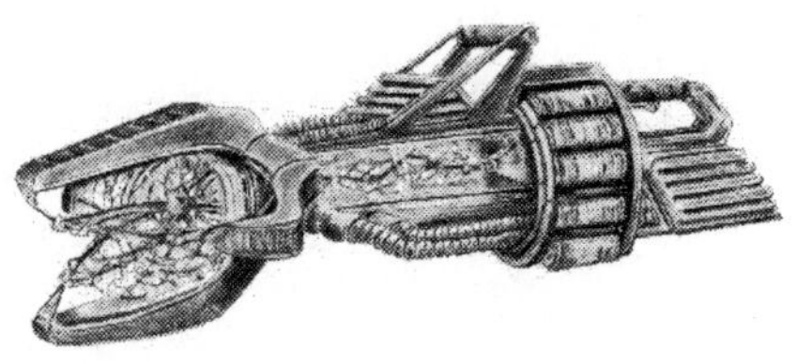

265

Both creatures lie dead at your feet. You look up into the tower for any more signs of these foul things, but thankfully it looks quiet.

The area is open and exposed, making it difficult to see hiding places. The ramp eventually disappears into a dark haze above. You would be very exposed if you went any higher, so you decide against going up. Wherever this strange place is, it's enormous. Across the floor from where you stand there is another door. What do you do?

Head back down the ramp and choose another path. Turn to **272**.
Stick close to the wall and make your way around to the other door. Turn to **248**.

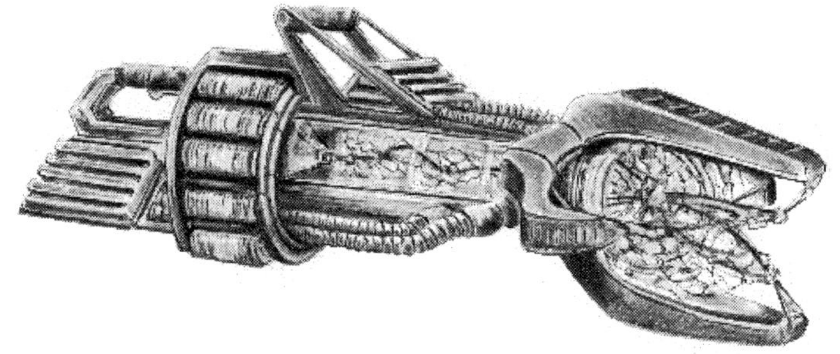

266

You charge at the mi-go as it hefts the weapon up to aim it in your direction. But you're too fast, colliding with the beast before it can fire and sending the gun skidding across the floor. The gun crackles for a moment, then the power seems to drain from it. The mi-go is stunned by your charge, enabling you to finish it off easily. You retrieve the gun, but find it inoperable. Turn to **222**.

267

You make a dash for the opposite side. The cavern floor is littered with mi-go eggs and large fungi which make it difficult to move with haste.

Make a Regular (2D6) **Dexterity** check.

If you pass, turn to **213**.
If you fail, turn to **543**.

268

You start searching for it among the devices on the counter and Edward joins in to help you. There's a variety of dangerous looking weapons here, including retractable claws and blades, and more versions of the lightning gun weapon.

There is no sign of the *Tok'llian*.

If you haven't already done so, you can:

Search the mi-go bodies. Turn to **570**.
Or search the adjoining room where the family had been. Turn to **575**.

269

To your relief, the platform rises again and rests in its original position. Now you must choose which of the two other buttons to try.

To try the diagonal button, turn to **470**.
To try the horizontal button, turn to **228**.

270

You hand Pete the two dollars and thank him – also adding you didn't mean any offence. You mention your desire to find the house on Sentinel Hill.
He nods. "No harm done so. I've got to get locking up now so best you be heading," he says. "If you're after the way to the house, best check at the post office just down the street there. Mrs. Wilkins knows this area better than anyone."
You thank him once again as he turns and heads inside the garage, shutting the door behind him.

Record in your Investigator Journal that '*Your car radiator was fixed*', and note the reference 94. Later in the story, if asked if you have earned this information, you will turn to 94. (Do not turn to that now).

You turn back to your car, then take another look up and down the street. No one is around. The place seems empty and uninviting. A cold breeze suddenly whips through the garage lot, blowing leaves up into a swirl.

Will you get into your car and head on (turn to **557**), or visit the post office and see if you can get directions there (turn to **218**).

271

You touch the black liquid with your fingertip and immediately recoil. The liquid singes your finger with a sizzle as though touching a hot stove, but you're quick enough to recoil and avoid injury. You then watch in horror as the black ooze starts to creep over the lip of the container. Suddenly, tendrils shoot outwards latching onto the shelving around it. It attaches itself to the container of red liquid next to it, causing it to tip over and smash to the floor.

The creeping black mass is extremely unsettling to watch. Make an Easy (2D6-1) **Composure** check. If you fail, deduct 1 from your current Composure.

You back away, wary of the noise made by the falling containers, as the black ooze slithers across the floor.

Record in your Investigators Journal '*Released a black slime creature*', and note the reference 12. +4 *Mythos* points.

You flee the room, hoping that you won't run into any mi-go, nor that this new horror can follow. You hastily pass through the door at the end of the corridor. Turn to **105**.

272

Not wishing to risk being caught here, you head back down the ramp, but as you do, you hear a buzzing noise from one of the creatures coming from over to your left. Two mi-go have entered the lower floor from the door you originally came from.

To avoid detection, you quickly dart through the door at the base of the ramp. Turn to **546**.

273

"Yes, I'm from the university," you reply, holding your hands up in a gesture of peace. "But I've been sent here to help you."
"Help me? You're here to take the pages of that accursed *Necronomicon* back. Tell Armitage he can't have them. He can't! I'm too close. Those pages hold the key to all of this.

I'm so close to figuring it out." He gets very agitated and pulls a revolver from his pocket and starts waving it around at you.

You back off, continuing to hold your hands up in a gesture of surrender. "Okay, I'll leave. I don't want any trouble."

Record in your Investigators Journal '*You were warned to leave the house alone*', and note the reference 335.

You leave Peabody to his madness, not wishing to agitate him any further. Turn to **210**.

274

You carefully tug at one of the pods hanging from the plant. It comes away easily and feels like paper in your hand. You hold it up to the light and can see that there appears to be something inside. What do you want to do?

Carefully break open the pod and see what is inside, turn to **259**.
Leave it here and be on your way by going through the door in the opposite wall. You get a sense you've lingered here too long here. Turn to **370**.

275

Hiding behind a jut of rock near the opening, you toss the seed among the eggs. It explodes with a sickening squelch as multiple eggs burst, spilling the writhing larvae to the floor. The ones that survive the blast wriggle and contort, with a high-pitched squeal emanating from wherever their mouths may be. Four adult mi-go enter the chamber from the tunnel opening, passing you, and immediately try to help the surviving young. With your distraction a success, you slip into the tunnel.

Do you take the tunnel in the right-hand wall (turn to **138**), or keep going straight to the chamber that was occupied by the mi-go (turn to **474**)?

276

A searing light and high-pitched squeal make you grip your head, but it passes as quickly as it began. You find yourself standing motionless until your senses reattune themselves, then look around. You are in a massive cavern with huge piles of rotten flesh and bone stretching as far as you can see in the dim light. Above the peak of each mound of meat and viscera a light is set into the cavern ceiling. Next to each light there appears to be an opening in the ceiling.

Make an Extreme (2D6+3) **Composure** check.

If you pass, turn to **216**.
If you fail, turn to **161**.

277

Ignoring the smell, you get on your hands and knees and move partially into the opening. The air is thick with the putrid odour, and you cannot see far as the fungus doesn't grow here.

Will you crawl in and explore (turn to **349**), or change your mind and back out, then head for the exit from this cavern (turn to **147**)?

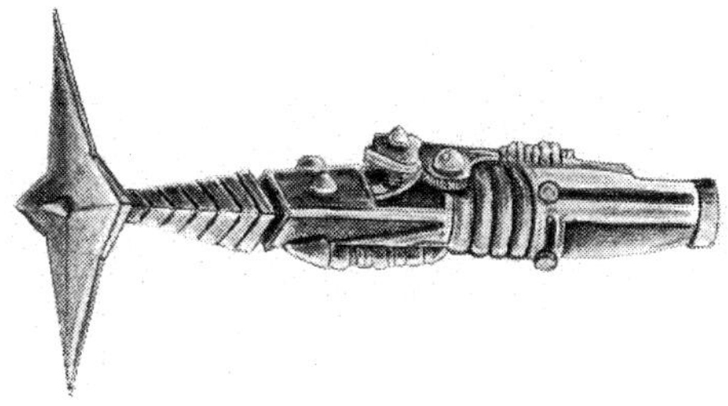

278

With a final heavy blow to the creature's head, it collapses to the ground. A pool of green blood oozes from its carcass. They are surprisingly fragile, you think to yourself, though still repulsed by the encounter.

If this truly is the domain of these monsters, just how many will you have to face?

You're about to step away when you notice a small metal tube with a star-shaped metal piece at the top lying next to the creature. You pick it up and examine it. A small switch on its outer casing piques your interest. When you press it, the star-shaped headpiece starts to whirr and spin. You're not quite sure what it could be for, but it's a curious enough thing that you decide to take it and place it in your satchel.

Record in your Investigator Journal '*Have a star-shaped tool*', and note these two references. The *first* is 475, and the *second* is 425. If asked about this entry later, be sure to confirm you go the correct reference mentioned, the first, or the second. +3 *Mythos* points.

As the chasm was a dead end, you decide to try the other door in the room you arrived in. Turn to **62**.

279

You take one of the seeds from your satchel and step back before tossing it between two cylinders guarding the door. The resulting explosion is bigger than you had expected. The cylinders are immediately destroyed. Shards of glass fly through the air, cutting you.

Lose 1 **Health**.

The machines collapse, spilling the fluid and brains to the floor with a sickening squelch. The remaining two cylinders (one of which is Eugene), cry out. "What have you done?"

They turn and flee, leaving you free to investigate the laboratory. Turn to **471**.

280

The more you attempt to remove it, the more it attaches itself. Panic starts to set in, and this leads to you becoming hopelessly entangled. With escape impossible, death is just moments away. The spider-thing finishes dispatching Yar'ith and turns its attention to you. With a sickening squelch, your head is speared by a talon-like leg. You die instantly.

Record in your Investigator Journal '*You were killed by a Spider of Leng.*' -5 *Mythos* points.

Your investigation ends here.

281

You charge at the mi-go as it hefts the weapon up to aim it in your direction. You are just a fraction too slow. The creature fires!

The blast from the gun is like a lightning bolt lifting you off your feet as the charged energy surrounds you, singeing your flesh. You lose all control of your bodily functions as the shock runs through your body. Hitting the ground in a heap, you twitch for a few moments as the mi-go surround you... then they start to disassemble your body piece by piece.

Record in your Investigator Journal '*You were shot and killed by a lightning gun.*' -2 *Mythos* points.

Your investigation ends here.

282

Your curiosity gets the better of you and you start to push the lever up. The machine starts to hum, softly at first, but as you continue to push it further it rises in volume. The disc in front of you starts to glow and suddenly the rock wall in front of the disc starts to liquefy and melt away. It gets so loud that surely it will attract unwelcome guests...
"Intruuuder!" That horrible, affected voice of a mi-go sounds from behind you. You turn and spot two of the creatures above on the walkway. One of the creatures is holding a metal rod and pointing it towards you. With a low *shunk* sound, a shard of metal shoots from the end of the rod and just whizzes by your ear, embedding into the rock wall.

You will have to think fast.

Will you dart across the room and over the conveyor belts to the large doorway (turn to **148**), or turn the disc machine around and aim it at the creatures (turn to **581**)?
Alternatively, you can attempt to escape via the nearest conveyor belt through the opening in the wall (turn to **285**), or stay where you are and face the creatures (turn to **453**).

283

You show the metal rod to Yar'ith. "Yessss huuuman. Ussseful." Yar'ith takes it from you, and without explanation, enters the cavern. Remove the metal rod from your *Investigator Journal*. It stays low, skittering deftly between the threads. Close to the location of the *Tok'llian*, the mi-go turns back and points the metal rod up into the mist. With a series of low ringing chimes, Yar'ith fires metal shards from the rod. A loud hiss emanates from the cavern ceiling as the creature within is hit. Like a stone, the bloated purple spider-like thing falls to the cavern floor. Yar'ith moves to take the *Tok'llian*, but the disturbed threads catch the mi-go and entangle it. The threads stick like glue to Yar'ith as it thrashes about, becoming hopelessly entangled. The spider-thing is still alive and starts to thrash about, causing the white threads to both flail and intertwine. The visage of this bloated, purple monstrosity, bores into your very soul.

If you have recorded in your journal '*Been inside the cavern*', then you do not need to make a composure check. If you do not have this entry, make an Extreme (2D6+3) **Composure** check. If you fail, you must lose 2 Composure. If you pass, lose 1 Composure.

There is now a clear path to the *Tok'llian* as the spider-thing limps towards the thrashing mi-go. Metal shards ricochet off the cavern rock as Yar'ith attempts to shoot the advancing spider, but Yar'ith's entanglement makes it too difficult to aim. You grab the *Tok'llian* to the sound of the mi-go being rendered limb from limb behind you, then reach the other side and exit the cavern.

You flee from the cavern and put as much distance as you believe is safe. Exhausted, you stop to examine the cube. Turn to **445**.

284

It appears to be some kind of fungus growing here, likely aided by the mist and damp air.

If you want to break a piece off and examine it, turn to **255**.
If you head for the door in the far opposite wall, turn to **546**.
Or you can head for the door over on the right-hand side. Turn to **7**.
Investigate the ramp going up to the next floor. Turn to **433**.
Or approach the well in the centre of the room. Turn to **327**.

285

You see an opportunity to escape and dash for the nearest opening into which a conveyor is depositing its load. You don't have time to think this through as another projectile is fired from the walkway above by one of the creatures. The missile glances off the floor with a loud *shring* just as you reach the opening. You pause and nearly retch as the guts, entrails, and other vile offal disappears into the opening. Your hesitation nearly costs you your life as another metal shard whizzes by your head.

Taking discomfort over death, you dive into the opening. Turn to **110**.

286

You turn left, hoping to see signs of the hill, or even the house. However, with the light fading you start to doubt what you're even doing. You contemplate turning around and taking a lodging in the town but decide to confirm the house location first.

Have you recorded in your journal that '*Your car radiator was fixed*'? If so, turn to the reference associated with that entry now.

If not, turn to **438**.

287

You ring the bell with the palm of your hand, twice. Looking over the counter, you see a door set into the wall on the left. Perhaps the attendant is in there? You're about to ring the bell again, when you hear a creak of the front door behind you. You turn and see a heavy-set man, possibly late fifties, standing in the doorway. He's wearing dirty blue overalls, with *Pete's* written across the breast.
"Yerp? What you be needing, sir?", he says, wiping his hand on an oily rag.
How do you respond?

Tell him you're looking for directions to Sentinel Hill. Turn to **373**.
Or inquire about the town and why it's so quiet. Turn to **35**.

288

The devices make little sense to you. One of them appears to be for extraction of the larvae, an articulated claw on the end of a tube. A single button on the tube extends it slowly before it snaps shut and retracts. It's too big and bulky to carry with you so you place it back down.

You can now make for the side tunnel. Turn to **138**.
Or try some of the yellow liquid on the other side of the room. Turn to **116**.

289

You turn the syringe towards him. "If it's so harmless, how about I stick you with it?" you answer, making a jabbing motion towards him. He doesn't flinch. "What are you doing in this house that requires... this?"

"I can show you. It's in the attic. If you would like to follow me." He places one foot on the stairs, and waits. "I'd recommend you take that first," he adds. He seems quite unfazed.

Tell him you won't be taking any unknown drug, but will follow him to the attic. Turn to **229**.
Or you can demand to see the lower floor of the house first. Turn to **374**.

290

You connect both devices to the empty cylinder, but nothing happens. Looking at the brains floating in the liquid of each of the other cylinders, you guess it's plain that this empty one would not yield any results.

If you want to instead try the cylinder with the **X** symbol on it (turn to **9**), the one with the **L** symbol on it (turn to **391**), or leave this unsettling machinery and try another route from the central chamber (turn to **235**).

291

The creature moves toward you, quicker than you'd have thought it capable of. When it's close enough to see clearly, it becomes a lot more terrifying – a dark mound of flesh twice your size. It has no legs, and seems more like a giant slug with its glistening wet skin. However, it is far more mobile than a slug, capable of shifting its bulk with rapid contortions of its body. Its mouth becomes all too clear as it lets out another beastly call. *Schreeeeeeeeeee!*

Six rows of flat teeth line its jaws, three rows top and bottom.

Make a Regular (2D6) **Composure** check. If you fail you must lose 1 composure as the creature's scream sends shivers down your spine.

You need to fight it off.

Giant Cave Slug
Combat 7
Health 6

If you win 3 rounds of combat in a row against the cave slug, you may flee the cave by turning to **147**.

If you decide not to flee and win against the creature, turn to **261**.

292

Yar'ith's body crumples into a mess of green blood and broken carapace. You kick the body away from you, allowing your utter disdain for these monsters to show through. From the corner of your eye, you spot a black shadow moving...

You turn just in time to witness a huge bloated purple spider-thing descend from the misty ceiling above and settle silently on the cavern floor. You knew this was coming... and you turn to flee.

If you have recorded in your journal '*Been inside the cavern*', then you do not need to make a composure check. If you do not have this entry, make an Extreme (2D6+3) **Composure** check. If you fail, you must lose 2 Composure. If you pass, lose 1 Composure.

Hoping the beast will pause to examine Yar'ith's body, you quickly make your way down the stepped ledges until you arrive back at the riverside. From the rock ledge, you follow the river flow, hoping to put as much distance as possible between yourself and the foul spider thing. Turn to **204**.

293

"Professor, I noticed some very strange green lights last night. Did you see? They appeared to be coming from around the house, or perhaps even from it," you say as you look about the hallway. You decide not to mention hearing that voice, as it's often told how that comes across.

"We are the lights," the professor responds, emotionless.
You turn, startled by that reply. "I beg your pardon?"
"Where were the lights, I asked?" inquires the professor, curious.
"Oh... I could see them from Durham. All around the hill. You didn't notice?"
"I was probably fast asleep. Early to bed is best for me." He gestures for you to take the stairs, his arm still stuck to his side.

Start heading up stairs. Turn to **69**.
Ask him if his arm is okay. Turn to **124**.

294

Turning quickly, you cross the threshold of the door into a gigantic cavern, and are suddenly terrified to see there is no pathway ahead. You attempt to stop yourself and keep your balance.

Make a Regular (2D6) **Dexterity** check.

If you pass, turn to **91**.
If you fail, turn to **125**.

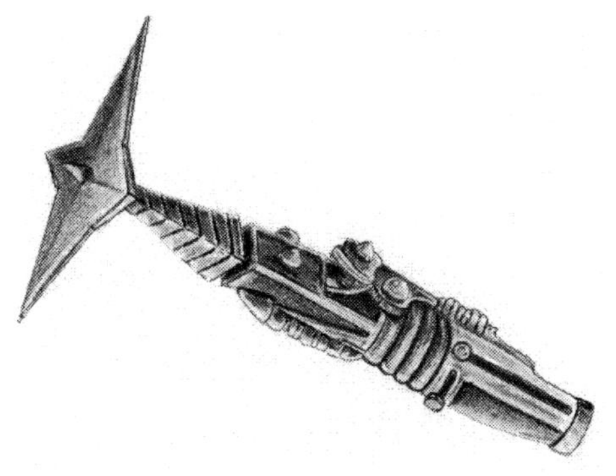

295

Reluctantly, you bring your finger to your mouth and taste it. It's as sweet as it smells. You feel a sudden urge to try some more, which you do. The liquid has a strong nourishing effect on you.

Restore 2 **Health**.

Thankful that it's possible to get some kind of sustenance here, you decide your next move.

Will you try the door on your right (turn to **7**), the door in the opposite wall near the ramp (turn to **546**), or investigate the ramp (turn to **433**).

296

You wait for a possible opening, then make a desperate dash towards the door. The spinning claws prove too difficult to avoid. You charge through them but not without suffering numerous serious lacerations.

Lose 4 **Health**.

If you survive, you stumble through the door, leaving a trail of blood behind you. Eugene calls out "You'll die, old chap. Should have listened to us…" His voice dies off as the door shuts, but it's not long before it opens again. They are coming after you. You immediately take the exit on your left and leave the area. Turn to **437**.

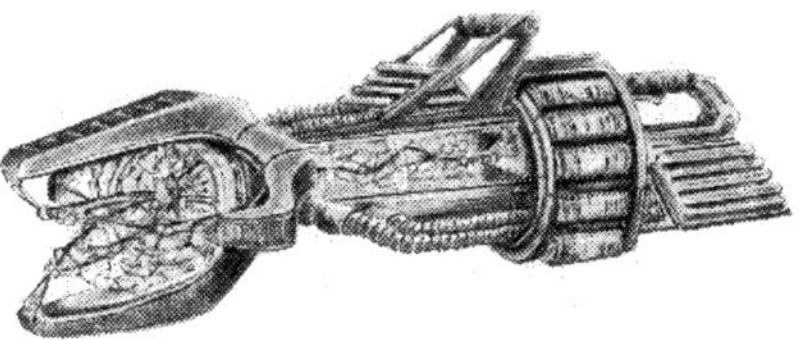

297

You thread carefully along the ledge, sticking close to the wall, and soon arrive at a natural rock formation from which the river is flowing. The ledge continues across the rockface to the opposite bank and then climbs steadily upwards. On the far side above you can see a return to the metal construction built into the rock, and another door.

Suddenly from above you hear a loud shriek. You look up just in time to narrowly avoid an attack from a winged beast. It swoops past you, missing you by inches, and glides over the river. You don't get much further before it deftly changes direction and swoops again. It lands directly ahead of you, spreading its wings to prevent passage. Its wings are rough and tattered as though it has been in many battles. Its body looks sickly, half-decomposed, with a head dominated by a huge beak on the end of a flexible elongated neck. Its head is more snake-like than bird-like, with little room for eyes and other sensory organs. Ignoring its wingspan, it is perhaps the size of an emu.

Make a Regular (2D6) **Composure** check. If you fail, lose 1 Composure.

What will you do?

Stand your ground and face the beast. Turn to **313**.
Flee along the ledge. Turn to **49**.

298

You lower yourself and hang from the walkway, trying desperately limit the fall distance. You quickly want to reconsider, but as you hang on, you know you'll never muster the strength required to pull yourself back up. You drop.

Make a Hard (2D6+1) **Dexterity** check. If you pass, you successfully prevent hurting yourself. If you failed, you land awkwardly, and must lose 2 **Health**.

If you survive the fall, you look around and see another door directly ahead that leads back into the main building you came from.

You get moving and exit the cavern through this door. Turn to **170**.

299

"You don't look well, sir. Perhaps you need to see someone, and then perhaps we could talk about what happened in the house? I don't know anything beyond the information contained in this news clipping from ten years ago," you reply, holding up the article that led you here.

"See someone?" he replies, sounding a little angrier than before. He reaches into his coat pocket. "You're from the university, aren't ya? Come to put a stop to my work! I won't return those *Necronomicon* pages. They hold the key to all this!" He gets very agitated and pulls a revolver from his pocket and starts waving it around. "Leave, now, before you can't leave any more."

You back off, holding your hands up in a gesture of compliance. "Okay, I'll leave. I don't want any trouble."

Record in your Investigators Journal '*You were warned to leave the house alone*', and note the reference 335.

Not wishing to agitate him any further, you leave Peabody to his madness.

Deflated and more than a little rattled, you head back to Durham. Turn to **210**.

300

"The basement? Nothing in there but junk. I don't use it," he says.
You insist, so he opens the door. A damp, mouldy smell, rises from the darkness below. It is mixed with something else – a chemical odour?
"You first, professor," you say, turning on your flashlight.
He starts to walk slowly down the steps with you following behind, lighting the way.

"See," says Peabody, his voice echoing in the open basement below.

Staying where you are on the current step you scan the basement with your flashlight. Peabody has turned and is facing you. His gaunt features are a frightful sight in the hard-shadowed light of your flashlight as you pass it across him to spy into the corners of the room. As your flashlight passes beyond Peabody, you see a green glimmer of light shine in his eyes. Suddenly, he lunges at you from the darkness, his contorted face positively frightening in the shadows.

Make a Regular (2D6) **Composure** check. If you fail, deduct 1 from your current Composure. If you pass, there is no effect.

Now, make a Hard (2D6+1) **Dexterity** check to avoid his lunge.

If you pass the Dexterity check, turn to **559**.
If you fail the Dexterity check, turn to **34**.

301

You contemplate rushing it... but you haven't faced one of these in a fight before and it's a rather unsettling prospect.

Make a Hard (2D6+1) **Composure** check.

If you fail, turn to **250**.
If you pass, turn to **101**.

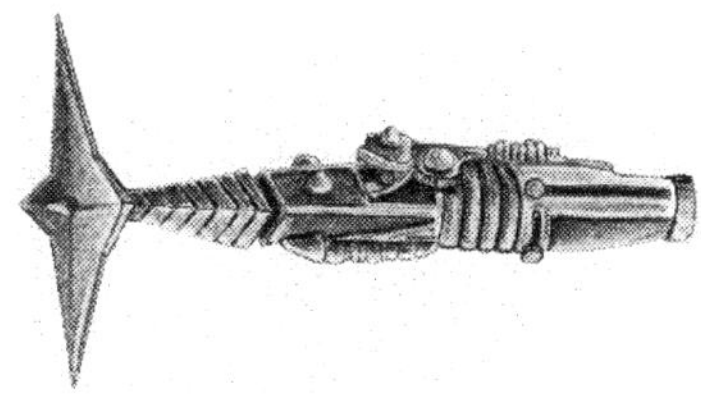

302

Conjuring up every last ounce of strength you manage to pry the claws apart. However, you feel yourself losing again when suddenly he lets you go of his own accord.

You step back in terror.

"I... am... sssssorry!" Edward says, backing away again into the darkness.

Feeling equal parts revulsion and pity for the thing before you, you pick up and turn the flashlight off.

You take this opportunity to ask questions. What do you want to ask?

Where has he been all this time (turn to **90**)?
How does he seem to be the still only twelve years old (turn to **77**), or to ask about his 'claw' and other physical changes (turn to **571**)?

303

You hold up the syringe and turn it about in your hand as though you could somehow judge its contents visually. The professor suggests you sit first, so you oblige. After a brief pause, and with a shaky hand, you inject its contents into your arm.

The professor stands there, emotionless, as your vision blurs.

You slump over the desk, and everything goes dark. Turn to **120**.

304

You wait for your moment, listening for the creature's footfalls. To your horror, the sound you hear is not the of creature coming around the corner of the slab, but instead of it landing on top of the slab just above your head. It's too late for you to react, as the beast wastes no time in firing another blast of the weapon. At this close range, your body is nearly ripped apart from the inside. Skin splits and melts away. Your screams are drowned out by the noise of the weapon itself... and when it has finished firing, you are nothing more than a half-melted puddle of flesh and blood.

Record in your Investigator Journal '*You were shot and killed by a lightning gun.*' -2 *Mythos* points.

Your investigation ends here.

305

Just as you touch the panel to the cell, the door you originally entered from opens. You turn sharply and see two mi-go enter the chamber. With a loud hiss of rushing air, the glass wall to the enclosure begins to descend into the floor. The two mi-go immediately stop when they realise what you've done. "Huumaan fooool..." one utters in those unnatural affected tones.

Before you stands the spider-thing, now free to leave its cell. It rushes past you. The legs of the spider-thing thunder on the floor as it moves with incredible speed. The two mi-go are torn asunder before your very eyes as the malice of this giant arachnid is unleased on its captors. The sight is utterly vicious and unrelenting.

Make an Easy (2D6-1) **Composure** check. If you fail you must lose 1 Composure. If you pass, there is no effect.

You make to flee, but the spider-thing is too quick. It sweeps across the floor, smearing the torn carcass of a mi-go behind it, and blocks the door.
"Human, wait. You freed me of your own free will. I mean you no harm."
"What... are you?" you mutter, backing away.
The creature follows you closely, seemingly oblivious to the dread its visage causes.
"I am Unlatha. That is all your kind need know of me. How have you come to Yuggoth, outpost of the mi-go?"
You tell her of your ordeal, how you arrived because of Edward and the Turne family, and your only desire is to be rid of this place.

She points a blood-soaked leg towards the dead mi-go. "They interfere much, and were it not for their technology, I would tear them all asunder. I will help you by letting you live, even though... I hunger. Mi-go are worthless to feed upon." With that, you're left standing there alone as Unlatha passes through the door ahead and disappears into the darkness with uncanny speed. You wonder how she was caught in the first place.

Record in your Investigator Journal '*You freed Unlatha*', and note two separate reference numbers carefully. The *first* is 431. The *second* is 126. If asked about this entry later, be sure to confirm you go the correct reference mentioned, the first, or the second. +5 *Mythos* points.

Suspecting more mi-go may be coming at any moment from the way you came, you leave through the same door Unlatha took. Turn to **144**.

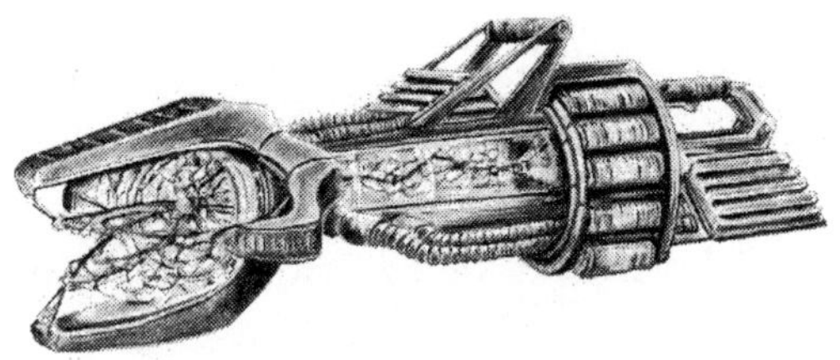

306

The counter is lined with a variety of devices, and many of them appear to be weapons. Blades and claw-like prosthetics of various shapes and sizes make up the majority of the items here, but there's something more eye-catching – a large bulky gun with coils and a glowing green panel on its side. You implore Edward to stay put as you rush back, armed with a lightning gun.

Unlatha turns to you. A trail of blood whips through the air from her proboscis and spatters the wall.
"You... DARE?" The body of the mother convulses on the slab. You step forward and pull the trigger!

Make a Regular (2D6) **Dexterity** check.

If you fail, turn to **224**.
If you pass, turn to **383**.

307

Sensing that taking the advantage is the only way you could defeat this beast, you sneak up behind it.

Make an Easy (2D6-1) **Stealth** check.

If you pass, turn to **156**.
If you fail, you accidentally kick a stone which alerts the creature. Turn to **392**.

308

You are utterly terrified. Lose 2 **Composure**.

You immediately turn and flee in terror from the spider, throwing caution to the wind as you leap down each of the ledges you had climbed to get here.

Make a Very Hard (2D6+2) **Dexterity** check.

If you fail, turn to **576**.
If you pass, turn to **134**.

309

You charge out from behind the containers to surprise the mi-go, but only now do you realise there's something different about this one!

With lightning-fast reactions, it turns to face you, ready to fight. Turn to **505**.

310

You cautiously take a peek and see the creature has its back turned to you. It replaces the lump of meat that fell from the conveyor and then starts to pick through the remains in front of it. As you watch, it holds up and examines an eyeball, turning it gently in its claw. The creature's head changes to a deep shade of green and then it places the eyeball in a small container, before resuming its search through the entrails. What do you want to do?

To sneak up behind it and attack, turn to **150**.
Or if you wait for it to leave, turn to **86**.

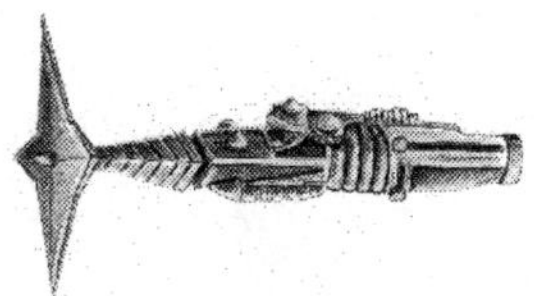

311

You take a run and manage to grip the edge of the walkway. Now comes the difficult part – you must try and pull yourself up.

Make a Hard (2D6+1) **Strength** check.

If you pass, turn to **19**.
If you fail, turn to **515**.

312

You follow the lit tunnel as it bends around to the right. You're suddenly feeling quite hungry, a feeling that brings some sense of normality to your desperate situation. Your thoughts drift back to the house, and Edward.

'Find my family!' he said. But they are dead.

'You promised!' he cried. You promised nothing. You had never met him before. Yet, he knew your name – could the professor have told him? His mind was clearly gone. He must have mixed up everything, and whatever the creatures did to him clearly prevented the aging process. A sudden pang of pity for him and what he endured washes over you. But now you're in this situation, and despair follows as you feel it could be *your* end.

Weary, you stumble on through the tunnel for another hundred feet before an opening appears ahead. You emerge into a large chamber. Turn to **154**.

313

Sensing you would be at a distinct disadvantage attempting to run on this ledge, you decide to stand and fight. The creature is a juvenile *Byakhee*. It appears to be wounded, likely a result from previous battles with the mi-go.

Its beak is particularly vicious and if you are hit, you will take 2 Damage in an attack instead of the usual 1. You must also reduce your Combat ability by 1 for this combat due to the precarious nature of fighting on the ledge.

Juvenile Byakhee
Combat 7
Health 4

If you win, you now must decide which way you will go.

Head onwards and make for the structure. If you're to find a way out of here, you suspect it will be through exploring the buildings. Turn to **170**.
Continue back along the ledge and follow the river flow instead. Turn to **204**.

314

You grab the gun and briefly look it over. It could be useful. The mi-go soldier twitches on the floor. You rush towards the door on the right and as it opens you stop in your tracks. There's no walkway or other path. It drops into a massive cavern that is swarming with hundreds of working mi-go, mining ore.

The door behind you suddenly opens as a group of mi-go enter. On seeing their dying companion in the centre of the room, the remaining soldier mi-go advance. You turn the weapon on them and fire, but are too late as they fire at almost the same time. The lightning guns fill the chamber with crackling light and energy. You manage to hit the group, destroying a number of them, but also at the very same moment, you are blasted off your feet through the doorway and fall hundreds of feet to your death in the massive cavern. The swarms of mi-go working in the cavern turn to look on curiously.

Record in your Investigator Journal '*You were shot by a lightning gun and fell hundreds of feet to your death.*' -3 *Mythos* points.

Your investigation ends here.

315

"No way am I going to end up like… like you! Step aside or there will be trouble!" you demand.
"My dear fellow," Eugene replies, "that is most disappointing to hear. I guess it will have to be by force. Our benefactors trust us quite enough to afford us a way to protect ourselves."
The claws on the end of their arms start to whirr and spin, becoming a deadly weapon. Eugene and another brain advance on you. You may not be able to fight them off without taking terrible wounds from those spinning claws.

Will you fight them regardless (turn to **579**), or attempt a charge for the door now (turn to **346**)?
Alternatively, if you have an explosive seed, you may use it on the two walking brains guarding the door. Turn to **279**.

316

You approach the table and are immediately surprised to see an array of everyday man-made objects.

On the table are metal tongs, assorted chisels, some screwdrivers, and jewellery such as earrings, necklaces, and bracelets. In stark contrast to the table, the containers next to it contain eyeballs of various shapes and sizes, what appear to be claws, teeth and other less recognisable viscera.

One of the larger screwdrivers could be used as a weapon. If you have no other weapon you can use this in a fight and add +1 to the Damage you deal. Mark it in your Investigator Journal. You may only use one weapon at a time, but you can carry this and any other weapon you currently have.

If you haven't already, you can examine the control panel. Turn to **523**.
Or exit the room and investigate further, going through the door next to the room. Turn to **405**.

317

The door opens into a similarly sized room with a single exit on the left, and to your right sits a stack of containers with various mechanical fragments and equipment parts. Suddenly that door on the left opens. Ducking down behind the containers just in time, you can see between two of them that a single mi-go has entered the room and is headed toward the back where a series of containment cells line the back wall. In one of the cells is another mi-go. That creature appears to be a prisoner. The mi-go guard, if that is what it is, hasn't spotted you.

What will you do?

Attempt to sneak up behind the creature and strike it down before it has a chance to react. Turn to **6**.
Toss a piece of metal from one of the containers as a distraction, then attack the creature from behind. Turn to **205**.
Surprise the creature with a full-on charge attack. Turn to **309**.

318

About halfway down you lose your footing and slip. You try to cling on with one hand.

Now you must make a Hard (2D6+1) **Strength** check.

If you fail the Strength check, you cannot maintain your grip and fall the rest of the way, landing heavily on your back. Lose 3 **Health** and 1 **Composure**. You are now on the bottom, turn to **323**.

If you pass the Strength check, you regain a firm footing and continue the climb down. Now, make a Regular (2D6) **Dexterity** check for the remainder of the climb.

If you fail the **Dexterity** check, you slip again, but are further down and manage to minimise your fall. Lose 1 **Health**, and turn to **323.**

If you pass the **Dexterity** check, you safely reach the bottom without further incident. Turn to **323**.

319

"We can't stop them coming through, Edward! Get out of here while you can, I will take Sara... " you call out in alarm. Edward doesn't listen. "No! *You* must save them... "
Before you can react, he charges through the portal to the other side. You see him charging at the machine through the haze and then... darkness. In a momentary flash the portal dissipates into the air. He did it! He gave his life and closed the portal from the other side.

Record in your Investigator Journal '*Edward sacrificed himself to close the portal.*' -20 *Mythos* points.

Your attention turns to the members of the family that survived.
If Sara, Melissa, and Jacob survived. turn to **430**.
If only Sara and Jacob survived, turn to **580**.
If only Sara survived, turn to **542**.

320

You grasp the claw with both hands and attempt to pull it apart, but he's too strong. He crushes your windpipe between his claws, your neck offering little resistance as he all but snips your head off your shoulders.

Record in your Investigator Journal '*Your neck was crushed by Edward's claw.*' -2 *Mythos* points.

Your investigation ends here.

321

You approach the door and wait a moment for it to open. When it does, you are immediately in shock. Standing in the corridor is a mi-go. It emits that buzzing sound, and the noise of its many feet click and clack on the hard metal floor. The creature turns towards you and advances, forcing you to back away.

You will have to defend yourself. Turn to **48**.

322

He closes the door behind you as you take in the dusty hallway. It darkens considerably as the door is closed.
"How long have you been staying here, professor?" you ask, feeling a little uneasy. You wait... he doesn't respond. Turning to him, you notice he seems to be staring blankly down the hallway, motionless. You're about to ask if he's okay when he suddenly comes to life.
"A few years, lad. I've been back and forth with the university over the years. Bunch of ingrates. If you'd go upstairs. please. What I have to show you is in the attic."

His right arm remains motionless by his side as he gestures you take the stairs with his left.

Do you start heading up the stairs? Turn to **69**.
Ask what is wrong with his arm. Turn to **124**.

323

The heat is just bearable down here. To your right, the river of black slime flows out of the cave wall behind you and disappears under the tower ahead, flowing beneath the wall. The structure is a towering convex wall of smooth black stone that rises three hundred feet to join with the cavern ceiling. The only visible feature is a large archway at the base, and darkness lies beyond it.

You take a deep breath and enter the structure. Turn to **99**.

324

A blast of lightning burns through the air from the doorway behind Unlatha. Her body convulses and crackles, smoke rising from her extremities. Edward stands in the doorway holding a lightning gun. Unlatha collapses in a heap, her legs folding inwards in a vain attempt to protect her body. Edward fires again, the weapon kicking him backwards as he tries to control its power. Unlatha's body twitches one last time, then remains still. She is dead. Edward throws the gun to the ground and runs to his mother. She is unharmed and alive.

You get to your feet. "Well done, Edward! Now we must wake your family so we can get out of here."
Edward nods. The boy is remarkably resilient to everything that has happened.

You grab Sara and carry her into the chamber with the portal machine while Edward attempts to wake his mother and father. When you return, they are still unconscious. You work together and move them into the room with the portal machine.

Record in your Investigator Journal '*Sara, Melissa and Jacob are alive.*' +60 *Mythos* points.

Edward examines the machine. "It won't turn on!" he shouts while frantically turning the dials.
You step in and find the slot for the power source – the *Tok'llian*. You remind Edward that is it required to power the device. Do you have it?

If you have recorded in your Investigator Journal '*Found the Tok'llian'*, then you must turn to the **FIRST** reference associated with that entry now.

If you do not have the *Tok'llian*, turn to **509**.

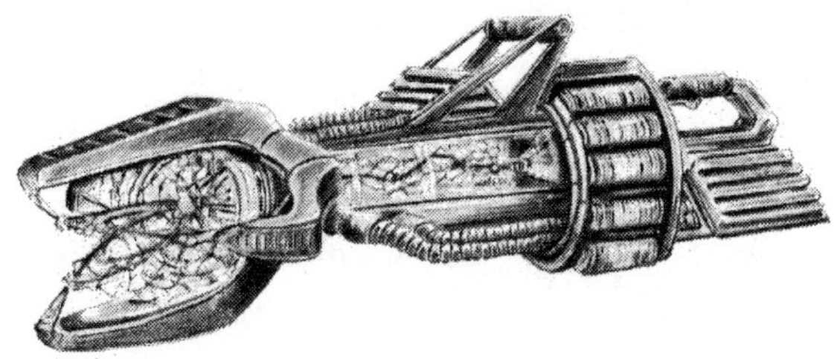

325

You maintain your composure and duck behind the large disc machine to scan the room for signs of mi-go. There is a walkway above, you but cannot see a way up to it. You'd have to climb up. These creatures have wings, so it seems they don't construct their buildings in a way that gives easy access to humans.

Above the walkway, a long opening in the wall can be seen running across the width of the room. It looks through into another room beyond.

On the ground floor where you are, each of the four conveyor belts would have to be crossed to reach the other side of the chamber. There, you see a large square doorway, easily twenty-by-twenty feet in size.

What's your next move?

Examine the disc machine. Turn to **220**.
Sneak across the conveyor belts and head towards the large door. Turn to **61**.
Wait and watch for signs of movement from the walkway above. Turn to **83**.

326

You enter a makeshift study on the first floor through the door at the foot of the stairs. A simple desk and chair sit against the far wall. The window above the desk faces out to the side of the house and is not boarded up like the front facing windows. Rain runs down the window, blurring the view outside. The desk is strewn with papers, open books, and notes. Filled bookshelves stretch the length of the room.

Where would you like to search?

Will you examine the bookcase (turn to **347**), or try the desk (turn to **494**)?

327

You approach the well in the centre of the chamber to find it is filled with a yellow liquid. An almost needle-thin pipe suspended from the ceiling above, releases a drop of the liquid into the well every few seconds.

You can touch the liquid (turn to **541**), leave the well alone and head for the door to your right (turn to **7**), or try the door in the opposite wall near the ramp (turn to **546**). Alternatively, you can investigate the ramp. Turn to **433**.

328

You proceed cautiously up the ramp but as you reach eye-level with the floor above the area opens out and you feel quite exposed here. You briefly stop and look around. To your horror, you spot two mi-go flying down towards you.

Have they seen you? You have only a moment to decide your next move.

Do you decide to stand your ground and face them (turn to **503**), or duck back down the ramp and into the nearest doorway, (turn to **412**)?

329

The door closes behind you as you cross the room that you first appeared in, and stand before the door opposite. It slides open, almost simultaneously as the door behind you opens. You realise you could be simply fleeing headlong into more danger, and possibly more of these foul creatures. You decide to turn and face it – better to try and put it down now. You're not even remotely comfortable with the prospect of battling this horrid thing, but nor are you willing to become its victim. You tighten your fists... ready to fight. The creature's head turns a deep shade of red as it advances.

Now you must fight for your life...

Mi-go Worker
Combat 5
Health 4

If you win, turn to **278**.
If you are reduced to just 2 remaining health, turn to **457**.

330

You try in vain to strip the thread from your hand, and using your other hand would be folly. It starts to hurt as you pull further, tugging at your skin. Suddenly you are almost pulled off your feet as the thread recoils back towards the cavern ceiling. Something is reeling the thread in! You desperately try to resist.

Make a Hard (2D6+1) **Strength** check.

If you fail, turn to **179**.
If you pass, you manage to release yourself and nearly fall over backwards in the process. You decide to turn back rather than risk becoming ensnared in these threads. Turn to **507**.

331

You get back in your car and roll away from the garage. You glance in your installed rear-view mirror, which you found vital for the crowded Boston streets, and see what appears to be the garage attendant walking out into the middle of the street. He’s watching you leave, rubbing his hands with a rag. You've picked up too much speed to bother stopping now.

Further on, the road narrows and gets a bit rougher. Turn to **557**.

332

He opens the door, then seeing your intention as you wait, he walks in first. The room is clearly a makeshift study. A simple desk and chair sit against the far wall. The window above the desk faces out to the side of the house and is not boarded up like the front facing windows. Rain runs down the window, blurring the view outside. The desk is strewn with papers, open books, and notes. Filled bookshelves stretch the length of the room.

Ask him what he is studying here. Turn to **98**.
Approach the desk. Turn to **214**.
Examine the bookshelves. Turn to **417**.

333

"Professor Peabody from Miskatonic University?" you call out.
"No one from 'round these parts knows I'm here. And you are?" he inquires, stepping through the gap to your side of the treeline. He looks around late fifties, about five-foot-five in height, and unshaven. Balding at the crown of his head, his remaining grey hair is a little long and unkempt.

You introduce yourself and explain your motive for finding the house.
"I see," he replies after a moment's contemplation. He appears to have trouble catching his breath. "And how would you go about helping me, exactly?"

How do you respond?

Show him the news clipping and explain that if he's still trying to discover what happened, you'd like to help. Turn to **477**.
Or first inquire about his health, as he doesn't sound well. Turn to **299**.

334

The spores fill your lungs, forcing you to your knees as you attempt to catch your breath. Choking hard, and with your eyes stinging and bloodshot, you can just barely see two mi-go enter the room. They approach you as you collapse to the floor and lose consciousness.

You awake and open your eyes. Turn to **564**.

335

You recall the professor's warning that you stay away from the house, but something tells you that if you could just convince him that you're here to help then he'll be more open to the idea. You pause for a breath and look out at the wet, desolate hilltop. The rain beats down thick and heavy. It's a grim sight. You turn back to face the house and look at the rusted metal knocker in the centre of the door.

What will you do?

Knock on the door. Turn to **472**.
Try the door instead and see if it's open. Turn to **166**.

336

You desperately fight on, unable to finish the mi-go off in time before the first mi-go scientist returns from through the doorway – armed with a large gun. The blast from the gun is like a lightning bolt, lifting you off your feet as the charged energy surrounds you, singeing your flesh. You lose all control of your bodily functions as the shock runs through your body. Hitting the ground in a heap, you twitch for a few moments as smoke rises from your body. The mi-go surround you… then start to disassemble your body.

Record in your Investigator Journal '*You were shot and killed by a lightning gun.*' -2 *Mythos* points.

Your investigation ends here.

337

You ensure Pete that your car is quite reliable, and you've had no trouble at all with it.

"Aye," he replies, "but the radiator valve needs checking when travelling a long way, or on the rougher roads out here. See here!" He gestures for you to take a look as he lifts the hood. "The cap here tends to loosen over bumpy terrain, and we have a lot of that about, as I'm sure you've noticed." He tightens the valve. "There, all sorted!"

Record in your Investigator Journal that '*Your car radiator was fixed*', and note the reference 94. Later in the story, if asked if you have earned this information, you will turn to 94. (Do not turn to that now).

You thank Pete and offer to pay for the repair, but he refuses, saying it was no trouble at all.

You can now ask him the way to Sentinel Hill (turn to **184**), or get in your car and drive on with the hope of finding a sign to the hill (turn to **557**).

338

As you reach the opposite side you hear the unmistakable clacking sound of multiple mi-go feet and the beating of wings. You duck behind a jut of rock near the entrance just as four mi-go rush past you into the egg-chamber. They've clearly come to defend their brood.

Will you watch to see what happens (turn to **238**), or take this opportunity to leave while they are heavily distracted by the creature (turn to **537**)?

339

The second mi-go falls to the floor dead just as you hear those unmistakable buzzing tones coming from the opening on the walkway above. More are coming!

You decide to take the metal rod for yourself.

Record in your Investigators Journal '*Have a metal rod*', and note the reference 283. +1 *Mythos* point.

Now you must think fast and get out of here.

Will you open the large square doorway by touching the panel next to the door (turn to **123**), or take the less desirable route, and escape via conveyor belt through the opening in the wall (turn to **110**)?

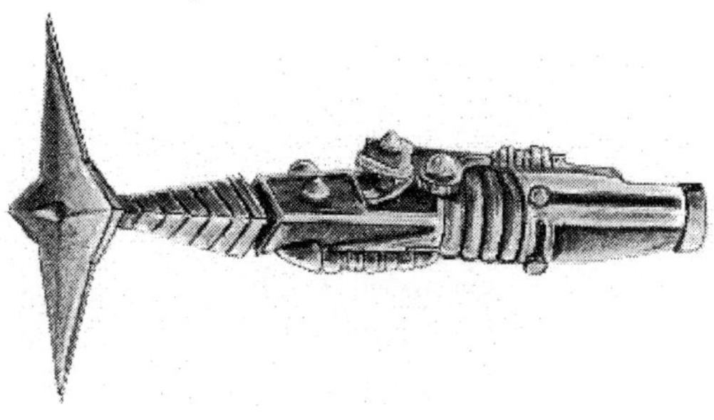

340

You hunker down lower to avoid being seen by whatever new devilry this thing is. Relying only on your ears now, you hear it sloshing through the soup of blood. Moments pass, then it starts coming closer...

Will you stay put and hope it moves away (turn to **393**), or start moving away from it by creeping around the mound you're hiding behind (turn to **439**)?

341

"A... a tribute," you respond, trying to sound confident in your answer.

"A pitiful offering. A senseless offering. I will show my subjects my displeasure, in time."

Before you can think how to respond further, the creature grasps you in its huge hand. A malice of impossible proportions washes over you, and your mind snaps almost instantly. Your very being is absorbed by Nyarlathotep. As you become a part of the Crawling Chaos, all sense of self and being are lost to you – there is now only madness and endless suffering.

Record in your Investigator Journal '*You were absorbed by Nyarlathotep and suffer eternal torment.*' -20 *Mythos* points.

Your investigation ends here.

342

You turn the first dial to what you would believe to be 90 degrees.

How do you want to set the second dial?

To set it to 45 degrees, turn to **521**.
To set it to 121 degrees, turn to **247**.
To set it to 37 degrees, turn to **489**.

343

You open the door into what appears to be a makeshift study.

"Didn't I warn you not to come here?"

The professor appears at the top of the stairs, bathed in darkness.

"Yes, listen, I wanted to..."

"Very well!" he cuts in as he takes a step down the stairs.

"Come on up, perhaps you can be of use to me after all." he adds.

You gingerly start climbing the stairway as the professor waits for you on the landing.
"Why the change of heart, professor?" you ask as you reach the landing.
"I was out of line, and too stubborn to ask for help. I see now that was foolish of me."
When you get to the top, he gestures for you to head down the hallway ahead of him.
"If you please."
You move cautiously ahead, and with good reason. From the corner of your eye, you see the professor raise his hand. Turning sharply, you see he has a syringe in his grasp.

Make a Hard (2D6+1) **Dexterity** check to dodge the blow.

If you pass, turn to **356**.
If you fail, turn to **406**.

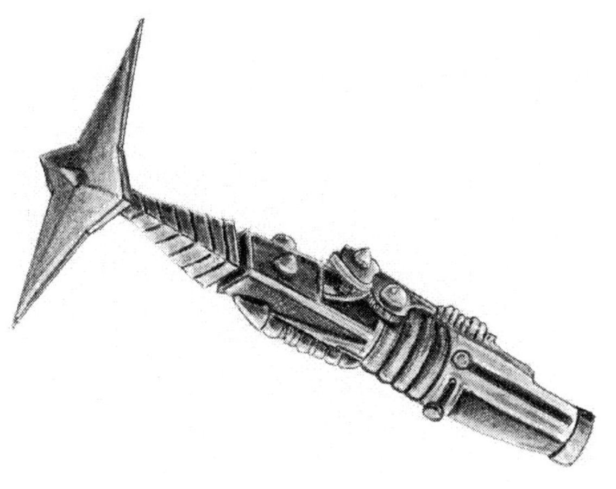

344

You find yourself once again standing by the bowl and statue in the temple. You feel strange and unsure of what good could come from a gift bestowed by a being of such malevolent form.

Record in your Investigator Journal '*Received a gift*', and note the reference 473.

If you haven't already done so, you can now explore the exits.

To exit through the archway to the right, turn to **437**.
To cross the chamber to the archway in the far wall, turn to **358**.
Or to investigate the archway on the left, turn to **230**.

345

In your haste you start pressing buttons, but as you press one the walkway starts to extend, pressing another cancels this action and it retracts again, attempting to extend in another direction. You've lost valuable time and the two mi-go catch up to you. The creature armed with the metal rod points it towards you. You must try to dodge this attack.

Make a Regular (2D6) **Dexterity** check. If you pass, you successfully dodge the shard, which flies harmlessly past you into the vast cavern behind. If you fail, you are hit square in the shoulder, and must lose 2 **Health**.

Now you must face them in combat. With the doorway narrowing the way, you can fight them one at time instead of both together. Fight the first mi-go, and if you survive then the second one steps up.

Mi-go Worker 1	**Mi-go Worker 2**
Combat 6	Combat 7
Health 5	Health 4

For this combat, keep track of the number of rounds you lose – as each lost round forces you backward. If you lose a total of 4 rounds against the mi-go, turn to **385**.
If you win, turn to **227**.

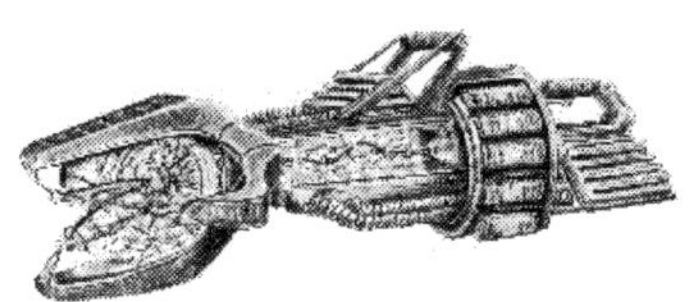

346

You charge towards the door in an attempt to escape this new nightmare.

Make an Extreme (2D6+3) **Dexterity** check.

If you pass, turn to **411**.
If you fail, turn to **296**.

347

The shelves are lined with books on scientific theories, physics, space, and gravity, and even some on human anatomy. Then, things get a little stranger – books on occult spells, incantations, books in Latin and various other odd volumes. There's nothing that would be easy to digest right now as each book is an extensive detail of its subject.

You can now examine the desk, turn to **494**.
Or leave this room and search the rest of the house, turn to **252**.

348

You tell her that you're thinking of moving out of the city, and want to see the property so you may attempt to purchase it.
She laughs, loudly. "Buy the house? Oh, you city folk. That place isn't for sale. It's all but condemned. I wouldn't bother, mister. If you want to move out of the city and live out this way, at least pretend you have a notion of life out here."

Her laughing would make you feel embarrassed, if it weren't for the fact you have no intention of buying the place. She composes herself, then bids you good day as she is shutting up shop.

You return to your car – the town is quieter than ever. The garage appears to have been locked up for the evening. You feel there's not much more you can do here, so you get back in your car, and turn on your electric lights.

Will you drive on? Perhaps the house might be easy enough to find along the main road out of town. Turn to **557**.
Or call it a day and look for a lodging to get a fresh start in the morning. Turn to **372**.

349

You move fully into the crawl space. It's dark and the rock is covered with a layer of slime.

Make a Regular (2D6) **Perception** check.

If you pass, turn to **50**.
If you fail, turn to **495**.

350

You raise the flashlight and flick the switch. The shape before you hisses loudly, raising its arms to cover its face. You are shocked by the sight!

His face is that of a boy, but gaunt and sickly. With a hunched, misshapen body, his torso is slightly twisted, while his right foot is turned and looks to be dead weight. His right arm is elongated, nearly twice the length his arm

should be, and worse still, at the end in place of a hand is a hideous engineered prosthetic of a metal claw. The claw is articulated, wired, and jointed. It looks jagged and sharp.
"Offff... turrrrn it OFFFFFF!" His cry of anguish chills your soul, but he also sounds angry.

What do you do?

Do as he asks and turn off the flashlight. Turn to **244**.
Press the advantage and get some answers first. Turn to **371**.

351

You turn to run in the hope of putting some distance between you and the emerging horror, but the black void is disorientating. You cannot tell if you're getting anywhere. Suddenly, your muscles tighten, forcing you to stop in your tracks while the air in your lungs is squeezed out. An invisible force is crushing you, and turning you back around to face whatever new terror is coming before you. The pain is intense for a moment until you're suddenly released, facing towards the tear again.

Lose 1 **Health** and 1 **Composure**.

You are forced to watch it emerge. Turn to **71**.

352

The armed soldier returns with four other smaller unarmed mi-go. One of the smaller variety steps forward to speak. You assume this is their master, or leader.
"Huumaan, your designation?" Its tone is more direct, less drawn out – more capable than the others you've heard.
"Eh, Frank. Frank Winston. Where am I? What is this place?

And more to the point, what are you?"
The mi-go skitter and turn to each other, their heads transitioning through a multitude of colours. They can communicate without the need for spoken words. The same mi-go speaks again.
"Frank. Huuman. You are witth usss on Yuggoth. We are the miii-go. Ruulers of Yuggoth. How did Frank geeet here?" It takes another step towards you, and seems to regard you almost curiously.

You explain the details of your arrival, the strange device, and the diamond-shaped object that was used to activate it. The moment you mention the *Tok'llian,* the creature's agitation becomes obvious. "Givvveee it to uusss," the leader demands, holding out a claw. "Give usss the *Tok'llian*!' Two of the mi-go train their guns on you.

If you haven't got it, you explain that the '*Tok'llian*' as they call it, is back on Earth in the house. Turn to **516**.
If you do have it, turn to **498**.

353

Edward inserts the diamond-shaped object into a recess on the side of the machine. It begins to hum. He then turns some of the dials in frustration. "Which issss it... ugggggh... Fraaank?" He looks up at you with a pleading look in his eyes.
"What do you need me to do?" you answer, horrified at the entire macabre scenario that is playing out before you.
He steps back pointing at the dials. "You musssst know how to activaaaaate? Like beeeefore!"
His frustration is growing and seems it may lead to violence. You don't know how much longer he will restrain himself. What will you do?

Approach the dials and attempt to operate the machine (turn to **195**), or tell Edward that you have never seen this device before, and that you do not know how to operate it (turn to **554**).

354

You feel your way in the dark hoping to eventually arrive at a new light source. Unfortunately, you take one step too many, and almost plunge down an open pit in the floor of the tunnel. You just manage to grasp the edge and attempt to pull yourself back up.

Make a Hard (2D6+1) **Strength** check. If you pass, you manage to pull yourself up from the edge of the pit. Terrified from what could have been a fatal fall, you edge onwards very slowly and carefully until a dim light appears ahead. Turn to **136**.

If you fail the Strength check, turn to **585**.

355

"Professor, is everything okay?" you call up the stairs and wait for a response, but the one you hear is not what you expected.
"Fraaaank. Coooome." The voice chills you to the bone.

It's not the voice of the professor, but instead the same raspy and slightly metallic voice from last night. It wasn't a dream!

Almost mesmerised, you continue up and step through the door. Turn to **511**.

356

You side-step his attempt to inject you with the syringe, but he's like a man possessed. He lunges at you again, giving you no option but to defend yourself in combat.

Professor Albert Peabody
Combat 5
Health 6

If you reduce his health to 3, turn to **96**.
If in any round of the fight the professor rolls a 12 for his attack AND beats your attack that round, turn to **237**.

357

The road appears to be in better repair, but before long you start to doubt that this was the correct route to take. The treeline fades to bush, affording you the chance to look about in dimming light. You spot the unmistakable outline of Sentinel Hill, and perched atop, the house, far off to the left and behind you. You're clearly heading away from it.

You curse your choice of direction and make to turn the car around.

As you head back, the lateness of the hour and your own tiredness makes you reconsider your actions. You now have a good idea of which way to go, and decide that doing so in the morning is the only sane choice.

You head on back to Durham. Turn to **127**.

358

The archway leads into another dark tunnel lined with similar intricate cravings to the main chamber, but this one ends with an oval shaped metal door.

If you approach the door, turn to **483**.
Or if you haven't already done so, you can explore the archway that is to your left (turn to **230**), take the archway that is to your right (turn to **437**), or examine the strange statue and bowl in the centre of the chamber (turn to **164**).

359

You creep along, trying to stay in darkness. After a few moments you spot a large black shape moving across the cave floor. You freeze and wait in the hope that it hasn't seen you, but suddenly it turns in your direction. A bulbous lumbering thing, about the size of a walrus, shifts its bulk towards you and starts to advance.

What do you want to do?
Ready yourself to fight the creature. Turn to **291**.
Make a run for it onwards and out of the larger cavern. Turn to **550**.

360

As you take a few steps forward the reverberation of your footsteps echoes strangely about the corridor. You reach out to touch the edge of the shape, and as you do the wall opens before you. It is a door. In one swift motion it sweeps aside to reveal a chamber on the other side. The chamber is undefined, blurred. Stepping through, you find yourself standing on uneven, rocky ground. The door closes silently behind you.

Ahead you see a hundred black stone needle like structures rising from the rocky ground against a starry sky. A faint green light shines in place of a sun, illuminating the strange landscape just enough for you to see the vista before you. Suddenly you're caught gasping for breath. You immediately fall to your knees, clawing at your throat. Your eyes bulge out of your head, your skin cracks and splits. Your vision blurs as something, a shape – a thing – lands silently in front of you.

Make a Hard (2D6+1) **Composure** check. If you fail, deduct 1 from your current Composure. If you pass, there is no effect.

Record in your Investigator Journal that '*You dreamt of an alien landscape, and suffocated in a vacuum.*' +4 *Mythos* points.

Then you wake up. Turn to **500**.

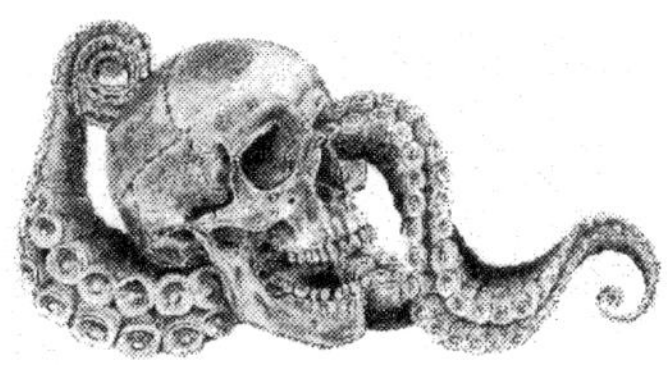

361

Your quick reactions and already cautious state of mind serve you well as you back away suddenly. The tendril of black slime snaps outwards then retreats into the spiny core. You decide to leave it alone.

If you haven't already, you can examine the tall plant with the black petals. Turn to **177**.
Examine the plant with the large orange petals. Turn to **386**.
Or decide you've had enough of these bizarre plants, and leave via the other door. Turn to **370**.

362

You turn the second dial to what you would believe to be 37 degrees.

How do you want to set the third dial?

To leave it as is on zero degrees, turn to **25**.
To set it to 90 degrees, turn to **418**.
To set it to 47 degrees, turn to **467**.

363

"Whooo... areee yooou?" A familiar, yet distorted voice calls from behind you. You turn to see Edward standing in the centre of the room. He looks confused! "Whaaat... what haapeened to meeee?" He raises his clawed arm and stares at it with a look of horror.
You rush to him. "Edward, it's me, Frank! Remember from the house?"
He looks up at you... his eyes are strange, and his expression offers no recollection. "Fraaank? I do noooot knooow you... my... faaamily... wheeere?" He recoils and turns towards the

slabs. "Mooother?" He limps awkwardly to the metal slab where his mother lies.
Unsure as to why he doesn't recognise you, your thoughts turn back to the machine. "Edward, I will try and get this machine to work, then we'll get your family home, okay?" He doesn't respond.

You approach the machine and examine it. You find the slot for the power source, but do you have it?

If you have recorded in your Investigator Journal '*Found the Tok'llian*', then you must turn to the **SECOND** reference associated with that entry now.

If you do not have the *Tok'llian*, turn to **102**.

364

You set the fourth dial to 100 degrees and step back from the device. Suddenly a bright flash of green light shoots upwards from the sphere atop the machine. A low thrum pulses in the air, and the light flickers, slowly at first, then faster and faster until it becomes a solid beam. You back away, not knowing what to expect. Edward stares intently at the beam of light. "Yesssssss!" he cries, excitedly. "You diiiid it!"

The sphere starts to tilt, sending the beam downwards, coming to rest parallel with the floor. Where it strikes the attic wall it seems to form what you can only describe as a doorway. A bright orange light penetrates from the other side of the portal, creating a haze that competes with the eerie green glow from the device.

"Goooooo, nooooow!!" Edward cries. "Goooooooo, befooore it isssss... .too late!"

Equal part terrified and fascinated, you step up to the shimmering doorway. The thrum of the machine pulses through your head. "Nooooooowww!" Edward cries from behind you. You consider the possibility of dashing to the attic stairs and getting as far away from this nightmare as you can, but before you can, Edward loses patience and pushes you through.

You stumble through the portal. Turn to **141**.

365

You've suffered too much at the whims of the mi-go to allow this creature take advantage of you any further. Your attack takes Yar'ith by surprise – the uncaring arrogance of these creatures seeming to make them susceptible to being unable to read your emotions. You manage to get one attack in, wounding Yar'ith. The mi-go turns on you, hissing...

Yar'ith (Mi-go Prisoner – Wounded)
Combat 5
Health 3

If the combat lasts to the *fourth* round, turn to **64**.
If you defeat Yar'ith in *three* rounds or less, turn to **292**.

366

There's a doorway to your right that you haven't seen any activity from, and decide that would be a possible way to escape. The mi-go guarding you seems uninterested in keeping its attention on you – perhaps it just assumes you wouldn't think of escaping. The skittish thing turns its back, giving you the opportunity you have been waiting for. You launch into an attack from behind, breaking its wing and then snapping one of its arms. With a sickening crunch, you pull it free from its socket. The unusual gun it was holding clatters off the floor and slides into the centre of the room.

Will you retrieve the gun (turn to **314**), or leave it and escape through the door on the right (turn to **424**)?

367

You pick up the journal and start flicking through the entries. It's a hand-written account of Peabody's work. The last entries are what interest you most.

> 14th September 1926
> I've decoded the equation! Now to use the numbers and see what happens. I knew that blasted book contained knowledge far beyond our understanding or reason – but I'll show those fools in Miskatonic now. Cowards, locking away secrets that would change our very existence. Bah! They'll be crawling at my feet soon... begging for the answers.
>
> 21st September 1926
> I'm close! I know it. The numbers are degrees for each dial!!! How did I not see it until now? 190 is not 190 degrees, its dial 1, 90 degrees, dial 2, 37 degrees, and dial 3, 121 degrees! Three-dimensional space! Dial 4, I have no reference for. I will leave that alone on zero. By my calculations I was only two degrees off as those dials are so sensitive. At this distance though (roughly 3 billion miles) two degrees is enough to miss the barn

right before you! I've made the adjustment – the next test should hit!!!!

23rd September 1926
I've managed to open it! GLORIOUS!!!! The lights! The glorious lights! Green and intense, yet somehow you can stare right at it without the need to blink. There's something on the other side. A room? Soon I can prepare for the crossing.

Record in your Investigator Journal '*Dial 1, 90 degrees, dial 2, 37 and dial 3, 121. Dial 4, leave alone.*' +5 *Mythos* points.

You don't find anything else of use. Mostly just rambling sentences about space and time and quantum theory.

If you haven't already done so, you can now look at the star charts (turn to **476**), or you can leave this room and search the rest of the house (turn to **252**).

368

Ahead of you are two tunnel openings in the wall. They don't appear to be carved, more like natural passages through the cave. One heads to the left and the other to the right.

To take the left tunnel, turn to **24**.
To take the right tunnel, turn to **527**.

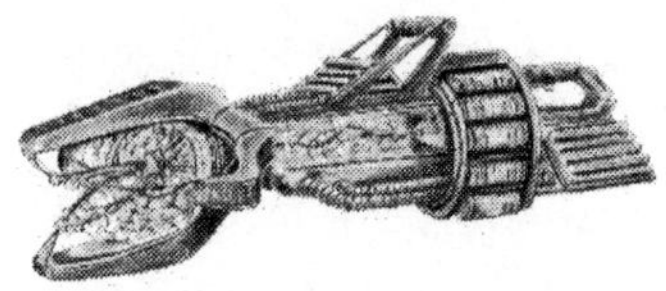

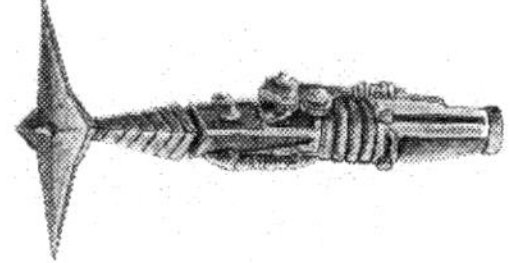

369

You gingerly follow the thing through the door, inquiring about what exactly it is.

"I'm Eugene. Pleased to meet you." it replies in a matter-of-fact manner.

Beyond the door is a laboratory. Rows of unidentifiable scientific equipment sit atop counters that run along the walls. The only exit is the door you came through. Three more of those walking brain cylinders are working at the counters, using their mechanical arms for mixing chemicals and operating the equipment – the purpose of which you couldn't begin to fathom.

Eugene announces your arrival to the rest of the brains. "Everyone, this is the intruder we were told about."

They gather behind you, blocking the door, then greet you in turn.

Eugene then turns to you. "We are scientists from Earth, experts in our field. What area of scientific study do you specialise in?" You tell Eugene that you're a reporter, and are here by mistake.

"Oh, well that explains the hubbub! All the same, we recommend getting out of that fragile body as soon as you can. You'll never survive up top in that skinsuit. This really is quite liberating, the mechanical body, I mean – and oh, the things we have learned! You're in luck, we have a spare right here. August Möbius has returned home." Eugene's mechanical arm points to the corner of the laboratory where an empty cylinder with mechanical legs lies unused. “There’s really no point in resisting…” adds Eugene. How will you get out of this situation?

Pretend to go along with the request and look for an opening to escape (turn to **480**), or threaten them to let you leave or you will attack them (turn to **315**).

370

As the door opens you're immediately surprised by a gush of air into your face. The air smells pungent. Beyond the door the metallic construction disappears completely, and instead this appears to be a large cavern formed of the black rock.

The cavern is lit by the soft blue bioluminescence of fungi covering the floor, walls, and ceiling, and blue algae also runs like veins up the cavern walls. There's an eerie beauty to it, but any sense of awe is quickly dispelled by the nature of your predicament.

A pool of still liquid blocks the path ahead. Water perhaps, you can't be sure. It glistens in the dim glow of the cavern.

On the far bank a roughhewn archway leads away out of the cavern into darkness beyond. There doesn't appear to be any cave fungi beyond that point to light the way. What do you do?

Head back and find another way. Turn to **107**.
Examine the pool of still water. Turn to **533**.
Examine the glowing fungi on a nearby wall. Turn to **538**.

371

You take a step forward, finding some reservoir of resolve and aim the flashlight directly at him. "Edward, you said. Are you Edward Turne?"

"Hrrrsssssssss... ..offffff!!!!" He turns about and tries to find a dark corner to retreat to, but there are none to hide in while you have the flashlight. His anger overcomes him, and he lashes out. The elongated arm and claw grasp you by the neck. You instinctively drop the flashlight and grip the claw with both hands to try and prise it open. The metal is cold to the touch.

"I saaaaid... ..OFFFFFFFFFFFFFFFFF!" he cries.

Make a Hard (2D6+1) **Strength** check.

If you pass, turn to **302**.
If you fail, turn to **320**.

372

You wander around looking for a vacancy sign, half expecting you won't find one given the run of poor luck the end of the trip has taken, but thankfully, you manage to find one. The landlords are a middle-aged couple. You apologize for the late hour, and explain your brief visit and the need to get off the road for the night.

After a late bite to eat and a long tiring day, you fall into an uneasy sleep.

That is, until you're suddenly awoken in the middle of the night. Turn to **168**.

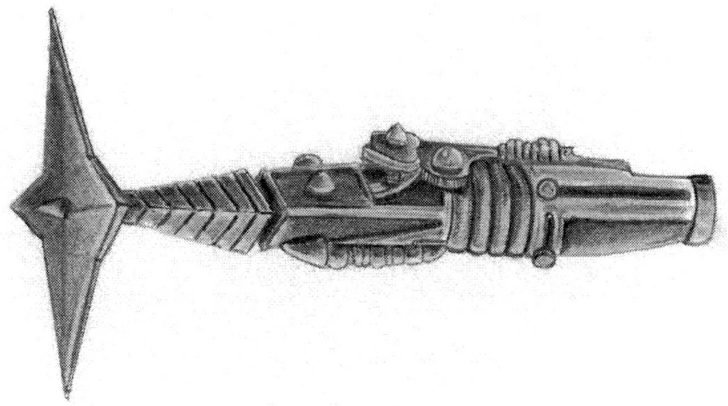

373

You ask about the way to Sentinel Hill.

"Ah, the old hill. House is still up there, too. Nasty business that. A blight on the landscape iffin you ask me. I haven't been out that way in years. And I'm sure it's even worse now." He looks you up and down for a moment, and then continues. "You a friend of that other chap, him that drives the truck?" he asks, his almost persistent smile fading away.

Not reading your confused expression, he continues.

"Another fellow. Much older than yourself, mind. He's been up at that house, oh, ages now, doing some work or whatever. A Mr. Smith. Never did catch his first name. Each time I sees him, he's less friendly again, and looking the worse for wear. Still, he's been here and back giving me the business. Filling his truck, I mean. So, I won't push those that want to be secretive."

Reply that you don't know who that man is, and ask again for directions (turn to **380**), or lie, and say the man is a colleague of yours. You're due to visit him up at the house, but lost the directions he had given you (turn to **584**).

374

He sighs heavily. "Very well," he replies. "Where would you like to start?"

Will you suggest the door to the basement (turn to **300**), the door at the foot of the stairs (turn to **332**), or the door at the end of the hallway (turn to **52**)?

375

You climb through into a disused kitchen. It certainly doesn't appear that anyone prepares meals here. With no other exits except a blocked up back door to the outside, you exit the kitchen into a dim hallway. Old picture frames line the wall on the right. The main staircase runs up on your left-hand side, and the hall ends with the front door leading outside. There's a door on your left that leads under the stairway (likely to the basement), and finally at the foot of the stairs is another door in the left-hand wall.

Where do you want to explore?
To try the basement door, turn to **78**.
To try the door at the foot of the stairs, turn to **499**.
If you want to go upstairs, turn to **131**.
Or if you'd rather stay put and call out to see if anyone is here, turn to **478**.

376

As you watch, a black amorphous blob of viscous slime appears over the crest of the mound of flesh and bone. It forms a new tentacle, retracts a previous one, and continues to morph and mould itself into different shapes as it glides down the mound, landing half-submerged into the soup of blood and other fluids. It's not much bigger than a large dog, but you watch with a breathless horror as it seems to form legs to raise its body up and out of the lake of blood.

Make a Regular (2D6) **Composure** check.

If you pass, you manage to remain calm enough to remain perfectly still. Turn to **153**.
If you fail, you are compelled to turn to flee. Turn to **106**.

377

As you reach the end of the corridor a door slides open. You step through into a large circular room about 50 feet in diameter with a high ceiling about 20 feet up. The air is damp and smells of mould. The walls here are made mostly from a black stone with only the doorways displaying a metallic sheen. A grey sponge-like material grows up from the floor and across the walls, obscuring much of the stone beneath.

Looking around, you see a variety of pillars of different sizes, each one roughly formed from the same black rock of the walls. At the top of each pillar is an opening through which a light mist is flowing out and blanketing the floor.

Finally, in the centre of the room is a circular well about 4 feet high, again carved from the stone.

You don't see any movement, but can hear the tell-tale signs of the denizens of this place – that strange buzzing sound reverberating through the air.

You see three possible exits. There's a door directly ahead across the chamber, and near it is a ramp that rises into an opening in the ceiling. To your right, mid-way across the floor is another door.

You evaluate your options.
Examine the grey growth on the walls. Turn to **284**.
Approach the well in the centre of the room. Turn to **327**.
Head for the door in the far opposite wall. Turn to **546**.
Head for the door over on the right-hand side. Turn to **7**.
Investigate the ramp going up to the next floor. Turn to **433**.

378

The professor gets a lucky blow in, knocking you down. You're momentarily dazed by the blow, giving the professor the opportunity to take the syringe from you and inject it into your back.

"I'm debating whether you're worth the effort, now," he says, leaning over you. Your vision blurs as the drug takes hold. Peabody continues talking, but his voice becomes an echo as you fall under. Turn to **120**.

379

"This is not for some curious fool who likes detective stories! This is far beyond any silly stories you've read or written about. This is the real science! The world will be changed forever! I just need more time."
He looks away, thinking for a moment. You wait expectantly.

"Very well... " he says, looking you up and down. "Yes... you'll do. Come back first thing tomorrow morning. Knock three times. I'm in no state to entertain... eh... guests, this night. I'll fill you in then, and if you have the stomach, and the mind for it, then perhaps you will be of use after all."

Record in your Investigators Journal '*You have been invited to the house*', and note the reference 215. +1 *Mythos* point.

You thank him profusely for chance to help him and promise to be back first thing tomorrow.

You return to the town, excited for tomorrow morning. Turn to **449**.

380

You explain to Pete that you don’t know anyone out here, and require directions because you are curious about the house due to the murders ten years ago.

“You some kinda reporter?” he asks, suddenly suspicious.

“No, no, nothing like that. Just interested in the stories.”

He hesitates before continuing. “Iffin you ask me, there is no-way, no-how, some young lad went and killed his own family in that way. I heard they were missing stuff. Like, the insides, eyes, and whatnot. A boy does that to his family? Pull the other one.”

He looks up, clearly thinking hard. “I'm sorry but I can't properly remember. I think you take the left fork for sure, but the path the house has been overgrown for years, so I don't right remember exactly where it was. Most folk that need help with their vehicles stay on the main roads.”

You thank him all the same. Looking around the town, evening is fast approaching.

It's time you got going on your way. You thank Pete once again for his help, and drive away. Turn to **557**.

381

You decide these creatures mean you nothing but harm, and you will not go quietly. They take your advance as a sign of following them and both creatures turn their backs on you. You have one surprise attack to give you an advantage.

Do you have a scalpel? If so, turn to **80**.

If you don't have a scalpel, you still manage to gain the upper hand and strike a solid blow to one of the creatures. Your intent known, the two beings turn towards you. You will have to fight them together.

Mi-go Worker 1
(wounded)
Combat 6
Health 2

Mi-go Worker 2
Combat 5
Health 4

If you win, turn to **265**.
If you lose, turn to **44**.

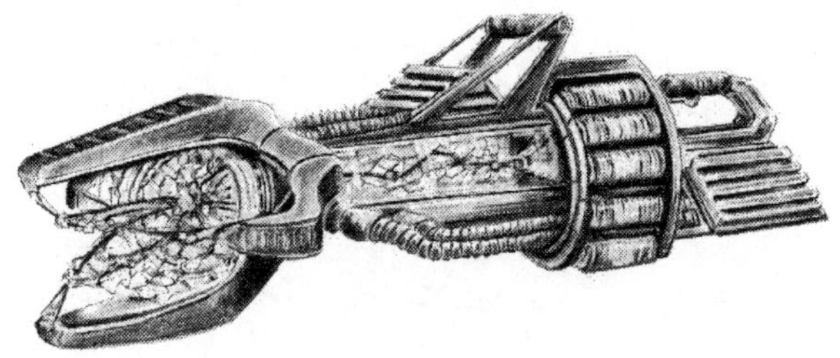

382

Staying close to the walls, you emerge from the ramp on to the first floor. The area is open and exposed, making it difficult to see hiding places. The ramp continues up, curving with the tower, before eventually disappearing out of view into a dark haze above. At various points along the ramp, you can just about make out a series of doors. You would be very exposed if you went any higher, so you decide against going up. Across the floor there is another door. What do you do?

Head back down the ramp and choose a less exposed path. Turn to **272**.
Stick close to the wall and make your way around to the other door. Turn to **248**.

383

A blast of lightning burns through the air from the tip of the gun, the kick sending you sliding backwards a few inches. Unlatha is enveloped by the twisting light. Her body convulses and crackles while smoke rises from her extremities. She collapses in a heap, her legs folding inwards in a vain attempt to protect her body. You fire again with a steady aim. Unlatha's body twitches one last time, then remains still. She is dead.

Edward runs in from behind you to his mother. She too, is dead.

"I'm sorry, Edward. But we must wake your father so we can try to get out of here." You grab the girl, Sara, and carry her into the chamber with the portal machine.

Record in your Investigator Journal '*Sara is alive.*' +20 *Mythos* points.

Placing her down next to the machine, you quickly return to help Edward. Turn to **54**.

384

You take the mushroom out of your satchel and hold it aloft. It's not as luminous as it first was then you picked it, but the soft glow is just enough to push back the suffocating darkness. You edge your way along the tunnel and eventually come to a pit in the floor of the tunnel. You can't see how far down it goes, and nor do you want to test it. There's an almost overwhelming stench of rotten meat rising from the pit. You carefully edge your way around it and carry on down the tunnel.

As you continue onwards, a light begins to form ahead at an opening. 'Not a moment too soon,' you say to yourself, as the glow from the mushroom fades completely.

You toss it aside and enter a wider tunnel. Turn to **136**.

385

Your wounds become too numerous as you desperately attempt to fight on. Each successful attack forces you to the edge of the walkway overlooking the larger cavern. The mi-go grabs you and starts to push you towards the walkway edge. With your last ounce of strength, you claw at its head, ripping a handful of the creature's feelers away. It tosses you off the end. A glancing strike off a lower walkway on the way down finishes you, snapping your back in half, before your lifeless body is swallowed up by a black river of slime that snakes its way along the bottom of the cavern.

Record in your Investigator Journal '*You died horribly, broken and discarded to the bottom of a vast cavern.*' -3 *Mythos* points.

Your investigation ends here.

386

This large flower stands out among the others due to the bright orange curled leaves. In its centre are dozens of blue filaments that sway slightly in a non-existent breeze. The rest of the flower is perfectly still. It gives off a strong odour, not unlike gasoline.

Will you examine the filaments more closely (turn to **524**)?
If you haven't already done so, you can examine the tallest plant (turn to **177**), or examine the cactus-like plant (turn to **190**)?
Alternatively, you can leave these strange plants and keep moving via the door in the opposite wall (turn to **370**).

387

You dart to the nearest door and impatiently wait for it to open. It does, and not a moment too soon. You dart inside and wait as the door closes behind you. Moments later you hear one of the creatures in the corridor. You wait with bated breath hoping the thing will leave... then the door opens!

You back into the room as the mi-go advances. "Huumaaan. Sssstop. No haaarm for yooou."
"Yesss... .cooome," its partner joins it from behind. You are now trapped, face-to-face with two mi-go.

Do you surrender and follow them (turn to **39**), or fight them off, suspecting they only mean you harm (turn to **506**)?

388

The track leads steadily upwards, twisting and turning through the blighted landscape. A tunnel of dead trees looms on either side of the trail. Despite the dull morning, you're immediately drawn to the sight between two twisted grey trees directly ahead of you.

The house.

Though the house stands atop the hill, the thickly knotted tree branches and dense lifeless briars lend the area almost complete privacy and inaccessibility, save for this one track you followed. The grey mottled wood panelling of the house seeps into the skyline behind, making the house look undefined, as though it were willing its surroundings to shadow it and hide it away.

Each of the downstairs windows are boarded up, with the upper floor windows in various states of disrepair. The attic window top and centre is the only fully intact window you can see. The front door also looks intact, though the porch is littered with loose timber wood panels, twigs, and other woodland debris. There is no sign at all of living vegetation. Dead crumbling creeper vines cling to the outer walls like grey varicose veins running upwards to the thatched roof. The roof tiles appear to be intact on this side, from what little visibility you're afforded on the ground.

The rain continues to beat down as you head up the porch steps, taking care not to trip over the myriad of loose branches littering the way. Thankful for the shelter, you stop to take a breath. Long streams of water run down each side of the porch and batter the muddy ground.

Check your Investigators Journal.
If you have you recorded '*You have been invited to the house*', you must turn to the reference noted with that entry now.

Or, if you have recorded '*You were warned to leave the house alone*', turn to the reference noted with that entry.

If you don't have either of these references you must choose one of the following instead.

You can knock on the door (turn to **212**), try the door to see if it is unlocked (turn to **160**), or head around the side of the house and look for another way in (turn to **502**).

389

Your thoughts wander as the tunnel continues to narrow. Is this petrifying city and cave truly undiscovered under the earth all this time? Or is it that all who have found their way down in the past – explorers, archaeologists, or just hapless wanderers such as yourself – have perished at the whims and instruments of these unrelenting insect creatures?

You become conscious of your heavy breathing and the sweat rolling down your brow. The heat is getting very uncomfortable the further you go.

You soon arrive a narrow crack in the rockface, just wide enough for you to pass through. On the opposite side is a sheer drop into another cavern below with signs of construction again. Below and to the right, a black river of slime flows away from you and disappears into a smooth walled building of stone on the opposite side.

If you have a cable that could be used as a rope, turn to **93**. Otherwise, you will have to find a way to climb down. Turn to **186**.

390

In a desperate attempt to survive, you launch yourself at the creatures.

For this combat you must defeat the creature armed with the metal rod first to prevent it firing on you. Only if you defeat it may you attack the second creature. The second creature stays back, allowing you to fight them one at a time.

If the mi-go with the metal rod rolls 11 or 12 for its **Attack** roll (*and* beats your **Attack Level**), then it manages to get off a shot, dealing you 3 Damage instead of just 1.

Mi-go Worker 1
(with metal rod, 11 or 12 – deals 3 Damage)
Combat 6
Health 5

After you defeat the first creature you can take this moment to escape by flinging yourself through one of the conveyor openings (turn to **110**).

If you decide to stay and fight the second mi-go, you must complete the battle as it manoeuvres itself between you and the possible escape route.

Mi-go Worker 2
Combat 7
Health 4

If you manage to win, turn to **339**.

391

You insert the two plugs into the sockets of the first cylinder and wait, unsure of what is supposed to happen. You are suddenly startled when a strange mechanical sounding male voice starts to speak from the connected speaker box.
"No! No! I don't want to be here anymore! Let me go, please!" The mechanical nature of the voice cannot hide the panic and distress of the speaker. With a whirring sound the lens turns in your direction.
"Who are you? Free me! Tell them I want to go back to my body! Or smash my accursed prison to the floor and let me die! Please let me go, or let me die!" The volume and pitch of the male voice rises to uncomfortable levels and starts to scream.

You attempt to respond but your meagre reassurances do little to keep it from getting louder. You pull the apparatus plugs from the cylinder, and mercifully the unnatural screaming noise cuts in an instant.

In the silence that follows, you then notice the skittering! It is the unmistakable sound of those vile mi-go coming this way. Thankfully just one of the creatures runs into the chamber, and upon seeing you it utters the words "Fooound the huuuman!" and immediately retreats to the central chamber. You rush to catch it, but it is too fast and disappears down the tunnel that is now to your left. You can't afford to be caught in a dead end.

You quickly cross through the chamber and exit via the tunnel on the opposite side. Turn to **437**.

392

The creature immediately turns, beak first, twisting around on that flexible neck, followed by the rest of its body. It walks on all fours with its wings acting as front legs.

The creature is a juvenile *Byakhee*. It appears to be wounded, likely a result from previous battles with the mi-go. Its beak is particularly vicious and if you are hit, you will take 2 Damage in an attack instead of the usual 1.

Juvenile Byakhee
Combat 7
Health 4

If you win, you can now search the area. Turn to **41**.

393

It gets closer and closer, to the point that it starts to disturb pieces of the piled-up bone and flesh you are hiding behind. Loose fragments roll down on top of you.

Make a Regular (2D6) **Composure** check.

If you fail, the fear of this monster is so great that you're compelled to run. Turn to **106**.
If you pass, you grit your teeth and remain perfectly still. Turn to **157**.

394

You pull out one of the solar system charts, noting that it's covered with annotations of equations and ruled lines converging to a point beyond Neptune. The area is marked with an 'X' and the text 'HERE?' is written next to it.

"Professor, what's the meaning of the marks on this chart?" you inquire, not looking up.
He approaches, making you wary.
"There's something out there. Something we haven't yet seen, but it's there," he says, pointing at the X. "I don't have time to explain. Come with me now to the attic and I'll show you."
"And the syringe?" you ask.
"Hang on to it if you wish. Makes no difference to me now."

Will you follow him upstairs now (turn to **229**), or if you haven't already done so you can look at the journal (turn to **16**)?

395

You begin to explain the nature of your arrival, when its head turns a deep red – then it attacks! With help from its wings to propel it forward, the creature's claws snap and scrape at you, cutting you badly as you try to defend yourself.

Lose 2 **Health** from the attack. You will have to fight the creature off or die trying...

Mi-go Worker
Combat 5
Health 4

If you win, turn to **278**.
If you are reduced to just 2 remaining health, turn to **457**.

396

You enter the pool and carefully start to wade across, feeling the way with your foot to avoid any unseen pits. The water is cool, but not too cold, and the ground remains even for the most part, but every now and then you feel a raised piece of rock and step over it. As you reach the halfway point, the water is up to your waist. It's then you feel something brush against your leg. There's something in this water!

Make a Regular (2D6) **Composure** check.

If you pass, turn to **234**.
If you fail, turn to **151**.

397

A restless sleep takes you as you lie against the cavern wall. The situation seems hopeless as you drift off. You're suddenly awoken by a familiar high-pitched squeal. You open your eyes to see a *Formless Spawn* moving through the bloody sludge. Another screech sounds off to your left, then another...

Three *Formless Spawn* writhe and contort their way towards you. You press yourself against the cavern wall, praying it will somehow give way and free you from this nightmare, but all that happens is a lightning-fast whip from one of the beasts catches you square in the forehead, smashing your skull against the wall. In seconds, as the life drains from your body, the creatures envelop you.

Record in your Investigator Journal '*You were devoured by Formless Spawn.*' -4 *Mythos* points.

Your investigation ends here.

398

You creep along, trying to stay in darkness. The rock formations create some natural cover, but could also provide hiding places for other lurking creatures. After a few moments you spot a large black shape moving across the cave floor. You freeze and wait in the hope that it hasn't seen you. A bulbous lumbering thing, about the size of a walrus, shifts its bulk over to one of the stalagmites and starts to feed on the fungus growing there. It stops, and loudly sniffs the air.

What do you want to do?

Continue to sneak past it and exit this cavern. Turn to **169**.
Wait and observe the beast some more. Turn to **454**.

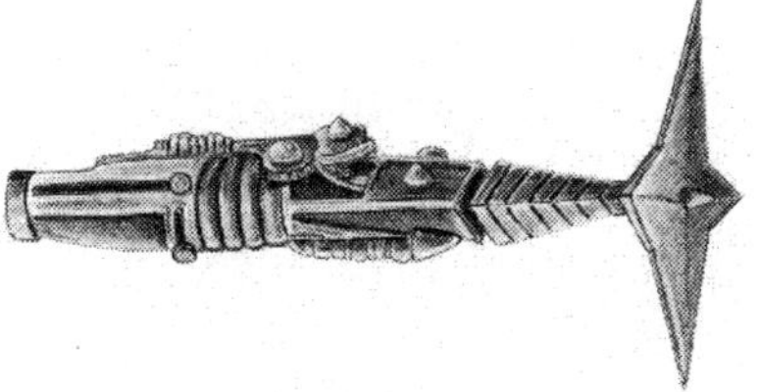

399

You wait, expectation building as the creature noisily makes its way down the tunnel towards you – then the door opens. Sweating profusely, you clench your fist waiting to strike.

The creature comes through the door...

Make a Regular (2D6) **Combat** check.

If you pass, turn to **171**.
If you fail, turn to **56**.

400

You rush to block Edward and cry out that Unlatha will kill him! But Unlatha is a creature of incredible speed… and she is upon you before you can get out. Looming over you, you properly 'see' her for the very first time. A fold of skin peels back on the front of her head to reveal a vaguely human-like skull. Her true face revealed, you hear her speak aloud. "Your blood will be sweeter than most, rebellious one!"

You'll have to face her with whatever weapon you've managed to find throughout your ordeal.

Unlatha is a formidable foe. She deals **2 Damage** each attack, but also gets *two attacks* for each one of yours. Each round, when you roll for your **Attack Level**, Unlatha gets *two* rolls against this due to her numerous leg-attacks and speed. For each one she succeeds at, you are hit and take 2 Damage. Therefore, it is possible for you to take up to 4 Damage in a single round.

While you engage with Unlatha, Edward moves to help his family.

Unlatha
(Daughter-Spawn of Atlach-Nacha)
Combat 10
Health 11

After two complete attack rounds, if you are still alive, turn to **324**.
If you are reduced to 0 health before the start of round three, turn to **240**.

401

Your refusal angers Yar'ith to the point that the mi-go attacks! "I will usssse your corpsseee... ", it hisses. As you fight Yar'ith off, neither of you notice the large dark shape descend from the mist on threads of silk. You block a blow from Yar'ith and get ready to strike back when suddenly a long spear-like appendage pierces Yar'ith's head, covering you in green mi-go blood. The spear is in fact the blade-like leg of a gigantic purple spider creature. With seven legs to spare, the bloated monstrosity wastes no time in repeating its attack on you. With a sickening squelch, your head is speared by a second leg, killing you instantly.

Record in your Investigator Journal '*You were killed by a Spider of Leng.*' -5 *Mythos* points.

Your investigation ends here.

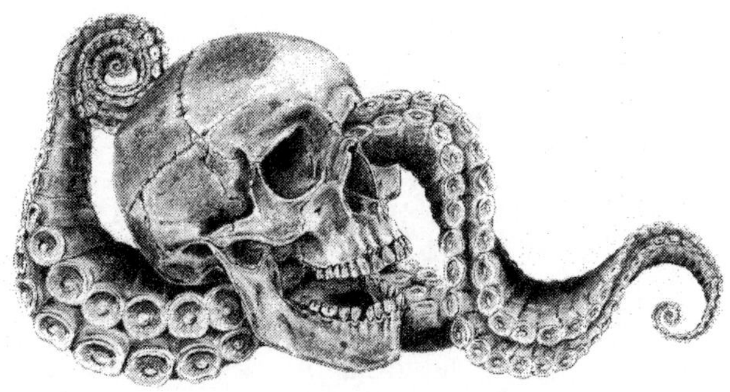

402

Despite the odds, you feel confident in your ability to take them out. You charge into the room and attack the mi-go that is attending to the table covered in various objects. Your strike catches it off-guard and slams the beast against the side of the table, wounding it badly.

The second mi-go is startled by the sudden attack and moves away.

You have 3 rounds of combat against the first creature before the second one can act. You can only attack this first mi-go in that time.

At the start of round 4, if you have *not* defeated the first mi-go, turn to **578**.

Mi-go Worker 1 (wounded)
Combat 6
Health 2

If you defeat the first mi-go in 3 rounds or less, you get the opportunity to attack the second. It moves to retrieve a metal rod from the shelf (a weapon perhaps?) but you engage it before it can utilise it.

Mi-go Worker 2
Combat 7
Health 4

If you defeat them both, turn to **262**.

403

You tell her you've known Professor Smith for years and have been called out here to help with the investigation at the house.
"Well why didn't you say so?" she replies. "It's not very well signposted. Carry on out of town and you'll come to a fork in the road, take the right fork, and from there you'll

see a few signs to help you on your way to the hill." She smiles broadly.

You thank her for her help.

When you get back to your car, the garage appears to have been locked up for the day. The evening light is fading. A cold breeze suddenly whips through the garage lot, blowing leaves up into a swirl. You turn up your collar against the cold and get into your car.

You can start the engine and drive on to find the house (turn to **557**), or call it a day and look for a lodging to get a fresh start in the morning (turn to **372**).

404

You stand back slightly and observe. He doesn't notice you, walks to the front of the car, then reaches down and the opens the hood.

Do you want to intervene now (turn to **208**), or wait some more (turn to **486**)?

405

You enter a short corridor that immediately turns left. There are two more doors here, one mid-way in the right-hand wall, and the second at the very end of the corridor, in the left-hand wall.

Try the door on the right. Turn to **197**.
Go past this door, and try the one at the end of the corridor. Turn to **105**.

406

Unable to avoid the blow, he plunges the syringe into your shoulder. "I'm debating whether you're worth the effort, now," he says, leaning over you.

Your vision blurs as the drug takes hold. Peabody continues to talk, but his voice becomes an echo as you fall under.

The drug has taken effect. Turn to **120**.

407

She turns about and looks you over again. "Bit young, aren't ya? Not like your friend. Tell me, do you know Professor Smith well?"

Make a Regular (2D6) **Perception** check.

If you pass, turn to **432**.
If you fail, turn to **403**.

408

You sprint across the room to engage the fleeing mi-go. These mi-go are slightly smaller than many you have encountered previously. They are mi-go scientists, and you hope they are less capable in combat. You catch up to the lone mi-go just before it reaches the door. It turns to face you knowing it will have to defend itself.

Mi-go Scientist
Combat 4
Health 4

If by the start of round *four* you have not defeated this mi-go, turn to **435**.
If you defeat it in *three* rounds or less, turn to **55**.

409

His lunge was off balance before it even began and so you manage to lean out of the way. He falls forward, landing on his hands and knees with a grunt. A syringe flies from his hand and rolls up the hallway.

Startled, you can take this opportunity to flee out the door (turn to **65**), or take advantage of your superior position right now – retrieve the syringe and then demand an explanation (turn to **201**).

410

You stop and try to remain perfectly still, listening and watching out for signs of movement. After a few moments, a black slimy tentacle slithers over the side of the mound to your left, followed by another, then another. Then, rising up behind it, a black amorphous blob of viscous slime appears over the crest of the mound of flesh and bone. It forms another tentacle, retracts a previous one, and continues to morph and mould itself into different shapes as it glides down the mound, landing half-submerged into the soup of blood and other fluids. It's not much bigger than a large dog, but you watch with a breathless horror as it seems to form legs to raise its body up and out of the lake of blood.

Make a Regular (2D6) **Composure** check.

If you pass, you manage to remain calm enough to remain perfectly still. Turn to **153**.
If you fail, you are compelled to turn to flee. Turn to **106**.

411

You wait for a possible opening, then make a desperate dash towards the door. You catch them unawares and miraculously manage to avoid the spinning claws.

You flee through the door as Eugene calls out "You'll die, old chap. Should have listened to us…" His voice dies off as the door shuts, but it's not long before it opens again. They are coming after you. You immediately take the exit on your left and leave the area. Turn to **437**.

412

You turn and flee down the ramp and through the door nearest the base of it, hoping you can evade the creatures. To your relief, you haven't run straight into the path of more of these nightmares, and scanning your location you see a potential hiding place here. A large square platform dominates the room, and on it sit a wide variety of potted plants of truly unusual shapes, sizes, and colours. You duck behind the platform hoping to be obscured by the plants, and wait.

You hear the subtle sound of the door opening, followed by the clacking of feet on the hard floor. The creatures don't speak. The door opens and closes once more. You wait, listening intently... nothing.

As you stand up to peek over the counter, a bright orange flower with large curling petals lets out a sharp hiss and sprays a mist of spores into your face.

Make a Hard (2D6+1) **Health** check.

If you failed, turn to **334**.

If you passed, you cough as the spores attempt to fill your lungs and sting your eyes. Though you manage to escape the worst of the effects, you must still lose 1 **Dexterity** for the slightly debilitating effect.

You decide that you must press on. Carefully avoiding getting close to any of the plants, you head for the door on the opposite side of the room. Turn to **370**.

413

You explain that you never asked for him to touch your car, and will not pay. He stands eying you for a moment, then says, "Suit yourself."

He folds open the hood, flips the wrench up, and adjusts something down inside the engine. You can't see what.

“Don’t worry,” he says. “I’ve only gone and put it back to how it was. Now, iffin you don’t mind, good day to ya!” He heads into his office, and shuts the door. The battered lock bounces and clangs as the door is pulled hard behind him.

You glance up and down the street. No one is around, and in the fading light the place seems uninviting. A cold breeze suddenly whips through the garage lot, blowing leaves up into a swirl. You turn up your collar and get into your car. Your vehicle got you all this way, so you’re not expecting any problems.

You drive on. Turn to **557**.

414

Yar'ith shows little interest in any of the possible weapons you have. "Weee mussst dissstract the feeder!" Yar'ith says, pointing a claw upwards into the mist.

Will you offer to distract the 'feeder', as Yar’ith calls it (turn to **468**), or suggest that Yar'ith distract the feeder while you retrieve the *Tok’llian* (turn to **264**)?

415

You simply can't trust this mi-go creature and turn to flee. Yar'ith's head turns almost black with rage. "Huuman... you will dieee here and become feed for Cxaxuklutha." The mi-go's words echo in your head as you quickly drop down each of the cavern steps. It does not pursue.

At the next junction, you turn left towards the river. Arriving back at the river edge, you turn left along the rock ledge and follow the river flow. Turn to **204**.

416

You approach a window in the wall to your left. It's almost large enough to fit a car through. The black sky is cloudless, but you can't see any stars. You look to the horizon, but all you see are endless black stone towers spearing the landscape like needles. Tiny figures appear to move erratically through openings in the towers, and out into the starless sky. A dreadful fear envelops you. You feel that something has seen you, knows you're here but you should not be. You're a cancer in their midst and must be cut out. Thoughts, screams, a voice... it all echoes in your head. "Helllp ussssss... " You fall to your knees as pain grips your skull. The things, the unknown things are coming for you, and you know it will be your end.

Make a Hard (2D6+1) **Composure** check. If you fail, deduct 1 from your current Composure. If you pass there is no effect.

Record in your Investigator Journal that '*You dreamt of an alien terror that will pursue you until you die.*' +4 *Mythos* points.

You wake up. Turn to **500**.

417

As you approach the bookcase, Peabody remarks, "We don't have time for this."

The shelves are lined with books on scientific theories, physics, space, gravity, and even some on human anatomy. Then, things get a little stranger – books on occult spells, incantations, books in Latin and various other odd volumes.

"Interesting reading material, professor."

"Like I said, I really don't have time for this. Either take that, now," he gestures at the syringe, "and you'll get your explanations, or put it away. You haven't heeded my warning, but I'll leave that up to you now. Come."

He waits for your response.

Give in and take the sedative. Turn to **303**.
Follow him upstairs. Turn to **229**.
Or if you haven't already, you can examine the items on the desk. Turn to **214**.

418

You turn the third dial to what you would believe to be 90 degrees.

How do you want to set the fourth dial?

To leave it as it is, set to 17 degrees, turn to **70**.
To set it to 100 degrees, turn to **364**.
To set it to zero degrees, turn to **447**.

419

Edward falls to his knees, tears running down his cheeks. You've managed to save Sara and Jacob from the hell on Yuggoth.

You remain with the family for a time, masquerading as helpful stranger that Edward sought on the road when the family took ill from a strange malady. Both you and Edward agree to deny anything happened other than his father falling ill with an unknown sickness of the mind. The disappearance of Melissa is decided upon as having left Jacob. It wasn't ideal, but it was the only way to keep the questions to a minimum. You both bury the machine deep in the woods.

Jacob, the father, is a changed man. Moments of lucidity reveal details of a visit to the hills of Vermont, where he discovered the machine, and some unusual individuals that showed him how to use it to help his farm prosper. But not much else he speaks of is worth delving into. You know it contains a hideous truth – of the mi-go and their possible influence on Earth – but you cannot allow those thoughts to become threads of a new story... for you, too, might eventually go hopelessly mad. Over time, Edward thanks you for your help, but soon the need for a doctor is discussed.

The date is October 11th, 1916. The newspaper clipping that brought you here remains as before, but tells a story that is no longer what happened. Your car is gone... or never existed. Only that which you brought with you to Yuggoth and back, remains as it was. The machine was more than just a way to traverse across space, it also had the power to transcend time. Edward and Sara hadn't aged because it sent you to Yuggoth ten years in the past – possibly only moments after they themselves had arrived. Now you realise just how powerful this device was for the mi-go, and why they were so tenacious in trying to recover the lost power source.

You settle in the town of Durham, get a job working as a store clerk for Mrs. Wilkins, and remain there as both support for the family you saved, and as a way to stay away from... yourself. A young reporter by the name of Frank Winston starts to write an article for the *Arkham Gazette*, which you have delivered by post especially to your door.

On September the 23rd, around 4:45 p.m., in the year 1926, you stand on the main road of Durham and wait for a Chevrolet to trundle down the road. You contemplated writing to yourself, anonymously of course, as a warning to stay away... but instead felt that you would simply be compelling the other version of yourself to question the warning and turn up anyway. When you thought about it, you know that is what you would have done.

No one arrives... there are no strange flashes of green lightning, and no voice on the air. The killings never happened, the article was never written, and thus the other version of yourself remained in Arkham writing for the paper. It is highly unlikely that your paths will ever cross.

If you have recorded in your Investigator Journal '*Received a gift*', then you must turn to the reference associated with that entry now.

If you do not have this entry, turn to **36**.

420

The creatures are preoccupied with their duties while you make your way down to the open doorway and choose the ideal moment to strike.

If you have a scalpel, you can ready it and get an advantage in the fight. Turn to **183**.
If don't have one, you can still choose your moment to get a free strike and attack. Turn to **402**.
Or change your mind against these odds, and try and silently exit the corridor. Turn to **74**.

421

He manages to jab a syringe into your chest. You let out a cry and pull it out as he backs away again. "What on earth?" you shout, confused.

The professor stands back, emotionless, as your vision blurs.

You fall to your knees, then black out. Turn to **120**.

422

You approach the large rectangular slabs. They are featureless and set low, close to the floor, but held up by a single column of metal underneath. As you get closer to the nearest slab it starts to move of its own accord, silently tilting up and forward as though your very presence has activated it. You wait to see what will happen, and when it's almost standing upright it stops. Suddenly the flat smooth surface morphs as the embossed shape of a man appears impressed into the metal. You feel compelled to approach it, and as you do you turn to face away from it and lie back into the man-shaped impression. Your head screams no, but your body disobeys. You can't move, locked somehow to the slab as it starts to tilt back to its original horizontal position. Your eyes close of their own accord, and suddenly you feel a presence by your side, standing over you. You can't open your eyes – they rest in a small container next to the metal slab. Your left arm is cut away, then your right foot, and then your ribcage is opened to the air. Finally, your brain is set down next to your eyes.

Make a Hard (2D6+1) **Composure** check. If you fail, deduct 1 from your current Composure. If you pass, there is no effect.

Record in your Investigator Journal *'You dreamt of being dissected by an unknown presence.'* +4 *Mythos* points.

You wake. Turn to **500**.

423

With a sudden lump in your throat at the thought that there may be someone under the bed, you quickly leap out and drop into a crouch to check. Nothing. A final flash of green light pours through the open window.

The voice, much fainter now, as though it were travelling on the wind, speaks one last time. "Cooome, Fraaaank. You... ..promised... ."

The speaker knows your name.

You approach the window. There is no one in the street. The sky fills again with a flash of the sickly green light. In the distance you see a hill and perched atop, the silhouette of the house. Could that be the source of the light? You wait, expecting more. Your heart rate eases, and nothing more is said. It's only then you notice the chill of the air blowing into the room and quickly latch the window closed as one last flash floods the room with a green haze.

You turn to get back into bed, but find it gone. Turn to **569**.

424

The mi-go soldier twitches on the floor. You rush towards the door on the right and as it opens you stop in your tracks. There's no walkway or other path. It's a sheer drop into a massive cavern that is swarming with hundreds of working mi-go, mining ore.

The door behind you opens as a group of mi-go enter. On seeing their dying companion in the centre of the room, the other soldier mi-go advance. They fire their lightning guns, filling the chamber with crackling light and energy. You are blasted off of your feet, through the doorway, and fall hundreds of feet to your death in the massive cavern as the swarms of mi-go look on curiously.

Record in your Investigator Journal '*You were shot and fell hundreds of feet to your death.*' -3 *Mythos* points.

Your investigation ends here.

425

The tool whirrs as it unlocks the panel in the wall, causing it to slide to the side. Behind the panel you discover a journal! Incredibly, it is a journal of human origin. You flick through it and notice it's in German. There are various diagrams and drawings of strange devices (some of which you now recognise from this laboratory), then something catches your eye. It's the machine from the attic! Detailed sketches follow of its components, and on one page you make a startling discovery. The coordinates you used to arrive here are displayed, and beneath those is the word 'Heimat', followed by another set of coordinates.

Record in your Investigator Journal '*You know how to get home*', and note two separate reference numbers carefully. The *first* is 535. The *second* is 254. If asked about this entry later, be sure to confirm you go the correct reference mentioned, the first, or the second. +15 *Mythos* points.

You place the journal in your satchel and leave the lab. Back in the main chamber you see the two remaining walking brain cylinders near a tunnel to your right. You immediately take the exit on your left and leave the area. Turn to **437**.

426

Equal parts terrified and fascinated, you step up to the shimmering doorway. The thrum of the machine pulses through your head. "Nooooooowww!" Edward cries from behind you. You reach out to touch it, but consider instead the possibility of dashing to the attic stairs and getting as far away from this nightmare as you can.

Suddenly, a strange bulbous head covered in multitudes of short writhing feelers or antennae, steps out of the light. Almost as large as a man, its body is a sickly pink colour, with a carapace similar to a crustacean, and two large insect-like wings protruding from its back. It has six limbs in total, two of which are large and fully formed arms, ending in vicious looking claws, two are legs with sharp pointed feet, and finally the remaining two are smaller middle limbs that fold into its torso. It appears to be comfortable on both two legs and on all-fours, using its clawed arms as front legs. Its whole body also seems to be constantly vibrating or resonating, creating a slight blur of movement which makes it difficult for you to fully focus on it as it moves about. It is a deeply unsettling sight.

Make a Very Hard (2D6+2) **Composure** check. If you fail, deduct 2 from your current Composure. If you pass, you still lose 1 Composure as both this terrifying sight and situation leaves a lasting impression on your psyche.

The doorway begins to fade, perhaps it is closing? Edward cries "It'ssss themmmm! The miii-gooo!! I willll ssstay! Goooo Fraaank... " He moves quickly and engages the creature. Before you can protest and consider an escape from this nightmarish situation, he lunges past the beast

swatting it aside.
"Huuumaaaansss! Forbidden!" the creature utters in a bizarre and unnatural buzzing tone. "Mi-gooo will not allooow passssage! Giiive us the poower souurce... the *Tok'llian*."
Edward holds the beast at bay with his elongated arm and claw and pushes you through the doorway. "Gooooo! Ssssave themmm!"

You stumble through the portal, terrified. Turn to **464**.

427

You take a run and manage to grip the edge of the walkway. Now comes the difficult part – you must try and pull yourself up.

Make a Hard (2D6+1) **Strength** check.

If you pass, turn to **84**.
If you fail, turn to **515**.

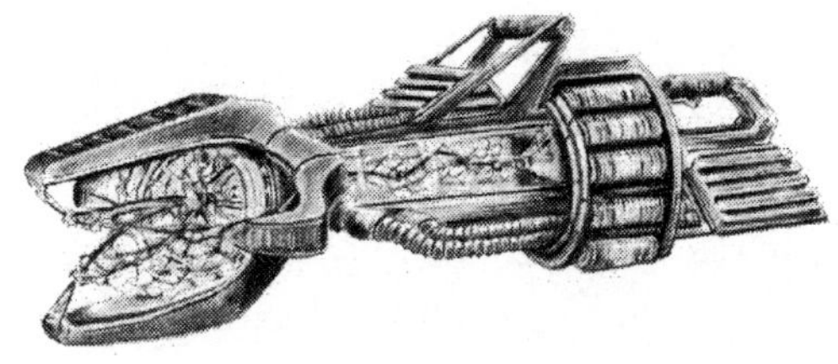

428

You take the right fork and continue on. The tree line starts to thin out a little when you arrive at another turn.

You can continue straight on. Turn to **357**.
Or take the turn to the right. Turn to **563**.

429

The second creature falls dead at your feet. Green ichor pools beneath the bodies as they lie in a heap, legs and arms curled inward. You look around, exhausted.

You don't think you can continually fight your way out of this place and will need to use your head. You attempt a search for the gun but with no success.

You decide to press on and cross the pool (turn to **396**).

430

It's a difficult and troubling conversation with both Jacob and Melissa as you attempt to recount the situation.

Jacob, the father, is a changed man. Moments of lucidity reveal details of a visit to the hills of Vermont, where he discovered the machine, and some unusual individuals that showed him how to use it to help his farm prosper. But not much else he speaks of is worth delving into. You know it contains a hideous truth – of the mi-go and their possible influence on Earth – but you cannot allow those thoughts to become threads of a new story... for you, too, might eventually go hopelessly mad. Over time, Melissa thanks you for your help, but soon the need for a doctor is discussed. The loss of Edward weighs heavily on her mind, but his bravery will not be forgotten.

The date is October 11th, 1916. The newspaper clipping that brought you here remains as before, but tells a story that is no longer what happened. Your car is gone... or never existed. Only that which you brought with you to Yuggoth and back, remains as it was. The machine was more than just a way to traverse across space, it also had the power to transcend time. Edward and Sara hadn't aged because it sent you to Yuggoth ten years in the past – possibly only moments after they themselves had arrived. Now you realise just how powerful this device was for the mi-go, and why they were so tenacious in trying to recover the lost power source.

You settle in the town of Durham, get a job working as a store clerk for Mrs. Wilkins, and remain there as both support for the remaining family you saved, and as a way to stay away from... yourself. A young reporter by the name of Frank Winston starts to write an article for the *Arkham Gazette*, which you have delivered by post especially to your door.

On September the 23rd, around 4:45 p.m., in the year 1926, you stand on the main road of Durham and wait for a Chevrolet to trundle down the road. You contemplated writing to yourself, anonymously of course, as a warning to stay away... but instead felt that you would simply be compelling some version of yourself to question the warning and turn up anyway. When you thought about it, you know that is what you would have done.

No one arrives... there are no strange flashes of green lightning, and no voice on the air. The killings never happened, the article was never written, and thus the other version of yourself remained in Arkham writing for the paper. It is highly unlikely that your paths will ever cross.

If you have recorded in your Investigator Journal '*Received a gift*', then you must turn to the reference associated with that entry now.

If you do not have that entry, turn to **36**.

431

A restless sleep takes you as you lie against the cavern wall. The situation seems hopeless as you drift off. You're suddenly awoken by a familiar high-pitched squeal. You open your eyes to see a *Formless Spawn* moving through the bloody sludge. Another screech sounds off to your left, then another...

Three *Formless Spawn* writhe and contort their way towards you. You press yourself against the cavern wall, praying it will somehow give way and free you from this nightmare, and suddenly find yourself lifted from the sludge and up the cavern wall! Fearing this is the end, you try to resist, but as you look up a familiar voice speaks in your mind.

"Be still, human... " says Unlatha. "I return to you the gift of freedom."

Held fast by her two front legs, Unlatha carries you up to the ceiling. It itself a scarily precarious feeling, it is nevertheless a welcome one as the *Formless Spawn* disperse into the cavern below. She slips both you and her bulk through a chute opening, climbing up until you both emerge into a tunnel above. You thank her, and feel truly grateful for this most unusual ally.

"A careless human will not survive here. Mi-go do not traverse these caves... more dangerous creatures do. Beware the cave of silken thread." And with that, Unlatha once again displays her impressive speed, disappearing into the darkness in seconds.

You're left alone in a narrow tunnel, and decide to head in the same direction she left. Turn to **136**.

432

"Smith? I think you mean Professor Albert Peabody, don't you?", you reply, remembering the name from the news article.

She smiles.

"Sorry, guess I'm getting my names mixed up. Ah yes, that's the fellow! He comes in from time to time in his truck. Always ordering the strangest of stuff from me. Don't suppose you'll tell me what it is you lot are doing up there in that old house, huh?" She appears to have perked up. Any hint of a suspicious nature has faded, replaced by an inquiring mind. You tell her that it's secret stuff, strictly hush-hush. She sighs, and falls silent.

Record in your Investigator Journal that '*You know who is in the house*', and note the reference 333.

What do you want to ask her?

Inquire about the types of items the professor has ordered. Turn to **53**.

Or you can ask for directions to the house on the hill. Turn to **549**.

433

The ramp is of metal construction and built into the rock. As you approach it, the buzzing in the air gets louder. It appears to be coming from the floor above. Sneaking a look upwards you see it opens out into a much grander chamber above. The black walls rise until they disappear into shadow above. This is some kind of huge tower, and you're currently at its base. With those creatures populating this place, you feel caution at every step is required.

Will you sneak up the ramp to the floor above (turn to **92**), or decide to check the door at the base of the ramp (turn to **546**)?

434

You make to move to the other side of the room, but stop dead in your tracks when you hear that dreaded clacking sound of mi-go feet in the tunnel. They pass the side tunnel, cutting off your escape with guns poised. There's nowhere to run from them, so you raise your hands in surrender, hoping they understand the gesture.

Captured, the mi-go lead you away. Turn to **39**.

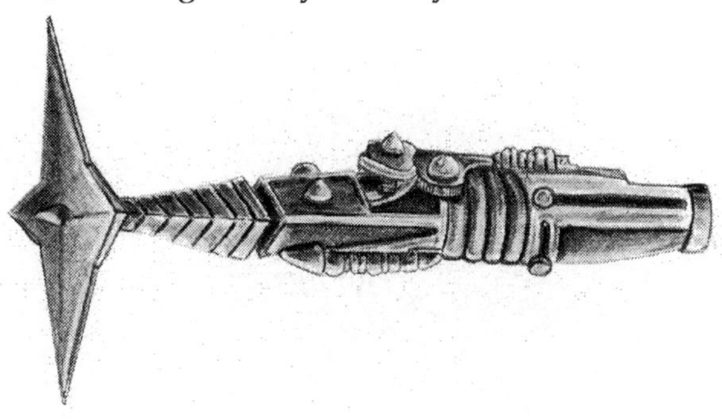

435

While you continue to fight the creature, the other two mi-go surround you.

You've no choice but to let it go and turn to the other two that have engaged you. The first mi-go sees the opportunity and flees through the door. You must face this other pair of mi-go together. Both attack at the same time.

Mi-go Scientist 1	**Mi-go Scientist 2**
Combat 4	Combat 5
Health 5	Health 3

If by the start of round *six* you have not defeated them both, turn to **336**.
If you win by round *five*, turn to **188**.

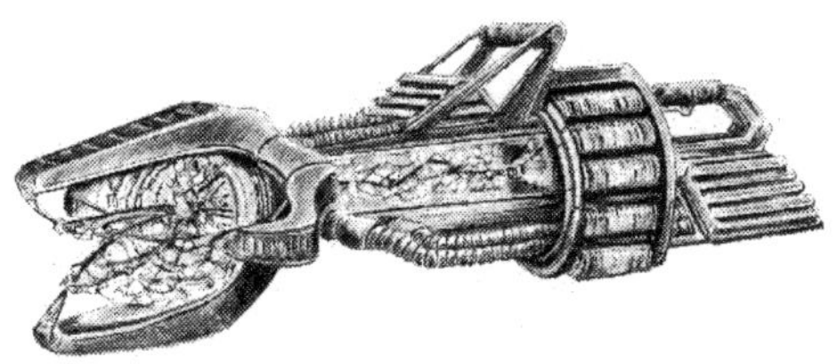

436

You pluck one of the mushrooms from the wall. To your surprise it retains its glow. You place the mushroom into your satchel.

Record in your Investigators Journal '*Have a glowing mushroom*', and note the reference 384.

You can move on and cross the pool of water, turn to **396**.
Or head back and find another way, turn to **107**.

437

The passage leads up, almost becoming a climb, but you're pleased to be going up rather than down. The tunnel widens quicky into a humid, sweet-smelling chamber with a ceiling nearly fifty feet high. The light is dim, emanating weakly from strands of fungus that grows across the floor and chamber walls. However, here, there is something new.

Covering the walls and floor are translucent orbs. Each one is about four feet in diameter, and on closer inspection they appear to be… *mi-go eggs*. Inside the translucent egg-casing you see a long thin worm-like larva. The tell-tale sign of a mi-go is the head. Even in larval form you see that the head changes colour and are beginning to form those horrid feelers. Small stubs are also forming where the legs and other limbs will be, and two large nubs on the back will become the wings. You place your hand lightly against the casing. The larva reacts to your touch with an audible jolt as it twists within the egg. You instinctively recoil. Feeling uneasy surrounded by this brood, you want to press on.

If you have recorded in your Investigator Journal '*Released a black slime creature*', then you must turn to the reference associated with that entry now.

If not, you carefully make your way through the eggs to the opposite side. Turn to **530**.

438

Your car bumps and jostles along the road, when suddenly you hear loud hissing sound coming from under the bonnet. A moment later, a gush of steam is expelled from the front of the car as it slows to a crawl. You take your foot off the gas and curse your bad luck as you pull in as close to the road edge as you can. You knock the engine off and step out. The radiator has overheated. You open the side panel, wincing as a bellow of steam flows out, forcing you to back away wafting the air. It'll need to be left alone to cool down. You ponder the situation for a while, looking both ways up and down the road. The light is fading fast. You decide the only option is to limp the car back to Durham. Turn to **127**.

439

You creep through the slop and offal, moving around to your right as you listen to the creature crawl up the opposite side of the mound.

Make an Easy (2D6-1) **Stealth** check.

If you fail, your movements through the soup of blood become too noisy. You stop as the creature comes closer. Turn to **410**.

If you pass, you manage to circumvent the mound and put more distance between you and the creature. Whatever it was, it moves away and disappears further into the cavern. You slowly continue onward. Turn to **519**.

440

You look around at the debris, but there doesn't appear to be anything potentially useful. The only way you would know for sure is to properly search through it. You're about to consider what to do next when you're suddenly startled by the screeching of the flying beast.

It has spotted you. Turn to **392**.

441

One window in particular looks to be quite poorly boarded up. You grip a board and attempt to pull it away.

Make a Regular (2D6) **Strength** check. If you pass, you manage to pull a board free, and then there's less effort required for the remaining planks. With the window cleared, you are free to climb in (turn to **375**).

If you fail, you can't work the board loose and must do one of the following instead:

Continue heading around the house towards the back of the house (turn to **568**), head back and knock on the door (turn to **212**), or head back and try open the front door (turn to **160**).

442

You pop the lid of each one and briefly smell it.

The black liquid has a sharp spicy smell.
The yellow liquid has a sweet fragrant smell.
And the red liquid, it's colour immediately causing you to pause before smelling, smells awful, like body odour.

Each one is looks to be quite viscous. What do you want to do?
If you taste the black liquid, turn to **271**.
If you taste the yellow liquid, turn to **443**.
If you taste the red liquid, turn to **258**.
Decide against trying these, as they could be poisonous, or the product of whatever it is these monsters do with the entrails. To head for the other door, turn to **105**.

443

After a brief taste you find it to be surprisingly sweet and refreshing. You immediately want more! It's nourishing and helps relieve some of the exhaustion you've been feeling.

Gain 4 **Health** and 2 **Composure**.
If you haven't already, you can try one of the others.

To try the black one, turn to **271**.
To try the red one, turn to **258**.
Or if you're finished with the containers, you can now leave the room and try the door at the end of the corridor. Turn to **105**.

444

Jacob charges wildly out of the room back into the tunnel and the huge cavern beyond. Edward pleads for him to return but it is to no avail. The door closes, shutting off his cries.
"Edward, he'll unwittingly alert the rest of the mi-go... we have to leave *now*!"
Edward nods, tears streaming in his eyes, and turns with you to the machine.

Record in your Investigator Journal '*Jacob has perished.*' -20 *Mythos* points.

Edward examines the machine. "It won't turn on!" he says, frantically turning the dials.
You step in and find the slot for the power source – the *Tok'llian*. You explain to Edward that is it required to power the device. Do you have it?

If you have recorded in your Investigator Journal '*Found the Tok'llian'*, then you must turn to the **FIRST** reference associated with that entry now.

If you do not have the *Tok'llian,* turn to **509**.

445

Turning the cube over and over, you find a diamond symbol etched into one side. You rub your thumb across the symbol and watch in amazement as the cube open almost flower-like, splitting into diamond-shaped panels and forming a flat metal star which you place on the cave floor. In its centre is a small glowing diamond-shaped jewel which illuminates the entire cave. It pulsates with a similar green light to the device that brought you here. The *Tok'llian*! This is what Edward used to activate the machine at the house. You press on the symbol and watch in amazement as the cube reforms around the *Tok'llian,* then place the cube back in your satchel.

Record in your Investigators Journal '*Found the Tok'llian*'. Note the two separate reference numbers carefully. The *first* is 232. The *second* is 572. +25 *Mythos* points.

You get to your feet and press on. Turn to **389**.

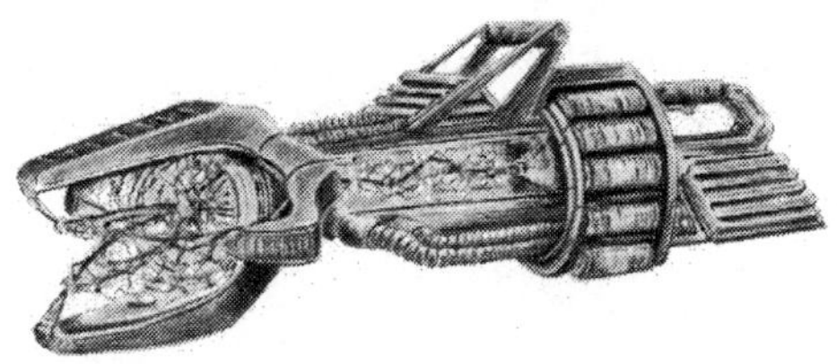

446

You clumsily attempt to pass over the third conveyor when a piece of bone falls noisily to the floor. You freeze, holding your breath, then when nothing appears to happen, you continue.

Suddenly a metal shard embeds itself into the conveyor where you stumbled just a moment ago. You look up to see two mi-go, one of which is aiming a metal rod at you, moving quickly along the walkway. They both leap and glide down, landing in front of you. You have just two choices here – fight, or flight.

Make a desperate dash for the opening where the nearest conveyor belt disappears into the wall. Turn to **110**.
Or turn and face the creatures in battle. Turn to **390**.

447

You set the fourth dial to zero and step back from the device. Suddenly a bright flash of green light shoots upwards from the sphere atop the machine. A low thrum pulses in the air, and the light flickers, slowly at first, then faster and faster until it becomes a solid beam firing upwards. You back away, not knowing what to expect. Edward stares intently at the beam of light. "Yesssssss!" he cries, excitedly. "You diiiid it!"

The sphere starts to tilt, sending the beam downwards, coming to rest parallel with the floor. Where it strikes the attic wall it seems to form what you can only describe as a doorway. However, you cannot see through it, there is nothing but darkness on the other side.

"Goooooo, nooooow!!" Edward cries. "Goooooooo, befooore it isssss... .too late!"

Equal part terrified and fascinated, you step up to the shimmering doorway. The thrum of the machine pulses through your head. "Noooooooowww!" Edward cries from behind you. You consider the possibility of dashing to the attic stairs and getting as far away from this nightmare as you can, but before you can, Edward loses patience and pushes you through.

You stumble through the portal. Turn to **490**.

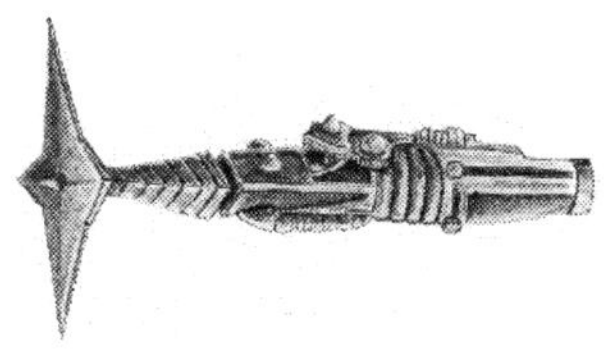

448

You keep low and move slowly to avoid alerting the creature to your presence.

Make a Regular (2D6) **Stealth** check.

If you pass, turn to **338**.
If you fail, turn to **219**.

449

Back in Durham you wander around looking for a vacancy sign. Thankfully, you manage to find one. Apologizing for the late hour to the landlady, you explain your brief visit and the need to get off the road for the night. The friendly middle-aged woman who, along with her husband, is happy to offer lodgings to visitors of Durham.
"You're a sight for sore eyes, young man. We haven't had a lodger in six months!"

After a late bite to eat and a long tiring, and trying, day, you fall into an uneasy sleep.

That is, until you're suddenly awoken in the middle of the night. Turn to **168**.

450

You try to recall the settings that got you here and set each one to the best of your recollection. When you get to the last dial, you move it, then recalling the machine in the attic, you set it back to zero again. The machine bursts into life. The low thrum starts up as you move away and clamber to your feet. The beam of green light shoots up from the sphere on top just like it had done in the attic of the house. It then bends downwards to rest parallel with the floor, striking the wall to form a shimmering portal. The entire room is bathed in the eerie pulsating light. It's difficult to see through the haze of the portal.

You rush back to Edward and explain how you can all leave this hellish place. Just as you are trying to convince him that you can help carry his unconscious family members into the portal chamber, the door on the opposite side opens – and in swarms a horde of mi-go. You're out of time!

You grab Edward and tell him you must flee. He refuses. You tell him that you'll come back for his family, but he doesn't listen. He turns on the mi-go and wades into them swinging his lethal arm. You turn and run as a blast from a lightning gun ionizes the air!

With one final push, you leap through the portal... and into the cold blackness of space. The machine was set incorrectly.

Record in your Investigator Journal '*You died in the cold blackness of space.*' -30 *Mythos* points.

Your investigation ends here.

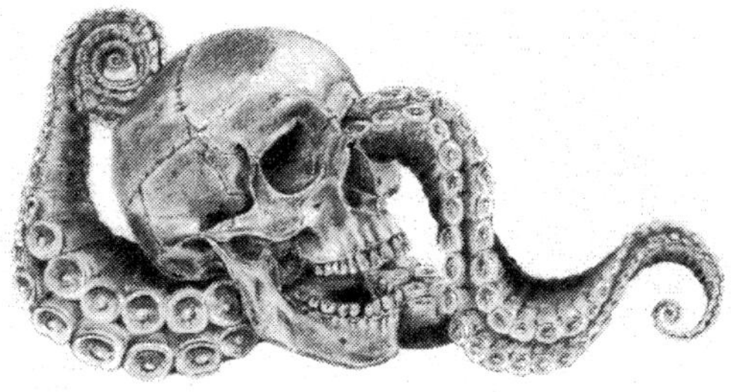

451

With the door fully ajar, you step into the hallway. The dusty unkempt interior is dark as very little light can penetrate in behind you. Looking around, you see a door immediately to your right at the foot of the stairs. Old picture frames line the wall on the left. Facing you at the end of the hallway is another door. Finally, there's a door under the stairs which likely leads to the basement.

You wonder if the intrusion might be pushing it and don't wish to explore too far. Will you call out to see if the professor is here (turn to **548**), or try the nearest door on your right (turn to **343**)?

452

You approach the window. There is no one in the street. The sky fills again with a flash of the sickly green light. In the distance you see a hill and perched atop, the silhouette of the house. Could that be the source of the light?

The voice, much fainter now, as though it were travelling on the wind, speaks one last time. "Cooome, Fraaaank. You... ..promised... ."

The speaker knows your name.

You wait, expecting more. Your heart rate eases, and nothing more is said. It's only then you notice the chill of the air blowing in the room and quickly latch the window closed as one last flash of light floods the room with a green haze.

You turn to get back into bed, but find it gone. Turn to **569**.

453

You step out, ready to fight these creatures, but they have other ideas. One of the creatures points a rod of metal at you. Fearing a possible weapon, you look for somewhere to hide, but it's too late. A thin shard of metal flies from the rod and pierces your shoulder, sending you stumbling backwards. You fall against the disc machine and to your horror get caught in its blast. Your flesh melts from your bones almost instantly. You've barely time to cry out in pain before the end comes.

Record in your Investigator Journal '*You died horribly, speared by a projectile weapon, then melted by a mining machine.*' -5 *Mythos* points.

Your investigation ends here.

454

The creature feasts on the various fungi for a few moments, then moves away. As you watch, it disappears into a smaller opening in the wall that is possibly its lair.

You decide this would be a good time to leave the cavern. Turn to **147**.

455

You emerge into a long circular tunnel. The walls of the tunnel are smoother, and every few feet a small green light has been set into the rock above. This tunnel is about twelve feet in diameter and is not a natural formation. It has been carved out with machinery. These creatures, whatever they are, are quite industrious.

You travel onwards down the tunnel until another branch appears to the left. Straight ahead the rows of lights continue then the tunnel bends to the right, preventing you from seeing too far ahead. Here at the side tunnel, you can't see very far at all, as there are no lights set into this tunnel. Which path do you take?

To continue straight on following the lights (turn to **312**), or take the branch on the left where there are no lights (turn to **2**).

456

You grab the claw and charge.
While using the claw you add 2 to Combat and 1 to the Damage you deal (for a total of 2 Damage each attack). Despite having this weapon, Unlatha is a formidable foe. She deals **2 Damage** each attack, but also gets *two attacks* for each one of yours.

Each round, when you roll for your **Attack Level**, Unlatha gets two rolls against this due to her numerous leg attacks and speed. For each one she succeeds at, you are hit and take 2 Damage. Therefore, it is possible for you to take up to 4 Damage in a single round.

Unlatha turns to face you, and for the first time you truly *see* her. Folds of skin peel back from her head to reveal a vaguely humanoid-like skull beneath. Her true visage revealed, you hear her speak aloud. "Your blood will be sweeter than most, rebellious one!"

While you engage with Unlatha, Edward moves to help his family. Record the number of rounds during this combat.

Unlatha
(Daughter-Spawn of Atlach-Nacha)
Combat 10
Health 11

If you are still alive by the start of the *fourth* attack round, turn to **324**.
If you are reduced to 0 health before the start of round *four*, turn to **240**.

457

You try to fight the horrid beast off, but its multiple limbs claw and scrape at you from various angles. You can't keep it at bay. Falling to one knee, you are unable to resist much longer. Rather than press the advantage, the creature backs away. Behind it two more mi-go appear. Your vision starts to fade, and terror overwhelms you as you are surrounded.

You await a killing blow, but it doesn't arrive. Instead, you are dragged away screaming. You are still clinging to life as the creatures begin to experiment on you, slicing off body parts, before you pass out.

You awake with a strange sensation and cannot feel your arms or legs. Turn to **564**.

458

You attempt to grasp the creature as it bores its way into your cheek. It's wet and slimy and difficult to grip, so you squeeze to get a proper hold of it and pull it away, resulting in both terrible pain and a tearing of flesh. You scream loudly as it comes away with a sickening squelch as the skin on your cheek is torn apart.

Lose 3 **Health** and deduct 1 from your current **Composure**.

If you survive, you toss the horrid thing back into the pool. Cursing your luck, this place, and why you insisted on investigating that accursed house, you struggle onwards.

The only exit is ahead through the natural archway, deeper into the cave. Turn to **455**.

459

Behind the huge disc you find what appears to be a control panel. Two metal bars are set either side of the panel for leverage and turning the device. A large lever protrudes from the panel.

Do you want to try and push the lever up (turn to **282**), or leave the machine alone and cross the conveyor belts (turn to **61**)?

460

You approach one of the displays for a closer look. The plant life is highly unusual looking. Bright and garish colours, strange, twisted shapes, and huge types of fungus can be seen within. Looking for movement, something catches your eye. A large insect, but the likes of which you have never seen, with huge, curled antennae and a stinger about four inches long, runs up the stalk of one of the plants. There doesn't appear to be any other type of creature in this display. What do you want to do?

Decide against lingering in this bizarre place and leave through the door at the end. Turn to **174**.
Examine another display. Turn to **534**.

461

With the last of your strength, you try to force the creature away from you, but to no avail. You fall across the conveyor as the mi-go slices at your flesh. Its claw pierces your eye socket and plucks your eye clean out. You've barely the strength to scream as it repeats this with your second eye. Slowly but surely the creature takes what it wants, and discards the rest of your dying body on the conveyor. You lie there dying as the conveyor is turned back on... then the end comes as you are plunged down a chute to join the other rotten remains.

Record in your Investigator Journal '*You died horribly mutilated by a mi-go.*' -2 *Mythos* points.

Your investigation ends here.

462

You rush out and advance to attack, but the creature is faster than you anticipated. The mi-go whips around almost immediately, its head turning a deep red. It lets out a shrill cry unlike what you've heard before from these monsters and prepares to defend itself.

Now you must finish it off.

For this combat, you must record the number of rounds it takes to fight the creature. If you haven't won (or lost) by the start of round *seven*, turn to **239**.

Mi-go Worker
Combat 6
Health 5

If you win in *six* rounds or less, turn to **30**.
If you lose in *six* rounds or less, turn to **461**.

463

Taking a chance with the door furthest from you, you reach it and impatiently wait for it to open. It opens, but almost simultaneously the door you came from opens behind you. You're standing there at one end of the corridor with a mi-go at the other end. It lets out a shrill cry and points its crab-like claw in your direction. The mi-go's head turns a bright yellow.

What are you going to do?

Launch yourself at the creature and attack. Turn to **531**.
Turn and flee though the open door. Turn to **294**.

464

A searing light and high-pitched squeal makes you grip your head, but it passes as quickly as it began. You stand there motionless until your senses reattune themselves, then you look around.

You are in a small dark room. Only a faint glow of light from a source you can't pinpoint makes it possible to see. The air here has a strange dampness to it, not quite fetid, but unpleasant all the same. The walls are plain, but appear to be made of a polished metal similar to the device that brought you here. You get a strange sense of *deja vu*.

Directly behind you there is no sign of the portal that brought you here, but instead you see two small pedestals about five feet apart. It would seem the doorway formed between them, but there is no other clue to their function. They are the only feature in the entire room.

The wall to the left and the wall on your right each have a large circular indentation about 7 feet in diameter. Likely they are each a doorway. Whatever this building or structure is, it is surprisingly barren of decor and other features.

Your mind goes back to the encounter in the attic, and you shudder at the thought of that creature, then curse Edward for forcing you through the portal. The hideous creature called itself a 'mi-go'.

You take a deep breath.

'Find his family,' Edward had said. Were they abducted and

brought here? But according to the article they are dead. It was ten years ago!

You won't find answers standing around, so you decide you've no other option than to figure out exactly where you are, and find a way back home. You do not expect to find any remains of the family, unless he expects you to bring their bodies back... and you shudder at the thought.

Record in your Investigator Journal '*You have passed through the portal.*' +10 *Mythos* points.

How do you want to start your search?

Try the door in the left-hand wall. Turn to **62**.
Try the door in the right-hand wall. Turn to **79**.

465

Nyarlathotep places a huge hand across your forehead. You try to recoil but are held fast by his indomitable will.

Suddenly, your mind becomes focused and sharper than ever before. Restore your **Composure** to its initial level and regain 3 **Health**. However, you feel less agile and must decrease your **Dexterity** by 1.

The void falls away like curtain tumbling to the floor. Turn to **344**.

466

Your thoughts linger for a moment at the hopelessness of your situation. No one will ever find you if you die down here...

Record in your Investigator Journal '*Been inside the cavern*', and note the reference 496.

You push yourself on, ever wearier. Turn to **481**.

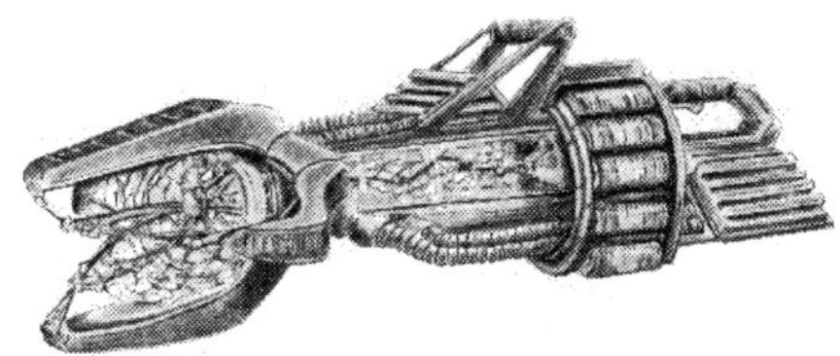

467

You turn the third dial to what you would believe to be 47 degrees.

How do you want to set the fourth dial?

To leave it as it is, set to 17 degrees, turn to **70**.
To set it to 100 degrees, turn to **364**.
To set it to zero degrees, turn to **447**.

468

Yar'ith's head changes to a mix of green and yellow at your offer to distract the creature in the mist. It suggests you rush towards the right-hand side of the cavern and disturb as many threads as possible, giving Yar'ith time to retrieve the *Tok'llian*. You wince, as it seems Yar'ith's plan is nothing more than to send you to your death while it escapes with the *Tok'llian*. Your mi-go 'ally' is as cold and uncaring as you suspected. You know this so-called plan is suicide and your options are limited.

What will you do?

If you still agree to go along with this plan, turn to **551**.
To refuse again and insist that Yar'ith be the distraction, turn to **401**.
If you wish to attack Yar'ith while its guard is down – the mi-go simply can't be trusted, turn to **365**.
Or flee! To head back down the stepped tunnel and find your own way out of this nightmare, turn to **415**.

469

As you get closer you see that the glint is from a metal cube. Without touching any of the threads, you bend down slowly to retrieve it. It sits in a small pool of green slime that clings to the cube as you pull it away from the ground. You suspect the slime is all that remains of a mi-go. Brushing it off, you place the cube into your satchel.

Yar'ith has realised too late what your plan has been. You glance back and see the mi-go crouch low and enter the cavern, its head the tell-tale deep red of an enraged mi-go as it skitters with surprising speed across the cavern floor.

Suddenly, a wrong move by the mi-go sees it ensnared by one of the threads. It sticks like glue to the creature, and as it thrashes about, Yar'ith becomes hopelessly entangled. Silently, like a shadow of death, a giant vaguely spider-like thing flows down from the mist and envelops the writhing mi-go. The visage of this bloated purple monstrosity bores into your very soul.

If you have recorded in your journal '*Been inside the cavern*', then you do not need to make a composure check. If you do not have this entry, make an Extreme (2D6+3) **Composure** check. If you fail, you must lose 2 Composure. If you pass, lose 1 Composure.

You turn away and head for the exit, praying that this thing finds enough sport in Yar'ith to allow you to go unnoticed. You manage to reach the other side without incident and exit the cavern.

When you believe it's safe, you stop to examine the cube. Turn to **445**.

470

The walkway begins to extend to your right, but also angles downwards and joins with a lower platform that leads back into the main structure. You quickly follow it, trying to stay out of sight.

You exit the cavern from this lower floor walkway. Turn to **170**.

471

The lab is a baffling array of scientific equipment and chemicals, none of which you have any knowledge of. However, as you search, you notice a wall panel with a star-shaped indentation set into it.

If you have recorded in your Investigator Journal '*Have a star-shaped tool*', then turn to the **SECOND** reference associated with that entry now.

If you do not have this entry, you leave the lab and return to the larger chamber. Back in the main chamber you see the two remaining walking brain cylinders near a tunnel to your right. You immediately take the exit on your left and leave the area. Turn to **437**.

472

The knocker squeaks and squeals as you lift it and knock on the door. Moments pass, and you're about to knock again when suddenly the door swings open. The professor stands in the doorway, wearing the same clothes he was in last night. He looks dishevelled, as though he didn't sleep.

"Hello? Sorry to intrude, but I had to come. I'm only here to... "
"Help me?", he cuts you off.
"Yes, listen, I wanted to... "
"Very well," he cuts in again as he takes a step to the side and gestures you to enter.
You gingerly move forward and pass him over the threshold. It's then you are surprised by a sudden sting in your shoulder. You stagger forward a little, reach back, and pull out an empty syringe. The professor stands there, emotionless, as everything fades to back.

Now, turn to **120**.

473

The years roll by, and on the 8th of February, 1930, the end comes. Though unbeknownst to you, the date has a special significance. It is mankind's discovery of the planet Pluto, or as you know it... *Yuggoth.*

On the evening of the 8th, you retire for night in your home on Church Street in Durham, when an incessant knocking on your front door bids you up again.

A very tall man, dressed all in black, stands motionless and silent in the doorway. You ask if you could help the stranger, and suggest that if lodgings are required, then perhaps the Bradburys (the very people you stayed with on the night of arriving in Durham all those years ago), could accommodate him. His silence is unsettling, his visage, unnerving. He seems familiar, or that is to say, invokes a familiar air of menace that you have near forgotten. You move to close the door, bidding the stranger good tidings and apologising that you could not be of help... but instead he reaches out a long arm, his long fingers coiling around the door, and steps in.

"Until such a time as your kind see... I, Nyarlathotep, offer this, to thee."

In a flash you know of this man, when he was not a man, you know why he has come, and what the price is going to be for taking his gift so willingly. The Crawling Chaos, Nyarlathotep, is here to settle a debt...

You are found three days later by your boss, Mrs. Wilkins from the general store. You hadn't turned up for work and she was worried. You lay in the middle of the hallway, just behind the front door, with a look of frozen terror on your face. The cause of death was put down to a heart attack.

Record in your Investigator Journal '*Your life was claimed by the Crawling Chaos as payment for your gift.*' -50 *Mythos* points.

Your debt was paid, and your story ends here. Now, turn to **586**.

474

The chamber here is a dead end, but would seem to be a guard station, perhaps for the protection of the egg chamber behind you. Numerous large containers, each with a yellow sweet-smelling liquid, line a low shelf on the wall to your right. On your left sit a variety of odd-looking contraptions, possibly for maintaining the care of the eggs, but you cannot be sure. You glance back down the tunnel, wary that the mi-go could return at any time.

What do you want to do?

Examine the strange contraptions. Turn to **33**.
Taste the sweet-smelling yellow liquid. Turn to **567**.
Leave and make for the side tunnel while you still can. Turn to **138**.

475

You place the head of the tool into the star-shaped recess and find it is a perfect fit. With a press of the button, it spins and with a click, the forearm detaches from the suit and drops to the floor. You pick it up and examine it. There's room to place your forearm through. You try it to find it fits well enough, with a grip on the inside that when twisted causes a vicious blade to unsheathe from the aperture. This is a lucky find as this could be quite lethal in a fight.

Record in your journal that you have a *Forearm Blade*. While using this in combat, you can add both 1 to your Combat skill, and 1 to the Damage you deal (for a total of 2 Damage each attack). Note that you cannot use it in conjunction with any other weapon. Its reinforced construction also adds 1 to your Strength during any Strength Check you attempt while you are using it.

You feel much safer armed with this formidable weapon and gain 1 **Composure**.

Now, if you haven't already done so, you can examine the skinsuits (turn to **45**), or continue onwards through the door in the far wall (turn to **317**).

476

You pull out one of the solar system charts and see that it's covered with annotations of equations and ruled lines converging to a point beyond Neptune. The area is marked with an 'X'. There's not much else written that clarifies what this means, but it is alluding to something beyond Neptune. +2 *Mythos* points.

If you haven't already done so, you can now pick up the hand-written journal (turn to **367**), or you can leave this room and search the rest of the house (turn to **252**).

477

You show the clipping and explain your interest in folklore and unexplained mysteries.
"You're so curious you've come all the way out here to see an old ruin?" He reaches into his coat pocket. "That doesn't sound right to me. Did the university send you?"

Lie and say, yes, you're from the university and they've sent you to help with the investigation. Turn to **273**.
Insist that you're not from the university, and instead simply wanted to discover the mystery of what happened ten years ago. Turn to **379**.

478

"You're trespassing, lad."
Draped in darkness, a figure stands on the landing above looking down at you. You apologise, but explain that you had to come in out of the rain, and had been looking for the house. The man descends the stairs, slowly. When he comes into the dim light of the hallway below you can see he is around late fifties, about five-foot-five in height, and

unshaven. Balding at the crown of his head, his remaining grey hair is a little long and unkempt.

"Sorry to bother you, sir. Frank Winston. I write for the *Arkham Gazette* and... "
"Arkham, you say? ARKHAM? Did the university send you?"

Arkham? University? "You're Professor Peabody, from the Miskatonic University?" you ask, putting the pieces together.
"Aye!"

You explain that you aren't associated with the university at all, and show him the news clipping.

"Best you come on up then, Frank from Arkham," his manner suddenly becoming more pleasant.

You get a sudden rush of excitement and follow him up the stairs. When you reach the top, he gestures for you to head on past him. You turn and continue on when suddenly you get a sharp pain in your back. The professor has stuck a syringe in you when your back was turned. You let out a cry while trying to reach back and pull it out. "What on earth?" you shout, confused. The professor stands back, emotionless, as your vision blurs.

You fall to your knees, then black out. Turn to **120**.

479

You turn the first dial to what you would believe to be 100 degrees.

How do you want to set the second dial?

To set it to 45 degrees, turn to **521**.
To set it to 121 degrees, turn to **247**.
To set it to 37 degrees, turn to **362**.

480

"What would I need to do?" you ask, feigning compliance.
"Ah, splendid, splendid. Avoiding bloodshed is our number one priority. Isn't it, team?"
"Yes, quite."
"Indubitably!"
"Indeed." Answer the three other 'scientists' in turn. Eugene moves towards the inert machine in the corner. One of the brains walks back to its station, leaving a possible gap to the door.

What will you do?
Make a dash for the door now a gap has opened up (turn to **491**), or threaten them to let you go or you will attack (turn to **315**).
Alternatively, if you have an explosive seed, you may use it on the two walking brains guarding the door. Turn to **279**.

481

The passage descends and opens into another huge cavern. You are standing on a narrow ledge overlooking a chasm fifty feet across. Below is a black underground river of slime snaking its way slowly through cavern, flowing away to the left. You suspect (or hope) it could eventually lead out of this hell hole. It's also a lot hotter here, the humid air is more difficult to breathe at times. The ledge looks wide enough to traverse safely.

Will you head left along the ledge, following the river flow (turn to **204**), or head right instead, against the river flow (turn to **297**)?

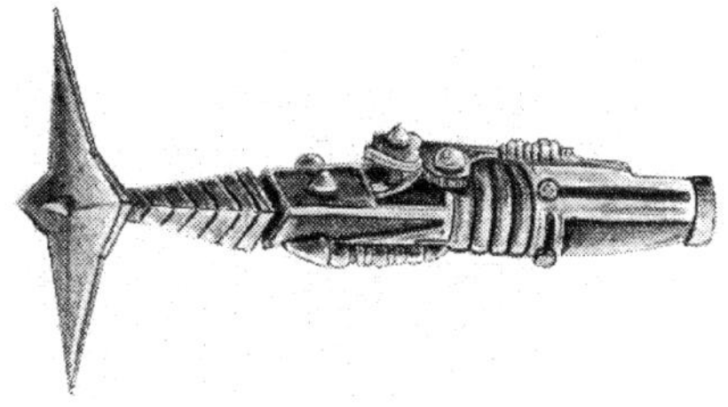

482

The lone mi-go takes the opportunity and flees through the door as you face the other two mi-go. Both attack at the same time.

Mi-go Scientist 1	**Mi-go Scientist 2**
Combat 4	Combat 5
Health 5	Health 3

If by the start of round *six* you have not defeated them both, turn to **336**.
If you win by round *five*, turn to **188**.

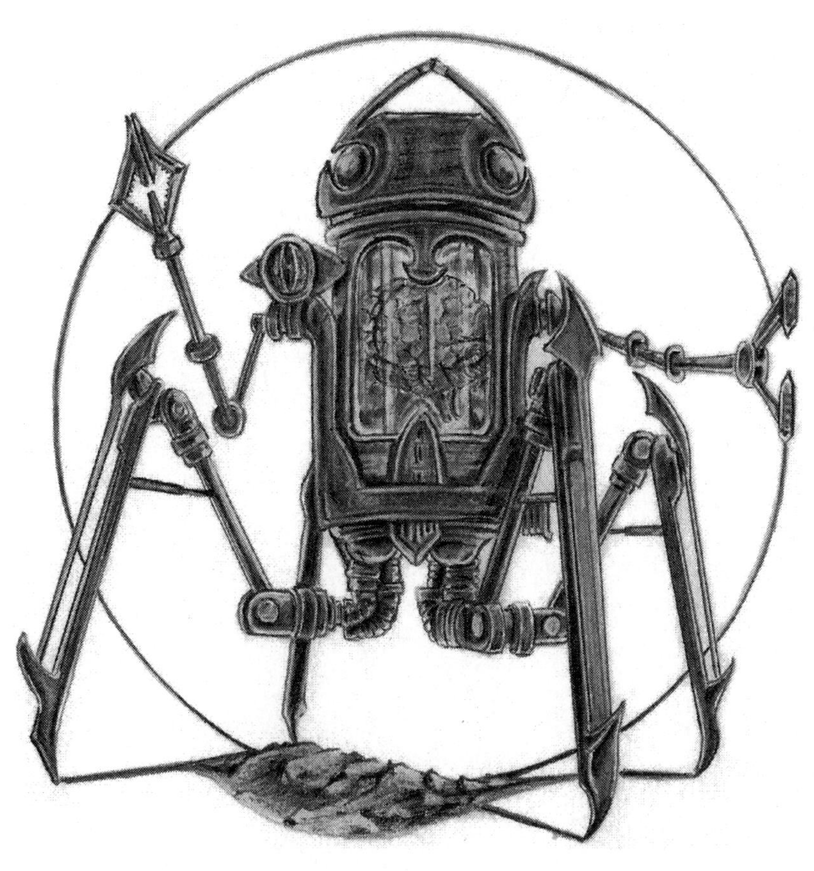

483

As you approach the door, it suddenly opens – but not because of your proximity. What you see coming through the door makes you step back in horror. A brain encased in a transparent cylinder sits on top of a mechanical walking frame with four legs. This walking brain stands about four feet high, with two articulated arms ending with metal claws for performing tasks. There's also a small open tube attached to the right-hand side, and on the left is an oval-shaped lens.

Make a Very Hard (2D6+2) **Composure** check. If you fail, lose 1 Composure. If you pass there is no effect.

The thing stops. The lens tilts and rotates to point directly at you. Then the thing speaks English in a strange metallic voice that emanates from the tube. "There you are! You have caused quite the stir among our benefactors. Follow me, please." It turns on the spot and walks back through the oval door, stopping in the doorway before speaking again. "Come, my good man." it gestures with its robotic arm.

Will you follow it through the door (turn to **369**), or turn and flee (turn to **577**)?

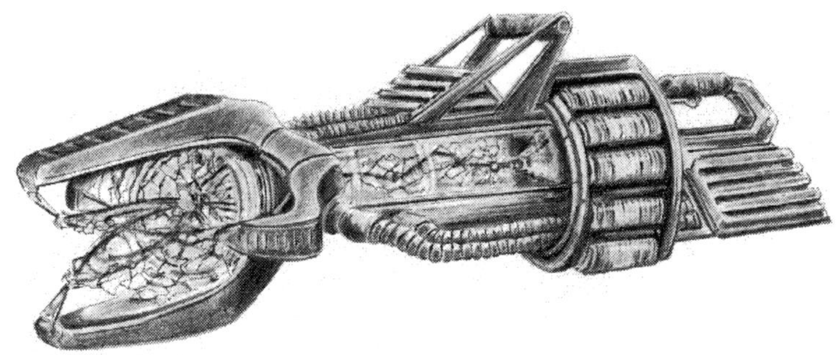

484

The door opens into a large kitchen that encompasses the whole back of the house; however, it is as expected, in poor condition. It doesn't look as though anyone prepares meals here. The counters and table are covered in dust, with numerous cobwebs stretching in all directions. There's nothing useful here. Now what?

Try the basement door. Turn to **78**.
The door at the foot of the stairs. Turn to **499**.
Head up the stairs. Turn to **131**.
Or call out and see if anyone is here. Turn to **478**.

485

You tell her that you're familiar with the stories about the house, and thought you'd look for yourself as you've always had a keen interest in such things.
"Oh, I see." She turns to face you. "Not stories though, sir. Fact. That Turne boy, bad 'un he was. He even gave Reverend Downe a tough time. The reverend left soon after the killings, never seen him since. But then, I suppose you know all of this already? Thing is, you can't go up there. No one is allowed, you see. So sorry you wasted your time. If you make a start home, perhaps you make it before it gets too late. Now if you'll excuse me!"
You return to your car. The town is quieter than ever, and the garage door appears to have been locked up for the evening.

What will you do now?
Drive on and search for the house. Turn to **557**.
Call it a day – look for a lodging and get a fresh start in the morning. Turn to **372**.

486

The man bends over your car and appears to put his hands down into the engine. You hear a clang of metal. You can't quite make out what he's doing now.

Now do you wish to intervene (turn to **208**), or wait and see what else he does (turn to **221**)?

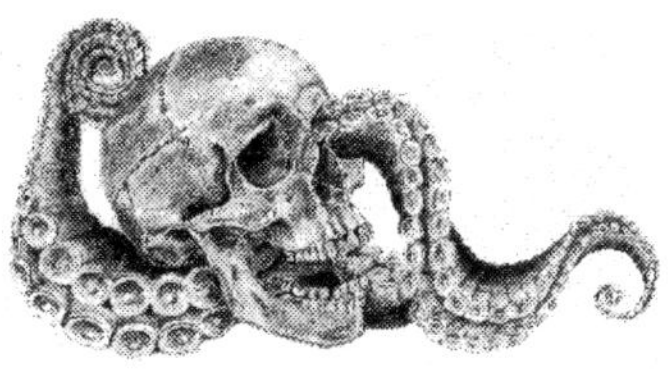

487

You strike the mi-go as hard as possible with the metal rod, but the blunt object is less effective than you had hoped. The wounded creature turns sharply, forcing you to jump back and avoid its menacing claws. Still, you've managed to inflict some damage before the fight, and now you must finish it off, or die in the attempt.

This mi-go is unlike the others you have encountered. It has a broad carapace and four fully formed arms ending in huge claws, instead of the usual two clawed arms with two smaller utility arms the other mi-go have. The extra limbs and claws are capable of dealing 1 extra Damage to you for each round you lose against it.

Mi-go Guard (wounded)
Combat 8
Health 6

If you win, turn to **562**.

488

Despite the risk of being discovered, you head into the tunnel in an attempt to get to the next junction without being spotted.

Make a Very Hard (2D6+2) **Stealth** check.

If you pass, you successfully reach the junction without being spotted and, after checking that it is clear, you turn and head that way. Turn to **138**.
If you fail, turn to **14**.

489

You turn dial two to what you would believe to be 37 degrees.

How do you want to set dial three?

To leave it as it is, set on zero, turn to **25**.
To set it to 90 degrees, turn to **418**.
To set it to 121 degrees, turn to **556**.
To set it to 47 degrees, turn to **467**.

490

A quick flash forces your eyes shut, then you open them again as you emerge on the other side. The air from your lungs is sucked out instantly, the bitter cold and blackness of space freezing your insides. Your eyes bulge as the blood vessels in your body explode – you die almost instantly, drifting forever in the vast emptiness of space. Your calculations were wrong!

Record in your Investigator Journal '*You went through the portal and died in the vacuum of space.*' -3 *Mythos* points.

Your investigation ends here.

491

You charge towards the door in an attempt to escape.

Make an Easy (2D6-1) **Dexterity** check.

If you pass, turn to **411**.
If you fail, turn to **296**.

492

Nyarlathotep places a huge hand across your forehead. You try to recoil but are held fast by his indomitable will.

You feel strange, and yet, more capable. It comes and goes, a bit like being in a daze then followed by moments of absolute clarity.

The gift bestowed upon you means that all attribute and skill checks you make from now on will be *Regular* checks (no modifier). Make a note of this in your Investigator Journal. Remember that while this means you benefit from *Hard* and more difficult checks, it also means that easier checks must now be taken as *Regular*.

The void falls away like a curtain tumbling to the floor. Turn to **344**.

493

You manage to escape the grip of the creature's talons, but not without taking numerous cuts, and must lose 2 **Health**.

If you survived, you reach the doorway into the building and fling yourself through it. Turn to **170**.

494

The desk is almost completely covered with notes, papers, charts, and various open books. There's a journal filled with notes, a couple of star charts held open by two large paperweights, a map of the solar system, and various books on studies of physics and the new quantum theories. Some loose pages catch your eye, old and torn as if ripped from an older book written in Latin. You push them aside as you cannot read them.

What do you want to look at?

To look at the star charts first, turn to **476**.
If you'd rather review the journal, turn to **367**.

495

There doesn't appear to be anything here, and the close air and heat are starting to bother you even further in this enclosed space. You back out then head for the exit from this cavern. Turn to **147**.

496

You recognize this cavern. The white hanging threads and the mist above... there is something in that mist that you do not wish to encounter!

"There, huuuman." Yar'ith points towards the back of the cavern. "There issss where the *Tok'llian* liesss. You willl retrieve it."

"I will not," you reply, trying to keep your voice low. "I know there is something in that cavern, waiting above in the mist!"

The mi-go's head changes to a deep red.

"Verrry weelll. Weee neeed a weaapon!" Yar'ith's voice sounds as cold and emotionless as it ever did, but whatever passes for mi-go anger, you believe you have just heard it.

If you have recorded in your Investigator Journal '*Have a metal rod*', and if you wish to give it to Yar'ith, turn to the reference associated with that entry now.

If you do not have a metal rod (or wish to keep it to yourself) but have any other type of weapon, you can choose to give a different weapon to Yar'ith. Turn to **414**.

If you would rather not give up any of your other weapons (or don't have any), turn to **211**.

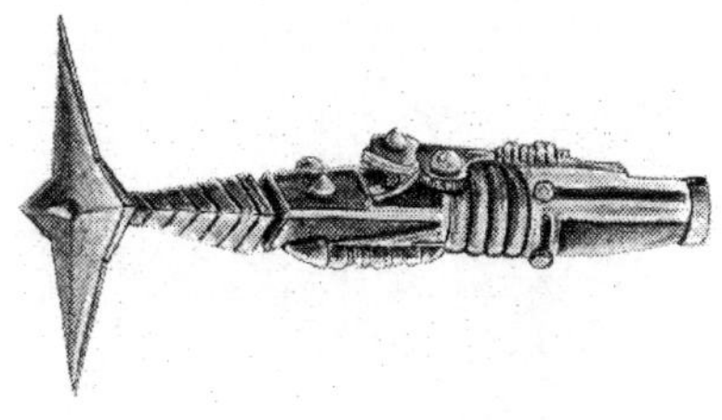

497

You grab hold of Edward as Unlatha leans over his mother. He cries out as you pull him away. Unlatha is a formidable creature as evidenced by the ease in which she dispatches the mi-go. It seems senseless and futile to attempt to engage her in combat. As Unlatha starts to feed on the mother, you drag Edward away screaming through the doorway.

Record in your Investigator Journal '*Melissa has perished.*' -20 *Mythos* points.

The room beyond contains more dead mi-go and something that you instantly recognise – the machine from the attic, or at least, an identical one! It sits in the centre of the room. Various items are resting on a counter that runs along the right-hand wall.

What do you do?

Examine the counter with the items. Turn to **306**.
Return and grab the young child, Sara, before Unlatha has finished feeding on the mother. Turn to **115**.

498

You take the *Tok'llian* from your satchel, contemplating how you might use it to bargain with the mi-go, but the moment you do, your wrist is caught in the claw of one of the soldiers. You cry out in pain as it locks on your wrist, forcing you to drop the powerful *Tok'llian*.

Their leader speaks, "Takeee away for proocessing!"

Your attempts to defend yourself are in vain as the creatures surround you. You cry out in agony as your eyes are plucked from their sockets, and eventually lose consciousness.

You awake with a strange sensation and cannot feel your arms or legs. Turn to **564**.

499

You reach for the door at the foot of the stairs when suddenly a voice calls from the landing above.

Startled, you look up the stairway. Turn to **478**.

500

You awake, not in the bed, but on the floor between the bed and the window. You feel tired as though you haven't really slept at all. You know you dreamt last night, but the memory of it has faded from your mind. Dragging yourself to your feet you immediately go to the window. It's raining outside. The morning is heavily overcast and grey. Still, with your mind made up you get dressed and prepare for the journey to the house. You do remember seeing flashes of green light, that much you recall, and you strongly believe that wasn't part of any dream. Once downstairs, you casually ask the landlady if she saw anything odd last night, or lightning, but she reports nothing, giving you a quizzical look.

You get your automobile checked over at *Pete's Fuel Depot* as you do not want to have any trouble in the rain. After some small talk, and further confirmation that nothing was seen last night, you drive on satisfied with the condition of your vehicle.

The rain is heavy at times, lessens, then returns with a vengeance. The road is muddy and bumpy. There's enough daylight to afford you a glimpse of the hill every hundred or so feet through a weakened treeline. Directions or not, finding the house in the day is a far easier task than last night proved.

You arrive at the track that leads to the house, and suddenly recall that strange voice from last night… an echo of a nightmare. Refusing to let your imagination get the better of you, you take a deep breath, and exit your vehicle. You turn your collar up against the rain and step through the treeline.

You head up the track to the house. Turn to **388**.

501

You grab the sphere on top of the machine and pull with all your remaining strength. Edward, seeing your intent, grabs it from the other side and pushes. The copper wiring that runs from the machine's base snaps loose as the device tips over. The sphere crashes through the attic floorboards. The portal hasn't closed! This machine is not connected to the portal in any way. You turn in horror to see through the haze that the mi-go appear to be arming themselves with the weapons from the counter. The portal is fully controlled on the opposite side!

If you have recorded in your Investigator Journal '*The black slime devoured the mi-go eggs*', then you must turn to the reference associated with that entry now.

If you do not have this entry, turn to **319**.

502

With some hesitation, you turn up your collar and leave the porch to head around the side of the house. Wet mud seeps into your shoes as you step over and around the myriad of dead tree branches that litter the yard. The windows are boarded up, though in rather haphazard and amateur fashion.

Do you want to try and pull some of the boards away from a window (turn to **441**), or keep heading around the house towards the back (turn to **568**)?
Alternatively, you can head back around to the front and knock on the door (turn to **212**), or head back around and try and open the front door (turn to **160**).

503

A lump forms in your throat as the two creatures descend and land on the floor ahead of you. "Huumaan! Intruuudeer. Coome wiith ussss!"
They don't advance. Instead, they take two steps back and call you again. "Coooome! Nooo harmmmm to huumaan."
What do you do?

Do as they ask and start to follow them, but stay a good distance behind them. Turn to **39**.
Turn and flee back down the ramp. Turn to **412**.
Or advance on them and fight them off. Turn to **381**.

504

You place your hand on the panel and it immediately retracts into the wall.

As the door opens, you step through. Turn to **123**.

505

This mi-go is unlike the others you have encountered. It has a broad carapace and four fully formed arms ending in huge claws. It is clearly built for combat. The extra limbs and claws are capable of dealing 1 extra Damage to you for each round you lose against it.

Mi-go Guard
Combat 8
Health 8

If you manage to win against this imposing warrior, turn to **562**.

506

Given the dead end, you feel that fighting is your best chance. You advance on the mi-go to give yourself some advantage.

One of the creatures is armed with the metal rod, and points it towards you. A shard of metal shoots from the end. You must try to dodge this attack.
Make a Very Hard (2D6+2) **Dexterity** check. If you pass, you

successfully dodge the shard, which flies harmlessly past you and clangs against the wall. If you fail, you are hit square in the shoulder, and must lose 3 **Health**.

Now you must face them in combat. The room gives the creatures the space to surround you, so you must fight both together.

Mi-go Worker 1	**Mi-go Worker 2**
Combat 6	Combat 7
Health 5	Health 4

If you win, turn to **181**.

507

Deciding this way is too dangerous, you turn around and start to make your way down the stepped ledges. Suddenly, you hear numerous thuds on the wall and ground from the cavern behind. You turn to find a truly terrifying sight. Lurching its bloated purple bulk through the opening is an enormous spider. The cave of silken threads is clearly its lair.

Make an Extreme (2D6+3) **Composure** check.

If you fail, turn to **308**.
If you pass, turn to **514**.

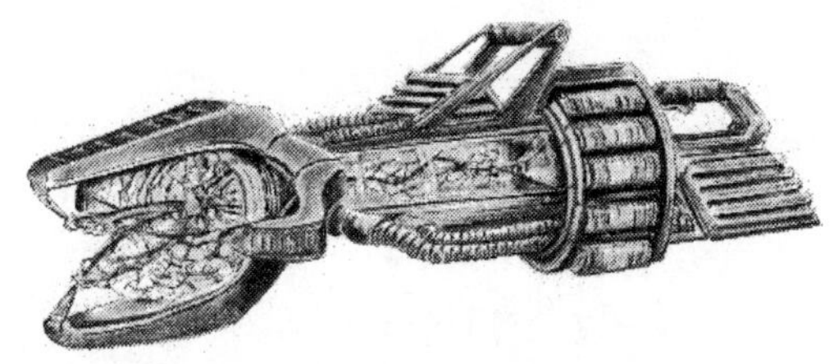

508

Reluctantly, you approach the table and look at the mess strewn across it.

The table is a grisly sight, and all of the items are now covered in a mess of blood and viscera. You turn away from wanting to look through the disgusting mess.

There's nothing else of interest in this room, so you leave. Turn to **405**.

509

You curse the machine when you see it doesn't have the power source attached. You will have to search for it.

Search through the mi-go remains. Turn to **570**.
Search the counter and devices. Turn to **268**.
Or return to the previous room and search there. Turn to **575**.

510

You desperately attempt to avoid the spinning claws, but it proves too difficult. You limp away, attempting to knock equipment from the counters across their path. They continue to advance. Eugene curses you for destroying their work. Backed against the wall, the whirring claws dig deep into your thigh, carving out chunks of flesh. "You brought this on yourself, old chap…"

Record in your Investigator Journal *"You die from massive blood loss on the laboratory floor."* -10 *Mythos* points.

Your investigation ends here.

511

The attic space is narrow but long, and strangely uncluttered as you would be used to seeing an attic space taken advantage of for storage. Standing in the middle of the attic floor is an unusual metal device about 4 feet tall. It is a pillar of polished metal that glints in the dim light of the attic, and like tentacles, many copper wires snake their way from openings in the device, running across the floor and disappearing into the walls. A perfect sphere of the same polished metal sits atop the device, set partway into the base. In an almost perfect circle three feet around the device, lies a ring of dead animals – everything from rats, mice, flies, beetles, and centipedes. Some look fresher than others. The possibility of a bad smell is masked instead with the odour of chlorine bleach.

What you see just beyond the device sends you into a mild shock. The professor is lying on the floor, his body twisted at the middle, while his lower half is facing almost entirely the wrong direction. Blood runs down into the seams of the floorboards. His eyes are wide open, frozen in terror.

Make a Very Hard (2D6+2) **Composure** check. If you fail, lose 2 Composure.

Something moves in the far corner. Lurking in the darkness is a small, hunched figure. You are about to ask who is there when it speaks first in a strained and raspy voice. You fumble to take out your flashlight.

"Fraaaaannnk! Where areeee myyy family? Yooou..mussst go... baaack."
"How… how do you know me?" you answer, both terrified

and overwhelmingly intrigued.
"Fraaannk? It issss me... Edward... You saaaved meeee... "
"Did... did you kill the professor?" you ask, your nervousness showing through.
"Yesssssss. I had to! He plannned to stop ussss. Heee isss working for... ..theeeem!"
It's then that you notice blood dripping from the serrated edge of the claw at the end of his arm. Edward lurches to one side and starts to shuffle out of the darkness towards you.

What do you do?

Decide this is all too much and flee the house. Turn to **198**.
Use your flashlight to get a better look at the figure. Turn to **350**.
Ask more questions to find out exactly how this could be Edward. Turn to **31**.

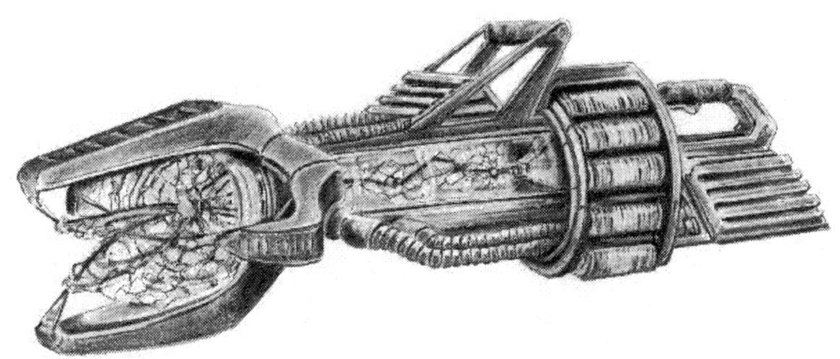

512

The sight and smell of the blood and guts rolling by on the conveyor belt makes you retch uncontrollably.

Deduct 1 from your current **Composure**.

Your dry retching is loud, and you're suddenly snapped out of your state as a shard of metal whizzes by your ear and embeds itself into the rock wall. You look up and see two mi-go up on the walkway. One of them is pointing a metal rod in your direction. You surmise it could have fired the projectile that just missed you by a whisker.

You will have to act fast.

Will you dart across the room and over the conveyor belts to the large doorway (turn to **148**), escape via the nearest conveyor belt through the opening in the wall (turn to **285**), or take cover behind the large disc machine (turn to **158**)?

513

You clear the first conveyor easily enough, but the metal floor doesn't make it easy to keep your footing. You slip and fall across the second conveyor, covering yourself in its disgusting cargo. One of the creatures lands close by, the other remaining above. You make at attempt to move across the belt when a metal shard from the weapon pierces your shoulder.

Lose 3 **Health**.

If you are still alive, you cry out in pain and fall across the conveyor as it pushes you towards the opening. Both mi-go are bearing down on you, and one more hit from that weapon could finish you off.

Your only escape is to dive into the opening in the wall and hopefully to relative safety. Turn to **110**.

514

Despite maintaining some level of composure, you must still lose 1 **Composure** as the terrifying horror behind you radiates malice and dread. Facing it seems impossible, so you turn and descend the ledges that led you up here. Balancing caution and speed. you manage to get back down safely and immediately follow the tunnel on the right. It quickly narrows, making it impossible for the beast to follow you.

Breathing a massive sigh of relief, you head on, wary and on edge for what else might be lurking in these caves of terror. Turn to **466**.

515

You try with all your might, but your current ordeal has already sapped a lot of your strength. You drop to your feet, your fingers aching.

You've no choice but to exit via the large door instead. Turn to **123**.

516

You explain that the power source, or *Tok'llian* as they called it, remains at the house. You reluctantly add the details of Edward and his family, knowing that they are already deceased. You remain constantly on guard, for you expect your confession here will not be favourable as you assume these mi-go are responsible for the death of the Turne family.

The creatures confer again in silence for what feels like an age before the leader speaks once more. "We do nooot know of what you speeak. Takeee away for proocessing!"

Your attempts to defend yourself are in vain as the creatures surround you. You cry out in agony as your eyes are plucked from their sockets, then lose consciousness.

You awake with a strange sensation and cannot feel your arms or legs. Turn to **564**.

517

You reach the door, and as expected it opens with a gentle swish sound. You wince, quickly passing through as the unmistakable sound of the creatures buzzing tones start to emanate from the control room behind, followed by the clack of their feet on the metal floor. They are coming!

You are in another short corridor that immediately turns left, and need to act fast. There are two doors, one mid-way in the right-hand wall, and the second in the left-hand wall at the very end of the corridor.

Do you take the door on the right (turn to **387**), or quickly pass this door and exit the corridor through the far door in the left-hand wall (turn to **463**)?

518

You reach the other side and approach the large doorway. It doesn't open of its own accord. You glance around and notice a square raised panel on the wall next to the door.

Will you touch the panel and exit through this door (turn to **123**), or attempt to jump and pull yourself up the walkway above (turn to **311**)?

519

Hours pass, and exhaustion starts to set in. You feel sick to your stomach but carry on until you just can't keep going. As unwelcome as it is, you sit on a small pile of remains against the cavern wall and close your eyes.

If you have recorded in your Investigator Journal '*You freed Unlatha*', then turn to the **FIRST** reference associated with that entry now.

If you do not have this entry, turn to **397**.

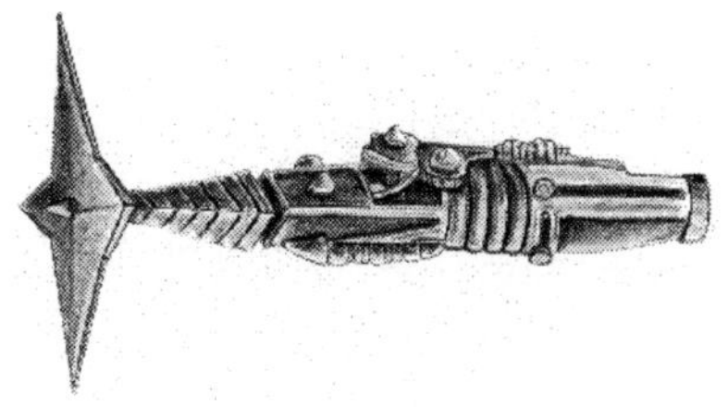

520

You approach the reflective glass. As you get closer an image appears as though a huge window has opened before you.

The image displays a room similar in size and shape to the one you're standing in. However, this room is not empty. It too has a large rectangular slab, but on the slab rests a naked figure. It appears to be a human female, but it's difficult to see as the image is slightly warped at the edges. On the right-hand side of the displayed image, you think you noticed something else moving.

If you want to continue observing and get a closer look at what is going on (turn to **88**), or you can back away from the glass (turn to **162**).

521

You turn the second dial to what you would believe to be 45 degrees.

How do you want to set the third dial?

To leave it as is, set on zero degrees, turn to **25**.
To set it to 90 degrees, turn to **418**.
To set it to 47 degrees, turn to **467**.

522

You cut the thread above your hand, and it springs back into place. Crossing the cave could be dangerous with so many of these threads to avoid. Your gut instinct is that this is a purposeful trap.

If you wish to attempt it anyway, turn to **194**.
Or if you decide to turn back and take the earlier right-hand branch, turn to **507**.

523

The control panel is what you've come to expect from mi-go technology, plain looking and devoid of any clear indication as to its purpose. You push a few buttons and wait.

Suddenly a panel opens in the wall next to the metal slab. A large amount of guts and bone slide out and deposit onto the slab, covering it entirely. Disgusted, you turn your head away. What is all this vile meat and flesh for, and more to the point, where… or who, is it coming from?

If you haven't already, and still wish to, you can examine the slab (turn to **508**), or return to the corridor and head through the door (turn to **405**).

524

As you lean in closer to get a better look at the swaying filaments, the flower suddenly lets out a sharp hiss and a mist of spores fly directly into your face.

Make a Hard (2D6+1) **Health** check.

If you fail, turn to **334**.

If you pass, you cough as the spores attempt to fill your lungs and sting your eyes. Though you manage to escape the worst of the effects, you must still lose 1 **Dexterity** for the slightly debilitating effect.

You decide you must press on. Carefully avoiding getting close to any of the plants, you head for the door on the opposite side of the room. Turn to **370**.

525

You've seen Unlatha in battle and know she is a formidable creature. You stall. But Edward is oblivious to this, and protecting his mother appears to override any sense of fear he might feel. Filled with rage, he charges at the nightmare that is about to drain his mother's lifeblood. While she is distracted by her hunger, Edward manages to clasp the claw around one of Unlatha's legs, and the serrated blade cuts in deep. Unlatha recoils for a moment, but with a flick of another leg she sends Edward sprawling backwards across the floor. The claw skids across the ground and lands at your feet. Unlatha retracts her proboscis as Edward gets to his feet, winded but unhurt, with hatred in his eyes. What will you do?

Will you pick up the claw and use it to fight Unlatha (turn to **456**), or intercept Edward and attempt to get both of you out of here (turn to **400**)?

526

Three particularly unusual looking plants catch your eye. Which one do you want to examine closer?

There's a tall thin plant with black petals lined with red veins. Small pods hang from its stem. To take a closer look, turn to **177**.
To examine the shorter thicker plant with large orange petals that curl outwards, turn to **386**.
Or examine a strange round spiny plant, not unlike a cactus, with a large opening in its centre. Something appears to be moving inside it. Turn to **190**.

527

The opening leads into a tunnel that becomes more difficult to traverse the further you go. It then starts to descend sharply, to the point you're having to slow yourself down and hug the wall for fear of losing your footing and sliding downwards.

Make a Regular (2D6) **Dexterity** check.

If you pass, turn to **95**.
If you fail, turn to **121**.

528

"Who's there?" you say, standing in the middle of the room. There's no feasible location for the speaker to hide. You approach the window. There is no one in the street. The sky fills again with a flash of the sickly green light. In the distance you see a hill, and perched atop, the silhouette of the house. Could that be the source of the light?

The voice, much fainter now, as though it were travelling on the wind speaks, one last time. "Cooome, Fraaaank. You... promised!"

The speaker knows your name.

You wait, expecting more. Your heart rate eases, and nothing more is said. It's only then you notice the chill of the air blowing in the room and quickly latch the window closed as one last flash floods the room with a green haze.

You turn to get back into bed, but find it gone. Turn to **569**.

529

You take his hand and shake. His grip is firm.

"Pleased to meet you!" He smiles and releases your hand.

Resisting the urge to look at your hand, you tell him your name.

"Here, look at this, Frank." He lifts the hood on your car again, and pulls a wrench out from his belt. "Your radiator wouldn't last too much longer with this valve loose the way it is." He tightens it, and closes the hood. "Now, no charge for that. So, what else you be needing?" He tucks the wrench back into his overalls and wipes his hand on an oily rag. Taking the opportunity to glance at your own hand, you see it's smudged with oil. You thank him for the repair.

Record in your Investigator Journal that '*Your car radiator was fixed*', and note the reference 94. Later in the story, if asked if you have earned this information, you will turn to 94. (Do not turn to that now).

What will you say?

Tell him you're looking for directions to Sentinel Hill. Turn to **373**.

Ask about the town and why it's so quiet. Turn to **35**.

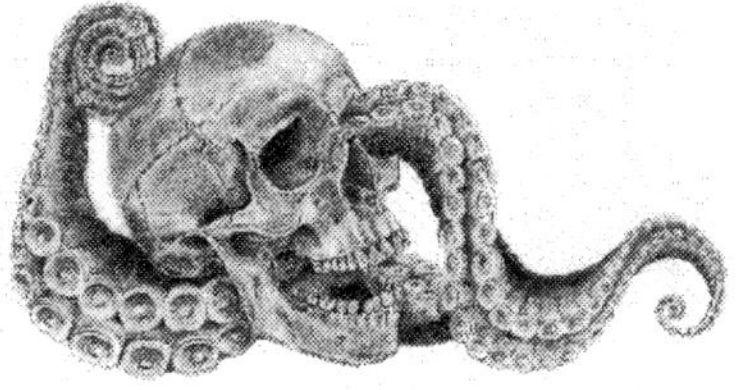

530

Stepping carefully through the fungus and around the eggs, you reach the exit on the other side of the chamber. It leads into a tunnel about forty feet long where, directly ahead, it opens into a larger chamber. In this further chamber you can clearly see at least three adult mi-go moving back and forth. Two of them are larger than the others, and carry what appears to be a large type of gun – possibly guardians for the eggs. About halfway through the tunnel before reaching the chamber with the mi-go, about twenty feet ahead, there is another junction in the right-hand wall.

Do you have an explosive seed? If so, you could use it in one of two possible ways.

To throw the seed into the chamber with the mi-go to try and kill (or maim) the armed creatures, turn to **555**.
To throw the seed back into the egg chamber as a distraction, and take the tunnel to the right while they are investigating the noise, turn to **275**.
If you do not have a seed (or do not wish to use one), you can sneak up to the tunnel on the right. Turn to **488**.

531

You charge the creature, and for just a moment, you imagine it is startled by your tenacity.

Mi-go Worker
Combat 4
Health 4

If you win, turn to **132**.

532

You land a heavy blow as you attempt to defend yourself, causing him to fall back against the wall and slump to the floor. You check for a pulse as best you can. Nothing. Placing a hand on his chest you check if he is breathing. Still nothing.

You've killed him. Make a Very Hard (2D6+2) **Composure** check. If you fail, deduct 1 from your current Composure.

Record in your Investigator Journal *'You killed Professor Peabody in self-defence.'* -10 *Mythos* points.

Your mind races. You think to yourself that no one will find out. Get a hold of yourself, Frank. You've killed someone. He attacked me; it was self-defence. You replay the scenario over and over but eventually calm down enough to decide your next action.

You place the syringe in your satchel. Record in your Investigator Journal that you *'Have the syringe'*, and note the reference 142. +2 *Mythos* points.

What will you do now?

Will you leave the basement (turn to **47**), or search it (turn to **87**)?

533

The pool sits perfectly still. You touch it with the tip of your shoe, causing it to ripple slightly. What will you do?

Make your way across. Turn to **396**.
If you haven't already, you can examine the glowing fungi on the walls. Turn to **538**.
Or decide against this, and head back the way you came. Turn to **107**.

534

Another display that catches your eye that contains large fungi and other strange varieties of vegetation. Partially hidden amongst the vegetation is what at first you believe to be a large black boulder. Then it moves! A long spindly leg unfurls from the black mass, then another, and another...

Eight legs in total unfold as the black mass they are attached to rises from the floor under their support. Six eyes catch the dim light of the room, and a series of long tentacle-like feelers drop from its mouth... or are its mouth? You can't be quite sure. This terrifying thing stands nearly eight feet tall.

Make a Hard (2d6+1) **Composure** check. If you fail, lose 1 Composure.

You turn to leave...

"No, don't go!" A voice, a harsh-sounding female whisper, speaks directly in your head. You dart your gaze around. "Human... I am before you." You turn at look directly at the huge spider-thing behind the glass. It's locked on your gaze, its position following every tiny move you make.

"What... what are you?" you ask out loud.
"I am... a prisoner. Free me, human. Before the mi-go return."
"Why would I do that? This is madness!" you reply.
"No, human, it is your salvation. Free me."

Every instinct in your body says to leave this creature alone. You can quickly leave through the door (turn to **144**), or touch the panel on the enclosure and free the spider-thing (turn to **305**).

535

As you set the last dial, the beam of green light shoots up from the sphere on top just like it had done in the attic of the house. It then bends downwards to rest parallel with the floor, striking the wall to form a shimmering portal. The entire room is bathed in the eerie pulsating light. Through the haze of the portal, you can see the attic of the house. You did it!

With Edward's help, you drag the remaining family members through to the other side. Each pass through the portal is slightly disorientating. When you've successfully got them through, you both collapse exhausted on the attic floor – however, the portal remains open. Through the shimmering portal you see movement! Mi-go have entered the portal room you escaped from. You must close the portal somehow...

Will you attempt to tip the machine in the attic over on its side (turn to **501**), or find something in the attic to block the doorway (turn to **66**)?

536

Doubting you'll get much service here, you head back outside. You're only just out the door when you see a heavy-set man, possibly late fifties, standing by your car. He's wearing dirty blue overalls, with *Pete* written across the breast. He appears to be lightly kicking one of your tires.

What do want to do?

If you want to approach the man and greet him, turn to **97**.
Or if you stay where you are and wait for the man to notice you, turn to **404**.

537

You enter another tunnel about forty feet in length, ending with an opening into a larger chamber ahead. Halfway along the right-hand wall is another passage.

To head down the passage to the right, turn to **138**.
To head on past this passage and examine the chamber at the end of the tunnel, turn to **27**.

538

The walls are covered with mushrooms and other fungi of various shapes and sizes. Most of them glow with a faint blue light, and there are enough of them present to illuminate the entire cavern. What do you want to do?

Take a sample of the fungi. Turn to **436**.
If you haven't already, you can examine the pool. Turn to **533**.
Or head back the way you came. Turn to **107**.

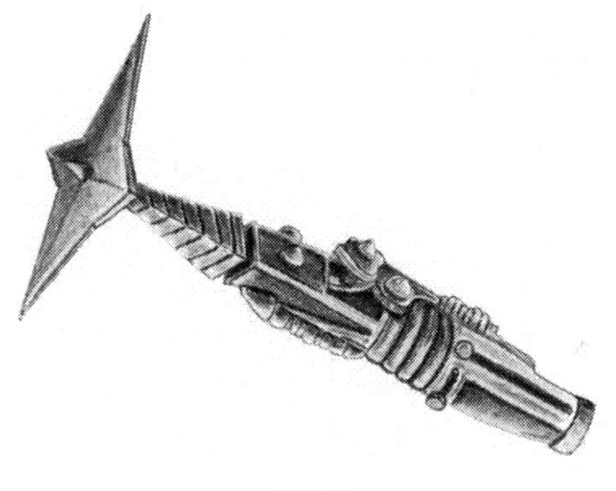

539

With some hesitation, you touch the surface of the dark liquid. It immediately envelops your finger. You recoil instantly and attempt to shake it off, but instead it absorbs into your skin and disappears. For a moment you feel fine despite the fright, but then a sharp pain wracks your body and forces you to your knees. Your eyes roll and turn black.

Then you open them.

You find yourself standing in a black void. There is no sound and nothing to see but your own body. That growing sense of unease that you felt while approaching the statue is now even stronger. You're about to call out when suddenly, a long thin vertical shaft of light pierces the void. Shielding your eyes for a moment, you watch as impossibly long fingers emerge from the light, coil around either side, and pull the void apart as though tearing a hole in space itself.

What will you do?

Turn and flee. Turn to **351**.
Stand your ground and see what comes through. Turn to **71**.

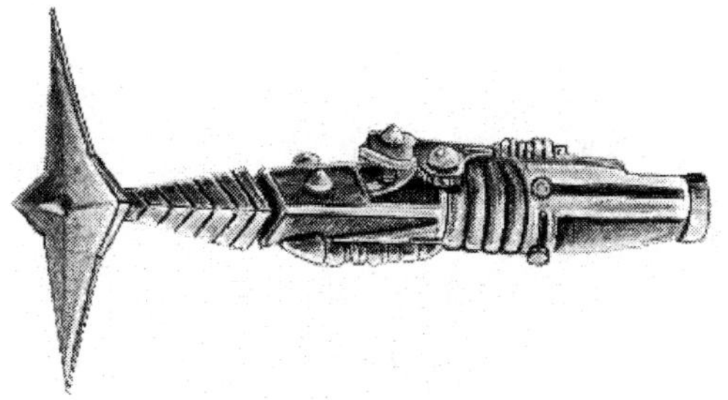

540

You retreat, allowing the door to close. Your first instinct is to run but you keep your composure, knowing that you will never make it across that pool in time, or even if the pool can be crossed. You wait patiently at the side of the door for the creatures to emerge. It is a desperate situation, but you plan to disarm the being with the weapon and fight them.

As they emerge you see your chance to go for the disarm.

Make a Regular (2D6) **Dexterity** check.

If you pass, turn to **566**.
If you fail, turn to **67**.

541

The liquid is viscous. As you lift your finger, a strand drips slowly back into the pool. It has a sweet odour.

Will you risk tasting the liquid (turn to **295**), leave it alone and try the door on the right (turn to **7**), try the door in the opposite wall near the ramp (turn to **546**), or investigate the ramp (turn to **433**)?

542

You fall to your knees, tears running down your cheeks. You've managed to save Sara at least, and with some luck she won't retain any knowledge of what has transpired.

Despite your weary condition, you manage to bury the machine in the woods. To your bewilderment, the house is in good general condition, with no boarded-up windows or abandoned rooms. You masquerade as a stranger happening upon a lost girl wandering the road near the house. You involve the police, give statements, and feign ignorance. The house is searched, but no clues to the whereabouts of the family is uncovered. No one knows, or will ever know, what actually happened.

You soon discover that the date is October 11th, 1916. The newspaper clipping that brought you here remains as before, but tells a story that is no longer what happened. Your car is gone... or never existed. Only that which you brought with you to Yuggoth and back, remains as it was. The machine was more than just a way to traverse across space, it also had the power to transcend time. Edward and Sara hadn't aged because it sent you to Yuggoth ten years in the past – possibly only moments after they themselves had arrived. Now you realise just how powerful this device was for the mi-go, and why they were so tenacious in trying to recover the lost power source.

Sara is fostered in the town of Durham, and in time seems happy and settled, with the terrors of the past buried, or hopefully completely forgotten. You settle in the town of Durham also, and get a job working as a store clerk for Mrs. Wilkins. You remain there as a way to stay away from... yourself. A young reporter by the name of Frank Winston starts to write an article for the *Arkham Gazette,* which you have delivered by post especially to your door.

On September the 23rd, around 4:45 p.m., in the year 1926, you stand on the main road of Durham and wait for a Chevrolet to trundle down the road. You contemplated writing to yourself, anonymously of course, as a warning to stay away... but instead felt that you would simply be compelling some version of yourself to question the warning and turn up anyway. When you thought about it, you know that is what you would have done.

No one arrives... there are no strange flashes of green lightning, and no voice on the air. The killings never happened, the article was never written, and thus the other version of yourself remained in Arkham writing for the paper. It is highly unlikely that your paths will ever cross.

If you have recorded in your Investigator Journal '*Received a gift*', then you must turn to the reference associated with that entry now.

If you do not have this entry, turn to **36**.

543

You move quickly across the chamber and are just about to reach the exit when you slip on a patch of fungus, and slide into one of the eggs. The egg sac bursts, covering you in its embryonic fluid. A whip-like black tentacle lashes through the air and ensnares your leg. You're quickly reminded that this creature is acidic to touch. You cry out involuntarily as it burns through your clothing and into your calf.

Lose 1 **Health** and 1 **Composure**.

Suddenly, four mi-go burst through from the exit. They don't appear to have noticed you lying among the fungi; instead, their focus is clearly on the rampaging creature that is devouring their young. Two of the mi-go fire large gun-like contraptions at the creature. The entire chamber lights up as sparks of lightning blast and crackle from the guns. It has little effect. You're instantly released as the creature turns its focus on the mi-go.

You don't hesitate to take this opportunity and flee through the exit. Turn to **537**.

544

"Who's there?" you ask, sitting upright in the bed. No answer. "Show yourself!" Still nothing.
You look about the room. There's no feasible location for the speaker to hide. Unless... a sudden thought goes to the bed you're in.

If you wish to check under the bed, turn to **423**.
Or instead approach the open window, turn to **452**.

545

You aim the forearm blade at the back of the creature and strike. The vicious serrated blade tears through the carapace, spraying green blood across the room. Though very badly wounded, the creature turns sharply to counterattack.

This mi-go is unlike the others you have encountered. It has a broad carapace and four fully formed arms ending in huge claws, instead of the usual two clawed arms with two smaller utility arms the other mi-go have. The extra limbs and claws can deal 1 additional Damage to you for each round you lose against it.

Mi-go Guard (badly wounded)
Combat 8
Health 4

If you win, turn to **562**.

546

The door opens and you step inside. A large square platform dominates the centre of the room, and on it sit a wide variety of potted plants of utterly alien shapes, sizes, and colours. Though exotic plant life is not your forte, these are clearly not normal plants – perhaps hybrids, or experiments? Another circular door leads out on the opposite side of the room.

Will you examine the strange plant life here (turn to **526**), or decide you can't afford to waste time and must find a way home, by heading for the door across the room (turn to **370**)?

547

Believing that the best way to accomplish this task is to stick to the distraction plan, you lightly brush one of the threads with your sleeve. As expected, the threads are extremely adhesive, and it will not come away from your sleeve. The more you attempt to remove it, the more of it that attaches itself. Panic starts to set in. Looking above, you see a long black appendage ease its way out of the mist... then another, and another...

Fear turns to terror as a huge, bloated thing vaguely in the shape of a spider, sails down silently towards you. In your horror you turn to flee for the entrance, only to entangle yourself in the threads.

The mi-go makes its move. Crouching down as low as possible, it skitters across the cavern floor towards the *Tok'llian*. With the threads largely cleared, Yar'ith reaches the *Tok'llian* with relative ease, its head turning the brightest green you've yet seen. Yar'ith skitters out of the cavern leaving you to your fate.

The spider-thing is upon you before you can react any further. With a sickening squelch, your head is speared by a talon-like leg. You die instantly.

Record in your Investigator Journal '*You were killed by a Spider of Leng.*' -5 *Mythos* points.

Your investigation ends here.

548

You let out a call, feeling anxious about your slight intrusion. "Hello? Sorry to intrude, but I had to come. I'm only here to... "
"Help me?" The professor appears at the top of the stairs, bathed in darkness. His words cut you off.
"Yes, listen, I wanted to... "
"Very well!" he cuts in again. "Come on up, perhaps you can be of use to me after all."

You gingerly start climbing the stairway as the professor waits for you on the landing. When you get to the top, he gestures for you to head down the hallway ahead of him.
"If you please."
You move cautiously ahead, and with good reason. From the corner of your eye, you see the professor raise his hand. Turning sharply, you see he has a syringe in his grasp.

Make a Hard (2D6+1) **Dexterity** check to dodge the blow.

If you pass, turn to **356**.
If you fail, turn to **406**.

549

She explains the way as best she remembers it, as she hasn't been out that way in years.

"It's not too hard to find. Just carry on out of town and you'll come to a fork in the road, take the left fork, then continue straight past the next junction. Finally, turn left at the next opportunity, and up a little from there you'll see a large boulder by the roadside. The trail to the house is there. Follow that trail up the hill and you'll be at the old place soon enough." She smiles broadly.

You thank her for her help and leave.

When you get back to your car, the garage appears to have been locked up for the day. The evening light is fading. A cold breeze suddenly whips through the garage lot, blowing leaves up into a swirl. You turn up your collar against the cold and get into your car.

Armed with the directions to the house, you drive on. Turn to **557**.

550

The thing lumbers in your direction as it seems to have very short legs, or perhaps no legs at all. Thinking you could easily outrun such a clumsy beast, you rise from your crouched position and make a dash for the opposite side of the cave.

Make an Easy (2D6-1) **Dexterity** check.

If you pass, you make it out of the larger cavern and the creature doesn't seem interested in following you. Turn to **147**.
If you fail, you stumble awkwardly in your attempt to run. The creature catches up to you and rears up to defend its territory. Turn to **291**.

551

"Very well... " you whisper to Yar'ith. Its head turns to a deep green at your agreement to adhere to the so-called plan. You approach the cavern entrance – the eerie silence and stillness of the scene is none-the-less unsettling. Above, in the mist, lies a malignant presence of pure terror. You feel it even now.

Stepping in, you weave your way between the threads, careful not to touch them. Yar'ith waits, watching, its head turning an unreadable mix of blue and yellow. It's then you spot the glint of metal that Yar'ith claimed to be the *Tok'llian*. You realise in that moment... why not go for it yourself? You need it, and this mi-go would betray even its own kind, hardly a being to be trusted. What will you do?

Make your way to the *Tok'llian* yourself, and flee the cavern through the opposite exit. Turn to **251**.
Or stick to the plan and when in far enough, disturb one of the threads as a distraction. Turn to **547**.

552

You enter, slowly, while looking the professor over. It's then you notice that one arm hangs loosely by his side, immobile. He appears to be holding something, but you can't quite see.

You look briefly at the hallway. Old picture frames line the wall on the left. The main staircase runs up on the right-hand side. At the foot of the stairs on your right is a door. Facing you at the end of the hallway is another door. Finally, there's a door under the stairs which likely leads to the basement.

You turn back to the professor. You almost felt he was reaching for you just then, but when your gaze meets, he's standing there motionless as before.

Will you ask him what he's holding (turn to **146**), ignore it for the moment and ask about the house (turn to **322**), or ask him about the green lights you saw last night (turn to **293**)?

553

The crates are piled to the ceiling. That strange chemical smell is more obvious now – chlorine bleach. You pull some crates down and see that they contain various pieces of electrical wiring, copper pipes, coils, mostly empty bottles of chlorine bleach. What could all this be for? Moving some more crates out of the way, you find a grisly sight. Piles of dead rats, what looks like a couple of dogs and a cat, and possibly even a hare or two lie rotting away in various states of decay. They look half eaten.

Make an Easy (2D6-1) **Composure** check. If you fail, deduct 1 from your current Composure.

The bleach is being used to mask what would undoubtedly be a far less pleasant odour.

There's nothing else to be discovered here so you decide to leave the basement. Turn to **47**.

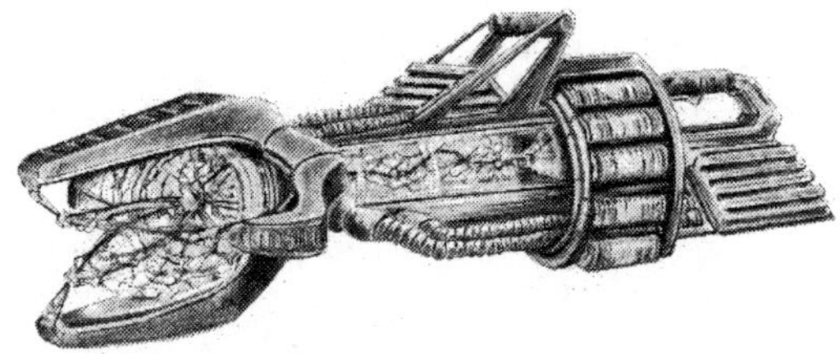

554

When you tell him you don't know how to use this machine, you are not very surprised by his response. Edward cries out in a rage and slams the floor with his claw. The floorboards splinter and crack as the metal appendage rips through it. Then faster than you possibly could expect, he comes at you and latches his claw around your arm. He drags you painfully towards the machine.

Lose 1 **Health**.

"You mussst trrry!" You don't believe he means to hurt you, but you plead with him to release your arm and he does so.

You decide it'd be best to try and do as he asks. Turn to **195**.

555

You approach as close as you dare to, getting increasingly anxious with each step. When you think you'd be able to throw with some accuracy, you throw one of the explosive seeds into the chamber. What happens next you are not prepared for. You're blasted off of your feet as an explosive force shoots through the tunnel.

Lose 1 **Health**.

The mi-go are utterly annihilated. The weapons carried by two of the mi-go are powerful, but volatile. The seed exploding set one off, causing a chain reaction. You climb to your feet and peer down the tunnel. What now?

Approach the chamber with the dead mi-go. Turn to **217**.
Leave the devastation and take the tunnel to the right. Turn to **138**.

556

You turn the dial three to what you would believe to be 121 degrees.

How do you want to set dial four?

To leave it as it is, set currently at 17 degrees, turn to **70**.
To set it to zero degrees, turn to **143**.
To set it to 100 degrees, turn to **364**.

557

It's almost 6 p.m. as you're rolling slowly along the leaf-strewn road through the woods, keeping an eye out for the house. The evening is fast approaching, and the low sun is now obscured by dark clouds. The overhanging trees are in cahoots with the clouds, darkening the evening more as they form a tunnel that envelops the road. You switch on the headlights to improve visibility and prevent you from missing any tell-tale signs of the houses' whereabouts. The road starts to slope upwards as you enter the hills that stretch across this side of Durham town.

A few minutes pass when you arrive at a fork in the road. The trees and brambles are thick, knotted together as though one wants to strangle the other. Even the electric lights from your car can't penetrate them to the other side. Protruding twigs and tree branches scrape off the car every few feet. There's no signpost at the fork.

To take the left fork, turn to **22**.
To take the right fork, turn to **428**.

558

Sticking to what looks like a pre-made trail, you move slowly, giving your eyes time to take in your surroundings. The trail leads to the left-hand wall of the chamber where a low semi-circular opening has been carved into the black rock wall. You would have to crouch down to enter this small tunnel.

Do you want to enter the tunnel (turn to **37**), or leave this and head on further into the larger chamber (turn to **368**)?

559

Being suitably alert to his presence, you manage to block his blow. He appears to be stark raving mad, and so you'll have to defend yourself.

Professor Albert Peabody
Combat 5
Health 6

If you reduce his health to 3, turn to **532**.
If in any round of the fight the professor rolls a 12 for his attack AND beats your attack that round, turn to **378**.

560

You inquire about the lack of people around (she's the only person you've seen). She lifts her head, and then looks you up and down.

"Being a city feller, you must think every place be full of people flapping around bumping into each other. Not here lad! People about, doesn't mean they want to be eyeballed by strangers. If it be unsettling for ya, how about you get on back to your mobs?"

She seems indignant, and starts to shuffle away mumbling to herself. You realise she hasn't told you how to get to the hill. You attempt to ask but she waves you away, saying you're best leaving it well alone.

What will you do now?

Enter the garage to ask in there. Turn to **59**.

Call it a day, look for a lodging and get a fresh start in the morning. Turn to **372**.

Or you can return to your car and drive on. Perhaps there will be a sign to point you in the right direction towards the hill. Turn to **331**.

561

You grab the bars and start to turn the device around. The creature fires again. It strikes the disc with a loud *shring*, and embeds into it. Two more follow in quick succession, spearing the disc as you duck behind it. What you hear next is a kind of sizzle, strange alien screams, and then this is followed by an unpleasant smell of burning. You glance past the machine to see the melting remains of both creatures oozing off the walkway to the floor below.

You power down the rock melting machine. There's no obvious way up to the walkway above but might be able to grasp it and pull yourself up. At the far end of the room is the large square door.

Investigate the large doorway. Turn to **582**.
Attempt to get up onto the walkway above. Turn to **427**.

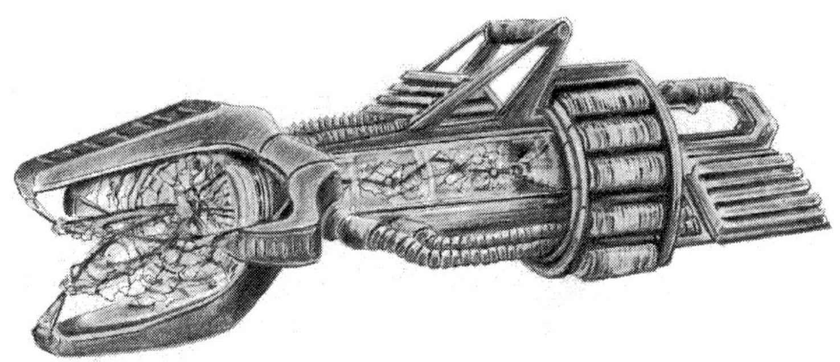

562

The mi-go guard lies dead at your feet – an impressive kill, but one that leaves your heart racing for a few minutes as you rest against a container to calm down.

"Huumaan." *Tap tap tap*. The mi-go prisoner raps on the cell wall with its claw. "Freee meee, huuumaan. Heeelp me... I help you."
"Why would you possibly help me? You're one of them!" you retort, pointing to the creature you have just slain. You let your disdain for these things show in your voice, even though you're not sure that these creatures can recognise such emotion.
"I am a prisssoner. To be deesstroyed. It is plain that I seek essscape and you do alsssso. I flew toooo close to the fooorbiden mooon! We trieeed to essscape. My companion and I. Sssstole poweeer."

The creature continues to talk, and you find out its name is Yar'ith, a rebel mi-go. There are others, but mi-go that do not follow the way are destroyed, or offered to something called the Crawling Chaos as tribute. Your inquiry into what the Crawling Chaos is yields no answer. Yar'ith does not want to talk about it. The rebel group of mi-go seek to prevent the ability to bring humans (and other beings incapable of interstellar travel) to and from Yuggoth so easily. The rebels secretly worship Cxaxuklutha, a being of great power that lies mostly dormant far below the city in a pit of black slime. The other mi-go are 'feeding' the great black river with the processing of body parts to keep Cxaxuklutha in a state of dormancy.

You explain the details of your arrival, the strange device,

and the diamond-shaped object that was used to activate it. The moment you mention the diamond-shaped object, Yar'ith's agitation becomes noticeable. "I knoow wheerre it is! The *Tok'llian*. We ssstole it." The mi-go elaborates further, and it becomes clear that your intentions may be aligned.
One *Tok'llian* takes two generations to construct, and thus they are immensely valuable and rare. Yar'ith tells you no more, and now repeatedly asks to be set free before another mi-go guard arrives.

You're naturally mistrustful of these vile creatures, but a mi-go ally could be the turning point in your desperate plan to escape. You ask about the Turne family and how they fit into all this, but Yar'ith doesn't know what you are talking about. What is clear to you from the paper clipping is that they are dead – victims of mi-go experimentation. It is not a fate you wish for yourself.

There is a panel on the side that looks to be the opening mechanism. What will you do?

To free the mi-go prisoner, turn to **117**.
Or leave it here, as you already know these alien creatures see humans as nothing more than playthings. How could you possibly trust it? Turn to **196**.

563

The road widens, and after a little while you come across what appears to be a main road junction. You stop and look around, spotting the unmistakable outline of Sentinel Hill, and perched atop, the house, far off to the left and behind you. You're clearly heading away from it. You curse your choice of direction and make to turn the car around.

As you head back the lateness of the hour, and your own tiredness forces you to reconsider your actions. You now have a good idea of which way to go, and decide that doing so in the morning is the only sane choice.

You head on back to Durham. Turn to **127**.

564

Your vision is narrowed and at first you find it hard to focus. Across from you on a metal slab lies the body of a man. One of the creatures is leaning over it and doing something to the head, but you can't quite see what is happening.

Moments later it turns towards you with a large flap of skin dangling from its blood-soaked claw. As it gets closer the creature's head turns a deep green while it holds up the flapping piece of skin before your eyes. It is your face dangling from its claw...
You spend the rest of your life as a brain in a cylinder,

occasionally given the power of sight, hearing, and speech through devices that are connected to the cylinder, so that you may be questioned further as to how you arrived in their city. You tell them of the machine and of the Turne family. They don't seem very interested in your responses. You beg them to let you go, but eventually they just stop questioning you and leave you to die slowly forgotten on a shelf.

Record in your Investigator Journal '*You died after many years as just a brain in a cylinder.*' -5 *Mythos* points.

Your investigation ends here.

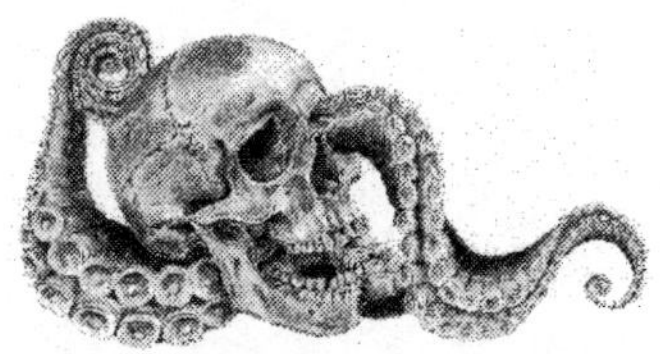

565

The huge spider's gaze is locked on you, its position following every tiny move you make.
"What... what are you?" you ask out loud.
"I am... a prisoner. Free me, human. Before the mi-go return."
"Why would I do that? This is madness!" you reply.
"No, human, it is not. Free me."

Every instinct in your body says to leave this creature alone. You can quickly leave through the door (turn to **144**), or touch the panel on the enclosure and free the spider-thing (turn to **305**).

566

The creatures are surprised by your tactic to ambush them. You pounce on the one holding the weapon and attempt to pull it free. With surprise on your side, the creature fails to grip the weapon and with a sharp tug it is flung through the air and lands with a splash in the pool.

The creature you disarmed calls out to you, "Huumaaan, waaaait! Cooome wiiith ussss!"
"Yesssss, intruuuder, weeee meeean nooo harrm," the other one adds.

How do you respond?

Having disarmed them, you can choose to forgo this invitation and face them in combat instead. Turn to **103**.
Or accept this gesture of peace between you, and go with them. Turn to **39**.

567

To your great relief, the liquid is palatable and nourishing. You take more until you've had your fill and begin to feel much better.

Gain 3 **Health** and 2 **Composure**.

Do you want to quickly head back and leave via the side tunnel (turn to **138**) or examine the strange contraptions on the other side of the room (turn to **434**)?

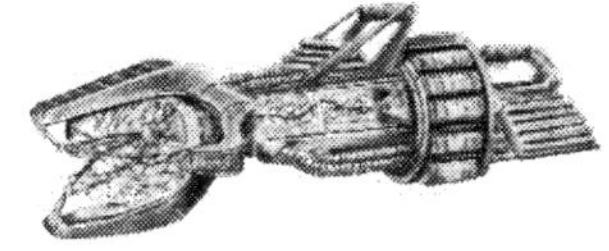

568

Around the back of the house the condition of the yard is even worse. The back door is also boarded up and looks like too much effort to attempt entry here. You don't have many options so decide to head back around to the front of the house.

Do you want to knock on the door (turn to **212**), or test the door and see if it is unlocked (turn to **160**)?

569

The green haze lifts and you find yourself standing in a long corridor. The floor, the walls, and the ceiling all glint of polished metal, smooth and cold to the touch. At the end of the corridor are three markings set into the walls. You see an oval marking in the wall ahead, a circle in the left wall, and a square in the right-hand wall. They are each large enough to be a door, but smooth and flush with the wall with no obvious way of opening.

There's a low thrum in the air. You cannot tell if it's from the floor, the walls or just in the air itself. The air smells of ozone after a lightning storm.

Call out to see if someone will answer. Turn to **574**.
Examine the circle marking on the left. Turn to **100**.
Examine the square marking on the right. Turn to **159**.
Or pass those and examine the oval marking at the end of the corridor. Turn to **360**.

570

The bodies of the mi-go are scattered all over the room. You sift through the pieces, but find only medical implements.

If you haven't already done so, you can search the counter (turn to **268)**, or search the adjoining room where the family had been (turn to **575**).

571

"They diiid thissssssss! Thosssse thingssss! Chaaanged meee. You saaaw they have my faaaamily! You prooomised to go baaack and sssave them!" He puts his head down and places his one good hand over it.
"Ssssave my family. You promisssed me!" He reaches into a pocket and produces something.

Holding up a small diamond-shaped object that glows gently, he moves toward the machine. Turn to **353**.

572

You nervously place the *Tok'llian* into the machine and are relieved when it starts to thrum. As before, there are four dials on the device, and you notice that each of these is currently set at what you denote to be zero degrees. Do you have any clues on how to set the device for the journey home?

If you have recorded in your Investigator Journal '*You know how to get home*', then you must turn to the **SECOND** reference associated with that entry now.

If you do not have this entry, you have little choice but to try. Turn to **450**.

573

The encounter immediately sets you into fight mode. You turn and make a run for it into the cavern, and on into the pool. The mi-go emerge through the door and one of them calls out, "Intrrruuuder, stooop!"

Wading through the pool isn't too difficult but it is certainly slowing you down. At the mid-way point it reaches waist height. The creatures reach the edge, then you hear a strange whirring sound, starting low but quickly becoming high-pitched. Suddenly there's a loud crack or snap in the air, and the water all around you lights up with a crackle of energy. You are immediately wracked with pain as the entire pool becomes electrified. You arch backwards, shaking uncontrollably, the hair on your skin standing on end and starting to sizzle and smoke. When it ends, you fall backward into the water, dead.

Record in your Investigator Journal '*You were electrocuted by an alien weapon.*' -2 *Mythos* points.

Your investigation ends here.

574

You call out, 'Hello, where am I?' and are immediately struck with the oddity of your own voice. The acoustic effect in the hallway brings your voice back to you in an echo that sounds eerily like the voice from your room a moment ago. No one answers. You decide to investigate the markings on the walls.

Will you:
Examine the circle marking on the left. Turn to **100**.
Examine the square marking on the right. Turn to **159**.
Or pass those and examine the oval marking at the end of the corridor. Turn to **360**.

575

You search back in the larger room where the battle with Unlatha took place, but it's looking more and more hopeless. Sifting through the bodies of the mi-go turns up nothing. You rise to your feet, hands covered in the green blood of the mi-go that Unlatha slaughtered. You've come so far, but the one thing you really need to get out of here is the one thing you don't have – the *Tok'llian*.

The door that leads back to the enormous mining chamber opens and in rush swarms of armed mi-go. You conclude that it is useless to resist. Remaining still, expecting your demise, the creatures surround you as others head onwards to take Edward and his remaining family members captive. You're taken away and placed on an operating table before being put under.

When you awake, you feel strange – your vision is narrowed and at first you find it hard to focus. Across from you on a metal slab lies the body of a man. One of the mi-go is leaning over it and doing something to the head, but you can't quite see what is happening. Moments later it turns towards you with a large flap of skin dangling from its blood-soaked claw. As it gets closer, the creature's head turns a deep green while it holds up the flapping piece of skin before your eyes. It is your face dangling from its claw...

You spend the rest of your life as a brain in a cylinder, occasionally given the power of sight, hearing, and speech through devices that are connected to the cylinder, so that you may be questioned by the mi-go. You see Edward, too, but transformed into a more complete version of the condition you first saw him in back at the house. You beg him to let you go, but his mind appears to be too far gone – a slave to the mi-go. And after a time, the final threads of your mind begin to snap also.

Record in your Investigator Journal '*You and the Turne family end up as experiments for the mi-go*.' -60 *Mythos* points.

Your investigation ends here.

576

You badly twist your ankle on the second leap down, crashing to the cave floor in agony. Your agony, however, is short lived, as the massive Spider of Leng looms over you.

It spears your shoulder with one of its legs, holding you in place. Rather than drag you back to its lair, it decides to feast on your insides here. It bites into your torso, injecting your body with a paralysing venom that starts to liquefy your internal organs.

Record in your Investigator Journal '*You were devoured by a giant Spider of Leng*.' -5 *Mythos* points.

Your investigation ends here.

577

You turn to flee. The brain-thing calls out after you – its legs noisily clambering on the stone floor as it follows. "You best come with us, old chap! We can save you from the mi-go."

The quickest route to flee is now to your left. Will you continue to run (turn to **437**), or accept that this walking brain might be helpful in getting out of here, and follow it (turn to **369**)?

578

As you battle against the first creature, trying desperately to put it down quickly, the second mi-go retrieves an object from the shelf. It turns, pointing a short metal rod at you, which then suddenly fires a sharp shard of metal. It pierces your chest, sending you reeling against the wall. Seizing the sudden advantage, the first mi-go pierces your eye socket and plucks your eye clean out. You've barely the strength to scream as it repeats this with your second eye. Slowly but surely the creatures take what they want, and discard the rest of your dying body on the table.

Record in your Investigator Journal '*You died horribly mutilated by two mi-go.*' -2 *Mythos* points.

Your investigation ends here.

579

The mechanical bodies are built for carrying out tasks in the laboratory, not for speed.

However, their mechanical construction also means that regardless of what weapon you currently have (if any), you can only deal 1 Damage in any attack.

The oval-shaped lens they use to see would appear to be a weak spot. If you can hit it and disable the lens, they'll be unable to fight back. In order to hit the lens, you'll need to roll a *double* on a successful attack roll (e.g., rolling two 1's, two 2's, etc.). If you hit the lens, count the brain as defeated. Their spinning claw is very dangerous – if you are hit, take 2 Damage instead of the usual 1.

You must fight them both together.

Eugene **Brain Cylinder 1**	**Brain Cylinder 2**
Combat 5	Combat 5
Health 4	Health 4

If you are defeated, turn to **510**.
If you defeat or disable the first two, the second two flee immediately, leaving you free to investigate the laboratory. Turn to **471**

580

It is a difficult and troubling conversation with Jacob to recount the events. He's incapable of looking after Sara. Moments of lucidity reveal details of a visit to the hills of Vermont, where he discovered the machine, and some unusual individuals that showed him how to use it to help his farm prosper. But not much else he speaks of is worth delving into. You know it contains a hideous truth – of the mi-go and their possible influence on Earth – but you cannot allow those thoughts to become threads of a new story... for you, too, might eventually go hopelessly mad. The loss of Edward weighs heavily on your mind, but his bravery will not be forgotten.

The date is October 11th, 1916. The newspaper clipping that brought you here remains as before, but tells a story that is no longer what actually happened. Your car is gone... or never existed. Only that which you brought with you to Yuggoth and back, remains as it was. The machine was more than just a way to traverse across space, it also had the power to transcend time. Edward and Sara hadn't aged because it sent you to Yuggoth ten years in the past – possibly only moments after they themselves had arrived. Now you realise just how powerful this device was for the mi-go, and why they were so tenacious in trying to recover the lost power source.

Sara is fostered in the town of Durham, and in time seems happy and settled, with the terrors of the past buried, or hopefully completely forgotten. You settle in the town of Durham, also, and get a job working as a store clerk for Mrs. Wilkins. You remain there as a way to stay away from... yourself. A young reporter by the name of Frank Winston starts to write an article for the *Arkham Gazette,* which you have delivered by post especially to your door.

On September the 23rd, around 4:45 p.m., in the year 1926, you stand on the main road of Durham and wait for a Chevrolet to trundle down the road. You contemplated writing to yourself, anonymously of course, as a warning to stay away... but instead felt that you would simply be compelling some version of yourself to question the warning and turn up anyway. When you thought about it, you know that is what you would have done.

No one arrives... there are no strange flashes of green lightning, and no voice on the air. The killings never happened, the article was never written, and thus the other version of yourself remained in Arkham writing for the paper. It is highly unlikely that your paths will ever cross.

If you have recorded in your Investigator Journal '*Received a gift'*, then you must turn to the reference associated with that entry now.

If you do not have this entry, turn to **36**.

581

The machine can be turned by grasping two thick handles either side of the control panel. You grip them both and heave.

Make a Regular (2D6) **Strength** check.

If you pass, turn to **561**.
If you fail, turn to **109**.

582

The large door doesn't open automatically when approached. You glance around and notice a square raised panel on the wall next to the door.

Will you open the door by touching the panel (turn to **123**), or attempt to get up onto the walkway above (turn to **427**)?

583

To your great relief, the liquid is palatable and nourishing. You take more until you've had your fill and begin to feel much better.

Gain 2 **Health** and 2 **Composure**.

Feeling stronger, you must decide your next move...

Do you want to quickly head back and leave via the side tunnel (turn to **138**), or examine the strange contraptions on the other side of the room (turn to **116**)?

584

You claim that the man staying at the house is a colleague of yours, and having misplaced your directions to the house, you're concerned about being so late. Pete eyes you up and down, then finally speaks. "Aye, you do look one of his type. Learned, I mean. Leastways you be a might friendlier." He looks up, clearly thinking hard.

"Like any of us folk here, he needs supplies and what-not. So, Mrs. Wilkins over at the post office would know more. It's her what told me he was up about on that hill in the first place."

You remind him you had asked about directions to the hill. "I'm sorry but I can't properly remember beyond taking the left fork out of town to the west. All my jobs are on the main roadways outta town. Not much call for going up into the hills. If you catch Mrs. Wilkins, she should be able to help more."

You thank Pete for his time, and he nods while wiping his hands with a grimy rag.

Do you want to head on your way in the hope you can find the house (turn to **557**), head to the post office in the hope of getting better directions (turn to **218**), or ask Pete to check over your car (turn to **18**)?

585

Try as you might, you can't hold on. You slide downwards at a steep angle before being deposited from an opening in the ceiling of a massive cavern. Luckily, your fall is broken by a large mound of piled up refuse.

You find yourself on your back, staring up at the ceiling. A light above the peak of the mound shows an opening of some kind – it is the tunnel you dropped from. As you hold your aching head you suddenly start to slide down the side of the slick mound. It's only then you realise what it is you're sitting on – a massive pile of entrails, bones, and offal. You're covered in it. You jump up and try to wipe it off, but it seems futile.

Make an Extreme (2D6+3) **Composure** check.

If you pass, turn to **216**.
If you fail, turn to **161**.

586

Congratulations on completing the story.

Throughout your investigation, the *Mythos* points you have accumulated have been recorded on your *Investigator Sheet,* along with the number of attempts you have made to reach this point.

1) Divide your *Mythos* points by the *Number of Investigations* to get your sub-total (round down).
2) Then, as a final addition to your *Mythos* points, you gain the following points based on who you managed save (if anyone). Add these to your sub-total.

Edward (altered)	+ 2 *Mythos* points
Edward (unaltered)	+ 5 *Mythos* points
Sara	+ 5 *Mythos* points
Melissa	+ 5 *Mythos* points
Jacob	+ 5 *Mythos* points

You now have your **Mythos Total**. Consult the list below to see your final rank.

Mythos Points	Final Ranking
0 to 9	Mi-go food
10 to 14	Just a Brain in a Cylinder
15 to 19	Hapless Wanderer
20 to 29	Apprentice Investigator
30 to 39	Master Investigator
40 to 49	Delver into the Mythos
50 +	Master of the Cthulhu Mythos

As this was a completed investigation, depending on who you managed to save, you might decide to try again. If you do, you must reset your Investigation attempts and your *Mythos* points.

The Making of The House on Sentinel Hill

The following contains some story spoilers, so best to read this after you finish the story. I've been a fan of the Cthulhu Mythos and of Fighting Fantasy Gamebooks since the 80's, and I am delighted to have been able to bring those two interests together to create this story. This tale originally started as a 'FLASH' game. Remember Flash? The animation/web and game creation tool for browser gaming and websites that was around for years before browsers stopped supporting it as a plugin (due to web security concerns).

The story started as an isometric point-and-click adventure and I'd gotten a fair way into it before flash updates (changes to the programming language 'actionscript') meant having to recode aspects of it, and just the overall scope of creating the game and graphics became too large. I had to abandon it despite having a fully playable demo right up to the point you meet Edward. It started at the house though, and not at the village of Durham. I did manage to finish two other flash games and release them – you can still find them on the web. They are called *The Necronomicon Card Game,* and the sequel is *The Necronomicon: Book of Dead Names*.

Then I moved on from games and started working on *Cthulhu Mythos Music*. Combining my interests in HP Lovecraft and the other authors that have contributed to the wider mythos, I have written a large library of music drawing inspiration from the stories and creatures and games based on Lovecraft's works, such as Chaosium's *The Call of Cthulhu*. I wanted to ensure the music had an orchestral sound, but included synths and effects underneath to represent the science fiction aspect of many tales in addition to the cosmic terror many of the characters encounter.

Soon enough after the music gained popularity, I decided I would love to revisit this story I always had for *The House on Sentinel Hill,* and by chance (having rediscovered some gamebooks), I decided that interactive fiction would be a viable approach to take. With this approach, I could create the detailed story I wanted, but still keep it as an interactive experience rather than a passive story.

As I started writing, the scope of the story expanded a little. I decided it'd be more interesting from a narrative point of view to start like many *Call of Cthulhu* role-playing game scenarios start. With an intriguing reason to investigate strange goings on or past disturbances in a secluded location, and a rather ordinary beginning with everyday people being encountered and questioned about those unusual events.

One of my favourite gamebooks is Steve Jackson's *The House of Hell,* but the world of the Cthulhu Mythos isn't really about full-on horror-at-every-turn – though some elements of 'pulp horror' can be fun and is often the premise of the wider Cthulhu games out there, I tried to keep it reasonably grounded in the work of Lovecraft. An ordinary man, not a hardened gun-totting investigator, stumbles unwittingly into a terrifying situation, and thus it becomes a fight for survival. But one that the main character may overcome and possibly be hardened against, instead of the usual fate of a Lovecraftian protagonist, which is to write how they are likely to just end up in an insane asylum. The book started this way, but how did it end for you?

This book has been the product of a few years of effort, a little at the start, a big push then to finish 70% of the work in two further years of solid writing and playtesting, editing, and finally, the wonderful art you see throughout the book.

Strong art is a gamebook necessity. Discovering Matthew's art and style was stroke of luck, and I was delighted when he agreed to take it on. Matthew took my image briefs and came up with something that exceeded my expectations each time. A personal favourite being the first time you see Unlatha, the spider-thing. When I was finished writing, being able to sit back and enjoy the art coming in was a very enjoyable process, as I didn't have to do much beyond describe my locales and characters/creatures, and watch Matthew come up with final look.

I hope you enjoyed playing *The House on Sentinel Hill* as much as I have enjoyed creating it.

About the Artist

Matthew Dewhurst is a Hampshire based artist who studied art, design and illustration at the University of Portsmouth. Inspired by sci-fi and fantasy artists of the 1980's, he produces artwork for gamebooks, roleplaying games, graphic novels as well as commissioned portraiture. Matthew wishes to thank Emma-Lee Elodin, and Alan Langford for their inspiration and support.

Printed in Poland
by Amazon Fulfillment
Poland Sp. z o.o., Wrocław
12 October 2023

cb0f536f-9f5e-44b5-9870-5a4e911e39a0R01